DRAGONWYCK

by
Anya Seton

THE SUN DIAL PRESS
Garden City, New York

SUN DIAL PRESS Reprint Edition, 1945, by special arrangement with HOUGHTON MIFFLIN COMPANY.

PRINTED IN THE U.S.A.

Author's Note

THIS STORY WAS SUGGESTED BY A NEWS ITEM IN THE *New York Herald,* 1849, but the main characters are entirely fictional. The historical framework—manor system, anti-rent wars, Astor Place massacre, and steamboat race—is, however, founded on fact, and I have tried to be accurate in presenting it and all background detail.

There was, on the Hudson, a way of life such as this, and there was a house not unlike Dragonwyck. All Gothic magnificence and eerie manifestations were not at that time inevitably confined to English castles or Southern plantations!

I want to thank the patient and helpful librarians at the Greenwich Library, and many kind people who facilitated my research in Hudson, Albany, Kinderhook, Cornwall, and other towns along the river.

I am particularly grateful to Mr. Carl Carmer, not only for his book 'The Hudson,' to which I am very much indebted, but for his personal help and interest.

A. S.

From childhood's hour I have not been
As others were—I have not seen
As others saw—I could not bring
My passions from a common spring.
From the same source I have not taken
My sorrow; I could not awaken
My heart to joy at the same tone;
And all I lov'd, I loved alone.
Then—in my childhood—in the dawn
Of a most stormy life—was drawn
From ev'ry depth of good and ill
The mystery which binds me still:
From the torrent, or the fountain,
From the red cliff of the mountain,
From the sun that 'round me roll'd
In its autumn tint of gold—
From the lightning in the sky
As it pass'd me flying by—
From the thunder and the storm,
And the cloud that took the form
(When the rest of Heaven was blue)
Of a demon in my view.

'Alone' by Edgar Allan Poe

1

IT WAS ON AN AFTERNOON IN MAY OF 1844 THAT THE letter came from Dragonwyck.

One of the Mead boys had seen it lying in the Horseneck post-office, and had thoughtfully carried it with him three miles up the Stanwich road to deliver it at the Wells farmhouse.

When the letter came, Miranda was, most regrettably, doing not one of the tasks which should have occupied the hour from two to three.

She was not in the springhouse churning butter, she was not weeding the vegetable patch, nor even keeping more than half an absent-minded eye on Charity, the baby, who had kicked off her blanket and was chewing on a blade of sweet meadow grass, delighted with her freedom.

Miranda had hidden behind the stone wall in the quiet little family burying-ground on the north side of the apple orchard as far from the house as possible. It was her favorite retreat. The seven tombstones which marked graves of her father's family were no more than seven peaceful friends. Even the tiny stone in the corner beneath the giant elm had no tragic significance though it was marked, 'Daniel Wells, son of Ephraim and Abigail Wells, who departed this life April 7th, 1836, aged one year,' and covered the body of her baby brother. Miranda had been ten during little Danny's short life, and he was now nothing but a gently poignant memory.

Miranda was curled up against the wall, her pink calico skirts bunched carelessly above her knees in uncharacteristic abandon. A green measuring worm inched himself unchecked across the smooth bodice of her dress. The May breeze, fragrant with appleblossoms and clover from the adjacent pasture, blew her loosened hair into her eyes. She pushed the strand back impatiently with one hand while the other clutched her book, as Miranda devoured the fascinating pages of 'The Beautiful Adulteress.'

So compelling were the beautiful adulteress's adventures, that even when Miranda's sunbonnet slipped off and hot sunshine fell through the elm trees onto her skin, she did not pause to replace the bonnet. And yet the transparent whiteness of that skin was the envy of her friends and part product of many a tedious treatment with buttermilk and cucumber poultices.

'The Beautiful Adulteress' had been lent by Phoebe Mead, and it must be finished by nightfall so that Phoebe could return it to Deborah Wilson, who had purloined it from her brother's saddlebag.

Despite Miranda's eighteen years and elegant education at Philander Button's Greenwich Academy, despite avid perusal of this and similar books, she had not the vaguest notion of the horrifying behavior that resulted in one's becoming an adulteress. But that point was immaterial.

It was the glorious palpitating romance that mattered. The melancholy heroes, the languishing heroines, the clanking ghosts, dismal castles and supernatural lights; all entrancingly punctuated at intervals by a tender, a rapturous—but in any case a guilty—kiss.

Her mother's first call went unheard. It was not until the cry 'Ranny—' changed to a louder and sharper 'Miranda-a-a! Where in tunket are you?' that the girl jumped. She shoved the book between two stones in the wall, and called hastily, 'Coming, Ma!'

She brushed bits of grass and drifted appleblossom off her dress and apron, straightened the black mesh net which confined her masses of soft curling hair during the work day, hair that in the sunlight shone nearly as golden as the buttercups in the pasture behind her.

Then she picked up Charity.

'Oh, shame, lambkin, you're wet again,' she said reproachfully.

The baby at once set up an anguished yell; even at a year she resented criticism.

Miranda laughed and kissed the soft neck. 'Never mind, pet. Sister isn't really cross.' But she sighed, rapidly checking the chores which must be done before dusk.

There was a big batch of the baby's never-ending diapers to be washed and sunned, the butter to be churned, and, worst of all, a fowl to be slaughtered, plucked, and drawn for the Sabbath dinner tomorrow. Miranda loathed this particular task above all others. The sight of blood sickened her. And whereas her brothers and sister found the antics of the staggering, decapitated chicken funny, Miranda always felt a little spasm of nausea. Equally unpleasant was the later necessity for plunging one's hand into the chicken's slimy entrails.

She usually spent quite ten minutes scrubbing her slender white fingers afterward. A process which Ephraim, her father, viewed with disapproval when he caught her at it.

'Quite the finicking young lady, aren't we, Ranny!' he growled, frowning at her beneath his bushy eyebrows. 'The Lord has mercifully provided us with food, and He has no patience with those who think themselves too fine to prepare it.'

Ephraim always knew what the Lord was thinking or feeling quite as well as the Reverend Coe did.

Miranda assumed that her mother's summons had to do with the chicken and she walked slowly, shifting the heavy baby from arm to arm and avoiding the barnyard where the destined victim clucked in happy ignorance.

As she walked, she noted absently that the north potato field was deserted and that therefore her father and three brothers must have finished the spraying and moved on ahead of schedule to the great field by Strickland brook. She also noted that the distant blue of the Sound was unusually clear and that she could even see the wooded purplish strip of Long Island on the horizon. That meant rain. But otherwise she saw nothing of the beauty of the rolling Connecticut countryside, the flowering meadows, the rustling wineglass elms and hemlocks greenish-black against the sky. The farm and the sturdy six-room farmhouse were simply home, and she had never been farther than ten miles away from them in her life.

As she entered the dark kitchen, she saw with relief that her mother's gaunt though still handsome face showed neither annoyance at Miranda's tardiness, nor even the habitual pucker of admonition with which she urged her children on to the next inevitable chore.

Abigail, who seldom rested from morning till night, was sitting on a reed-bottomed chair and staring at a paper which lay unfolded on the kitchen table.

She looked up as her daughter came in. 'Here's a strange thing, Ranny. I don't know what to make of it. Can't tell till I've talked with your pa.'

Miranda followed her mother's puzzled gaze to the paper on the table. 'Why, it's a letter, isn't it!' she cried with lively interest. Not three letters a year came to the Wells farm. 'Can I read it?'

'I guess so,' said Abigail. 'But change the baby first, then knead down the bread dough while I nurse her. Time's wasting.'

The girl cast a longing glance at the mysterious letter, but she did as she was told. Abigail flew around the kitchen, cutting bacon with quick, decisive stabs, poking at the embers beneath the oven where the bread would soon be baked. Finally she unbuttoned her bodice, snatched up the hungry baby, and settled on the low nursing chair.

When the dough was set to rise again, Miranda seized the letter. She examined the envelope first. The thick creamy paper was pleasant and unfamiliar as was the bold, rather illegible writing unadorned by the copper-plate flourishes or shaded capitals which she had painstakingly learned at the Academy. The envelope was addressed:

To Mistress Abigail Wells
The Stanwich Road
Horseneck, (or Greenwich)
Connecticut.

It was postmarked 'Hudson, New York,' which conveyed nothing to Miranda, who had never heard of the place. But as she put down the envelope and picked up the letter a thrill of excitement ran through her. It was an intuitive flash of certainty that this bland piece of paper was of importance to her, and, though this intuition was pleasurable, it also contained a fleeting apprehension. She read eagerly.

Dragonwyck, May 19th, 1844.

My dear Cousin Abigail:

Though we have never met, we are related, as you doubtless know, through our mutual grandmother, Annetje Gaansevant.

My wife and I, having discussed the matter at some length, have decided to invite one of your daughters into our home for an extended visit. We shall naturally be able to offer her many advantages which she could not hope to enjoy in her present station. In return, if she pleases, she may occasionally occupy herself with the teaching of our six-year-old child, Katrine, but she will in all ways be treated as befits my kinswoman.

I have had inquiries made and was gratified to find that you and your husband enjoy the honor and respect of your little community. Be so good as to let me know at your earliest convenience which of your daughters you select, and I will make all suitable arrangements for her journey to Dragonwyck.

Believe me, madam, your sincere friend and cousin.

Respectfully yours,

Nicholas Van Ryn

Miranda read the letter twice before turning in amazement to her mother. 'I don't understand this at all, Ma. Who in the world is Nicholas Van Ryn?'

'He is, I believe, a very grand personage,' answered Abigail with a half-smile. 'He is lord of a large manor up on the Hudson River somewhere near Albany.'

'And you're his cousin?' persisted Miranda, still more astonished.

'It would seem so,' replied Abigail dryly. 'I remember my mother telling me of the Van Ryns, though I haven't thought of them in years. Bring me the Patterson Bible.'

Miranda moved toward the shelf where her father kept his ponderous Bible.

'No, not that one, child,' Abigail stopped her. 'That one has no records from my side. I want the Bible I brought with me at my marriage. It's in the attic next your Grandfather Patterson's musket and powder horn.'

When Miranda had brought the great gilt-edged volume, they examined the records on the fly leaves between the Old and New Testaments.

It was clear enough. Annetje Gaansevant of Rensselaer County, New York, had in 1779 married Adriaen Van Ryn, patroon of the Van Ryn manor, and borne him a son, Cornelius, who must be the father of Nicholas.

Then after Adriaen Van Ryn's death, Annetje had married again, a Connecticut Yankee named Patterson, and thereupon produced a great many children, the eldest of whom had been Abigail's mother

'So this Nicholas' grandmother is also my great-grandmother,' cried Miranda at last. 'I had no idea I had such fine relations.' She looked down at her tapering hands. She had always privately thought them aristocratic, and it was pleasant to have confirmation.

'You haven't a scrap of Van Ryn blood,' snorted Abigail, 'so you needn't go puffing like a peacock. The connection is only through the Gaansevants; Dutch farmers they were like ourselves. And it's just as well, for the Van Ryns are a wild, strange lot with some kind of a skeleton in their closet, for all their money and land and hoity-toity ways.'

'Truly, Ma?' cried Miranda, her hazel eyes sparkling. 'How vastly romantic! Do tell me, please.'

Abigail shifted the baby to the other arm. 'I don't know anything to tell. You and your "vastly romantic"! You've a head stuffed with nonsense now.'

'But you must know something about this Nicholas who writes the letter. I suppose he's quite an old man; it's a pity his birth date isn't in the Bible.'

'Oh, he's somewhere in middle life, I guess,' said Abigail. 'About my age. And I know nothing about him except that he has great estates and a town house in New York, and that four years ago, when Van Buren was President, Nicholas often visited at the White House, for I read about it in a newspaper.'

'Oh, Ma—' breathed Miranda, quite overcome. 'He must be very grand indeed.' She considered these revelations for a moment, then she burst out, 'You haven't said a word about his letter, the invitation.'

She clasped her hands together in a suddenly childish gesture. 'Oh, but wouldn't I love to go!'

'And if we should send a daughter, which I think unlikely, why should it be you, miss?' asked Abigail. 'Why not Tibby, I'd like to know?'

Miranda frowned. Tabitha was sixteen and even now at the Academy finishing her last term. There was no reason why she should not be chosen except that Miranda felt that she could not bear it if she were.

'Tibby wouldn't want to go,' she said slowly. 'She's not like me. She doesn't—' Her voice trailed off. Impossible to explain that Tabitha did not hunger after romance, change, adventure, as Miranda did. That she actually enjoyed cooking and washing and housekeeping, that she asked for nothing better in life than to settle down on the next farm with young Obadiah Brown and likely have a parcel of babies right off. But I'm different. I *am,* thought Miranda passionately.

Abigail watched her daughter and read some of these thoughts on the downcast face. Though she would never have admitted it, her first-born girl was closest of all to her heart. She secretly gloried in Miranda's delicate, small-boned beauty, in her fastidiousness and dainty ways. She thought her remarkably like one of those exquisite creatures in *Godey's Lady's Book,* the same graceful height, small nose, and full, pouting lips.

She pretended not to see when Miranda fussed over her complexion, guarding its pink and whiteness from freckles or sunburn with as much anxious care as might a fashionable New York lady. And she sympathized with the girl's restlessness and vague youthful dreams. Abigail had had them, too, long ago before she married the estimable

Ephraim and life flattened into a monotony of never-ending work and baby-tending.

'So,' she said with her normal crispness, 'just like that, and with your usual lack of prudent thought, you "want to go." You don't consider whether I might be able to spare you, nor do you even seem to think that you might miss us here.'

Miranda looked up, stricken. She rushed across the room and put her arms around her mother's thin shoulders, resting her cheek on the brown head that was already finely threaded with gray. 'Oh, Ma, dear, of course I'd miss you. It's just that—that it seems so rarely exciting an opportunity.'

Abigail smiled faintly, and Miranda knew that, whether or not she would be allowed to go to Dragonwyck, there would be no real question of Tabitha's going.

Her mother straightened, buttoned her bodice, and placed the sleeping baby in the cradle. Then she seized the holystone and began scouring the oak drain board. 'We'll say no more about the matter now. Hurry up and kill that old white hen; she'll be a mite tough, but the others are laying well, and she'll have to do.' She glanced at the Seth Thomas banjo clock that was her great pride. 'We're shockingly behind with the work. The men will be in from the fields before supper's near ready.'

After the evening meal, the May night being warm, the family gathered in the parlor instead of the kitchen for Scripture reading and prayer.

Ephraim seated himself in the armed Windsor chair beside the cherry-wood center table. His open Bible lay before him and he kept one blunt finger in readiness on the chapter heading. Not a hair of his brown beard quivered. His eyes were stern and nearly motionless while he waited for each one's respectful attention. They were all there, his wife and five older children, seated on stiff chairs in a prim row. Only the baby, gurgling in her cradle by the kitchen fireplace, was exempt.

Next to Abigail sat Tom, the oldest of her brood. He was staid and responsible, already despite his scant twenty years a duplicate of his father whom he greatly admired.

Seth and Nathaniel, the two other boys, aged fourteen and twelve, cast longing looks out the window and wondered if the light would hold long enough for a game of Run Sheep Run with the Reynolds boys. But they knew better than to wriggle. Many a strapping in the woodshed had taught them that.

At the other end of the row, beside Miranda, sat Tabitha. Her hands were folded demurely in her lap, her plump freckled face was set to the proper expression of piety.

Only Miranda found it nearly impossible to restrain her fidgets. She knew that Ephraim had read the startling letter, and knew also that any discussion of it was impossible until evening worship was concluded.

During the fifteen of her eighteen years that Miranda had taken part in family worship, she had heard the Bible read through six times; and though Ephraim read well, rolling the sonorous phrases and giving considered emphasis to every word, she had long ago perfected a method of enjoying her own thoughts from which she emerged only to say 'Amen' with the others at the end of each chapter.

And yet, in spite of herself, she had soaked in a great deal of the poetry and imagery. Sometimes certain phrases mingled with her daydreams, and seemed to touch off delightful little explosions in her mind. It was so tonight, despite—or perhaps because of—her preoccupation with the letter from Dragonwyck.

Ephraim read from the twenty-sixth chapter of Ezekiel, and her attention was caught by verses which meant nothing to her consciously, though they had power to strike through mist and show her glimpses of a dim, enchanted country.

'Then all the princes of the sea shall come down from their thrones . . . they shall clothe themselves with trembling,' said Ephraim's measured voice. It didn't make much sense, thought Miranda, but somehow it was beautiful.

Ephraim dropped to a lower, menacing note. 'How art thou destroyed, that wast inhabited of seafaring men, the renowned city, which wast strong in the sea, she and her inhabitants, which cause their terror to be on all that haunt it.'

A little shiver ran through her, and a sensation of strangeness. She would not have dared move her head, but her eyes roamed round the familiar room. There was the wide, seldom-lit fireplace with the pewter candlesticks on the mantel. There on the whitewashed walls hung the sampler her Grandmother Finch had worked, and the silhouette profiles of her mother and father which had been cut on their wedding day.

On the oak plank floor lay the hooked rugs that she and Tabitha had labored through many a winter's evening to finish. There in the west window through which glanced the last red rays of the setting sun was the cracked pane, result of an impulsive snowball thrown by Tom years ago.

Everything was commonplace and dull. What had they all to do with 'princes of the sea, renowned cities, terror or hauntings'?

'Fine linen with broidered work from Egypt . . . blue and purple from the Isles of Elisha,' intoned Ephraim, now well into the next chapter . . . 'occupied in thy fairs with chief of all spices, and with all precious stones, and gold.'

Miranda felt a wave of sharp yearning. She saw them heaped about her in a marble courtyard, the fine embroidered linens from Egypt, the spices, the precious stones and the gold. She looked at her parents, at her brothers' and sister's expressionless faces. How could they listen so calmly! Even the Bible admitted that the world was full of mystery and beauty and golden perfumed luxury. How then could they be content with sweaty homespun, with the odors of stable and barnyard, and with no gold but potatoes and little spring onions?

The low room was full of the smell of onions. The boys had been pulling them all day, and the white and green shoots lay neatly stacked in open crates outside the kitchen windows waiting for the dawn, when Tom would pile them in the wagon and drive them to the Mianus docks for shipment to New York.

There was a small scuffle, and Miranda fell to her knees with the rest of the family as her father shut his Bible and began to pray.

He always talked to God in much the manner of a senior member of the faculty reporting progress to a respected principal. He touched on the faults of each one of the family, not excepting himself sometimes. He occasionally reported some commendable act (though this honor was usually reserved for Tabitha), and he finished with an intimate and entirely confident request for guidance. Tonight there was an added clause.

'This day, O Lord,' said Ephraim, 'there has come to me a matter of some slight perplexity. Deliver us, we pray, from the pitfalls of rashness or hankering after the fleshpots.' Here he looked briefly at Miranda. 'And deliver us from the sins of arrogance and false pride.' This time Ephraim's stern gaze rested upon his wife.

The situation was therefore clear to Miranda. Her father did not approve of the letter. Disappointment overwhelmed her, nor was it lessened by Ephraim's final words. 'However, O God, Thy will be done, and whatsoever Thou decidest for Thy servants we shall try to do with all our might. Bless and preserve us through the night. Amen.'

God's will usually seemed to coincide with her father's, and against this partnership there was no hope of appeal.

But I'm not going to give up, thought Miranda hotly. During the hours since she had first seen the letter, its invitation had grown from a delightful possibility into an obsession. She had never in her life had a desire that approached this one in intensity. The fantastic name 'Dragonwyck' enchanted her. She repeated it over and over to herself and it was as though it pulled her to it, and beckoned.

Ephraim rose, and her spirits revived a little, for apparently there was at least to be a conference. Usually at the conclusion of evening worship her father went straight to his black cherry desk, where he entered items in the leather account book: so many bushels of potatoes from the north field, so many heads of cabbage or pecks of peas; wharfage charges, wholesale prices in New York. His cramped figures accounted for every penny while he squinted painfully. His far-sighted eyes blurred on close application.

But now he remained standing behind the table and said: 'Abby and Ranny, ye'll stay in here, I want to speak to you. Tom, water the stock and look to Whiteface, she's freshening. Tibby, is that young spark Obadiah likely to come mooning around again tonight?'

Tabitha cast down her eyes, and her round face was suffused with a peony blush. 'Oh, Pa!' she said in tones of demure horror. 'I'm sure I've no notion of his plans, and I can't see why they should concern me, anyway.'

A grim twinkle appeared in Ephraim's eyes. 'Well, if he should happen to turn up, you may sit on the steps where your mother can keep an eye on you. Though I must say that Ob is steady enough, and you, praise be, aren't the flighty kind.'

'Thank you, Pa,' said Tibby, and from between her pale lashes she flung Miranda the tiniest complacent glance. Tabitha was perfectly aware that her piety and domesticity pleased her father, and that she never gave him a moment's anxiety as Miranda did.

Seth and Nat did not wait to see if their father had directions for them; they sidled through the door and pelted away down the road toward the Reynolds Farm.

Ephraim reseated himself and indicated with a gesture that his wife and Miranda might do likewise. He pulled the Van Ryn letter from his pocket.

'I don't like this letter at all,' he said heavily. 'And I'd see no reason even to discuss it, if it wasn't that you two foolish women read it and Abby acts like it was important.' He frowned at his wife. 'Far as I can see there's only one answer.'

Abigail very seldom disagreed with her husband, indeed in most matters her opinions coincided with his. But now her firm mouth compressed. 'It is important, Ephraim,' she said. 'Mr. Van Ryn is my cousin, and seems to me he's making a generous offer. Might be a good thing for Ranny to live for a while in a great house, learn something of the world outside this farm.'

Miranda threw her mother a grateful look. 'I'd like to go, Pa,' she said temperately, knowing that emotion of any kind always annoyed him.

Ephraim snorted. 'Your opinion is of no consequence whatsoever, miss. You're always hankering after new, foolish things. You haven't the sense of a tom-tit. You should be thinking only of helping your mother until you settle down with one of the young sparks hereabouts. You're past eighteen and comely enough in a namby-pamby way, I suppose. I don't know what's the matter with you. There's Zach Wilson, now. He'd make a fine husband and he seemed to fancy you. And how did you treat him!' Ephraim suddenly empurpled, banged his hand on the table, and Miranda's heart sank. She knew what was coming.

'I've seen you many a time,' growled Ephraim, 'mincing around, your nose in the air and crying, "Oh, Zach, don't come so near, you smell of the stable. Oh, Zach, don't play that vulgar dance on your fiddle, can we not have 'Love's Sweet Bloom' or some ree-fined ballad?" Faugh! No wonder he had his fill of your ladyship and is courting Mead's girl.'

Miranda stirred unhappily. Zach's interest in her and her discouragement of it had been a sore subject for weeks.

She had never liked Zach. He had coarse red hair and pudgy hands, and his idea of love-making had been scuffling in dark corners, a moist smacking kiss on the cheek, and on one occasion a playful pinch on that portion of her body that, even to herself, Miranda designated only as 'the sitting-down place.' Not one of the neighbors' sons, no man she had ever seen, had stirred in her any emotion but distaste. This realization made her feel guilty.

There was bitterness in being different from the others. Many times she had forced herself to romp through the boisterous square dances, and joined in the horseplay and practical jokes which delighted her friends, simply that they might not think her too uppity and queer.

'As for this letter—' went on Ephraim, returning to the subject, 'I think the tone of it offensive. This fine relation of yours, Abby, writes as if he thought himself the King of Spain. What right has he, I'd like to know, to be making "inquiries" about us, or to think I'd fair leap at the chance to send him one of my girls?'

'He doesn't mean it like that, I'm sure,' said Abigail quickly. 'It's only that the gentry have different ways of putting things.'

That was a mistake, thought Miranda, watching her father's face blacken.

'Oh, indeed,' snapped Ephraim. 'And since when, ma'am, do ye know all about the ways of gentry? Come to that, since when do we have gentry in this country where all are free and equal? A Yankee farmer is as good and mebbe a little bit better than many in this land. We'll say no more about this.' He put the letter back into his pocket. 'I'll sit down now and answer it.'

'Oh, Pa, please . . .' Miranda, galvanized into action, ran around the table and seized her father's arm. 'Pa, listen—' She spoke breathlessly, her wits sharpened by desperation. 'I have a—a feeling that I'm meant to go. I mean during worship tonight, I had a leading, truly I did. I think the Lord wants it. At least put it to the test, Pa, please, and see what happens.'

Ephraim paused. He stared down into his daughter's flushed, pleading face. 'Are you speaking the truth, daughter? Search your heart.'

Miranda nodded earnestly. It crossed Ephraim's mind that the girl, whom he usually thought far too pale and thin for beauty, did have a certain delicate, appealing charm.

'Well, you may try the test,' he said in a softer voice. He shoved the Bible over to her.

Miranda sighed with relief. There was still hope. The Bible test was used only in moments of grave crisis when its advice was urgently needed, and its decision was always abided by, as the manifest guidance of God.

She rested her hands on the great volume and sent up a fervent little prayer. If God wanted her to go to Dragonwyck, He would give her a sign. But, just in case, and without more than a fleeting stab of conscience, she intended to do what she could as well. For God helps those who help themselves. Had not Ephraim said so a hundred times?

Her mind darted over the various Bible stories while Ephraim and

Abigail watched her. Of course. Hagar! And the page would fall open because Ephraim so often re-read the story of Abraham.

She shut her eyes, as was necessary to the test, opened the book, stole a lightning glance through her long lashes, then placed one slender finger-tip on a verse. She passed the Bible back to her father, who cleared his throat and read.

'And Abraham rose up early in the morning, and took bread and a bottle of water and gave it unto Hagar, putting it on her shoulder and the child, and sent her away; and she departed and wandered in the wilderness of Beersheba.'

Ephraim stopped and looked suspiciously at his daughter, who bore the scrutiny calmly. For after all, the Lord had given a sign. She might so easily not have found the right chapter or verse.

'It's none too fitting,' said Ephraim grudgingly, 'but it does seem to have some bearing. I'll sleep on the matter and pray over it.'

Miranda's spirits soared. She knew that during the night Abigail would find means to bring Ephraim round to their point of view, so long as the decisive letter of refusal had not actually been written.

She felt a sudden urge to get out of the stuffy house into the cool twilight. She avoided the back steps where Tabitha sat with Obadiah, though she heard her sister's high-pitched giggle and little murmurs of coquettish protest.

She flung herself headlong on the grass beneath an apple tree, and wished on the evening star. Then she lay quiet, her face upturned to the sky, and dreamed of travel and far places; of New York. She pictured it vaguely as a vast city of towers and castles, peopled with elegant silken ladies and dark romantic gentlemen. Amongst the latter perhaps there might be one who would press his hand to his heart, though he dared not speak. Perhaps she would drop a handkerchief as Esmeralda had done in the 'Deserted Rose,' and when he, bowing, returned it to her, their mingled glances would reveal the message of their souls.

It was all very formless and exciting.

2

EPHRAIM'S STIFF LETTER OF ACCEPTANCE HAD BEEN promptly answered by a note of instructions about Miranda's journey to Dragonwyck, and at three in the morning of Monday, June the fourteenth, Miranda awoke at a light touch on her shoulder. She opened her eyes to see her mother, candle in hand, standing beside the bed.

'It's time, dearie—' said Abigail, and the unaccustomed endearment startled the girl into realization of what this day was to mean. She was leaving home, leaving the ordered safety of the familiar, leaving this quiet woman on whose love and sympathy she had always instinctively leaned. Suppose something happened to Ma, thought Miranda in sudden terror, suppose something happened to any of them here at home, she wouldn't even know about it for days.

She thrust her bare feet over the edge of the bed and looked up at Abigail. 'Perhaps I oughtn't go,' she said slowly. 'Something might happen. You'd need me. And— Oh, Ma, I'm going to miss you so.'

This woke up Tabitha, who yawned and said virtuously, 'Don't worry about Ma, Ranny. I don't mind doing the extra work when you're gone.'

The mother knew this to be true. Tibby would not only take over Miranda's work, but do it far better than her sister had. Miranda was full of the most regrettable faults, she was vain and lazy and heedless. She thought far too much about worldly things; she was, as Ephraim constantly pointed out, finicking; while Tabitha was of an upright rectitude that had made it unnecessary to chide her since she was six.

How was it, then, thought Abigail, that possessing the very model of daughters she could look upon that plump and dutiful little person unmoved, while the sight of Miranda always gave her a sensation of melting and warmth? She had much ado now not to take that curly golden head and press it against her breast as she used to long ago. Instead she said:

'Nonsense. Of course you're going, Ranny,' and put the candlestick on the washstand. 'No shilly-shallying now, miss. You've got what you wanted, so you might as well enjoy it.'

There was no answer to this, and Abigail's brisk voice was comforting.

Miranda dressed quickly. She put on her church dress of brown merino. It had been impossible to find the money for a new dress, but she had furbished this one as much as possible with a snowy white fichu and starched her petticoats until they stood out stiffly and pushed the merino skirt into a creditable imitation of a bell-shaped crinoline. She fastened the fichu with the beautiful hair brooch that was her only piece of jewelry. It had been given her on her thirteenth birthday while she was convalescing from scarlet fever. It had a real gold rim enclosing, under glass, a braided rose made from the combined hair of the whole family; Ephraim's grizzled strand twined with Abigail's brown and the children's reddish chestnut to form a pleasing russet shade with a sheen like that of the walnut chair in the parlor. Ephraim had had it made by a jeweler in Stamford, and Miranda was very proud of it. It certainly set off the dress and nearly matched the elegance of her new bonnet.

The Misses Lane, milliners in Cos Cob, had made the bonnet after many devout consultations with *Godey's* and the one copy they possessed of *La Mode à Paris*. It was of natural straw trimmed with rose satin ribbons, and in lieu of the ostrich feathers which appeared in the illustration it was embellished on either side by a large red cotton rose. The egg money which had provided the bonnet could not be stretched enough to include ostrich feathers.

Miranda tied the ribbons of this creation beneath her chin, peered into the tiny cracked mirror, then looked to her mother for approval.

Abigail thought the girl beautiful. 'That bonnet's a mite giddy, but you'll do,' she said crisply. 'Here's your shawl; say good-bye to the children and hurry. I hear Tom hitching up.'

Miranda picked up her traveling basket, which had been made by old Hardy, the last Sinawoy Indian who lived over in the Stanwich woods. It was capacious and sturdy, quite adequate to her scanty wardrobe. Then she leaned over Tabitha, who was half asleep again.

'Good-bye, Tibby,' she said.

Tabitha sat up and the sisters kissed tenderly, forgetful in this parting moment of all their little squabbles.

The younger children, Seth, Nat, and the baby, did not wake up as

Miranda kissed them, and her eyes filled, premonitory pangs of homesickness assailed her.

Fortunately there was little time for emotion during the next half-hour. The market boat for New York would leave Mianus at five, and they must be at the dock in plenty of time to unload the wagon and get the produce on board.

At four o'clock, just as the first gray streaks of dawn showed over the distant ridge of Palmer Hill, Miranda clambered up onto the wagon seat beside Ephraim. Tom, who must accompany them to drive the ox-team back, settled himself on a bag of potatoes in the rear, Ephraim shouted to the oxen and they started, with no more drama than that.

Miranda waved to the diminishing figure of her mother, barely discernible in the dim light, and thought of a hundred things she might have said to her. 'Ma, I'll write often. If you need me, I'll come home at once. Don't work too hard, will you, Ma, dear? And take care of yourself—please.'

She had said none of these things, nor had Abigail said much except, 'Behave yourself now. Make yourself useful to Mr. and Mrs. Van Ryn. Say your prayers every night and morning.'

Miranda swallowed, the familiar countryside blurred. The wagon rumbled up and down the stony hills on the Catrock road, the brakes squeaked as they slid down the last steep pitch into the Mianus River valley. Many other farm wagons were clustered on the turnpike below the Dumpling Pond Bridge. Isaac Taylor in the wagon next theirs greeted Ephraim cordially and then peered in astonishment at Miranda.

'You folks going somewhere?' he asked. 'Mighty early in the day to see a young lady all togged out in finery.'

Ephraim nodded. 'Ranny and I're off to New York with the boat. She's going to visit some of her ma's relations up the Hudson.'

Isaac whistled. 'You don't say. Mind you don't get lost in the big city. Last time I was there in thirty-nine, what with all them horsecars and cabs and hacks and the twisting streets and the hawkers wanting to sell you something I got plumb confused. Was mighty glad to get home again. You never been there, have you, Ephraim?'

'No,' answered Ephraim stiffly, his eyes on the potatoes and bushel baskets of onions Tom was loading onto the boat.

'Well, they got a lot of slickers down there,' continued Isaac. 'There was one fellow with a gold watch chain and a satin suit tried to sell me the City Hall, hundred dollars down and the rest monthly. I told him

I wasn't born yesterday and he'd have to be a lot smarter than that to diddle a Connecticut Yankee.'

'I guess we'll manage all right,' said Ephraim. 'With the Lord's help. Come on, Ranny, get on board. Looks like they're getting ready to sail.'

She hurried down from the wagon and across the plank to the market boat. There seemed to be no place to sit, so she made her way to the stern through the piled vegetables, dusted off a sack of potatoes, and settled gingerly on that.

Tom emerged from the hold and came over to her. 'Good-bye, sis,' he said, holding out his hand. 'Good luck.' He hesitated a moment and reddened. 'I sure wish I was going too, like to see the city.'

'Oh, I wish you were, Tommy—' cried Miranda warmly. 'Come on, why don't you?'

Tom shook his head. 'Got to get back and hoe up the north field. Can't everybody go junketing off at once.'

'I guess not,' answered Miranda. Tom was so responsible. He never forgot a duty or left one undone. I suppose I am selfish and flighty, she thought unhappily. But nevertheless her spirits began to revive. This was adventure and travel and change. Even Ephraim, she saw, as the boat got under way and slid down the river toward the Sound, was beginning to enjoy himself. His stern face had relaxed, he actually smiled as he chatted with the captain.

In the Sound they picked up a strong southeasterly breeze. The Dora J. skimmed past Port Chester, Rye, New Rochelle, with a skittishness belied by her squat sturdy hull. Miranda had much trouble keeping her precious bonnet on, the wind caught its scoop brim until the confining ribbons beneath her chin nearly strangled her. When a shower of salt spray descended on her head, she finally untied the bonnet and examined the red roses anxiously. They were a trifle limp, so she protected them under a fold of her skirt and allowed the wind and spray to make havoc of her smooth braids. It wasn't at all proper to sit hatless in a public place, but after all there was no one on board but the sailors and her father, and she hoped they wouldn't notice or think her a trifle free in her manner.

The tide was with them and the trip passed quickly. At half-past eight she saw the New York skyline, and nearly fell over the rail in her excitement. How very tall the buildings were! some of them actually had four stories. And how many church spires there were! Sunshine glittered off the far-flung jumble of slate and shingled roofs, confused distant noises clamored from the shore. The river swarmed suddenly with ships; dories, ketches, market boats, schooners, and an occasional steam packet all apparently bearing down on the Dora J. Miranda several times braced herself for what seemed an inevitable collision, but nothing happened. They forged steadily ahead, rounding Corlear's Hook to make fast finally at a dock on South Street.

Miranda hastily put on her bonnet as Ephraim came aft to her.

'Looks like we're here,' he said. There was a lack of certainty in his manner, and as they stepped off the boat into a bustle and uproar the like of which Miranda had never imagined, she was both surprised and comforted to know that her father was for once a bit unsure of himself.

They stood a moment on South Street while the traffic whirled by them; heavy drays whose horses' great hoofs clattered on the cobblestones, private carriages and hacks, milk wagons and bakers' wagons, a dustman and a scissors-grinder man with his little bell.

People jostled them, a small boy strolled by, took a long, impudent look at them, then turning his eyes to heaven said, 'Lord love us if I don't think there's something green around here.' He lowered his eyes and fixed them on Ephraim. 'Don't you see nothing green?' asked the urchin chattily.

Ephraim frowned. 'Why no, my lad, I guess I don't know what you mean.'

'Whee, crickey,' said the boy. 'It's greener than I thought for and it's got hayseeds on it!' He contorted his grimy visage into a prodigious wink, burst into hoots of laughter, and strolled away.

Miranda flushed. 'I guess he meant us,' she said in a small voice.

'Little limb of Satan,' Ephraim growled. He pulled the Van Ryn letter angrily from his pocket and consulted it. 'He says to go to the Astor House. We better get started.'

But after they had twice asked their way and received conflicting impatient directions, Miranda was relieved when a cab drew up beside them, and the driver said: 'You people strangers, ain't you? You want I should take you somewheres?'

'Oh, yes, Pa, please,' said Miranda.

'How much to go to the Astor House?' asked Ephraim cautiously.

The broad Irish face on the box looked concerned. 'Oh, yez wouldn't be wanting to stop there, would ye, now? That's a high-falutin' place where they charge a dollar to turn around, let alone what they want for room and vittles. I'll take yez to me brother Paddy's foine little tavern on Morris Street. They'll treat you grand.'

'I said the Astor House,' said Ephraim icily.

The cabby shrugged his shoulders. 'Then that'll be a shilling.'

'What!' roared Ephraim. 'Be on your way, then, you conscienceless ruffian!' and Miranda could not but agree with him, tired and bewildered as she was.

Isaac Taylor was right, the city was full of slickers. But how did people know right off like that that they came from the country?

It took them almost an hour to reach the Astor House because they got lost three times. But when they finally trudged up Broadway, each clutching a wicker basket, and saw between Vesey and Barclay Streets the great pile of granite that was the hotel, Miranda had the answer to her question. It wasn't only the wicker baskets, it was their clothes. No one wore a shallow round beaver like her father's, no one had a fringe of beard under the chin, or long coattails or such wide trousers. And as for the fashionable ladies who were out on Broadway for the morning shopping, their satins and cashmeres, their ruffled and plumed bonnets, no more resembled Miranda's attire than a peacock resembles a wren.

Though most women love clothes there are not many with a real flair for them, an understanding of line and color, a swift instinctive certainty as to what will be becoming, or an ability to measure and apply the first vague indications of fashion change. Yet Miranda was one of these—though her faculty had had small scope in Greenwich—and now she suffered accordingly. She followed her father up the wide steps of the Astor House and wished passionately that she might fade into eternal invisibility before she faced the grand new cousin.

Everything about her was wrong. Fashionable ladies did not wear fichus, or brown merino, nobody had darned cotton gloves, and alas, though the Misses Lane had done their best, the bonnet was worst of all. It was too deep and too high. Its pink ribbons and red roses were ridiculous. It looked cheap, tawdry, and just what it was, an adapted provincial imitation of a French style of four years ago.

'Stop sidling along behind me like that,' commanded Ephraim sharply. 'Hold your head up and don't act like a scared rabbit. Ye're entering one of the marts of Mammon, and you'd better hold yourself like a God-fearing girl with nothing on her conscience.'

'Yes, Pa,' and Miranda stiffened her spine trying hopelessly to look like the haughty young lady in green satin who swept by them into a waiting barouche.

They entered the lobby and she gave a gasp. They seemed to be swimming over a vast sea of red plush carpeting. She had a confused impression of thousands of mirrors which reflected thousands of gilded gas jets, of marble columns interspersed with hordes of people. No one paid the slightest attention to them, and again they wavered uncertainly, until Ephraim discovered a marble desk at the far end of the lobby. Behind this stood a bored young man drumming his fingers.

'Must be the tavern-keeper,' muttered Ephraim. He lumbered across the carpet with Miranda in his wake.

The bored young man looked them up and down, lifted one black eyebrow, and said, 'Well, my good man, what can I do for you?'

'We're to meet a Mr. Nicholas Van Ryn here,' said Ephraim. 'Perhaps you could tell—' He stopped in an amazement shared by Miranda.

The bored young man was galvanized. He bowed, he smiled not once but in a rapid succession of ever more ingratiating smirks, he rang bells, he beckoned to underlings who materialized from behind the pillars. 'But, of course!' he cried. 'You are Mr. and Miss Wells. Mr. Van Ryn wrote me. All is in readiness for you. I beg that you will come with me, I will conduct you to your apartment. Mr. Van Ryn will arrive this afternoon. He directed that you were to have anything you wished. Anything,' he added with an impressive emphasis which suggested that if they expressed a preference for the British crown jewels or an African lion, it would not daunt him.

Miranda was dazed. She and Ephraim both made a quick reflexive gesture as two of the bellboys seized the precious baskets. 'I'll carry 'em!' cried Ephraim, but they were already out of sight. Miranda and her father found themselves herded up a tremendous staircase, down a brightly lit corridor, and into a large parlor crammed with rosewood furniture. 'Your bedchamber to the right,' said the clerk to Ephraim, throwing open a door with a flourish, 'and the young lady's in there.'

'You mean we're supposed to use these three rooms just for us?' said Ephraim in bewilderment. 'Seems like a sinful waste.'

The clerk looked pained. 'Mr. Van Ryn was very anxious that you should be comfortable, sir. I trust that you will be.'

'I guess so,' Ephraim answered. 'Much obliged to you, young man.'

When the door finally closed behind the clerk and bellboys, Ephraim sat down heavily on the settee. 'This Mr. Van Ryn must be very rich and very wasteful. What do people want with all this flummery anyway?' He stared resentfully at the blue plush curtains, the five carved chairs, the desk, the center table, the flowered rug, then through the opened doors at the four-posted beds, dressing-tables, black walnut armoires, and footstools. 'All any sensible body needs is a table, a chair, and a bed.'

His daughter did not answer; she stood wide-eyed in the middle of the room. Through the open windows came the steady clatter of the traffic. She took the bonnet off and flung it into a chair, she walked to the windows and looked out for a minute while her hand caressed the lush blue curtain fringes. She turned and examined the glass and gilt knobs that held the tie-backs. She leaned over and pressed her finger into the pile of the festooned red-and-gray carpet. When she straightened her eyes were dreamy.

'I've read about it, but I didn't know people lived like this, really,' she said half to herself. 'I think it's wonderful.'

Ephraim made an impatient sound and stood up. 'Miranda, you're a very light-minded female. You've always given too much weight to material things. I doubt very much that this excursion into Babylon is good for you. I've a mind to tell Mr. Van Ryn ye cannot go.'

'Oh, you couldn't do that, Pa!' she cried. 'You've given your word.'

Ephraim's mouth tightened and he turned away. He had never in his life broken his word and he would not do so now, but he was uneasy. He had little sympathy with Miranda, still she was his daughter and he was worried about her soul. All the frivolity and worldly tendencies which imperiled it he had tried to eradicate, with but dubious success, he knew very well. It looked now as though she were going into an environment where her worst nature would be fostered by luxury and the general atmosphere of ease and softness that he abhorred.

He walked into his room and shutting the door fell to his knees in prayer for Miranda.

His disquiet was increased later by the girl's behavior. Mr. Van Ryn, it seemed, had no limit to his forethought—or from Ephraim's viewpoint, foolish extravagance. He had ordered dinner for them. It arrived on trays borne by two black waiters just as Ephraim and Miranda were preparing to eat the bread and sausages and slices of pie that Abigail had packed in Ephraim's basket.

The dinner was colossal and composed entirely of items that neither of them recognized. Nor were they helped any by the gilded menu which was presented to them by one of the negroes.

It was written in gibberish—French, the waiter said in response to Miranda's timid question. She thereupon seized the menu and repeated the outlandish words to herself. '*Gigot d'agneau roti*,' murmured Miranda, pronouncing every letter carefully. 'I wonder what that is. *Tournedos de volaille. Compote de fruits glacés.*' She darted from one dish to another, sampling each. 'Oh, but isn't it all tasty! And so many different things!'

Ephraim pushed back his plate, and pulled Abigail's sausages from the basket. 'Lot of disgusting messes, if you ask me. Good food ruined by a mort of gluey gravies and sauces. Can't tell what you're eating. Don't touch that!' he thundered suddenly as Miranda put her spoon in a mixture of frozen fruits. 'It has spirits in it. I can smell it!'

The fruit had indeed been soaked in rum. Miranda put her spoon down. 'But Pa,' she said wistfully, 'it looks so good. Couldn't I just try to see? One bite couldn't really be intoxicating, could it?'

'Miranda!' cried Ephraim, shocked. 'Would you ever touch liquor in any form just because it looked good?'—

'No, Pa. I'm sorry. I wasn't thinking, I guess.'

'Child, child,' said Ephraim not unkindly. 'How many sins you commit through thoughtlessness. You must wrestle with your spirit like Jacob wrestled with the angel. Here, I have something for you.'

He fished in his basket and brought out a small leather-bound Bible, quite new. 'It might be hard sometimes for you to read in the Van Ryn's Bible. I want you to keep this with you in your room. Study in it every day. I've marked some passages for you.'

'Oh, thank you, Pa!' she cried, touched. With the exception of the hair brooch, and that had been Abigail's idea, it was the only present she had ever received from her father. Ephraim had written her name on the fly leaf:

Miranda Wells, June, 1844, from her Father.

'Read me the Ninety-First Psalm now,' ordered Ephraim.

'Now!' protested Miranda unhappily. She was in a fever to look out the window at the fascinating street, to examine her sumptuous bedroom again, to rip some of the trimming off the unfortunate bonnet, and perhaps something could be done about the fichu; it might be turned under, made less conspicuous. Moreover the early afternoon in a hotel room seemed a strange time and place for Bible reading.

But to Ephraim there was never an unsuitable time for the contemplation of Holy Writ, and he felt its need now as a disciplinary measure for Miranda and as an antidote to the disintegrating influence he felt around him.

'Now,' he said inflexibly. 'I want to hear you read.' He sat straighter in his chair, folded his large gnarled hands, and waited.

When she came to the tenth verse, he stopped her and repeated it himself in his measured voice ' "There shall no evil befall thee, neither shall any plague come nigh thy dwelling."—I pray that may be so, Miranda, in the new life you're going to.'

Oh, pshaw, she thought impatiently. What evil could possibly befall me in a rich old gentleman's house on the Hudson? Pa makes too much fuss about all this, he's not—not— She did not know the word she looked for: 'sophisticated' perhaps would have best covered her meaning. Nor did she realize that this was the first time in her life that she had been consciously critical of her father. She finished the psalm and jumped up before Ephraim should order her to go on. 'Pa, I must red up a bit before Mr. Van Ryn comes,' and she fled into her room.

By five o'clock Miranda had done what she could to improve her costume. The fichu had been turned under to form a collar. The roses were gone from the bonnet, and she had loosened into ringlets the tight honey-colored braids which had been coiled on either side her face, giving thanks as she did so that her hair curled naturally.

And still Mr. Van Ryn had not arrived.

'I think,' said Ephraim, giving the curls a disapproving frown, 'we'd better go downstairs and ask that oily jack-a-napes at the counter if maybe he knows when his high mightiness is coming.'

The lobby was even fuller than before, and the noise, compounded of chatter and laughter and the constant swish of taffetas, seemed to Miranda to be a roar. The air was loaded with tobacco smoke, the fragrance of rose and verbena water, and hair pomatum.

They made their way toward the desk, which was half-hidden by a newly arrived family from Philadelphia; Mama in black satin, a young girl in a Paisley shawl and green silk bonnet, and Papa, large and pompous, who was arguing with the clerk about the accommodations.

'Excuse me—' began Ephraim, craning over the stout back which cut him off from the clerk, when an indefinable murmur ran over the crowded lobby. There was a bustle around the door.

Miranda, conscious of the heightened interest, turned with everybody else.

A tall man walked through the door, and even in that first glimpse against the light, she received an instant impression of careless dignity and of an almost regal indifference.

She wondered vaguely who it might be, when she heard a whisper behind her. 'That's Nicholas Van Ryn, you know.' And at once the place seemed full of whispers as one told it to another. She heard the name Van Ryn repeated a dozen times.

The family from Philadelphia had ceased arguing, for the clerk, darting out from behind his barricade, had run to greet the new arrival.

'That's the Van Ryn patroon, Nellie,' said the Philadelphia mother importantly to her daughter. 'He lives on his manor up the Hudson like an English belted earl. I can't think what he's doing in an hotel; they say he's very proud and exclusive.'

'Oh, Ma!' answered Nellie in a subdued squeal, staring with all her might. 'Mercy, but isn't he handsome!'

And he was, thought Miranda, bewildered by this development, and trying rather frantically to rearrange her ideas.

Followed by the smirking clerk and perfectly indifferent to the gaping around him, he came straight to Miranda and Ephraim with his hand outstretched in cordial greeting. 'How do you do, Cousin Miranda and Mr. Wells. Let's go at once to my sitting-room where I can greet you properly, for this is too public a place.' And his lean dark face which was somber in repose broke into a charming smile.

As Miranda responded to it sudden excitement possessed her.

While they walked down the hall to Nicholas' suite she stole glances at him through her lashes. He was tall, over six feet and of a slender build. His fawn-colored trousers strapped to Wellington boots, his brown coat and traveling cape, were worn with the easy grace of a man who buys the best, is dressed by a valet, and then thinks no more about the matter. His hair, nearly as black as his boots, was abundant and slightly waving. He wore in his buttonhole a very small red rose, and she was later to learn that the flower in his buttonhole was almost as much a part of him as his long narrow hands.

As for his face, it was so nearly the embodiment of the descriptions of heroes in Miranda's favorite books that she was awed. Here were the full flexible mouth, the aquiline nose with slightly flaring nostrils, the high and noble forehead accented by stern black brows. There was only one discrepancy. Heroes invariably had dark eyes, large and flashing. But Nicholas' eyes were not large and they were blue—evidence of his Dutch ancestry. A peculiarly vivid light blue that was startling and somehow disconcerting in a face that might otherwise have belonged to a Spanish grandee.

When they were settled in a sitting-room which was even more luxurious than their own, Nicholas said: 'I beg your pardon for not being here to greet you, but the Swallow has only just now docked. I trust you've been comfortable.'

'Oh, to be sure, Mr. Van Ryn!' cried Miranda, so carried away with gratitude that she interrupted her father. 'Everything's wonderful and grand!'

Nicholas noted the faint provincialism in her clear voice and he turned and looked at her swiftly, the briefest glance, but it missed nothing: the tall grace of her slim body under the clumsy clothes, the delicate face with its unrealized potentialities for real beauty, the long hazel eyes innocent of any emotion but excitement and a transparent admiration for himself. She shows her blood, he thought with satisfaction. Thank Fortune she's not a hulking farm girl.

He had had misgivings about the invitation after it had been sent. Strangers were not lightly introduced at Dragonwyck, and despite the relationship, which was the only reason he had acceded to his wife's request for a companion to the child, he would have suavely packed Miranda back to Greenwich, had he thought her impossible.

'You're a powerful sight younger than I thought for,' exclaimed Ephraim suddenly. He had been examining Nicholas, and his conclusions though based on the same evidence were different from his daughter's.

Nicholas laughed. 'I'm thirty-one.'

'Well, ye don't look it,' answered Ephraim doubtfully. This fellow had the kind of slimsy looks that might turn a silly girl's head, and he certainly didn't have the feel of a good solid family man. Was it proper to let the lass go off with him tomorrow on a day-long trip? And what was this dumfool business he'd let the women talk him into anyway, thought Ephraim with a spurt of baffled irritation.

This irritation and its cause were obvious to Nicholas, who could usually read people's minds when he troubled to do so. He was completely indifferent to anyone's opinion, and the viewpoint of a New England farmer interested him not at all, but this man was his guest and the father of his kinswoman. It therefore amused him to charm Ephraim out of his doubts. So he talked a while of Johanna, his wife, and little Katrine, stressing the pleasure they anticipated from Miranda's arrival.

Then he flattered Ephraim by asking his opinion on politics and listening with intent interest to the answers.

Ephraim believed in the annexation of Texas and rather favored Henry Clay as candidate for the presidency in the coming election

Nicholas did neither, but politics bored him, and beyond a wish to see his old friend and neighbor Van Buren back in office, he took no part in them, so he agreed courteously with all of Ephraim's opinions.

Even when Ephraim outlined the religious observances which he would expect from Miranda and tried to exact a promise that she would be kept up to the mark, Nicholas remained smoothly gracious and reassuring, though he committed himself to nothing. As it never occurred to Ephraim that there could be a respectable family which did not hold morning and evening prayer and attend church twice on Sundays, the real though unrecognized obstacle to Miranda's departure on the morrow was averted.

For Nicholas was a hedonist and an atheist, and Ephraim would have regarded him with greater horror than he would a leper had he known. But he did not know, and by evening after they had supped, he had come to feel that Van Ryn was pleasant and solid enough after all.

They disagreed once. In speaking again of the elections, Nicholas said casually: 'My farmers will of course vote for Van Buren, unless this unknown Polk should get nominated. In that event I shall decide what would be best for them to do.'

Ephraim sat up with a jerk. '*Your* farmers! What in tunket d'you mean by that?'

'Why my tenant farmers on the manor land,' answered Nicholas. 'There are nearly two hundred of them.'

'Don't they own their own land?' asked Ephraim, frowning.

Miranda, who had sat quietly in a corner unnoticed by either man during the lengthy conversation, which did not interest her, turned her head from the window where she had been entranced by the coming of evening to New York and the myriad lights that leapt from the windows. She saw Nicholas' eyebrows raise, and an expression of annoyance on his face.

'Of course they don't own the land,' he said. 'It belongs to me as it did to my father before me and straight back to Cornelius Van Ryn, the first patroon, who took title in 1630. The tenants pay a very small yearly rent, and in return we have done a great deal for them.'

'How much land have you altogether?' pursued Ephraim.

'Only a few thousand acres; my grant is not nearly so large as that of the Van Rensselaers or the Livingstons.'

'Can the farmers not buy the land they've been working if they have a mind to?' Ephraim was still mulling over this new problem.

'No,' said Nicholas curtly, and Miranda saw, as her father did not, that behind his polite expression Nicholas was displeased. She saw no reason for it; all this talk of land and tenantry conveyed nothing to her. She had no means of knowing that Nicholas, who preferred to forget the matter, had of late had unpleasant evidence of unrest amongst his tenants. He refused to believe that the richly productive and gratifying feudal system which had supported himself and his ancestors for two hundred years could ever be seriously threatened. He treated his farmers with aristocratic indulgence, built them schools and chapels and bridges, bought them new machinery, entertained them with feastings, settled their differences, and kept a disciplinary eye on their lives. In return he expected them to be grateful and loyal as they always had been, and to share with him a just proportion of their produce.

'I would rather,' said Ephraim suddenly, 'own one half-acre of barren stony land myself free and clear, than work the richest farm in the country for someone else.'

'Then you're very foolish,' said Nicholas sharply, but controlled himself at once. 'I daresay it's just that we don't understand each other's viewpoint.— This must be very dull for you,' he added, getting up and walking over to Miranda.

'I don't know what it's all about,' she confessed. 'But I'm happy looking out the window, the park looks so pretty and cool with all the lights and that fountain. What's the big building, Mr. Van Ryn?' She pointed. 'And that one?'

'You mustn't call me Mr. Van Ryn, Miranda; call me Cousin Nicholas,' he said, smiling. He stood close beside her and a warm delightful sensation came to her as they looked out onto Broadway. 'That's the City Hall,' he answered her question. 'And that building across the street is the Park Theater.'

'Oh—' she breathed. 'How dearly I'd love to see a play.'

'Ranny!' exclaimed her father angrily. 'She knows better than that, Mr. Van Ryn. I can't think why she often talks so wildly.'

Miranda flushed and lowered her lids, but not before she had seen the amusement on Nicholas' face. Was it for her or her father or what, she thought unhappily. She couldn't bear it if he were laughing at her, because already she wanted desperately to please him. Of course he was really quite old, and married for so long. But someone like him, only younger and with dark flashing eyes, would fit perfectly into that daydream where souls commingled as they had for the lovely Esmeralda.

3

MIRANDA SLEPT LITTLE THAT NIGHT. EVERYTHING was strange; the street lights that filtered through her tightly drawn curtains, the amazing softness of the bed, the absence of a bedfellow. It was the first time in her life that Miranda had slept alone, and she would have missed Tibby's breathing and restless little mutters except that there was so much unaccustomed noise. There was the ticking of an onyx clock on the mantel, the rattle of wagons over the cobblestones, the hourly peal of bells from Saint Paul's Church next door, and there was the voice of the watch on the street below. 'It's one o'clock of a fine summer's night. All's well in the Third Ward.'

And later as dawn was breaking, the watch, as though inspired by near release from his duties, became more eloquent. 'It's Tuesday of a June morning. Four o'clock and all is well. John Tyler's still our President. The weather's fine, bless the Lord.'

By five o'clock Miranda gave it up.

She had been dressed and at the window for an hour when the waiters appeared in the sitting-room with breakfast. She was too excited to eat much, and when Nicholas appeared, smiling and courteous, telling her that his barouche was waiting at the door, she suppressed a belated instinct to cling to her father.

Ephraim had no stomach for sentiment this morning. The girl was going, and he was impatient to get back home. He also had slept badly, and he was not of those who enjoy a break in routine.

So their farewells were hurriedly said on the steps before the Astor House. 'God in His providence'll guard you, Miranda. Remember always that you're the Lord's handmaiden. Serve him diligently,' said Ephraim, putting his round beaver hat firmly on his head. 'And farewell to you, sir.' He turned to Nicholas, who stood beside them, his uncovered dark hair slightly ruffled by the morning breeze. 'Chastise her when she needs it. I pray that you'll make her useful to you and your wife. She's inclined to be lazy, I'm warning you. See that she writes home often, and don't let her neglect her prayers.'

Miranda flushed and Nicholas bowed gravely, saying, 'I will treat her in every way as though she were my own daughter.'

But I couldn't be, thought Miranda, he's but thirteen years older than I. And this sudden thought startled her.

'Good-bye to ye, then,' said Ephraim. He picked up his straw basket and walked rapidly away down Broadway.

At once a sensation of forlornness seized Miranda. He might have kissed her, she thought, aware that this was folly. Ephraim did not hold with cozening and cuddling. And he's not very fond of me, anyway, she thought wistfully. She knew that Ephraim was, so to say, through with her for the present. He had done his duty, albeit unwillingly, had turned her over to her new cousin, and was anxious to get back to his real interests.

She sighed as Nicholas handed her into the barouche. As they rode west on Barclay Street she was too despondent to notice her surroundings. She had never been in a private carriage before, but even the liveried coachman on the box and the two sleek bay horses did not capture her attention.

She vaguely supposed them to be hired, having no conception of the way men of Nicholas' standing lived. He kept a full stable and two carriages in New York for use during his infrequent visits. And he had recently built himself a town house on Stuyvesant Place for the same purpose. The house had been closed, its furniture swathed in dust sheets, and it had not seemed worth while to have it opened for one night, hence his choice of a hotel.

But when they reached the Hudson River pier and Miranda saw the enormous white-and-gold steamboat which awaited them, she was startled out of her depression. 'Oh, do we sail on that?' she cried. 'I never saw a boat so big—and beautiful.'

Nicholas smiled. Her naïveté amused him. It would be interesting to form this immature mind, to teach it and mould it. She would have much to learn before she would do him credit as his cousin. Those hideous clothes must be rectified. She must lose the flat drawl that proclaimed her Yankee upbringing. He had noticed her uncertainty with forks and knives; her table manners in general needed correction. She must learn how to walk with dignity instead of apologetically. She was unpoised, her movements were jerky, she seemed not to realize that she must always precede a gentleman and hung back in an awkward way whenever he tried to usher her through a door. But she would learn easily. Fortunately Nature had given her delicate bones and a graceful slenderness—very different from Johanna.

As always at the thought of his wife a black curtain descended in his mind.

They reached the gangplank, an ornate affair of mahogany and red plush carpeting. Miranda stopped uncertainly at its foot, instinctively waiting for Nicholas to lead the way.

He shook his head. 'You must go first. Always a lady precedes her escort.'

'Oh, to be sure,' she said quickly. Pa had always led his flock but this was different, the ways of gentry. She would not make that mistake again.

The Swallow was overpowering to Miranda. It was, as the newspapers proudly called it, a 'floating palace.' From the carved golden eagle on the bow to the gaily flying flag at the stern, every available surface had been embellished with scrollwork painted white and tastefully accented with gilt. Inside the main saloon—two decks high—Corinthian pillars supported Gothic arches which merged in turn into a vast ceiling painted with cupids and garlands. The satin draperies, the inch-thick carpets, and enormous chandeliers eclipsed even those at the Astor House.

Whereas, yesterday, Miranda had sat on a sack of potatoes in the market boat, today she had a rosewood-and-velvet armchair in a sheltered recess of the broad white deck. And there was music. A German band in the saloon rendered one after another, without interval, the popular tunes.

'An infamous racket,' commented Nicholas disdainfully as he sat down beside her, so that she did not dare admit that she thought the music beautiful. But as the Swallow got under way the band's efforts were drowned out by the swishing of the paddle wheels, the pounding of the walking beam, and chugging blasts from the smokestacks.

They gathered speed after they passed Yonkers, and Miranda was grateful for the protected place which Nicholas had found, for the firemen brought up pressure by the addition of fat pine knots to the anthracite, and less sheltered passengers must either be deluged with soot and flying sparks or seek the stuffy saloon.

When they left the Tappan Zee, Miranda gave herself eagerly to admiration of the scenery. Nicholas pointed out to her the peaks of Dunderberg and Anthony's Nose, the tiny Pollopel's Island, on which in Dutch times a goblin had dwelt to plague the sailors. He told her this and other legends of the river so that she listened in wide-eyed fascination. Nicholas, when he chose, was a brilliant talker, with that inborn and unteachable gift for making any topic interesting. At the moment it amused him to entertain Miranda.

The Swallow was leaving the Newburgh landing when several passengers ran down the decks to the stern and the boat seemed to leap forward, the pistons banged to a new frenzied rhythm, and sparks flew thick as red flies from the stacks.

Nicholas stood up and gazed down-river where another ship had appeared around the jut of Denning's Point. 'It's the Express,' he said. 'She's after us. Now we shall doubtless race her to Poughkeepsie.'

'Race?' questioned Miranda, surprised. 'Whatever for?'

'For the pleasure of proving that the other boat is inferior.'

She looked at him quickly, thinking it an odd reply, and wondering if he were laughing at her, but he was intently watching the Express's progress as she gained on them. The Swallow's pounding and straining increased until it seemed that her decks would burst open, and the sparks from the smokestack coalesced into tongues of actual flame. Suddenly the race frightened her.

'Isn't it dangerous?' she cried as the deck grew hot under her thin soles.

Nicholas shrugged, never taking his eyes from the pursuing boat whose bow was now flush with their stern. 'There's danger everywhere, I suppose.'

She shrank into her seat clutching its arms and telling herself that she must not be a silly coward. Certainly everyone else was enjoying himself hugely. The passengers surged from bow to stern cheering or groaning as now one boat gained and then the other; they made hoarse wagers on the outcome, shouting across the hundred yards of water to the Express, whose own passengers and crew answered back in kind.

And then it was all over. The Swallow slid first up to her Poughkeepsie dock; there was deafening applause on the decks around them, while catcalls and oaths came from the vanquished boat.

Miranda felt foolish, and glancing apologetically at Nicholas she saw that though he had taken no part in the enthusiasm of the passengers, he yet wore an expression of exhilaration and triumph. An expression which vanished at once as his face returned to its usual reserve.

She had a moment of puzzled uneasiness, for though she did not in the least understand him, she knew that his reaction to the race was not like that of the other passengers; she felt that the contest had had for him an inner meaning, and that in some way its outcome represented the vindication of his will.

The Swallow proceeded decorously up-river from Poughkeepsie, but Miranda continued to suffer uneasiness out of all proportion to the cause. This uneasiness had in it a quality of foreboding and of prescience, as though the boisterous and senseless contest between two boats held for her a future significance. And yet the summer afternoon was tranquilly blue, and the narrowing river flowed peacefully past their vessel as the wooded shores came nearer. By the time that the western shore reared itself up into the purple masses of the Catskills, she had regained her eager expectancy and cried: 'Oh, Cousin Nicholas, how high they are! I'd no notion mountains were so big!'

Nicholas thought of the Alps, in which he had spent the summer of 1835 while making the Grand Tour before his marriage, and he smiled, but forebore to disillusion her. Instead he pointed out the Mountain House, whose thirteen white columns were visible even at that distance.

'That's Rip Van Winkle's country back of the Mountain House,' said Nicholas. 'They say that on hot summer days one can still hear the little men playing at ninepins.'

Miranda looked blank.

'Don't you know Diedrich Knickerbocker and "The Sketch Book"?'

She shook her head.

'Tales by Washington Irving, a fine writer and a friend of mine,' Nicholas explained. 'No doubt you'll meet him some day.'

Nicholas settled back in his chair. This touched on one of his dominant interests. He was well grounded in the classics, of course, though it had never occurred to his father to send him to college; that type of education open to almost anyone, even tradesmen and farmers' sons, was not fitting to an aristocrat. There had therefore been a succession of tutors, German and English, to prepare the boy for the cultural climax of the Grand Tour.

He had spent two years traveling elegantly through England, France, Spain, Italy, and Germany before returning to Dragonwyck to find that his father had died and he was now Lord of the Manor.

Nicholas, then, knew the classics, but in the last five years he had developed a lively interest in contemporary American writing. In this he differed from most of the young men of his class, who aped the European and persisted in regarding the United States as crude and negligible.

Nicholas, true to his birth and an upbringing far less democratic than that of an English nobleman, delighted in the rôle of patron. He had patterned himself half-consciously on a Lorenzo de Medici or a Prince Esterhazy.

He enjoyed entertaining the intelligentsia at Dragonwyck. He read the new works of Bryant, Hawthorne, and a startling young writer called Poe, with a sincere appreciation which was only slightly patronizing. For Nicholas' conviction of his own superiority was so interwoven with his flesh and bone that he had no need to prove it to others as do those not quite secure. He was a Van Ryn of Dragonwyck Manor, a law unto himself and beholden to nobody on earth—or in heaven.

He glanced again at Miranda who sat forward gazing first at one shore then the other. The breeze had whipped color into her white skin, her lips were slightly parted, her small breasts under the brown merino bodice rose and fell rapidly. There was a strong aura of femininity about her, and her long eyes, gold-flecked in green between thick dark lashes, were really magnificent. Except that they were innocent of all sex-consciousness, they were the seductive eyes of a passionate woman.

He was suddenly reminded of a French marquise he had met in Paris and of whom he had been enamored until she offended his fastidiousness. This memory annoyed him and he said coldly:

'I fear you're rather ignorant, Miranda. I shall map out a plan of reading for you.'

She smiled nervously, hurt by his tone. He had seemed so cordial and charming on the trip that she had felt at ease with him, almost as though he were her own age. It was therefore startling to see that his handsome face had grown indifferent and remote, and to have him speak to her as her father did. She felt suddenly that she bored him, and was sure of it when he wrapped his cloak about him and rose abruptly, saying, 'I'm going to take a few turns about the deck; you'll be quite safe here.'

She would have liked to walk with him, she was unused to sitting still for hours on end, and her healthy young muscles ached for exercise, but she dared say nothing. Nicholas had turned sternly unapproachable. It was her first experience of his dark moods, and far more experienced and mature people than Miranda had found them impossible to understand.

In an hour he came back, and she saw at once that the darkness had lifted. He approached her with his rare smile, a smile devoid of merriment and yet magnetic and intensely personal so that the recipient invariably felt flattered.

'In half an hour we'll arrive at Dragonwyck, Miranda. This town is Hudson.'

She obediently inspected the small neat collection of buildings and wharfs, but she was somewhat sated with new sights and privately thought Newburgh or Poughkeepsie more attractive.

'I've wondered about the name Dragonwyck, Cousin Nicholas,' she said timidly. 'Please don't think me prying,' she added, fearful that she might offend him again.

But Nicholas was pleased to explain anything that bore on the history of his family or Manor.

He sat down at once. 'The name is typical of the place in that it's a mixture of Indian legend and Dutch now anglicized—made into English,' he added, seeing that she did not understand the word. 'You see, when my direct ancestor Cornelius Van Ryn, the first patroon, acquired our lands here, he sailed up from New Amsterdam to inspect them and choose the site for the Manor House. He decided on this cliff by the river. But there was a party of Mohican Indians camped near-by and he soon found that they were afraid of this cliff on which he had started to build the house. They avoided it always, and though he was kind to them they feared him too, nor would they touch one stone or brick which went into the building. After he knew them better he discovered the reason. They believed that under the cliff there lived a great winged serpent which devoured everything which encroached on its territory.'

'And did he build there anyway?' asked Miranda.

'Of course he did. And he called the place *Drakenwyck,* "place of the dragon" in Dutch, and so it has been for two hundred years.'

'The dragon hasn't ever bothered you?' asked Miranda, half-seriously.

Nicholas was amused at her question. 'No. There are many other legends and superstitions of this region; I hope you're not too impressionable or old Zélie will frighten you with her spook rocks and phantom ships and witches—' He stopped abruptly as though he had been going to add something else.

She waited politely to see if he would go on. But he did not, and just then the steamer gave one sharp blast and veered to the eastern bank. 'We're here,' he said.

She turned from her puzzled contemplation of his face.

In after years Miranda knew that her first sight of Dragonwyck was the most vivid and significant impression of her life. She stared at the fantastic silhouette which loomed dark against the eastern sky, the spires and gables and chimneys dominated in the center by one high tower; and it was as though the good and evil, the happiness and tragedy, which she was to experience under that roof materialized into physical force and struck across the quiet river into her soul.

While the steamer made fast to the private landing she stood by the rail close to Nicholas gazing up at his house with a fascinated repulsion, while the setting sun touched half the hundred windows into fiery rectangles against the blackness of the vine-covered stone.

Nicholas seeing her awe-struck face was content to let her gaze in silence.

His home was part of him, an externalized expression of his will, for upon his inherited Dutch Manor house he had superimposed the Gothic magnificence which he desired. He had been attracted by the formulations of Andrew Downing, the young landscape architect who lived on the river at Newburgh and whose directions for building 'romantic and picturesque villas' were changing the countryside; but it was not in Nicholas to accept another's ideas, and when five years ago he had remodeled the old Van Ryn homestead, he had used Downing simply as a guide. To the original ten rooms he had added twenty more, the gables and turrets, and the one high tower. The result, though reminiscent of a German Schloss on the Rhine, crossed with Tudor English and interwoven with pure fantasy, was nevertheless Hudson River American and not unsuited to its setting.

The Dragonwyck gardens were as much an expression of Nicholas' personality as was the mansion, for here he had subdued Nature to a stylized ornateness. Between the untouched grove of hemlocks to the south and the slope of a rocky hill half a mile to the north he had created along the river an artificial and exotic beauty.

To Miranda it was overpowering, and she felt dazed as they mounted marble steps from the landing. She was but vaguely conscious of the rose gardens and their pervasive scent, of small Greek temples set beneath weeping willows, of rock pavilions, violet-bordered fountains, and waterfalls. She was acutely conscious of her travel-stained brown dress, and the sharp, contemptuous stare of the liveried footman who had met them on the pier and was gingerly carrying her wicker basket.

It wasn't credible that she was to live in a place like this, and her steps as she followed Nicholas to the great front door dragged slower and slower even as her heart beat faster.

They entered the great hall which ran sixty feet through the house to open on the back lawns by the drive. It was dark inside, for the tapers had not yet been lit, and she shrank toward Nicholas as two people glided through a door at the right and confronted them bowing. They were Magda, Mrs. Van Ryn's housekeeper and personal maid, and Tompkins the butler.

They both ignored Miranda while they greeted their master, but from the woman's thick back and round averted head Miranda felt hostility.

'Where's Mrs. Van Ryn?' asked Nicholas, allowing the butler to take his cape and hat.

'In the Green Drawing-Room, my lord.' The butler was a Yorkshireman who had accompanied Nicholas back from England years ago and with the special snobbery of the British servant had always addressed his master by this title, insisting that in any civilized country the owner of such lands and name and estate would have been a peer. Nicholas, agreeing with him, had not objected, though the matter was indifferent to him. A Van Ryn had no need of title or distinction borrowed from Europe.

'This way, then, Miranda,' said Nicholas, ushering her down the hall to a doorway on the left. 'You shall now have the pleasure of meeting my wife.'

Was there a peculiar intonation in his voice or did she imagine it? She had no time to wonder, for they entered the Green Drawing-Room.

Johanna Van Ryn sat by the window embroidering. She started and her gold thimble rattled on the floor as Miranda and Nicholas walked in.

She looked up at her husband and the dull colorless eyes came to life with longing and a mute appeal. 'You're back!' she whispered.

Nicholas picked up the thimble and placed it on the tabouret beside a half-eaten cruller. He bowed to his wife and taking her extended hand, which was loaded with rings, barely touched it with his lips. 'Yes, I'm back as you see. And here is Miranda.'

Johanna's eyes dropped and she gave a nearly inaudible sigh. 'Welcome to Dragonwyck, child,' she said, not looking at the girl. 'I trust you'll be happy. Nicholas, did you bring me the pastries?'

Miranda stared at the figure in the rocking chair. Johanna was enormously fat, the plump pale fat that makes monstrous dimples at elbows and knuckles. On her face, which was round and white as one of the crockery plates in the kitchen at home, there were two unskillfully applied spots of what even Miranda, who had never seen any, recognized as rouge. The scanty flaxen hair was tightly drawn back and covered with a coquettish lace cap embellished with blue ribbons none too fresh. There were delicate laces covering her bosom, and on them were scattered small brown crumbs whose origin was no farther to seek than the cruller on the tabouret.

Miranda, suddenly remembering her manners, said: 'It's most kind of you, ma'am, to let me come here. Please to accept Ma and Pa's respects.'

Johanna nodded. 'I'm sure they're most worthy people, and I'm sure you'll be a good girl. Nicholas, did you get those pastries?'

Her husband stood looking down at her a moment without answering, then he spoke pleasantly. 'I did, my dear. Will you have them here now, or can you wait until supper time?'

'Did you get the Napoleons, the honey puffs, and the mocha bon-bons?'

'All of them.'

She contracted her tow-colored eyebrows. 'Well, I think I'll have the bon-bons now. Tell Tompkins to have the others served at dinner. Be sure he keeps them well chilled so the cream won't melt.'

Nicholas bowed slightly. 'It shall be done, my love.'

How sweet he is to her, thought Miranda. I suppose he was awfully in love with her and hasn't noticed that she's so fat and untidy. Farther than that she did not go in her thoughts, for she was determined to like Johanna.

'One of the servants will show you to your room,' said Johanna, at last realizing that the girl was still standing there, 'and after a while you'd best go and find Katrine. I never can keep track of that child. You might read a story to her.'

'I think we can hardly ask our guest to occupy herself with a child tonight,' said Nicholas. 'She must be tired.'

Johanna shrugged her massive shoulders, and thrusting out an incredibly small foot in a purple velvet slipper began to rock slowly back and forth.

'Oh, to be sure, you must rest if you're tired, my dear. You'll feel better after a good supper. You may eat it in the nursery.'

'Oh, I think not,' said Nicholas again. 'Our cousin would hardly eat in the nursery. It will be a pleasure to have her with us.'

Johanna pursed her mouth. 'As you like, Nicholas. Only do hurry and tell Tompkins about those pastries or they'll be quite ruined.'

Miranda listened to all this with dismay. She didn't know what a nursery was exactly, but it was plain enough that Johanna expected to consider her as a kind of upper servant. She was correspondingly grateful to Nicholas for his attitude. But neither this nor the luxurious magnificence of the bedroom in which she presently found herself obliterated a spasm of homesickness and a yearning to return to the dearly familiar and simple farmhouse. It seemed a week since she had bade her father good-bye that morning and a month at least since she had seen Abigail's shrewd, affectionate face.

She threw herself on the bed and indulged in bitter tears which were not quenched by the realization that she had wanted to come to Dragonwyck and here she was, that she had yearned for luxury and elegance and now she had it to an extent a thousand times beyond her dreams. She felt defenseless and out of place, frightened of the servants, unable to like Johanna, appalled by the size and grandeur of the house, which she had barely glimpsed as Nicholas led her upstairs. Nor did she altogether like Nicholas. He gave her a strange sensation that was half pleasurable and half a shrinking discomfort.

I wish I hadn't come, she thought, and in the thinking knew that it wasn't true. She had been impelled toward Dragonwyck from the first moment of hearing about it, and now that she was here it still seemed to be pulling her closer, as though there were a magnet hidden in its gray stone turrets.

She sat up and dried her eyes and looked around the room. The bedroom at the Astor House had been only a pallid introduction to this. Her three windows faced south and commanded the whole sweep of the river downstream, while in the distance rose the Catskills, hazy in the dusk. She was on the second floor, on which there were six large bedchambers, as she later discovered, and hers the middle one on the south side. It was furnished with massive black walnut pieces in the Gothic style and its draperies were of peacock blue brocade, as was the tester of the four-posted bed. The rug was an Aubusson specially woven for the room in a pattern of golden wheat sheaves garlanded with blue and green. The washbowl and ewer, even the doorknobs, were made of engraved silver. Miranda's youth and her temperament combined to raise her spirits, and to her other discoveries was now added an excited wonder. Imagine a bathroom across the hall with a silver tub! Imagine above all the small private closet which opened from her room and was obviously for her exclusive use! She thought of the embarrassing and chilly trips across the yard to the outhouse behind the bushes at home, and felt for them all there an impatient pity. How little they knew of real refinement. They hadn't even sense enough to want a different way of living. Except Ma, she thought with swift love; how dearly I'd like to have her here too!

She unpacked the wicker basket and hung her three calico dresses in the painted Dutch Kas, where they looked lost and bedraggled. She longed to change the brown merino, which now seemed to her incredibly ugly, but there was nothing to change into. The calicos would be worse.

Supper was a silent meal. The food, served by Tompkins and a young footman, was delicious, but Miranda had no appetite. The profusion of strangely shaped spoons and forks dismayed her, and so did the wineglasses which stood beside her plate. From one of these she took a sip because the Van Ryns did, feeling very defiant and wicked as she thought of her father, but the stuff tasted sour, and she pushed the glass stealthily away.

Nicholas, at the head of the table, scarcely spoke except to make conventional inquiry as to her comfort. It seemed impossible that he could have been the entertaining companion of the first part of today's journey.

As for Johanna, she concentrated on her food and her only remarks had to do with that subject. The roast was overdone, but the potato cakes were tolerable. Annetje must remember not to get the jellies so hard. When she had mopped up the last bite of honey puff, Johanna looked up at Miranda. 'Where's Katrine?' she asked.

'I don't know, ma'am, I'm sorry. I've not seen her yet,' answered the girl nervously, wondering if she had already failed in a duty.

Johanna frowned. 'That child—she's always down with the servants. Now that you're here I hope you can keep her upstairs where she belongs. That's why I wanted a companion for her.'

'I'll try hard, ma'am.'

Johanna gave Miranda a dissatisfied look. 'You're not quite the type I expected, but I suppose you'll do your best. You seem very sweet,' she added with a vague smile and a quick glance at Nicholas, who was peeling himself a nectarine and had not looked up.

Johanna heaved herself up from her chair and waddled on her tiny feet into the adjoining room.

'Send Miss Katrine in to us, Tompkins,' ordered Nicholas, rising and motioning Miranda to follow his wife, who had already ensconced herself in an armed rocker by the central table.

This was one of the many rooms that Miranda had not yet seen. It was called the Red Room from the color of its carpet and plush curtains, and it was comparatively small because it was part of the original house and Nicholas had left it alone. Around its fireplace ran still the old blue and white Dutch tiles representing the story of Adam and Eve and the Fall, and the furniture was simple for Dragonwyck; besides the center table with its fringed red velvet cover there were only three chairs, a horsehair sofa, and in the corner an old and shabby harpsichord.

At first Miranda decided that it was more homelike and cosy than the rest of the house. She sat timidly in the corner by the harpsichord, Johanna rocked while jabbing with a clumsy hand at the white lawn handkerchief she was embroidering. Nicholas with his back to the unlit fire buried himself in the morning *Tribune* which he had brought from New York. Ten candles lit the room and in their soft light the reflected reds glowed warmly. It was a reassuring domestic scene, but as she sat there an indefinable discomfort crept over Miranda, and at the same time she shivered from a sudden sensation of cold. Dare I ask them to light the fire, she thought, and knew that she did not. The June night was warm, and she could see Johanna's forehead and upper lip glistening.

Miranda shifted uneasily in her seat, and the formless discomfort mounted within her until between one second and the next it ceased to be discomfort, and she knew it for blind unreasoning fear. Fear of what? She moistened her lips and looked about her. There was nothing but the comfortable room. Nicholas turned a page of his newspaper, and the small rustle mingled with the rhythmic creak of his wife's rocker; both these sounds seemed to Miranda to come from a vast and chilly distance. She clasped and unclasped her hands, struggling with a violent urge to run headlong from the room.

The door opened and a little girl walked in dragging her feet. At once the fear and the feeling of cold vanished.

'Oh, there you are, pet,' said Johanna vaguely. 'You're a naughty girl to stay away so much.'

Nicholas took the child's arm and led her over to Miranda. 'This is your new cousin, Katrine.'

The child put her finger in her mouth and gaped at Miranda, who smiled and held out her hand. Katrine would someday be a replica of her mother. She was a plump and stolid child now, with the same scanty tow-colored hair and small colorless eyes like pebbles.

'Shake hands with your cousin,' said Nicholas sharply, and Katrine slowly obeyed.

'We'll be friends, won't we, dear?' said Miranda, trying to draw the child toward her, but the chunky little body resisted.

'Yes, Cousin M'randa,' answered Katrine without interest. 'Can I go find my kitty now, Mama?' she added, scuffling her slippers and twisting a corner of her plaid skirt.

'Oh, I suppose so—' began Johanna fretfully, but the child did not wait for more. She gave her father a quick, apprehensive glance, and seeing that he was not going to stop her she darted from the room away from the mother who was always discontented and ineffectual, and the father who frightened her, back to the simple delights of the kitchen and Annetje's welcoming presence.

Nicholas' eyes followed his daughter, and Miranda saw that the dull, unprepossessing child was a disappointment to him, though how bitter a one to a man of his nature she could not guess.

Johanna sighed and bent over the monogram she was embroidering, Nicholas' monogram, Miranda now saw, and saw also that the letters were botched and straggling.

'I can't think,' said Johanna, 'why Trine's always wanting to run to the servants. She can't get those tastes from my side, or yours either, Nicholas, except possibly the Gaansevants; they were certainly common people.'

Miranda looked up startled. Johanna must be aware that she was insulting her guest, whose only connection with the Van Ryns was through these same Gaansevants, but one look reassured her. Johanna was simply following a familiar train of thought and was perfectly insensitive to any overtones or ramifications which it might develop.

'No one could possibly doubt that your ancestry is of the bluest and most aristocratic, my love.' And again Miranda was struck by the extraordinary sweetness of Nicholas' tone.

Johanna smiled. 'My papa,' she said to Miranda, 'always used to say that he despaired of finding a suitable match for his girls in view of the sad way the country had gone lately. There are so few of the fine river families left. But he was pleased when I married Nicholas. He thought that a Van Ryn would do very well, though he would perhaps have preferred a Livingston or Van Rensselaer.'

'I'm profoundly grateful that he found me acceptable,' said Nicholas. 'Miranda, do you play the pianoforte? We might have some music.'

She shook her head. 'I'm sorry.'

'Well, anyway, come and turn the pages for me.'

She looked at the harpsichord, but Nicholas shook his head. 'No one ever touches that old instrument. It belonged to my great-grandmother, Azilde de la Courbet.'

'I wish you'd get rid of the thing, Nicholas,' said Johanna suddenly, putting down her work. 'It's not in keeping with the rest of the furniture and then there's that old story. I vow the servants are afraid to dust it.'

'Servants are always superstitious,' answered Nicholas indifferently. 'You know very well that I never "get rid" of anything that belonged to my ancestors. Their material possessions are as precious to me as the blood and traditions which I also inherited.—Come, Miranda, let's go to the music room.—You don't care to come, I suppose, my love, since you never do.'

Johanna bent her fat neck and stared down at the embroidery. 'Isn't it rather late? Miranda must be tired; you said yourself she was tired.'

'I'm not tired now,' said the girl quickly with some resentment, for why should she be sent to bed like a child when Nicholas had paid her the compliment of wishing her company? Besides, there was an undercurrent here that she did not understand.

Without further words Nicholas led the way to the music room, a nearly empty chamber with a vaulted ceiling and an oriel window beneath which stood the pianoforte.

As they entered the room a figure slid out from the shadowy hall and lit the tapers. Miranda soon grew accustomed to the noiseless and almost invisible service at Dragonwyck, though it took her some time to realize that it was part of Nicholas' plan of esthetic living.

The machinery of labor must never intrude. The synthetic perfection of his surroundings must seem to spring effortlessly into being as from the touch of an enchanter's wand. For this reason the pleasure gardens, even the lawns and fruit orchards, were always romantically deserted. The necessary digging, weeding, hoeing, and trimming was done at night by an army of gardeners with lanterns and torches.

Nicholas sat down on the piano stool and it soon developed that she could not possibly turn the pages, for though she read the soprano part of hymns, she could not follow the complicated sonatas which suited his mood that evening.

He was a musician of distinction; he played with passion and a fastidious brilliance. These qualities she felt, though the cascades of sound meant nothing to her uneducated ear. She watched his flexible hands and his profile against the green curtain behind the piano. His eyes were fixed on the distance, a point far beyond the instrument, and she knew he had forgotten all about her, but she felt again at ease with him.

He executed a chromatic run and stopped. 'That was Beethoven, Miranda.' He turned and giving her an understanding look, smiled at her. 'But here's something you *will* like, I think.'

He drew a sheet of music out of the carved chest beside the piano.

'This is something new from England, an opera called the "Bohemian Girl." I'll play the air through once and then you sing it. Oh, yes, you can; it's very easy.'

So Miranda stood beside him and sang, 'I Dreamt that I Dwelt in Marble Halls.' And when her first self-consciousness wore off she thrilled to the singular appropriateness of the words. Had he guessed her dreams and was that why he had picked this music? But the song was about love as well, and her voice wavered as she thought, Love there can never be for me in *these* marble halls—this is then not my dream, how could it be?

The song ended and Nicholas raised his head. Their eyes met for a second and a faint color flowed under her white skin.

'You have a pretty voice,' he said softly. 'And you sing with feeling. Is there perhaps someone at home whom you've promised to "love just the same"?'

She shook her head, and turned away, gripped by an obscure unhappiness.

Nicholas nodded, satisfied. It would be a pity to educate Miranda from a farm girl into a lady only to have her go back to some yokel on whom everything would be wasted. I must try to find her a worthy husband, he thought, and rising abruptly he closed the piano. 'Good night, Miranda.'

What have I done now, she thought, that he should dismiss me so sharply? She murmured something, confused because he stood motionless beside the piano waiting for her to precede him from the room.

'Pay your respects to Mrs. Van Ryn and then you may retire,' he said, seeing her uncertainty.

In the Red Room, Johanna still sat, but the embroidery had disappeared. She was engaged in sipping port wine and munching sugar biscuits.

How greedy she is, thought the girl with distaste, while she politely said good night. Johanna responded amiably, smiling her indeterminate smile, but her pale eyes slid from Miranda's face to seek those of her husband. He, however, had his back turned to both women while he riffled the pages of a new copy of *Graham's Magazine* which had been lying on the table.

He bowed as Miranda left them, then returned to his magazine.

To her mortification Miranda could not find her way back to her own room. She took the wrong turn in the great hall and missed the staircase which led up through an archway. She wandered through a maze of dark rooms until she encountered the silent young footman who had lit the candles.

'This way, miss,' he said tonelessly, and directed her up the stairs to her own door.

She noted with amazement all the things which had been performed by the invisible hands in her absence. The sheet turned down on the bed, the coverlet neatly folded, candles lit long ago, judging by the length that had burned. Her basket had disappeared and her poor little toilet articles were laid out upon the dresser, where they looked lost and unappetizing on the brocaded scarf. There were hot water steaming in a copper can and fresh lavender-scented towels, and a silver pitcher of drinking water placed beside some luscious peaches on the table by her bed.

Peaches—in June! But she was long past amazement. A delicious sensation of comfort lapped around her, enfolding her as softly as did the immense bed. The sheets were of a linen so fine that they felt like silk, and they were also scented, not with lavender, but with rose petals and verbena.

Miranda stretched voluptuously like a little cat. It was warm in the room and she had a sudden desire to feel the cool silkiness upon her body. Her cotton nightdress seemed hot and coarse. On impulse she took it off, thinking how horrified Tibby would be. She flung her bare arms above her head and gloried in her privacy. No one to tell her to move over, no one to tell her to hurry and go to sleep. No need to get up at five and cook, and wash. She felt a pang when she thought of her mother and the baby. Still, they'll do all right without me, she thought, and after all I'll be back soon—but not too soon. Not until she had sated herself with the strangeness and the adventure and the delectable savor of great wealth and luxury, not until—

She sat up, clutching the sheets tight around her neck, for there was a sharp tap at the door.

'Who's there?' she quavered.

The door opened and a strange woman walked in, shutting the door behind her. A thin old figure in a shapeless black dress who came over to the bed and gazed down at the frightened girl. The woman was nearly six feet tall and erect, her coarse black hair, which showed no gray, drawn back into a scraggy knot, her face a ruddy brown crisscrossed with wrinkles from which peered two shrewd little eyes as black as dewberries.

'What do you want?' whispered Miranda.

'Me old Zélie,' said the woman in a harsh accented voice, touching her slab-like chest. 'I want to see what you look laike.'

Miranda let her breath out. Cousin Nicholas had mentioned Zélie on the boat, someone who might try to frighten her with tales of spooks and witches. It must be an old servant, a bit touched in the head, no doubt, though the unwinking black eyes looked sane enough. They traveled slowly from the girl's apprehensive face to the masses of golden hair which fell across the bare shoulders and down to the bed.

Zélie shook her head. *'Pauv'e petite.'* She spoke with a sort of sad resignation. 'What for you coming in dis house? There will be badness. Azilde will laugh again.'

'You're talking nonsense,' said Miranda. 'Please go away; I want to sleep.'

The shriveled lips parted in a grim smile. 'You been in Red Room tonight. I think you feel somesing. Yes?'

'I don't know what you—' She stopped. Those few seconds of cold and unmeaning fear had certainly been imagination, they had not recurred, and now she doubted that they had happened. 'Of course not,' she finished angrily. 'Do go away.'

The old woman nodded. 'Yes, you feel somesing. But you no listen. You will rush into trouble wiz open arms singing as you go. Maybe it is the Will of God!' She made a gesture in the air, palm up, and then the sign of the cross.

'Why do you want to frighten me?' cried Miranda, trying to laugh.

'Not frighten, *p'tite,* but warn.' Zélie's gnarled hand shot out and closed around a strand of Miranda's hair. The old woman held the bright curl gently, almost tenderly, in her closed hand. She shut her eyes and over her seamed face there stole a listening look. 'You must believe—' Her voice rose to a higher note, a sing-song chant. 'There is blackness, and badness and bloody water round about you. There is love too, two kinds of love, but you not knowing in time.' She opened her eyes, and the strand of hair fell from her hand. 'You think old Zélie crazy, *hein?* You lie there with naked body and your gold hair like a web and you not knowing what I mean. Pah! you are a child yet, and your soul is blind, blind as the little mole that burrows beneath the lawn out there—the beautiful quiet lawn.'

The black eyes glittered with a contemptuous pity. The gaunt figure turned and walked out of the room, shutting the door behind her.

'She *is* crazy,' whispered Miranda.

She got out of bed and locked the door. It had not occurred to her before, for there were no bedroom locks at the farm. Then she put on her cotton nightdress and braided her hair into tight plaits. She clambered once more into the high bed, but this time she took with her the Bible her father had given her, and which she had forgotten to read earlier.

She said her prayers, and then opening the Bible read the Ninety-First Psalm with a passionate and guilty concentration.

4

IT WAS POSSIBLE TO LIVE AT DRAGONWYCK WITH the Van Ryns and twenty servants and yet be virtually alone, Miranda soon discovered. Nicholas was busy with estate affairs, and divided the rest of his time between his study on the top of the high tower and the greenhouses where he pursued his hobby of horticulture. A hobby shared by many wealthy landowners at that time, but astonishing to Miranda, who perfectly understood a man's growing plants for food or barter but found it hard to comprehend an interest in ornamental and quite useless shrubs.

It was Nicholas' pride to have one example of every tree which could be grown in that locality, and many of these he had imported by schooner from Europe and the Orient straight to the Dragonwyck dock—the Incense Cedar, the Weeping Cypress, the Judas Tree, the Ginkgo with its fan-shaped leaves, and the delicate bronze Japanese Maple—these were hardy enough to live outside; but the palms and aloes, the oleanders and the orchids, grew in the elaborate greenhouses or in the conservatory off the dining-room.

Johanna too had her own pursuits, if food and spasmodic attempts at genteel handiwork—china painting, purse netting, or crochet—could be called pursuits. Her weight made her lethargic and she kept much to her room unless there were guests.

Miranda accepted this sense of separateness in the household, just as she accepted the surprising discovery that husband and wife occupied different rooms. Here at Dragonwyck all was to her strange and surprising, no one aspect more than another. These were the ways of aristocracy, the exalted group whom she envied, and to whose pattern she longed to shape herself.

She seized upon the luxuries of her new life with the avidity of a kitten after cream. It was delightful to sleep until eight, and then to eat delicious food of which she need never think until it was on the table. It was amazing how soon she got used to having other hands make her bed and clean her room, and how many charming ways there were of filling the leisure thus acquired. For Nicholas had made her free of the music room and library, and if one tired of strumming the piano or reading the Waverley Novels—which he had recommended and she found to be nearly as exciting as her contraband romances—there were always walks through the gardens or along the river where the boats passed endlessly up and downstream.

Her only duty consisted in trying to teach Katrine. Every morning after breakfast the two of them retired to the sunny schoolroom, where Miranda patiently repeated, 'B-A-T, bat. C-A-T, cat. R-A-T, rat. Now you spell them, dear.' The child was docile and did her best, but she was slow and her memory was poor; her attention continually wandered. She gradually grew fond of Miranda, who was always kind, but the little girl continued to prefer the company of her beloved Annetje, who fed her sweets and told her stories. So Miranda had little to do, and during the first weeks the novelty of this method of living sufficed in itself. It never occurred to her that it might be the occasional contacts with Nicholas which gave meaning and excitement to Dragonwyck. But she did know herself to be passionately grateful for an act of generosity which he had shown her.

On the day after her arrival, Magda the housekeeper had presented herself at Miranda's door, armed with a tape measure, paper, and pencil. She would explain nothing except that Mynheer had sent her. Her lips were compressed to a thin line. She pushed and pulled the girl about roughly while she took measurements.

A week later at dusk as she mended a rip in the despised merino, there came a tap on Miranda's door, and the housekeeper entered followed by a footman. They carried bundles, boxes, and a small cowhide trunk.

'Some things from New York Mynheer ordered,' said Magda sourly in answer to the girl's exclamation. The woman paid no attention to Miranda's cry of excitement, but unpacked the bundles and the trunk with swift efficiency. She laid the clothes on the bed.

There were two silk dresses, one green with black velvet trimming on the flounces, one a rose evening gown festooned with blond lace. And besides a blue cashmere morning dress, there was a pelisse, a green bonnet, two pairs of kid shoes, an ivory fan, a beaded reticule. There were also more intimate garments at which Miranda stared with dazzled confusion; a flowered muslin négligée, linen nightshifts trimmed with fine lace, petticoats, camisoles, even a pair of whalebone stays.

'But how could Mr. Van Ryn—I mean— For sure he didn't order all these things—' cried the girl, blushing and divided between embarrassment at the nature of the garments Magda was phlegmatically spreading on the bed, and delight at their daintiness.

Magda shot the girl a contemptuous look. 'You don't think the patroon bothers himself with such business. He sent an order to Madame Duclos in New York. Last summer we had a French orphan from New Orleans visit here. He did the same.'

'Oh,' said Miranda. The color deepened on her cheeks. There was then an unpleasant aspect of charity to this gift, and her staunch Yankee heritage gave her an unexpected twinge. And was it quite proper to accept things like this from a gentleman—even a cousin? But what nonsense! she told herself hastily. He would be annoyed if she made a fuss or refused the clothes, he would think her countrified and silly. And the clothes were so beautiful. She smoothed the rose satin of the evening gown, entranced to discover that beneath its heavy folds there was the small bell-shaped hoop for which she had yearned.

Madame Duclos had neglected nothing to fill Nicholas' written order. 'Send complete wardrobe for young lady, fair-haired, quite tall, and of the following measurements.'

The modiste had also included a plush-lined box containing Guerlain's lustral water for the hair, *Sirop de Boubie*—'Warranted to enhance even the most delicate complexion'—orris toothpowder, rice powder, and a vial of heliotrope perfume.

'It smells just like Ma's little garden on a summer night,' cried Miranda, sniffing the vial. 'Oh, Magda, isn't everything lovely, gorgeous!'

The woman did not answer. She knelt before the bureau neatly folding away the lingerie. The belligerent set of her thick shoulders under the black bombazine expressed rigid disapproval.

'Why don't you like me, Magda?' cried the girl on impulse. 'Have I done anything wrong?'

The woman rose heavily. 'It's not my place to like or dislike, miss. Mevrouw is waiting.' She clicked the last drawer shut and walked out to go to Johanna.

Is it because Johanna doesn't like me that her maid is so unfriendly? thought Miranda, puzzled and rebuffed. But she was not yet sure of

Johanna's dislike, that broad flabby face seldom showed any emotion at all, and on the rare occasions when she spoke to the girl it was with her usual vague amiability. She's like a turnip, a fat white turnip, thought Miranda, and forgot Johanna in the excitement of dressing herself in the green silk gown. It fitted perfectly, the bodice taut across the small high breasts and slender waist, the skirt full and gracefully billowing over the hoop which she had transferred from the ball dress. If her skin and her hair had been pretty above the muddy merino, now against the clear leaf-green silk they were startling. The color enhanced her blondness as it brought out new lights in her hazel eyes.

Perhaps, with luck she might find Nicholas alone downstairs and thank him for his thoughtful kindness. There was still half an hour before supper time. She hurried downstairs and the rustle of silk that accompanied her gave her new assurance. She held her head high and swayed her hips a little so as to increase that luxurious swish.

She found Nicholas in the conservatory examining a slipper orchid which he had just had brought in from the greenhouse. He turned and surveyed her as she approached through the dining-room.

But the girl's really beautiful! he thought, astonished. She has the body of a dancer.

'Cousin Nicholas—' she said shyly, 'I don't know how to thank you. All these grand clothes—they—you've made me so happy.'

'I'm gratified that it takes so little to make you happy, Miranda.'

Usually she was daunted by his tone of repressive irony, but this evening she had more courage. She smiled, thinking that men never liked to be thanked—at least Pa and Tom didn't; and she moved close beside him and touched the striped green orchid.

'How queer a little flower it is!' she said. 'Is it doing well here?'

As she bent her head over the marble urn which held the orchid, a faint perfume floated to him from the massed golden braids at the nape of her white neck. He raised his hand, then let it drop to his side. 'The orchid does well enough. Shall we sit down awhile until Mrs. Van Ryn comes?' He indicated the filigree iron bench against the south wall where there were massed oleanders and hibiscus. Beside the bench, water trickled from a lion's mouth into an alabaster basin, thus evoking in the steamy room the cool fresh sound of the forest.

It occurred to her that at last she had a moment alone with him in which to ask about Zélie. She had seen nothing of the old woman since the inexplicable midnight interview and time had erased the impression of eeriness, but she was curious.

She brought out her timid question and Nicholas turned sharply. 'You've seen Zélie? Where?'

She gave a brief account, suppressing some of Zélie's more fantastic utterances, which now sounded extremely silly.

'Did she frighten you?' asked Nicholas, frowning.

'A bit, though I don't know why now. There was a lot about somebody laughing and the Red Room and me bringing—bringing badness. I know it's all nonsense,' she added hastily, hoping he wouldn't laugh at her.

He was not amused, he was annoyed. 'She's really getting impossible with her claptrap. I'd no idea she'd ever venture upstairs. I shall speak to her.'

'But who *is* she?' said Miranda, persisting in the face of his evident wish to close the subject.

Nicholas stood up and she saw with dismay that her insistence had spoiled the rare moment of intimacy.

'The old hag must be ninety; it's time she died and her stupid tales with her.'

She was astonished at the venom in his tone, but he went on more quietly with controlled irritation. 'My great-grandfather Pieter Van Ryn married a New Orleans belle in seventeen-fifty-two. Her name was Azilde Marie de la Courbet. He brought her back here, and with her, her body slave, Titine. Zélie is the daughter of the black Titine and a Mohican Indian. She's always lived here at Dragonwyck.'

'She talks so queerly—' ventured the girl after a moment, feeling that what she had heard was no explanation at all.

'She speaks with the Creole patois she learned from her mother, I suppose.'

'I didn't mean that, I mean the things she says—spooky things. And I remember now. It was Azilde she said would laugh again.'

Nicholas shrugged. 'There's some ridiculous legend kept alive by Zélie. Azilde was not happy here; after the birth of her son she—' He paused. 'She died, and that's all the basis for the arrant foolishness invented by Zélie involving a ghost and a curse. Now shall we talk of something more sensible? Did you read those Essays by Addison that I suggested?'

'Not yet,' she confessed, looking up at him contritely. 'I'm still reading "Ivanhoe." Oh, but it's a grand story, Cousin Nicholas!'

'My dear child, you're an incorrigible romantic, and may I suggest that the English language contains many more appropriate adjectives than "grand," of which you seem to be immoderately fond?'

The embarrassed color flew to her face, as it always did when he reproved her, but she saw with startled joy that this reproof was different, for there was no censure in his tone, rather an unexpected lightness as though he teased her, and there was warmth in his piercingly blue gaze as he looked down at her.

'Tompkins announced supper, Nicholas.' Johanna, panting a little from the effort of having searched throughout the lower floor, stood in the conservatory archway.

As though the flat and breathy voice had been a rock thrown into a still pool, the warmth and the shared instant of subtle expectancy shattered.

'I'm extremely sorry to have kept you waiting, my love,' said Nicholas, in a tone conveying nothing but courteous apology. 'Miranda and I were discussing literature. Her new dress becomes her, doesn't it? Madame Duclos has done well.'

Johanna turned and looked at the girl in the green silk dress. The fingers on which a half-dozen magnificent rings made deep channels through the fat twined themselves tight together. The pale eyes slid back to Nicholas. 'The gown seems to suit her very well,' said Johanna.

During the first weeks of Miranda's stay at Dragonwyck there had been an occasional guest—Mr. and Mrs. Newbold en route from New York to Saratoga, the portly Mr. Solomon Bronck, who looked after Nicholas' valuable real estate holdings on Manhattan. But these had stayed only for a night or a meal and Miranda had scarcely seen them.

Now there was to be a Fourth of July celebration at Dragonwyck, festivities of dazzling magnitude, a banquet and ball on the night of the Fourth and a garden party the following day. All of the guest rooms were to be occupied by people whose names meant nothing to Miranda, but she speculated about them with excited interest, particularly the guests of honor, the de Greniers, a real French count and countess for whom the Florentine suite in the north wing was being prepared.

Despite the inevitable extra work and the days of preparation, no confusion or signs of bustle were in evidence. Tompkins and Magda directed their underlings, a few extra servants were hired from the village, there was a subdued hum from the basement kitchens where labor continued far into each night; but that was all that anyone could have detected. And yet it was Nicholas who by means of an occasional order or a brief tour of inspection coordinated all the elaborate machinery which would produce the dreamily gracious atmosphere, the lavishness, that imbued Dragonwyck. He was entirely guiltless of the vulgarity of wishing to impress his guests. It was simply his desire for perfection, for creating from the raw stuff of life, rather than on canvas or on paper, a finished artistic effect.

On the afternoon of the third of July the dayboat stopped at Dragonwyck and landed the de Greniers. They were a disappointment to Miranda. A French nobleman, fresh from the court of Louis-Philippe, would be tall and languid and haughty like Nicholas perhaps, only more so. And the Countess—here Miranda's imagination had run wild, and she endowed the lady with a white wig, satin panniers, and a mournful high-born beauty which were patterned on a dimly remembered picture of Marie-Antoinette.

The reality was a shock. The Count was plump and nearly bald. He was shorter than Miranda herself, and though he had fierce little black mustachios, they were the only impressive thing about him. His round face wore a perpetual expression of amusement. Life was to him a diverting panorama which he richly enjoyed. His speech—and he spoke good English, having spent five years in London—bubbled with wit and, to Miranda's mind, an astounding frankness. This frankness she would have considered shocking vulgarity in anyone but a count.

'But then, you see,' remarked the little Frenchman while they sat at supper, '*mes chers amis,* I am not an aristocrat *de l'ancien régime.* We are *parvenus!* The good Louis-Philippe has rewarded my family for some little services rendered. Our only connection with the Bourbons is perhaps a certain pretty little milkmaid who caught the Old Louis' eye one day in the Midi. She caught more than his eye—*parbleu!*' And the Count chuckled.

Miranda looked down at her plate. Surely the Count didn't mean—but what could he mean exactly?

The Countess was a dumpy little woman in black who spoke no English and listened to her husband with a tolerant smile.

'You have here a most *magnifique* establishment, *mon cher,*' said the Count to Nicholas. 'A luxury one would hardly expect in such a new country, and your cuisine, madame—' Here he looked at Johanna, his shrewd eyes traveling over her immense bulk in blue silk. 'Your cuisine—' he went on, bunching his fingers together and kissing them gustily, 'is superb!'

Johanna put down her fork. 'Is it true, Count, that you eat frogs' legs and snails in your country?' she asked seriously, and as he nodded, she said, 'How extraordinary!'

'No more extraordinary, my love, than the sheep's brains and fish eggs of which we are so fond,' said Nicholas.

The Count looked around. *Tiens,* he said to himself. Here is something interesting. The man is too polite to his wife; there is a repressed violence about him beneath his calm. Silent for a minute while the crawfish mousse was removed and the pheasant patty passed, the Count sipped his excellent Romanée-Conti and surveyed the party with lively speculation.

At the head of the table was this Nicholas Van Ryn whom he had met briefly in Paris years ago, and whose invitation he had been delighted to accept, for it was entertaining to see all aspects of life in the strange new country. Already he had had his fill in New York of the hysterical lionizing vouchsafed to all visiting foreigners with a title. He had expected more of the same here. But he saw at once that he had misjudged the Van Ryns.

The man was a *grand seigneur,* as self-contained as a Talleyrand or a de Lamballe, nor were his possessions and manner of living apparently inferior to these. And yet the man was not a nobleman. The mere possession of hereditary landed estates could hardly produce a nobleman in this country that shouted so loudly and so belligerently of its perfect democracy. He is then a type of anachronism, perhaps, thought the Count. For a minute he watched Nicholas, who was conversing with the Countess in careful accurate French. Decidedly the man was good-looking, and must appeal to women except that there was a coldness about him, there was no fire, no sentiment. Still there might be passion—there was sensuality in that full, compressed mouth.

By a natural sequence of thought the Count once more examined Johanna. But the woman was a cow! She would give no satisfaction at all in bed. Van Ryn then must have a mistress, though already the Count had learned that these matters were regarded differently in America. They had prudish conventions here; their English or in this case Dutch blood was sluggish, lacking in amorous vehemence.

'Miranda,' said Nicholas suddenly, 'after supper will you fetch for the Countess that volume of Mr. Cooper's which I believe you were reading? She wants to see it.'

The girl raised her eyes. 'Certainly, Cousin Nicholas.'

Sapristi, said the Count to himself, here is someone I've overlooked! He had accepted Johanna's offhand introduction, gathering that the girl was some sort of governess, and scarcely more than a child herself. She sat in the shadows at the far end of the table, and had not up to this point said a word. The three words that she had now said were not revealing, but the unconscious expression of her eyes as she looked at Nicholas was. But she's really charming, *cette petite,* thought the Count, craning very discreetly so as to see over the massed centerpiece of roses, and she is well on the way to falling in love with Cousin Nicholas.

She does not know it yet, nor does anyone else. How bizarre these people are! The fat one had better look out. He chuckled inwardly, wiped his mouth, and said chattily: 'I am all on the *qui vive* to take part in your great Fourth of July celebration tomorrow. What is the day's program, monsieur?'

Nicholas turned to his guest with his instant polite attention. 'Why, in the morning we have a party for my tenants, and I fear you must endure listening to a speech from me since it's a tradition with us.'

He smiled, and the Count said: 'A patriotic speech? It will be a pleasure.'

Nicholas continued: 'In the late afternoon there will be a banquet, followed by a small ball. We've asked some of our neighbors to meet you.'

'Also a pleasure, monsieur, and I am *passionné* for dancing. I bounce about like a little gutta-percha ball, but I do my best. You also must be fond of dancing, mademoiselle.' He deliberately addressed Miranda, who started and changed color.

'I—I don't know,' she said, confused by the sudden notice. 'I'm afraid I can't dance well, I don't know the polka or the waltz. I don't believe I'll be at the ball.'

She looked uncertainly at Johanna, who said: 'I thought Miranda should stay with Katrine; the child will be upset with so much noise and people in the house.'

'One of the servants may sit with Katrine,' said Nicholas. 'Of course Miranda must be at the ball. She'll soon manage the steps.'

'Oh, well, it makes no difference,' answered Johanna, burying a spoon in her vanilla ice.

Aha! thought the Count. The fat one is not so stupid after all. She tries to suppress the little one, to keep her in her place. Cousin Nicholas then comes to the rescue and Mademoiselle's superb eyes caress him gratefully. All this, so far, is instinct. Madame is perhaps too lazy and too smug to realize what is happening. Monsieur is too much bound by the consciousness of his position to permit himself to realize it. As for the little one, she is not awake. Simply, as yet, a pretty little animal.

They all rose and the Count examined Miranda with a connoisseur's eye, admiring the long slender limbs, the high breasts outlined by her tight basque, the fairness of her skin. He liked that *blond-cendré* type; he particularly liked the tiny black mole which emphasized the right corner of her mouth, and the slightly retroussé nose. This type was often capable of great passion. He sighed, wishing momentarily that he might be the means of awakening her.

He watched her graceful body as she followed the other two ladies out of the dining-room, and its innocent carriage and youthfulness touched him. *Pauvre petite!* He could teach her the arts of love with a tenderness that she would never get from this Nicholas for all his handsome face and exquisite manners. Then the Count's sense of humor returned. *Eh bien, c'est la vie!* The emotional complications of this household were none of his business.

He settled down to superlative port and conversation with his host, whom he found to have broad knowledge and well-expressed opinions on any subject. They touched on foreign affairs, France's Moroccan war, England's recent peace with China, the Foundation of the German Catholic Church. They passed quickly over the proposed annexation of Texas and the possibilities of James K. Polk's winning the Presidential election. Here the Count found himself out of his depth, so that Nicholas tactfully introduced the topic of science, in which the Frenchman was an amateur dabbler.

'What wonders we have seen in the last few years!' said Nicholas. 'The steam engine, the electric telegraph, the daguerreotype, this new illuminating gas, which I find harsh and hideous.'

'True,' said the Count, looking around the great dim room with its soft yellow points of candlelight. 'You have none here, and yet I should have thought that in a palace like this you would want all modern improvements.'

Nicholas shook his head. 'To me there is no beauty without mystery and shadow. There's a young American author, Edgar Allan Poe, whose writings express my feelings perfectly; do you know his work?'

The Count said no, and Nicholas continued, 'I think you will some day. I believe he's a genius. Sometime I shall go to him and tell him so. Listen—' And Nicholas began to recite.

> By a route obscure and lonely
> Haunted by ill angels only,
> Where an eidolon named Night
> On a black throne reigns upright
> I have reached these lands but newly
> From an ultimate dim Thule—
> From a wild weird clime that lieth, sublime
> Out of Space—out of Time.

Toward the end of the poem his voice took on a deeper vibration and he lingered over each musical word so that the Count, who detested sitting still and listening, was impressed in spite of himself. Who would have suspected here so much latent dramatic power, or for that matter so much appreciation of the mystically macabre?

'Tiens,' he said, 'it creates an atmosphere certainly. Not too gay, but exquisite, *mon ami,* quite exquisite. What is it all about—these sad dead waters, melancholy nooks, and shrouded forms?'

Nicholas leaned back, crossed his legs, and offered his guest a cigar.

'Ne me demandez pas des énigmes,' he quoted lightly. He regretted having exposed even a small portion of his inner emotions. He had been seduced into it because he seldom found an intellectual equal and had foolishly expected instinctive understanding from the Count.

'What do they think in France of these new experiments with ether?' he asked, changing the subject.

'Ah, that is a miracle indeed! If it works it will stop so much pain.'

'And it will provide a most easy death for those who deserve it.'

The Count looked startled. 'What the devil do you mean by that, "those who deserve it"?'

At that moment Tompkins came into the room, stepped softly around the table pouring more port. Nicholas waited until the butler had gone, then answered: 'I believe that death is inherent in our lives, that we get the kind of death which our natures attract. The mediocre die in bed where they began; the brave die adventurously.'

'And those who are murdered deserve to be murdered?' asked the Count, amused.

Nicholas' eyes lingered a second on the other's face. 'Perhaps,' he said. 'There's a vast amount of twaddle and sentimentality in the commonplace mind about death. It would be far better for the race if the ugly and useless ones were eliminated.'

'But monsieur!' expostulated the Count, laughing. 'This is barbaric. Who is to decide which one is ugly or useless enough for death? Who would dare?'

Nicholas lifted his glass and took a delicate sip. 'I would dare—if the occasion arose.'

The Count swallowed. The candles had burned down and some of them were guttering. The corners of the room flickered in shadow, but such light as there was illumined his host's impassive face.

The Count made a secret sign of the cross and was immediately ashamed of himself. This was no more than the jejune atheistic talk one heard from many a young sophisticate in Paris salons. All the same he was uncomfortable.

There was a small silence. Through the shut door there came the distant tinkle of a gavotte from the music room. He recognized it. His wife must be playing the piano for those other two strangely assorted women. Poor Marie Louise, he thought, it must be very dull for her, imprisoned with people whose language she did not speak. He longed to go and join them. But Nicholas, for once negligent of a guest's wishes, showed no sign of moving. He sat quiet, abstractedly fingering one of the Madame Desprez roses which had fallen from the centerpiece.

The Count cleared his throat and brought out a topic which he thought would be pleasant. 'You have a magnificent estate to leave to your sons, monsieur.'

Nicholas put the rose down. 'I have no sons.'

'*Eh bien,* they will come. There is much time yet,' said the Count hastily.

Nicholas slowly turned his head. 'You have seen my wife. Do you think she will bear me sons?'

Quelle question extraordinaire! thought the unhappy Count. But apparently one must answer something.

'Madame Van Ryn has quite a bit of embonpoint, certainly, but that is nothing. Why, the Marquise de Laon weighs ninety kilos and she has had eight—all boys. One must not be discouraged, and if there is something a little wrong, some *petite maladie,* why, that is easily fixed; you have good doctors here, I think—' He broke off, astounded at the expression that came and went so quickly on the other's face that almost he doubted that it was not a trick of the candlelight.

'Johanna will bear no more children,' said Nicholas, and rose at the same time, adding casually, 'You seemed interested in my Persian oleanders. I have a fine crimson specimen in the conservatory. Would you like to look at it on our way to join the ladies?'

While he dutifully admired the oleander, the Count was engaged in renewed conjecture, piecing together this last peculiar conversation. Did the man then find his wife so repugnant that he did not sleep with her? Was this his meaning? The fat one was unappetizing certainly, but when one wanted legitimate sons one must overlook such matters and do one's best. One can always find an outlet for romance elsewhere, after one has done one's duty. Perhaps as an older and more experienced man he would find an opportunity to point out this view to Monsieur Van Ryn. He would seize a chance tomorrow.

But the chance never came. Nicholas had allowed himself to be more personal with the Count than he had with anyone in years, and he was now annoyed at this momentary weakness.

The Countess having exhausted her repertoire, the ladies had retired to the Green Drawing-Room, where the men joined them, and after sitting down beside the Countess and while chatting with her in French, Nicholas did what he always avoided. He turned his eyes on his wife and deliberately looked at her.

He watched her attempt to respond to the little Frenchman's persiflage while she stifled the yawns which always assailed her after the evening meal. He noted how her scanty hair lay lank despite Magda's efforts with the curling iron, and how the pink scalp showed beneath the strands. He noted, too, the clumsy coquetry of her glaring rouge and that she had tried to darken her eyebrows with an unskillfully applied pencil.

His eyes descended to the pendulous bosom stuffed into the straining blue satin. It supported tonight the Van Ryn diamonds, a delicate necklace of the rose-cut gems which had been bought for Azilde by Pieter Van Ryn. They were fine stones, but they seemed lusterless, as everything, thought Nicholas, which touched Johanna, became by some malevolent alchemy tarnished and unkempt.

He no longer remembered or wished to remember that he had not always viewed her with this pitiless disgust.

She had been plump seven years ago at the time of their marriage, but passably pretty. Though she was two years older than he and of a stolid temperament, she had not been unattractive. She was placid and well bred, from Dutch stock as proud and long established as his own.

Upon his return from the Grand Tour to find himself an orphan, for his mother had died when he was twelve, Nicholas had discovered amongst his father's papers a letter designating Johanna Van Tappen as a suitable choice for Lady of the Manor. He had accordingly wooed her, without passion but without reluctance either. The change had come after the birth of Katrine. The child's sex had been a bitter blow then, but with the eventual certainty that Johanna was henceforth barren he had withdrawn into a cold and remote endurance which gradually crystallized into physical repulsion. For three years he had not shared her bed, and during those years she had become as she was now.

But she was his wife and the Mistress of Dragonwyck; to that position he had always given and would continue to give outward respect and punctilious courtesy.

He replied to the Countess, who had happily embarked on a long account of her children's beauty and *sagesse,* and seeing that for this fascinating topic she wanted only a listener, Nicholas turned his head a fraction of an inch. His eyelids drooped and his veiled gaze rested upon Miranda.

She sat across the room, her head bent over the embroidery hoops and the same lawn handkerchief on which Johanna had been working Nicholas' monogram. This transfer was at his suggestion, for upon seeing that Miranda was as skilled with the needle as Johanna was clumsy, he had remarked that he thought it foolish for his wife to waste her time, 'If Miranda will be kind enough to do them.' She had, of course, been delighted, and she took great pride in her exquisite stitches and the neatness of the letters which Johanna had bungled.

From the silver sconce on the wall above Miranda's head candlelight fell directly on her hair and burnished it to gold fire. The color and texture of this hair gave Nicholas yet again a sensation of pleasure which was deeper than admiration, a curious pleasure which had in it both voluptuousness and solace. But for the origin of this sensation he had never troubled to search. Introspection was alien to his nature.

He continued to watch the pure oval of the girl's averted cheek, the long white throat and the youthful shadows at her collarbones, while her nimble fingers continued to manipulate the embroidery silk, which had much the same sheen and whiteness as her skin. She had scarcely attended to the conversation, in which as befitted her youth and anomalous position in the household she had taken no part. Her thoughts ran on the anticipated excitements of the ball.

Suddenly, in unconscious response to the steadiness of Nicholas' gaze, she raised her eyelids and looked full at him. A shock ran through her. Her heart beat in slow thick strokes. They looked across the room into each other's eyes for a half a second only, then Nicholas turning to the Countess said smoothly: 'Ah, that is most interesting, madame. Tell me more about your little Blaise.'

But Miranda knew that for all the triviality of the incident something cataclysmic had occurred. Their relationship had changed and from this point there could be no going back.

That night she had a dream in which her father came to her at Dragonwyck, and she ran to him with a joyous affection that she had never felt in reality.

'I've come to take you home, my girl,' he said, caressing her. And she clung to him crying for happiness, and yet she could not go. For a while she struggled frantically while her father receded and beckoned to her from across a shadowy gulf. Then she looked down at her body and saw that it was bound around with many colored flashing chains like jewels. 'You see I can't get free!' she cried. 'The chains are holding me.' Her father's face grew angry. 'You can free yourself if ye'll but try!' he shouted. She shook her head and he vanished. At once the chains grew light as clouds. She gathered them up in her hands and fell to kissing the jeweled links. And as she kissed them fear came to her, a fear so sharp that she awakened.

For a while she lay shivering in bed, but soon in the growing light she felt the security of her familiar room. She watched the bureau and the great Kas dwindle from dim monsters to useful pieces of furniture. The first rays of the summer sun slanted across the distant Taghkanic Mountains into her windows. She got up and looked out. The Catskills seemed near and distinct. She could make out scattered rooftops down the river at Coxsackie. The Hudson's waters were brightly blue and ruffled by nothing except the wake of a great schooner bound for Albany.

Below the houses on the vast lawns, booths covered with red, white, and blue bunting, picnic tables, and a carrousel had been set up during the night. From a distant grove of hemlocks came the squeak of a fiddle and the wheeze of a hand organ where the rustic musicians were practicing.

It would be a fine day for the festivities.

5

BREAKFAST THAT MORNING WAS HURRIED AND EATEN to the accompaniment of confusion from outside. Nicholas' tenants were beginning to arrive in their rattling farm wagons and there was a constant stamping and whinnying of heavy draft horses, shouts from the men, excited squeals from the children as they spied the carrousel and the picnic booths, a quacking and cackling of poultry, and the bleating of lambs which had been brought as tribute to the patroon.

This was one of the semiannual rent-days, and before Nicholas' speech and the merrymaking which would follow it must come business. A platform had been set up under a large tulip tree and upon it were an armchair, a table, and several smaller chairs.

At ten o'clock Nicholas mounted this platform accompanied by Dirck Duyckman, his bailiff, the Count, and Miranda. Johanna had not attended this recurring ceremony for several years. It bored her, and she disliked being gawked at by the yokels, one of whom had once made loud and uncomplimentary remarks on her figure. The man had been punished, not as Nicholas' grandfather would have punished him, by a day in the stocks, but in a more modern way—by confiscating a portion of his farm on which he had been laggard in paying rent. But after this Johanna appeared no more on rent-day until the tenants had gone home.

The Countess also preferred to remain in her room and rest, but the Count was interested in this feudal custom, and as for Miranda she was always glad to be near Nicholas and take part in the life of Dragonwyck whenever she was invited to do so.

Nicholas seated himself in the traditional 'rent-chair' of carved oak black with age, for it had come from Holland with the first patroon and been used for this purpose ever since. The bailiff stood beside him holding a great gold-stamped ledger. He cleared his throat and called importantly, 'Let the tenants come forward, single file, with their payments. The patroon is ready!'

The crowd of farmers who had been kept on the back lawn by a rope shuffled, and sheepishly removing their hats arranged themselves in order. Two of the Van Ryn footmen lowered the rope.

A wizened little man in brown homespun stepped up to the platform clutching two gray geese and a bumpy sack of potatoes.

'Tom Wilson,' said the bailiff, thumbing through his ledger. 'Hollow Farm on the north road. Poultry and potatoes. Co—rect.' He eyed the geese narrowly. 'Them birds is a mite skinny, Tom. Couldn't you bring no better than that?'

The wizened little man shook his head, casting an anxious glance at Nicholas, who sat silently attentive. 'I couldn't do no better, sir. My corn give out and the crops is bad so far. We ain't getting enough rain. 'Sides, my old woman she's powerful sick; she can't feed the poultry like she used to.'

Nicholas leaned forward. 'I'm sorry to hear that, Tom. Has she had the doctor?'

'No, she ain't. She don't hold with no doctors, they won't do her no good. She thinks there's someone witching her, maybe old Molly Clabber lives down the road.'

'Nonsense,' said Nicholas. 'If she's sick she needs a doctor. Duyckman, look into this later and report to me.'

The bailiff nodded. Tom Wilson said, 'Thanky, sir,' dubiously, and touched his forehead. He deposited the geese and potatoes in a large pen to the right of the platform and walked over to a keg of beer which had been provided for the tenants.

The bailiff signaled and another farmer came up. The procedure was repeated. Jed Ribling had brought a spring lamb, a side of bacon, and a sack of flour ground at the village mill. He too was entered in the ledger, placed his stuff in the pen, and joined Tom Wilson at the beer keg.

They filed slowly by, the Dutch names, the English names, a scattering of German ones. Nicholas spoke to each one asking after the health of some member of the family, or inquiring into the condition of the crops.

Miranda from her corner of the platform watched him breathlessly, admiring his infallible memory for names, his detailed knowledge of his tenants' lives, the graciousness with which he said just the right word to everybody.

'*Ma foi,* he is like a young king,' whispered the Count, leaning over to her. 'Though I have never seen a king so 'andsome.'

'Oh, yes,' she whispered back enthusiastically. 'He is like a king, isn't he! No wonder they all admire him!'

The Count suppressed a smile. He was not sure that all the peasants who filed past depositing their geese and their sheep and their vegetables were as worshiping of Nicholas as Miranda was. He had noticed sullen looks, and some of the faces had not responded to the patroon's undeniable charm and rather condescending graciousness. But they kept on coming docilely enough. And the kermiss was now in full swing on the far lawn: the young people were jigging back and forth to the music of the fiddles. The carrousel, propelled by a white horse, was crowded with children and twirling merrily. Mug after mug was filled with beer, and the sweetmeats counter with its sugared olykoecks, its seed cakes and rock candy had to be continually replenished by servants running to and from the great house. The bowling green was extremely popular, and beyond it by the privet hedge which separated the kermiss from the forbidden grounds near the house several boisterous games of knuckle bones were in progress.

Scarcely a half dozen farmers were left, and Miranda, whose interest had slackened a little, was wondering if it would be all right for her to join in the kermiss, which represented far more gaiety than she had ever seen in her life, when she jerked around, startled by a small commotion.

A tall farmer of about thirty stood defiantly below the platform, his hands in his pockets, his under jaw thrust forth.

'Klaas Beecker, two bushels of winter wheat and—' began the bailiff, then checked himself angrily. 'Take your hat off to the patroon, man.'

Klaas raised his grimed red hands and jerked his hat down on his head. 'I take my hat off to no man. I'm a free American citizen.'

The bailiff swelled, his fat belly quivered. 'Take your hat off or I'll knock it off. And where's yer rent?'

Klaas turned his back on the bailiff; his small narrowed eyes fixed themselves on Nicholas' face with a malignance that frightened Miranda, who had not the vaguest idea what it was all about. The Count hitched his chair forward, delighted at this interesting incident in rather dull proceedings.

'I've brought ye no rent, Nicholas Van Ryn,' said Klaas harshly, 'nor will ye ever again get so much as a grain of wheat from me.'

Nicholas' eyebrows raised a trifle; except for a slight tightening of the lips his expression remained as calm as before.

'Indeed?' he said pleasantly. 'And do you propose to farm my lands, and enjoy the many privileges which I allow you, without making any return?'

Klaas's face contorted, he made a violent gesture and turned to the small group of farmers who were yet to follow him.

'Do you hear him, friends!' he shouted. 'The damned patroon! He talks of *his* lands. 'Tis my own farm he talks of, 'twas my father's and his father's before him. For nigh two hundred years the Hill Farm has belonged to Beeckers, and he dares to call it his.'

The men he addressed shifted uneasily, one of them nodded, another clenched his fist, but they all kept a wary eye on Nicholas, who said softly: 'But it happens that it *is* my land and always will be, no matter how long you have been there or intend to stay. Nor may you stay unless you pay your just rent.'

'By God! This is the blackest injustice that ever was. We've paid the worth of the land many times over in rent and ye know it. There ye sit lolling in your easy-chair grinding out of us the pitiful little results of our sweat that we may keep the lands that rightfully belong to us. I'll stand it no longer, I tell ye, and there's many another who feels like me. Ye'll find out, my fine young squire!'

'Klaas, be reasonable, man,' interposed the bailiff with a frightened look at Nicholas. 'True, ye cannot actually take title to the lands, but look what the patroon does for you. The church he has built, and the mill, the market boats he runs so you may sell your stuff, the doctor he sends when you're sick.'

'Faugh!' The farmer filled his mouth with spittle and aimed it directly at the platform. 'He does nothing for us, ye fat nincompoop, that we could not do better for ourselves.'

The ball of spittle landed on Nicholas' shoe. He pulled a handkerchief from his pocket, wiped his shoe, and tossed the handkerchief to the ground.

'Ye crazy fool,' cried the bailiff, really alarmed. 'Have ye no sense at all, no gratitude? Don't you know what will happen!'

'Hush, Dirck,' said Nicholas, raising his hand. He rose and faced the little group of farmers. The corners of his nostrils were white and sharply indented. 'You will all be glad to know that since Klaas Beecker feels this way, he need no longer be troubled by living on my land. He will leave the farm tomorrow morning. Doubtless he and his family will find lands to suit them in the West where they won't be bothered by rents or laws.'

A stifled gasp ran through the listeners. Klaas choked. His defiant face crumpled. 'Ye—ye can't, ye wouldn't turn me out like that overnight, Mr. Van Ryn. Why, we've no place to go.' He wet his lips and swallowed. 'I—I was born on that farm, ye know that, sir; ye couldn't be so cruel hard, Mr. Van Ryn.'

Nicholas looked down at his shoe, then up at the farmer. 'Since you are dissatisfied here, you will doubtless be happier elsewhere. You may apply to Duyckman after the kermiss. I shall authorize him to give you some gold pieces.'

The man's face twisted, turning a dull red. 'I don't want no charity, I—I won't go. Ye'll see. I've got friends—ye'll be sorry for this. We'll break up your damned manor—' His voice trailed off as Nicholas looked through him; he shuffled slowly back to the wagons. After a moment he picked up the reins and his horse started wearily down the road.

There was a dead silence around the platform, then Nicholas spoke. 'Will the remaining tenants come forward with their rents.'

The men did not look at each other but came quickly. Gebhard, a cousin of Klaas Beecker's, was empty-handed. The bailiff cleared his throat. More trouble. Miranda leaned forward anxiously. How could they treat Nicholas like that when he did so much for them, watching out for their interests, providing them with this beautiful kermiss? It was so unfair. Wicked, vulgar men, she thought angrily. Surely this Gebhard would not also refuse to pay his rent.

Nor did he. He stood uncertainly a moment before the platform, shuffling his hobnail boots and staring at the ground while Nicholas waited. Then, still not looking above the base of the platform, he removed his hat, and mumbled something about an accident to the farm wagon and added: 'I'll bring the stuff tomorrow, sir. If that will suit.'

'Certainly,' said Nicholas. 'That will do very well. I've no wish to be hard or unreasonable. Will you call the others from the kermiss, Duyckman. I want to say a few words to my tenants, as usual.'

The bailiff bustled off and lumbered amongst the merrymakers. 'The patroon is going to speak. Come to the platform, all of you.'

They straggled up reluctantly, loath to leave the fun, but they came. They gathered around their lord as they had been accustomed to do and as the manor tenants had always done.

Nicholas, looking down at their faces, was reassured. There had been rebellions before on the manors, small ones, quickly dissolved.

This new unrest would be equally easy to handle by a blend of firm authority and tactful kindness.

There could be no real disaffection amongst them. They were his people attached to his land. They felt for him an affectionate loyalty, just as he felt for them a paternal responsibility which embraced their physical and material welfare, and, if necessary, their discipline. The discipline he had administered to Klaas, and he knew that word of this had run through the group. It was time now for a lighter, more sympathetic note.

So he bowed to them and began: 'Tenants of Dragonwyck, I am more than happy to welcome you all today, on this glorious anniversary of our nation's independence, and I won't keep you long because I know you're anxious to be back at your sports and games. Whenever you feel hungry I hope that you won't hesitate to help yourselves. My servants will supply you with food and there are two sheep roasting on the spit behind the carrousel.'

'Our own sheep, very like, thanks for nothing,' murmured a feminine voice near Miranda, who looked about indignantly but could not identify the speaker. She could not tell whether Nicholas had heard or not, for he went on smoothly and, to her, very movingly to talk of patriotism, the beauties of their country, its superiority to all others. 'For I have traveled in many, and have a basis of comparison,' said Nicholas. He went on to assure them of his interest in their welfare, telling them that he was always ready to help with their problems. 'It is surely unnecessary for me to enumerate the great advantages that you as manor-tenants have over the struggling and insecure little farmer who has an empty title to his acres. It would never even occur to me to mention this were it not that I've heard that a few misguided men on other manors have seen fit to render themselves ridiculous by masquerading as Indians in calico nightshirts and trying to inflame the tenantry against their landlords. I know you all, your staunch integrity, your sense of fitness, too well to fear that any of you could be inveigled into any such childish mummery. So I'll say no more about it.'

He ended with a few more sentences wishing them health and happiness and directing them to enjoy themselves well at the kermiss.

There was a spatter of handclapping, one quavering cheer, 'God bless the patroon,' but for the most part they flocked silently back to the kermiss ground.

Miranda saw the suppressed dismay in Nicholas' face, and she grew warm with sympathy. She did not know that he was remembering former times when his father's speeches had produced a frenzy of cheers and foot stampings, a passionate surge of loyalty.

The manorial system was bred in Nicholas. He saw in it no inconsistency, no aspect which anyone might legitimately criticize. It annoyed him that they did not realize that the very modest rent payments which he required were only a symbol and a hereditary custom. Certainly their poultry and vegetables represented no valuable revenue, whatever they might have done in his great-grandfather's time. Nicholas, thanks to real estate holdings in the city and thanks to the pleasing way in which wealth begets wealth in a developing country, was a very rich man.

His tenants were of no financial use to him whatsoever, rather the contrary in fact; but he would have cut off his right hand rather than sell one piece of his manor, though since the Revolution there was no longer a law forbidding him to do so.

He watched them all enjoying the music and games which he had provided, glutting themselves on his beer and food. Then, turning, he met Miranda's eyes. She lowered her lashes quickly, having already learned that one did not offer sympathy to Nicholas. At once his own eyes resumed their characteristic opaque blueness and his mouth thinned to its usual line.

But he had not resented her sympathy. He smiled slowly and took her arm. 'You must be tired, Miranda, we've all been up so long. Wouldn't you like to rest awhile so that you will be fresh and very beautiful tonight?'

She did not want to rest, she wanted to join the kermiss, but she shivered a little at his unaccustomed touch, and the new caressing note in his voice. 'I'm afraid I could never be very beautiful, Cousin Nicholas,' she said, looking at him through her lashes with the first hint of coquetry she had ever used, 'but perhaps it would do me good to rest.'

Nicholas kept her arm as he helped her from the platform and he bent down and said quickly, 'I believe you're far more beautiful than you realize.'

The Count, trailing along a little behind them, heard this and thought, So—Monsieur, we are waking up a bit. Matters are progressing faster than I expected; and he yawned, for the sun was hot.

He looked at them both as they walked together, the tall slender man with his dark head and the tall slender girl with her fair one. They both moved with much the same fluid grace. They made a striking couple. It's a pity, thought the Count, that it can never be. Then he ceased to think at all. He wanted his dinner.

That evening when Miranda had completed hours of excited preparation for the party, she revolved before her mirror and her heart swelled with a new sensation of power. All of Madame Duclos' clothes had been successful, needing but a touch here and there from the girl's clever fingers, but the rose satin ball dress was a triumph.

The hair brooch looked well enough on the blond lace which filled in the low *décolletage,* though Miranda no longer thought the brooch as elegant as she once had. Before she pinned it to the lace she gazed at the intertwined strands and felt a faint pang of homesickness. But they all seemed so far away, and a letter yesterday from Abigail had told her that they were well. Miranda had tried to feel interested in the news contained in her mother's stiff, inarticulate sentences—Buttercup had calved, lightning had struck the old elm by the well, the Ladies' Missionary Society was to hold a quilting party. These things were remote and unimportant. It seemed to Miranda that there was no connection at all between the girl who lived in the little farmhouse and this dazzling creature in rose satin who was going to a banquet—and a ball.

How lucky I am! she thought, vainly powdering her cheeks, which were unfashionably flushed with excitement. The excitement was increased when a footman knocked on her door and presented her with a bouquet of flowers specially ordered by the patroon: rosebuds, tiny mauve orchids, and maidenhair fern. How like him! she thought joyfully. She had been longing for some ornament to put in her hair.

She fastened a nosegay on either side her face above the ringlets, and sewed the rest to a velvet band for a bracelet; then, sure that she could hold her own with any fashionable lady, she gave a last tug to the precious hoop, lifted her shoulders, and undulated into the hallway. The sliding doors between the Green and Italian drawing-rooms had been opened; both of these great chambers, the library, and even the small Red Room were filled with people moving to and fro, greeting each other, chatting a moment and passing on to other groups.

Johanna, enthroned in a gold chair near the entrance to the Green Drawing-Room, was behaving with unusual animation. A tall man with ginger-colored whiskers bent over her flatteringly while she flirted her fan and smiled and talked with an archness Miranda would have thought impossible. The Lady of the Manor was overpowering in yellow brocade especially chosen to set off the most splendid of the Van Ryn jewels, a ruby pendant set in a sunburst of seed pearls and diamonds. They were all admiring this jewel, the man with the ginger whiskers and several other ladies and gentlemen who came up to pay court to the hostess. Miranda, standing helplessly in the doorway not knowing what to do, heard them all begging for the history of the stone, which had come from India to Amsterdam in the seventeenth century, and complimenting the wearer on its becomingness. Indeed Johanna did look unusually well tonight, impressive rather than gross. Once she turned her head and her eyes rested for a moment on the unhappy girl in the doorway who was suffering the painful embarrassment of the young and uncertain amongst strangers. Johanna neither beckoned her over nor gave any sign of greeting, before turning back to her friends.

Miranda's cheeks grew hotter. Did Johanna mean her to stand all night on the edge of things, an outsider? And with the hurt resentment came envy. For all her physical handicaps, Johanna's position was forever assured, she was a Van Tappen and a Van Ryn, she was Lady of the Manor and on her breast was the beautiful jeweled heirloom that proclaimed the security of her title. The girl looked down at the hair brooch and the cluster of flowers on her own wrist. A passing couple stared curiously as they rustled by to greet the hostess; she thought she heard an acid murmur of comment.

She backed from the doorway with a confused notion of flight, then stopped as Nicholas crossed the hall from the Red Room. For a second they looked at each other silently. In a dark blue suit relieved by cascading white ruffles and stock, he was more strikingly handsome than he had ever been, and in that second under his unsmiling gaze her misery vanished.

His eyes were inscrutable as he said quietly: 'The flowers become you, Miranda, as I thought they would. Come, I want to present you to my friends.' He paid no attention to her nervous protest, 'Oh, no, please, I wouldn't know what to say—' but taking her arm ushered her through the drawing-rooms, pausing at each group. 'This is my cousin, Miss Miranda Wells.'

The faces, some kindly, some indifferent, some appraising and faintly hostile, were a blur through which the names floated disembodied. There were a great many Van Rensselaers, Livingstons,

Schuylers, and more which she did not hear at all. The only two who penetrated the blur were Mr. Martin Van Buren, the ex-President, a bald elderly gentleman in plum satin, and his son John, who turned out to be the tall man with the ginger whiskers to whom Johanna had been talking.

These she curtsied to with respectful awe. Her shyness had lessened by the time they had been the rounds, but then Nicholas settled her with a group of young ladies by the fireplace and left her. And without his support she was again at a loss. The three young women with whom he had left her all seemed to be Van Rensselaers; they made a few coldly civil remarks, then sped back to an unintelligible conversation about dear Cornelia's wedding.

She sat ignored and forlorn until Tompkins, red with importance, announced to Johanna that dinner was served. At once a pleasant-faced young man of about twenty-five came up bowing. 'Miss Wells?' he said. 'I believe I'm to have the pleasure. I'm Harman Van Rensselaer.'

She smiled timidly and took his arm, wondering what in the world one said to a dinner partner for hours and hours, and praying that he wouldn't guess that she had never been to a real party in her life.

But she need not have worried. Harman was a lively young man, fond of talk, and the evident admiration that she saw in his eyes restored her confidence.

'You're a stranger to the up-river country, are you not, Miss Wells?' he began. 'I hope you like it here.'

'Oh, yes,' she said. 'Though I've seen little of your country yet. I suppose you come from up around Albany?'

Harman shook his head. 'No, I belong to the Claverack branch of Van Rensselaers.'

He laughed as she looked blank. 'All this must be confusing for you. Those across the table are the Ford Crailo Rensselaers from the upper manor—some of them, that is. The man in black seated beside the Widow Mary Livingston is Stephen Van Rensselaer, the present patroon. Yonder is his son Stephen and there are two of his daughters, Cornelia and Catherine. I've seven sisters myself, but you won't have to try and identify them, for only two are here.'

She smiled. 'I'm afraid I'm stupid about it. There do seem to be so many Livingstons and Van Rensselaers.'

'The gentleman on your right is neither, at any rate,' said Harman. 'You know who he is, of course.'

Miranda stole a look at the heavy middle-aged man who sat beside her, gravely eating brandied eels in aspic. She shook her head.

'Why, that's Fenimore Cooper, the author. He and his wife often come down from Cooperstown. They're visiting the Schuylers.'

'Oh, of course,' said Miranda hastily, wishing she had had time to read 'The Last of the Mohicans,' which Nicholas had recommended.

When it came time to talk to Mr. Cooper, she found him taciturn. He seemed far more interested in the exotic creations which flowed unendingly from the kitchens than he did in her timid remarks. Until, in a desperate angling for conversation, Harman being engaged with his left-hand neighbor, she brought forth something about the kermiss that morning, and the farmers.

Cooper immediately put down his fork. 'Did Van Ryn have any trouble collecting his rents?' he asked, so sternly that Miranda was taken aback.

'Why yes, he did—in one case,' she faltered.

'Disgusting!' The author raised his hand and banged it down on the damask. Glasses tinkled, and Miranda jumped. She had no idea what it was that the suddenly excited gentleman found so disgusting, but she soon found out. Mr. Cooper turned his back on her and cutting peremptorily across the conversation at his end of the table, he addressed the Van Rensselaer patroon. 'This monstrous thing is spreading, Stephen. Van Ryn's having trouble too.'

Everyone stopped eating and looked up astonished. Stephen Van Rensselaer's placid face showed dismay, not so much at the news, which was no news to him, but at the introduction of an unpleasant subject amongst ladies in a social gathering. 'I'm sorry to hear it,' he said, and turned back to Mary Livingston, making some trivial remark about the weather. The good lady's forceful face beneath the white widow's cap expressed her perfect understanding of his tact, and she made haste to answer him as lightly.

But Cooper would not be checked. Though there was not upon his own land any such system of tenantry, he had perhaps often regretted that there was not. He never forgot that his wife was a De Lancey, once of Scarsdale Manor, and in any case his inclination and convictions had made him a thoroughgoing Tory.

He turned vehemently to Nicholas and all but shouted across the half-dozen people between them: 'I suppose you know, Van Ryn, about Smith Boughton, this tuppenny little doctor who has moved into Columbia County and skulks about preaching rebellion and defiance of the law. By God, were I one of you landowners, I'd track down the rogue and string him up to the nearest tree!'

Nicholas also found this vehemence in poor taste, though he agreed with the sentiments. 'No doubt you're right, sir, though I hardly think the fellow is of sufficient importance to trouble us; and after all, the law is entirely on our side. We need not resort to violence.'

'*You* may not, but they will. The lower classes are ever head-strong and stupid; they'll follow any leader who promises them change and power. They use no logic, and you need never expect gratitude, for you won't get it. If you'll not bestir yourselves, I'll do it for you with my pen as a cudgel.'

Along the table there ran an uncomfortable pause. Cooper's last speech had carried, and with the exception of the Count, who was observing everything with detached amusement, and his Countess, who understood nothing, each person there found the author's subject highly distasteful. Bound together as they all were by a kindred way of life and thought, they naturally refused to believe that it could be threatened, and resented any suggestion of such a threat even from an avowed champion. It was impertinent of anyone to imply that they needed championing.

Martin Van Buren stretched his plump legs and remarked: 'There is indeed much unrest in the country today, but it'll pass, as all things pass. Van Ryn, I never saw a finer show of pinks. I swear they're as big as butter-plates.' He indicated the set floral piece on the table. 'You must send your head gardener over to Lindenwald to instruct mine.'

'With the greatest pleasure,' answered Nicholas, and the company, seizing on the genteel and popular topic of horticulture, relaxed again into casual talk.

Miranda observed that Mr. Cooper rather grumpily returned to his dinner, and she was saved from further conversational embarrassment by Harman's asking her if she would dance the first polka with him.

She colored unhappily. 'I—I should like to, Mr. Van Rensselaer, but I don't know the polka.'

Harman stared at this surprising admission. Where in the world had the girl come from? He knew nothing about her except her Van Ryn relationship. She was delightfully pretty, her manners were charming if a trifle shy and uncertain. She looked like a fashionable young lady, and yet somehow she did not sound like one. He glanced at his sisters. Yes, decidedly, they both had a poise and a sophistication that this girl lacked. But what matter! He recovered quickly. 'I can think of nothing more delightful than teaching you, then, Miss Wells.'

Miranda murmured appreciation, but her eyes went wistfully to Nicholas. She had dared to hope that he would be the one to teach her, and she saw now how presumptuous the hope had been.

Nicholas, adroitly applying himself first to the Countess on his right, then to Mrs. Stephen Van Rensselaer on his left, was once more infinitely remote. He never once glanced in her direction.

What, she thought with increasing heartache, had ever caused her to think that they had established a special understanding? One mingled glance, his touch on her arm, a compliment or two. I must have been mad, she thought; of course I don't mean anything to him.

And there was Johanna at the other end of the table, smiling and hospitably urging more pudding on Martin Van Buren, who sat at her right, while pursuing with Stephen Van Rensselaer a discussion of the difficulties encountered in raising daughters. Johanna—the Lady of the Manor, and Nicholas' wife.

The drawing-rooms had in their absence been cleared of furniture in readiness for the ball, so that after leaving the gentlemen to their port and liqueurs the ladies gathered in the Red Room and the library. Seeing that Johanna was settling herself in the latter room, Miranda trailed along after the Van Rensselaer girls, who made for the Red Room.

And at once upon crossing the threshold she was conscious of the peculiar penetrating chill which she had experienced on the first evening and never since. Again she felt that formless uneasiness and oppression—the merest trickle at first but bringing with it the sensation of mounting force as though flood waters were rushing through an ever-widening breach, not touching her yet—but she knew that when they did she would be swamped with the remembered suffocating fear.

So desperate was her desire to circumvent that moment that she broke violently into the conversation of the two ladies nearest her. 'Isn't it awfully cold in here, I mean cold for July? I wonder if I should shut the window!'

Catherine Van Rensselaer from Fort Crailo stopped in mid-sentence and stared at Miranda; so did her cousin Harriet from Claverack. Both young women were handsome brunettes with a decided family resemblance.

'I don't find it cold,' said Harriet stiffly. 'Rather on the contrary. And it seems to me that the windows *are* all shut.'

'Oh, yes, so they are,' babbled Miranda, aware that she was talking nonsense but unable to stop, for the uneasiness was receding as she had hoped. 'Perhaps it'll be warmer in the other rooms when the dancing starts. Yes, surely it will be warmer when we start dancing.' She drew a long sigh of relief. The sensation had vanished, and was replaced by the doubt that she had ever felt anything strange at all. She was left with the unpleasant realization of having made a fool of herself over nothing, and the quick blood flowed up under her sensitive skin.

The ladies exchanged a look. The girl was either very silly or feverish or worse—was it possible that she had had too much wine? With one accord the two Misses Van Rensselaer drew in their billowing skirts.

'Dancing is certainly most agreeable,' said Catherine, with a vague smile in Miranda's direction; then, having done her civil duty, she turned to her cousin and added: 'Have you cards for the Downings' soirée in Newburgh next week? I think we'll go, for Mr. Downing is most gentlemanly and gives delightful parties, for all that his origin isn't quite—quite—'

'Yes, I know what you mean, love,' said Harriet, 'but after all he married a deWindt, and Mr. Downing's taste is so artistic, he has so much talent fror architecture and landscaping that I think we may consider him quite one of ourselves. Shall you be going to the Van Cortlandts' ball?'

Miranda, effectually silenced by this talk of people whom she did not know, listened a minute perforce, because she did not know how to withdraw. But why did they shut her out? She longed so to be accepted on equal terms by all these people. She didn't want to nibble at their fringes, she wanted to be woven into them, stuff of their stuff. At last she escaped upstairs to her own room with a murmured excuse of repairing her dress, to which neither lady paid any attention.

She walked at once to her mirror and consulted it mournfully. 'I *am* pretty, aren't I?' she whispered, 'and I *am* well dressed. What is wrong about me?'

She soon learned. As she emerged from her room into the thick-carpeted hallway, she heard the same two voices she had left in the Red Room. Catherine and Harriet with several of the other ladies had also gone upstairs to do a little necessary prinking. They were in one of the guest chambers, and the door was ajar. Miranda stood transfixed in the hall at the sound of her own name.

'But who in the world is this Miss Wells?' asked a voice she did not recognize, to be answered by Harriet's well-bred laugh, tinged now with annoyance. 'Nothing in the world but a sort of governess for Katrine. Johanna told me so.'

'Yet she seems ladylike, and Mr. Van Ryn introduced her as his cousin,' persisted the first voice.

'One of those poor unfortunate Gaansevant relations, actually off a farm, I believe. Nicholas has befriended her. You know how clannish the Van Ryns are. He's trying to make something of her.'

'Your brother Harman seems to find her attractive, at any rate,' said the other with a touch of malice.

'Oh, Harman likes a pretty face as well as the next man, but there's no danger of his getting involved when he knows her position. I can't think why she should be present tonight: Johanna thinks it most unsuitable. I'm sure my governesses never mingled with guests. The girl's manner is odd too; shows her lack of breeding.'

Miranda leaned her hot cheek against the cool walnut paneling. The hateful snobs! It wasn't like that at all; she wasn't like that. And hard on the first angry impulse that had almost sent her dashing into the room to confront Harriet came an even more disagreeable thought. They had said nothing that was not the literal truth. She was a farm girl and a poor relation, she was a sort of governess for Katrine. As for the odd manner and the lack of breeding—was that true too?

A sick discouragement washed over her. She took three steps toward her own room. She would not go down to the ball, she would stay upstairs. No one would really miss her—even Nicholas; Johanna would be pleased. As for the others, if they thought about it at all they would consider it most suitable.

While she stood there irresolute the musicians below, who had been tuning up, glided smoothly into the music she had learned for Nicholas. 'I dreamt that I dwelt in marble halls,' sang the violins. Miranda lifted her head and listened. It seemed to her to be a sign.

I won't go skulking back to my room, she thought, I'm going down. She drew a deep breath, clutched her fan and her handkerchief tight, and descended the staircase just ahead of the other ladies—who came out in a bevy and abruptly stopped talking at the sight of her erect, defiant back.

This defiance carried her through the evening. Let Johanna glare from her throne, let the older ladies on the side chairs whisper and look at her if they wanted to. The gentlemen at least were kind. Harman claimed her at once, and as she was naturally quick she soon managed to do well enough in the polka and waltzes.

She danced with Livingstons and Van Rensselaers and she danced with John Van Buren, whose wife was ill at home. Though his ginger-colored whiskers tickled her forehead, she particularly enjoyed this dance because Mr. Van Buren told her at once that she had something of the grace of the young queen. Miranda was immensely flattered but embarrassed too, for she had no idea to what queen he might refer and was wondering how to find out when the gentleman relieved her worry.

'I had always heard that the English were not particularly good dancers,' he continued, expertly twirling Miranda, 'but I must say that the Princess Victoria—she wasn't Queen yet, you know—quite altered my opinion.'

Miranda looked up at him. 'You mean you danced with Queen Victoria of England?' she whispered.

John Van Buren for all his sophistication was annoyed. Surely everyone knew of his sojourn in England with his father, and of his intimacy with royalty. An intimacy that had even in some American quarters prompted hints at a match between the President's son and the young princess. This would have been preposterous, of course, and he was entirely happy with his Elizabeth; but though he deprecated it he enjoyed his universal nickname of 'Prince John' which had clung to him since those hallowed months now seven years in the past.

Miranda, whose knowledge of men had broadened in the last weeks, and who was not handicapped in this instance by the dismay she would have felt if it had been Nicholas whom she had somehow offended, brilliantly redeemed her mistake.

'I don't wonder that the Queen enjoyed dancing with you,' she said. 'You dance so well, and then—then—' Miranda cast down her lashes.

'Then what—?' prompted Van Buren, already mollified.

'You're so very handsome,' finished Miranda with a shy little smile.

'Nonsense, child,' said Van Buren, laughing; but he revised his opinion of her. Really the little thing was charming. He was sorry when her next partner claimed her. A sorrow not shared by Miranda, for her next partner was Nicholas.

This was the moment for which she had been praying all evening.

Dance after dance had gone by and she had nearly given up hope that he would ask her. Indeed, now the Count had already approached her and begun, 'Mademoiselle, will you do me the honor—' when Nicholas came up to them.

'You're already engaged to the Count for this dance, Miranda?' he asked.

'Oh, no,—' she cried with a vehemence most unflattering to the round little Frenchman. 'No, indeed, Cousin Nicholas.'

The Count made a little face and smiled to himself, murmuring, 'At any rate I am in the discard.' Aloud he said, 'I hope I may dance with Mademoiselle later; but now I shall console myself with Mademoiselle Van Rensselaer.' He walked to one of the gilt chairs on the farther wall where Harriet sat waiting dolefully for a partner.

At least, thought Miranda swiftly, *I* don't lack for partners even if my manners are odd and I do lack breeding; but this thought vanished as all other thought vanished when the orchestra began to play the Coryantis Waltz, and she found herself in Nicholas' arms.

His gloved hand barely touched her rose satin waist, he held her even further away from him than the prescribed twelve inches; but as they followed the sugary strains of Coryantis she was overwhelmed by his nearness. It was as though they were imprisoned together in a shimmering bubble through which she could see the image of the drawing-rooms and the other dancers distorted and diminished.

Nothing was of any importance but Nicholas and the closeness of their bodies. Her heart beat furiously, the hand which he held in his trembled, her breath kept catching in her throat and starting with a sharp sigh. She rushed wildly into speech, babbling of the party, the music, telling him in incoherent detail of the episode with John Van Buren, of her earlier talk with Harman Van Rensselaer. Suddenly Nicholas cut across this flow. 'Keep still, Miranda,' he said curtly. He had not been looking at her; his dark chiseled face was raised and his eyes fixed on some point far beyond her head. Now as he spoke he still did not look at her, but to the rebuke which dismayed her he added two words, 'My dear.'

At first she doubted that she had heard them right, afraid to hope that he had said those words not casually, or impatiently, but with emphasis, giving them their full force of intimate endearment. But his hand tightened on hers, and she knew that she had indeed understood him.

To the other dancers the waltz seemed interminable. The musicians, watching Nicholas and waiting for a sign, received none and, cleverly dovetailing Coryantis' finale into its introduction, began again.

The Count, bouncing around with Harriet and perspiring freely, for she was a well set up young lady considerably larger than he, watched Nicholas and Miranda from the tail of his eye and thought: He is indiscreet, that young man, people will certainly begin to guess something. The girl's face is transparent as a piece of window glass.

But before Nicholas and Miranda had become really conspicuous, in fact at the very moment when Mrs. Stephen Van Rensselaer leaned toward the Widow Mary Livingston and whispered behind her fan, 'Were it anyone but Nicholas one might almost think—' the Count himself created a diversion.

He had not meant to; his altruism and interest in the young couple would never have included physical discomfort for himself. It was sheer accident.

His plump little legs had been tiring, his steps showed less and less of their habitual bounce until the orchestra, gathering speed for Coryantis' second finale, infused him with new, desperate vim. He seized Harriet firmly around her shrinking waist and pirouetted magnificently into the reverse. One of his tight black pumps shot out from under him, his ankle twined itself around the leg of a near-by chair. The Count and Harriet crashed to the slippery parquet with mingled cries of pain and fright.

Harriet was soon righted with the help of a dozen solicitous hands and retired precipitately to repair alike her dignity and dress. But the Count lay on the floor, resisting all efforts to raise him with floods of hysterical French and a Gallic abandon of cries and groans.

'Un médecin! Un médecin!' wailed the Countess, wringing her hands and fluttering around her prostrate husband.

'Certainly, Madame,' agreed Nicholas. 'Please calm yourself. I'm sending for a doctor. Count, I do think you'd be more comfortable off the floor, whatever the nature of your injury.'

Four footmen slid the protesting Count onto a table top and bore him from the drawing-rooms, while Nicholas directed the procedure and then disappeared with his suffering guest.

The others stood about for a moment discussing the accident, then the orchestra struck up a polka and, true to their code of ignoring the unpleasant, they settled back into the proper ballroom decorum. Johanna, who had waddled a few steps toward the scene of the catastrophe, resumed her chair in the farther room, but she caught

Miranda's eye and beckoned to her. Miranda obediently walked over to the gilded chair.

'Go and wait in the hall for the doctor,' ordered Johanna. 'The servants are all upset, those who aren't amusing themselves below stairs. When the doctor comes take him up to the Count.'

'Yes, ma'am,' said Miranda. She perfectly understood that she was being banished from the dancing, but she did not care in the least. After that dance with Nicholas everything else would be drab anticlimax. As it was she preferred to be alone, to re-create each moment of the last half-hour, the moment he put his arm about her, the pressure of his hand, and the tone of his voice in those two low words—'My dear.'

The hall by the front door was dim and deserted. The sounds from the drawing-rooms were muted here. She sat in a carved black Gothic chair, her chin cupped in her hand, and waited. In twenty minutes there was the thud of galloping hoofs outside, a sharp whinny.

Miranda opened the door and a young man strode in. He was hatless, his gray homespun suit was wrinkled and smelled of horse lather. He was several inches taller than Miranda but heavy-boned so that he looked shorter than he was. He had a great deal of rather untidy sandy hair, a freckled face, and alertly humorous gray eyes.

'You can't be the doctor—' said Miranda, who had been prepared for a reproduction of Doctor Lynch at home—silk hat, pointed beard, dignity and maturity at least.

The young man waved the shabby black bag which he clutched in his muscular fist. 'I'm a doctor. Jeff Turner from Hudson. I was tending Tom Wilson's wife. I got word I was wanted here.'

He spoke in a quick, forthright voice. 'Where's the patient?' he went on, examining Miranda coolly. 'One of the fine gentlemen take too much wine? Or one of the elegant ladies get a fit of the vapors?'

'Certainly not,' she retorted, annoyed at the carelessly contemptuous look he cast at the somber magnificence of the great hall. 'One of our guests hurt himself dancing—a French nobleman, the Count de Grenier.'

She had expected to impress him and was sadly disappointed. Jeff Turner snorted, 'No doubt an injury to a count hurts far worse than one to lesser mortals. You're Miss Van Ryn, I suppose, since you say "our guests."'

Miranda blushed. Odious man. 'Miss Van Ryn is six years old,' she answered stiffly. 'I'm Miranda Wells, the patroon's cousin.'

'Oh, to be sure,' said Jeff. He paused and gave her a look of amusement tinged with pity. 'I've heard about you.'

Miranda resented the look in its entirety. 'I'm sure I don't know how you could have.' She lifted her chin with a haughtiness she felt would have done credit to the Widow Mary Livingston.

To her fury Jeff burst out laughing. 'What a little goose you are!' he said, not unkindly. 'The humble people do occasionally dare to gossip about their superiors, you know. Now be a good girl and show me to the ailing Count.'

Miranda, seeking a withering retort, couldn't find one sufficiently devastating. As she led the way upstairs, even her preoccupation with Nicholas was banished by anger at this officious young country doctor. Why shouldn't she say 'our guests,' why shouldn't she try to show him his place? And he was the first person she had met who seemed to have no respect for the Van Ryn standing.

Nicholas, as hospitality demanded, had remained at the Count's bedside. He rose when Miranda and the doctor entered. The Countess continued to pat her husband's pillow and give vent to little shrieks.

Jeff did not greet the patroon. He gently pushed aside the Countess and made a swift concentrated examination.

'Sprained ankle, nothing more,' he said, addressing no one in particular. 'Bring me linen bandages.'

Nicholas gave a brief order to a hovering maid, then turned back to the bed. 'Are you quite sure the leg isn't broken?'

Jeff straightened up and leaning against the ornately carved bedpost answered quietly, 'I'm quite sure, Mr. Van Ryn.'

The two men looked across the bed at each other for a moment of steady appraisal. At last Nicholas nodded, satisfied. 'I've faith in your ability, and I've heard about you from my bailiff. It's fortunate that you happened to be on my lands tonight.'

A hot rejoinder rose to Jeff's lips, but he checked it. Though he had never before met the patroon he had always despised him, considering him as a contemptible oppressor living in fantastic opulence and denying to his tenants not only independence but the simplest justice. Were it not that this sudden call to Dragonwyck had been represented as acute emergency, he would have angrily refused to come, because a tragic sequel to the rent ceremony this morning had still further inflamed him against Nicholas. But now having met him he found some of his hostility evaporating. For in that instant of mutual stock-taking,

Jeff received an unexpected impression—Here is a lonely man and a very unhappy one.

While he deftly wound linen strips about the Count's swollen ankle Jeff made the rejoinder that he had started to, but he made it without heat. 'These would not be your lands if justice were done, Mr. Van Ryn.'

Miranda gasped and sent the young doctor an angry look, but Nicholas merely said, 'Indeed?—I'm sorry to hear you're an anti-renter.'

'Pour l'amour de Dieu!' cried the Count suddenly from his pillow, where he had been quiet during Jeff's ministrations. 'Do not, I beg of you, have the argument over my bed! I am suffering, I am exhausted, and forgive me, messieurs, but this rent business I do not understand. I do not wish to understand it!'

Jeff grinned in spite of himself. 'No, they do these things better in France, where they'd simply have a revolution and settle everything.' He turned to Nicholas and his eyes hardened. 'But maybe your tenant farmers aren't so different from the French, Mr. Van Ryn.'

'And maybe you're being a trifle melodramatic?' answered Nicholas. 'Come, Doctor, this subject is boring my guest. If you've finished here, I hope you'll join me in a glass of wine downstairs.'

Jeff straightened his coat and snapped shut his black bag. 'That would be charming, I'm sure, except that I'm busy. Tom Wilson's wife is critically ill with consumption, and Klaas Beecker, whom you turned out of house and home this morning, had an unfortunate accident with his scythe. It cut—' said Jeff with cold emphasis, 'the veins in both his wrists. I doubt he'll pull through.'

There was a pause. Nicholas' eyes flickered. 'Didn't he get the money I told Duyckman to give him?'

Jeff gave a brief laugh. 'I believe he did, but three gold pieces don't necessarily prevent—unfortunate accidents.'

Nicholas' mouth tightened. 'I direct you to do everything possible to hasten Klaas' recovery. Spare no expense.'

Jeff walked to the door and turned on the threshold. 'This is exceedingly kind of you,' he said in an expressionless voice which deliberately mimicked Nicholas' last speech, 'but I would do everything possible for Klaas without your gracious authorization.'

He made a dignified exit into the hall, thinking: Lord, that was a bit pompous of me, it's my red-haired temper again. He descended the stairs ahead of Miranda and Nicholas, preparing to let himself unobtrusively out the front door. He was a trifle ashamed of his rudeness, anxious to be gone from this oppressive palace back to the farmers whose way of life he understood, and to whose cause he was passionately dedicated.

But he reckoned without Nicholas, who walked swiftly around in front to bar the door, at the same time turning on Jeff the full force of his slow, rare smile.

'I beg you to join me in one glass of wine before you go out again into the night. It'll give me very great pleasure.'

'Well—' said Jeff to his own surprise, and found himself ushered into the library. He was puzzled by the intensity of will that he felt behind his host's natural enough invitation. He disliked the arrogance and ruthlessness which emanated from Nicholas in almost tangible waves, he disliked the luxuriant elegance of the patroon's dress, the white rose in his buttonhole; and yet he did not quite dislike the man himself. For Jeff was a good doctor, shrewd and intuitive, and he felt beneath the complex picture which Nicholas presented to the world a quality which one could not diagnose, a divergence from the norm, a cleavage—which inspired a faint, uncomfortable pity.

This impression wore off after Jeff had galloped two miles through the warm July night and once more entered Klaas Beecker's gray farmhouse.

Klaas lay semi-conscious on the corn-husk bed, his arms swathed in blood-soaked rags, his face as pale as the whitewashed walls behind him, while his wife, sobbing hopelessly, crouched on the floor amongst a huddle of chairs, tables, and carpetbags—the household goods which had been gathered for the eviction on the morrow.

6

FOR THE REST OF THE SUMMER THERE WAS GREAT activity at Dragonwyck, a constant stream of guests with entertainment for them from morning until midnight. There were musicales and soirées, there were elaborate charades played in the rose gardens by the light of flares and twinkling paper lanterns. There were picnics and boating parties on the Hudson. There were even swimming parties, though these were popular with no one but Nicholas, who was an expert swimmer, having learned the art abroad in the waters of the Mediterranean. Very few of his guests could swim, nor did they share with their host the pagan triumph of mastering the elements.

Nicholas, therefore, usually swam alone at sunrise, and one morning Miranda, unable to sleep, slipped out of the house and wandered down to the river. Attracted by the sound of rhythmic splashing, she innocently followed it to its source. She stood frozen on the bank while Nicholas, who had not seen her, started to come out of the water. She saw the tan neck, naked chest and shoulders, before she turned and fled frantically back to the house. In her room she flung herself on her bed. She was shamed and shocked. Stronger than these ran a deeper emotion. That glimpse of him with his head thrown back and his wet hair curling on his forehead—like that statue of the young Apollo beneath the pergola in the willow garden from which all the ladies quickly averted their eyes.

But she thought the statue beautiful, and now Nicholas—she pushed this violently down. But it returned again and again to torment her.

Much tormented her these days. Since the night of the ball he had avoided her. Worse than that, he had ceased to champion her against Johanna, and without his backing Miranda found that she had insensibly slipped into precisely the position which that lady desired. She met few of the guests and then very briefly; she was included in the entertainment only on the rare occasions when Katrine was; she now took most of her meals with the little girl in the school room. That this was a reasonable adjustment and exactly the type of life which she and her parents had expected for her at Dragonwyck, did not prevent her from lapsing into a dull misery. It had been so different at first when, though she had seen little of Nicholas, his attitude had been interested and personal. Only two things sustained her: the intuitive certainty that he was not as unaware as he appeared, and his remembrance of her birthday. She had become nineteen on September thirteenth, and upon returning to her room at noon after teaching Katrine, she had found upon the table a single large rose, ivory white with a golden center; and beneath it a book, 'Twice-Told Tales' by Nathaniel Hawthorne. Inside the book there was a note. 'The flower is like you, the stories may interest you, both convey my esteem on this memorable occasion.—N. V. R.'

Little enough cause for the uprush of joy which it brought. And though she wore the rose in her bodice until it faded he made no reference to it, nor to the birthday, and her joy soon dimmed.

On a day in early October the Van Ryns and their house guests of the moment, the Beeckmans and Philipses, were invited to dine with the Van Rensselaers at the Manor House in Claverack. Miranda, who had of course not been included in the invitation, disconsolately watched their departure from the window in the upstairs hall.

It was the state coach which had been ordered today, an enormous vehicle painted dark gray and upon its doors the Van Ryn coat-of-arms, three black leopards on a red field. None of the Van Ryn carriages needed any such identification, they were all as well known through the countryside as the matched cream-colored horses that drew them; but in that era those who possessed heraldic insignia displayed them, not from ostentation, but as the conventional badge of the privileged.

Miranda, watching from the window, saw Johanna emerge first from the house, a huge figure like a hogshead in purple velvet, her plumed hat awry, her ears, fingers, and chest all blazing with the Van Ryn diamonds. With the help of the liveried groom she clambered into the coach, which tilted violently and swayed on its springs. Mrs. Beeckman and Mrs. Philipse followed with their husbands. But Nicholas mounted the box and sat beside the coachman.

Why doesn't he go inside with the others? thought Miranda, pressing against the glass to get a last glimpse. From deep inside her the answer came. He never gets any nearer to Johanna than he can possibly help. Startled, she considered this. It was a new idea, and yet it seemed as though she had known it for a long time. Still, even if it's true what difference does it make? she thought, and turned listlessly from the window. The great silent house pressed down about her. She felt vanquished—dwarfed. She might go to her room and write to Abigail, she might try to pick out music on the piano, to which lately she had not had access since the guests were always in the way; but neither of these occupations attracted her. Suddenly and desperately she wanted to talk to someone, anyone. And she thought of Zélie. She had not seen the old woman again, but Miranda knew through Katrine that she lived down somewhere in the kitchen quarters. Perhaps Nicholas wouldn't like it, but it would at least be something to do, and Zélie, though she had been silly and mysterious, had also been interesting.

On impulse Miranda went downstairs, moving with a frightened quietness because the deserted house seemed full of whispering shadows. The door to the basement stairs led off from the pantry behind the dining-room and she had never before used it. The family, except of course Katrine, never penetrated into the sub-world. The stairs ended in the servants' hall and a dozen faces gaped at her in astonishment. Tompkins, in shirt sleeves and with a foaming mug in his hand, half-rose and then sat down again. 'What can I do for you, miss?' he said resentfully.

'I—I wanted to see Zélie, please.'

The butler shrugged. 'In the corner of the far kitchen as usual.' He pointed, having no intention except under Nicholas' eye of putting himself out for this little nonentity.

Miranda passed through two kitchens lined with cook stoves, ovens, and shelves full of gleaming copper pans. In a farther room there was a fireplace. Over the hickory logs a spitted pig rotated slowly while a small boy turned the crank. In a corner by this fireplace sat old Zélie, rocking. Across the room by a spinning wheel sat a placid Dutch woman, also rocking. This was Annetje, the head cook, and on her capacious lap she held Katrine while she sang to the child an old Dutch lullaby.

Trip a trop a tronjes
De vaarken in de boonjes—

The purring flames, the homely smell of roasting meat, the motherly voice singing and the two women rocking, sent a pang to Miranda's heart. No wonder the child preferred it down here. She smiled at Katrine, who smiled back sleepily but did not move.

Zélie raised her wrinkled face and her chair stilled. 'You want me, *petite.*' It was a statement not a question. She motioned to a hassock beside her, and the girl obediently sat down.

Across the room the foolish little song began again more softly.

Trip a trop a tronjes—

'What you want with me?' said Zélie. 'You no listen.' She shook her head sadly. 'Azilde will laugh. I tol' you before.'

'Oh, don't start that again, please!' cried Miranda, exasperated. 'I didn't come down to hear that claptrap. I don't know why I came. I guess I was sort of lonely.'

'Lonely!' Zélie spat the word out. 'You not knowing what lonely is —yet.—Why you not go home where you belong?'

Miranda's eyes dropped, she clasped her hands tight on her lap. Home, yes. Back to Abigail and safety. Back to the cosiness of fire like this. But never to see Nicholas again—to abandon all hope that someday, somehow— Further than this she never went. There was neither reason nor possibility in that formless hope.

Zélie watched the girl's downcast face and she gave a sharp, grim laugh. 'The Devil reads your soul. When you want a thing so much, it make that thing happen *sure*. Always if we want thing bad enough it happen.'

Miranda shook her head. 'That's nonsense, Zélie.'

The old woman stiffened, she jerked forward, her glittering eyes angry and threatening; but as quickly as it came her anger passed. She sighed and slumped back. She fell to rocking again.

The kitchen was quiet except for the hissing noises made by the hot grease on the fire. Katrine slipped off the cook's lap; clutching her doll she stole over to Zélie and laid her hand coaxingly on the bony old knee. 'Tell a story about the old time, Zélie,' she begged. 'Tell about Azilde. M'randa'd like to hear too. Wouldn't you, M'randa?'

The girl started. 'Why, yes, I suppose so,' she said unenthusiastically. She was no longer curious about Azilde, who seemed to be connected with nothing but superstitious fear and disaster. But the prospect of leaving the warm kitchen and even this tepid companionship for the silence of the great house upstairs was less inviting.

'The patroon don't like that I tell about Azilde,' said Zélie. 'It make him afraid.'

'Oh, how ridiculous!' said Miranda, smiling. 'He's not afraid of anything.'

'Ah—' Zélie sighed with a weary patience. 'How the young are blind! Everyone is afraid of something, *p'tite*. Yes, I think I tell you the story. Listen well.' She was silent for several minutes and then she began to speak in a flat, chanting voice as though she repeated words learned by heart long ago. 'Marie Azilde de la Courbet was mos' beautiful girl in New Orleans, always she singing and laughing and lighting flames in the heart with her so big so soft black eyes.'

While Zélie talked, Miranda at first listened absently, finding the high inflected speech hard to follow; but gradually as the old voice went on it evoked a hypnotic power. Azilde grew real and Miranda forgot that she was hearing of a girl who lived in an unknown city a hundred years ago, or that Zélie was recounting a tragedy which she knew only at second hand through her mother's stories—the black Titine who had been Azilde's body servant.

The past was vivified by intimate details until it seemed that she stood on the scrubbed kitchen flags beside them—Azilde with her breathless gaiety, and her dark curls powdered white and piled high. In these curls she always wore a golden flower—jasmine or a rose. Her elaborate panniered gowns were usually yellow too, for Azilde loved the color of sunshine and laughter. 'All day long she sing like a mockingbird,' said Zélie. 'And all night long she dance at the Governor's Palace with fine French gentlemen in white perukes.'

Azilde had loved a handsome Creole youth, aide to the Marquis de Vaudreuil, and there had been many a stolen meeting beside the fountain in the de la Courbets' palm-fringed courtyard behind their house on Royal Street.

Until Pieter Van Ryn came to New Orleans on an October day in 1752. He had come on his own brig to buy a cargo of Louisiana indigo which he could sell at immense profit in New York. Theoretically the French colonials were forbidden to sell produce to any but the mother country; still there were ways of getting around that. Pieter's flat blue eyes, his square stolidity, above all his cold persistency unrelieved by a single smile or conventional compliment, disconcerted the gay colonials. He got his indigo, and he got Azilde too.

'You mean he fell in love with her?' asked Miranda eagerly.

Zélie hunched her shoulders. 'There was no love in the patroon. He wanted her. He prove to her parents he was rich man, great lord, he took her with only a tiny dot. They think they make fine bargain.'

Even Titine had never known what actually happened on the long, stormy voyage to the North. But she had seen her mistress transformed overnight into a faded little wraith whose dark eyes now held but two expressions: a glassy blankness which changed when her husband was near to bewildered terror. There were no more songs or laughter. Day after day through the harsh snow-bound winter Azilde crouched beside a tiny fireplace, her hair no longer powdered, its curls strained back under the Dutch matron's white cap, her delicate body shivering under the shapeless black dress.

The next fall Adriaen was born. The patroon had been momentarily pleased with his wife for having produced the requisite heir. In all other matters she had sorely disappointed him. The beauty and gaiety which had first attracted him had not survived her outward metamorphosis into Lady of the Manor and Dutch housewife. But he overlooked her shortcomings upon the birth of Adriaen, presented her with a diamond necklace and the little harpsichord which stood in the Red Parlor. Azilde never wore the necklace. After the baby's birth even the patroon could not fail to see that it was not Azilde's body alone that shrank from him. Her spirit had retired into a misty far-off land from which she never tried to return.

'All day she sit and stare out the window,' said Zélie. 'She no answer when people speak. Only sometimes she go down to Red Room and play on the harpsichord when the patroon is out. Always she play a little Creole song she learn as a child. The patroon hate that, it make him savage. Then one day—'

Zélie paused. She glanced down at the child by her knee, but Katrine had lost interest. She was bent over her china doll, frowning a little with concentration as her pudgy fingers unbuttoned one of Cristabel's starched petticoats.

Miranda leaned forward. 'Do go on, Zélie—' she urged.

The old woman nodded slowly. 'One day a disaster happen. The patroon's ship went on the reefs. All the hands were lost and all the cargo. Titine was sitting with Azilde trying to make her look at her baby, when the patroon came roaring in like a bull. He grab Azilde by the shoulders and shake her. "You won't understand—you witless thing—" he shout at her. "But I am ruined."

'At first Azilde just stare at him, and then very softly she start to laugh. Titine say the sound make her hair creep. The patroon's hands drop. He back away. "Why are you laughing?" he whisper.

'And she answer him for the first time in months. "Because—" she say still laughing, "misfortune has come to this house of hatred. Always I will laugh at that."'

Zélie's chanting voice stopped abruptly. In the fireplace one of the hickory logs fell apart and a shower of sparks flew into the kitchen. Miranda drew a deep breath. 'What a horrible thing for her to say—she was crazy then, poor thing?'

'Crazy with fear and misery, *p'tite*. A tropic flower cannot live without sun. A soul cannot live without love.'

'But she had her baby,' protested Miranda.

'Yes, but it was too late. The madness had come. One week after the patroon tell her about the ship, she creep downstairs in the night. She play her little Creole tune and she laugh to herself. Titine heard. She come running to Red Room, but not in time. Azilde had taken knife from dining-room drawer.' Zélie raised her hand and made an eloquent gesture toward her throat.

Miranda swallowed, staring at the grim old face.

'And still she laugh—' said Zélie calmly in her ordinary voice, 'when badness come to Dragonwyck. Only those of her blood can hear, but sometimes others feel warning though they cannot hear her. I have felt—and you too, I think.'

The girl was silent. For a moment she almost believed, as she thought of the two occasions on which she had battled the nameless mounting fear, but since then she had sat a score of times in the Red Room with no eerie sensations at all; and both her common sense and her reverence for Nicholas, who had expressed the greatest scorn for Zélie's superstition, decided her.

'That's a shocking story,' she said, feeling reasonable and mature. 'But it all happened a long time ago. One should forget old tragedies. I quite agree with Mr. Van Ryn that the story shouldn't be repeated.'

Zélie, apparently not listening, pulled a clay pipe and a nubbin of tobacco from her pocket. She thrust a broom straw into the fire and, lighting the pipe, shut her wrinkled eyelids while she inhaled a mouthful of smoke.

'You know there couldn't really be "badness" at Dragonwyck,' went on Miranda, a trifle disconcerted. 'It's a beautiful place and I love it—why I only wish—' She stopped.

Zélie opened her eyes, the shiny black pupils fixed themselves on the girl. 'Aha!' she said with malice. 'You only wish—' She crossed her skinny shanks and inhaled again. 'Go back upstairs. I'm tired, I want to rest.' She turned her face away.

Discomforted and annoyed, Miranda got up. She should never have encouraged the daft old thing in the first place. She walked over to Katrine, who was now playing with a litter of kittens in the corner behind the spinning wheel. 'Let's go upstairs, dear,' she said, 'and I'll read to you.'

The child shook her head mutinously. 'I want to stay here. Annetje's making me a gingerbread man.'

There was nothing for Miranda to do but retrace her way through the kitchens and the hall full of servants, alone.

In her absence all the tapers had been lighted. The house was no longer dark and threatening. It was filled with the scent of flowers mingled with the aromatic smoke of the cedar-wood fires. She walked through the downstairs rooms, her head high in a mood of defiance.

It seemed to her that they all welcomed her, the gilded and carved furnishings, the moss-thick carpets, the marble statues, the porcelains from China and Dresden, the tapestries and brocade draperies. All the intoxicating perfume of luxury.

I *do* belong here, she thought angrily. I'm Nicholas' cousin. How dare that old hag try to frighten me away!

She came last to the Red Room. It was as quiet and fragrant as the others, except that as usual its smallness and the warm crimson of its curtains made it cosier. She walked to the harpsichord and threw back its cover. She hesitated, then quickly touched one of the yellowed keys. A thin tinkling note responded. Her heart beat faster and she waited. Nothing happened. No queer sensations, no warning chill. Nothing. And I never had any either, she thought. So much for Zélie.

She pulled out the stool and seating herself played 'I Dreamt I Dwelt in Marble Halls.' She played it faster than usual, and the old instrument so long untouched gave forth sounds that were reedy and jangling, but the effect was gay.

She played it through twice before she lowered the cover, pushed the stool back, and went up to her room. She took off her dress and slipping into the frilled India muslin négligée, curled up in the armchair before the fire. On the inlaid walnut table beside her were several books, and the Bible her father had given her lay squat and heavy in the middle of them. She looked at it with a stirring of conscience. How long had it been since she had read the required daily stint? There were no religious observances at Dragonwyck except that on some Sundays, when it was convenient, the family attended the village church, where they sat on one side near the pulpit under a carved-oak canopy and listened to very dull sermons from Dominie Huysmann.

It was weeks, thought Miranda guiltily, since she had even remembered God or salvation. She pulled the Bible onto her lap and riffled the pages. On impulse she shut her eyes and put her finger at random on a verse. It fell in the twentieth chapter of Job.

'He hath swallowed down riches, and he shall vomit them up again: God shall cast them out of his belly.'

Miranda made a disgusted face. How coarse and uninspiring! The Bible no longer opened windows into an enchanted world. It had become tiresome. She let the cover fall to with a plop. She put the Bible back on the table and took up her 'Twice-Told Tales.' On the fly leaf she had pasted Nicholas' note, which she now re-read for the hundredth time. She had read all the stories too, but they brought her closer to Nicholas because he had read them and once remarked that the author had talent and might some day be famous.

She began again on 'The Minister's Black Veil.'

7

THE RIVER FROZE EARLY THAT YEAR AND WITH THE cessation of the regular boats, guests too ceased coming to Dragonwyck. That Nicholas had used the distraction of entertaining this continual horde of guests for a purpose of his own, Miranda had no idea, but now in November with no one but the Van Ryns and herself in residence she was suddenly much happier.

Nicholas was aware of her again. It was as though he had held her in abeyance during those summer weeks, but he had not apparently abandoned all interest in her as she had sometimes feared. Though no overt word was spoken, she felt that their relationship again approached that of the night of the Fourth-of-July Ball.

On a Tuesday morning in the middle of November, Magda rapped on Miranda's door. 'Mevrouw wishes to see you in her room,' snapped the maid. 'At once,' she added harshly, as the girl started for the bureau to smooth her hair and shake out the immaculate ruffles at the wrists of her blue morning gown.

Somewhat troubled, Miranda followed the maid down the hall. She had never before been summoned to Johanna's bedroom.

The Lady of the Manor lay in the ancestral Van Ryn bed. Like the Rent-Chair it had come from Holland with the first patroon, and on its headboard were carved the three leopards amidst an elaborate design of bosses and leaves. Anyone else would have been dwarfed by the four colossal oaken posts and the scarlet-and-gold tester which they supported, but Johanna's unrestrained flesh overflowed most of the mattress.

This room was gracefully proportioned and very large, but it gave no impression of space, for it was cluttered with a heterogeneous collection of shabby furniture brought by Johanna from Albany. And despite the maids' constant efforts all the little tables were littered with half-eaten boxes of bon-bons, torn clippings from magazines, and crumbs of colored wax. Johanna had lately taken an indolent interest in making the wax flower pieces which had become so fashionable. Though outside the front windows dazzling sunshine sparkled on the partly frozen river, the brown plush portières were still tight-drawn, and the room had a sour airless smell.

If this were only my room, thought Miranda, who had examined everything in one quick glance, how beautiful I would make it. It could be the loveliest room in the house.

Johanna was finishing her breakfast. She wiped her mouth and pettishly pushed an empty cup toward Magda. 'Tell Annetje to have more cream whipped into my morning chocolate. This was thin as dish water. Take my tray away.'

The maid silently complied.

Johanna hoisted herself up on the frilled pillows and acknowledged the girl's presence with a discontented sigh. 'Oh, good morning. I wanted to talk to you.'

'Yes, ma'am,' said Miranda anxiously. 'Is anything wrong?'

Johanna's expression of vague peevishness hardened as she surveyed the girl. Against the vivid blue of Miranda's dress the carefully arranged ringlets shone brightly gold. Johanna's resentful gaze lingered on the tiny waist, which Miranda's new stays pinched down to eighteen inches.

'Such tight lacing can't be good for you,' she said sharply. 'It's not suitable to your station. Nor is the way you wear your hair. It should be confined neatly in a net.'

A slow wave of rose washed up to the fluffy curls on Miranda's forehead. 'I'm sorry ma'am,' she said with difficulty. 'Is that—is that what you wanted to speak to me about?'

'No. I'm not satisfied with Katrine's progress. You don't pay enough attention to the child.'

'I try to, ma'am,' returned the girl unhappily.

'Well, I want you to take her into Hudson today. She has a whitlow on her finger. Let Doctor Hamilton on Diamond Street treat it.'

Miranda was bitterly disappointed. She had been looking forward to this day. Two nights ago at dinner, Nicholas had said suddenly, 'Miranda, do you skate?'

'Oh, yes, indeed I love it,' she had answered, thinking of happy winter outings on Dumpling Pond at home.

He had nodded, his brilliant eyes on her eager face. 'The creek behind Bronk Island is well frozen. On Tuesday if the weather holds we'll cross the river and skate.'

This was Tuesday, and the weather had held clear and sharp in spite of bright sunshine. There would have been the joy of exercise; her muscles often rebelled against the ladylike inactivity which was now expected of her. And then she would have been alone with Nicholas.

'I don't think it's a whitlow, ma'am,' she protested. 'Trine had a splinter that I took out; you can hardly see the place now.'

Johanna pursed her mouth. 'Magda says it is a whitlow. Besides, the child must go to the cobbler's on Union Street and have her Sunday boots mended, and here's a list of things which you may get for me in the town.' She held out a scrawled piece of paper. 'You will go at once.'

'And where is Miranda to go at once?'

Both women jumped. Nicholas stood in the doorway, on his mouth an inquiring smile. He ignored Miranda, fixing his gaze on his wife.

Johanna's pasty face disintegrated into shapelessness. She moistened her lips.

'You—you startled me, Nicholas. You so seldom come in here—'

He inclined his head, and continued to wait for his answer. Johanna with a nervous motion pulled her bed jacket tight across her great breasts, straightened her crumpled nightcap.

'Miranda must take Katrine to Hudson today. The child needs a doctor,' she said at last.

His eyebrows arched. 'Could a doctor not come here, as usual?'

'It would take too long; besides, there are other commissions in Hudson.' She added on a defiant note: 'I ordered the carriage. It's waiting now.'

Nicholas inclined his head again. 'I see. The trip to Hudson is very important. Miranda and Katrine must certainly go. It changes my plans a trifle, but no matter. I've been meaning to talk with the county sheriff for some time. Your wishes are always paramount with me, my dear, as you know.'

Johanna drew a labored breath. 'What do you mean?'

'Why, that I shall of course accompany them to Hudson,' said Nicholas gently. 'They could hardly get back before nightfall, and with the temper of the farmers what it is, the roads are unsafe. The Livingston coach was waylaid last week.'

Miranda could not suppress a delighted glance at Nicholas. But he still ignored her, his unwinking gaze on Johanna's face, over which now passed an expression of helpless bewilderment, and something else. Can it be that she's frightened? thought Miranda in amazement. Nicholas was always so courteous, just as he had been now. And it was quite true that he usually did exactly as Johanna wished, especially in these last months. What a fool she is! thought the girl impatiently, and forgot Johanna, whose wishes were negligible now that Nicholas had taken hold of the situation.

That November day in Hudson was to be one of those vivid days which come seldom and unannounced, when every slightest incident is gilded with emotion. Of the dark undercurrents beneath that glowing day, she had no conception then, nor for many years.

It was enough that from the moment Nicholas seated himself beside her in the closed barouche, she should feel for the first time with him at ease—excited, adventurous, and beautiful. She wore the green silk, into which she had sewn a fresh ruching of cream lace. Over this, for warmth, went a wadded fawn-colored pelisse, and her gloves and reticule were lemon yellow. Though she had had few occasions to wear it she knew how becoming the green bonnet was with its satin ribbons and ostrich plumes. Her handkerchief was perfumed with heliotrope, and the seductive yet delicate scent added to her sense of confidence.

For the first mile, as the two cream horses drew them smoothly through the village, then slowed down for the icy puddles and ruts on the river road, Nicholas said little. But she felt him looking at her, felt the electric atmosphere within the warmed carriage, and was content. Katrine sat on the seat opposite them crooning to her doll. Now and again she examined her bandaged finger with satisfaction, pleased with its importance. It didn't hurt, but Mama said it was very bad. That's why Miranda was taking her to Hudson. It was a treat to go to Hudson. Perhaps there'd be ices to eat, and maybe Papa would buy her something.

The child looked doubtfully at Nicholas. It was queer to have him there. Sometimes for days she didn't see him at all, and when she did, usually he didn't pay any attention to her. But sometimes he gave her presents. I wish Annetje could have gone with us too, thought Katrine.

'Straighten your pantalettes, dear,' said Miranda, smiling. 'They're all rumpled.' She leaned over to help, and her golden curls fell across Katrine's pudgy legs. This tickled and Katrine was pleased. She liked Miranda, who was so pretty and gentle. Besides, she always smelled nice.

'Will we have ices in Hudson?' asked the child suddenly. 'Papa can we?'

Nicholas' face darkened, and Miranda thought, he's wondering if she is going to be like Johanna. Then he relaxed, leaning easily against the brocaded padding of the carriage seat. And he laughed, seeming much younger.

'Certainly you may have ices. We'll go to the Hudson House for dinner. I'd planned to drive down to the Widow Mary Livingston's and trespass on her hospitality. But perhaps you'd rather dine at an inn.'

'Oh, yes, please, Papa,' begged the child with unusual animation.

'What would *you* like to do, Miranda?' said Nicholas. At the intimate note in his voice her breathing quickened.

'The inn, please,' she said eagerly. This was no day to visit another Manor House where the awesome widow would immediately engulf Nicholas, leaving Miranda stranded as usual.

After that Nicholas began to talk in his most charming manner. He told her about the country through which they were driving. By now they had passed out of his own manor, but he knew every step of the road to Hudson. At Nutten Hook he showed her a shanty where lived a witch. 'At least my farmers think so,' said Nicholas, laughing. 'She sells love potions and on moonless nights flies as far as Kinderhook on her broomstick.'

Miranda laughed too, not at what he said but for delight that he was talking to her like this. Nicholas was so rarely light and gay, and now for all the dark reserve which he never lost, he was gay. He seemed to be living only in the moment as she was.

'Look!' he cried as they crossed the Stockport Creek. 'Do you see the falls upstream?'

She nodded.

'Once when I was a boy I made a wager with friends that I could dive down the cataract.'

'But that was terribly dangerous. How could anyone do that?'

'I did,' said Nicholas. 'And though I broke my leg, it was worth it. It's always been my pride to master circumstances.'

Yes, thought Miranda. Even as a boy he must have been able to master any situation.

The carriage jounced over a deep rut and she was thrown against him. Her cheek brushed the shoulder of his blue broadcloth coat. There was a faint odor of starched linen, *peau d'espagne,* and the leather of his boots. As it had been at the ball, her will and her body both seemed to melt like soft wax at his nearness. In his eyes there was a peculiar expression. He picked his tall beaver hat from the floor where it had fallen, and she noticed that his hands trembled slightly.

By noon they reached the Dugway Road and pulled up the sharp hill on Second Street into Hudson.

'How pretty the town is!' cried Miranda. She would on that day have thought a collection of squatters' huts on a mud flat pretty. But the little town did have charm. Its neat houses were of brick or fieldstone and plainly showed their New England origin. Hudson had been settled by Nantucket Quakers who sought after the Revolution a newer and safer whaling port, and though encircled by land-loving Dutch farmers, the Folgers and Macys and Coffins had been profitably going down to the sea in ships for fifty years.

'Where's Diamond Street?' asked Miranda. 'Cousin Johanna said that Doctor Hamilton lived there—for Katrine's finger.'

Nicholas shook his head. 'Hamilton's an old fogy. He knows no remedies but calomel, bark, and brandy. Take the child to that young Turner. He seems very capable.'

'But he's so rude, and he's a down-renter!' cried Miranda, startled into protest by the aversion she had felt to the brusque young doctor.

'All the more reason to flatter him with my patronage,' answered Nicholas easily. 'He'll soon lose his silly views if I make him the Manor physician.'

'Oh—' she said. 'I see.' How clever Nicholas was!

He gave the coachman instructions, turned back to her. 'I'm going to see Mayor Curtis and the sheriff. There's been more trouble in collecting the rents. I'll order this ridiculous business settled once for all. Then I'll meet you at the Hudson House at two.'

He got out of the carriage, stood hat in hand until the horses started. She watched his tall figure—made even taller by the high beaver hat—walk rapidly down the street. People stared, whispering. Once he uncovered his head and bowed to an old lady in gray and his wavy hair shone black in the sunlight.

The carriage turned down Union and she could no longer see him. It stopped at a low brick cottage on Front Street near the river. A tin sign nailed on the whitewashed door said 'Jefferson Turner, M.D.'

Miranda sighed. 'Come, Katrine. This is the doctor's.'

The child, hugging Cristabel, obediently followed. As Miranda lifted the brass knocker she was astonished to hear a confusion of voices from inside, and a male one louder than the rest shouting, 'Blast them, 'tis no time for half measures, I tell ye!'

Miranda's knock produced a dead silence. Someone said 'Hush!' She waited five impatient minutes before the door was opened by Jeff himself. His sandy hair was tousled, his shirt sleeves rolled up, disclosing heavily muscled arms with freckles and red hairs on them.

The girl's lip curled. She drew up her green skirts and lifted her chin. 'Miss Van Ryn has a sore finger,' she said haughtily, putting her hand on Katrine's shoulder. 'The patroon desires that you look at it.'

Jeff continued to stare. His sharp gray eyes looked past the two on his step to the waiting Van Ryn barouche with the coat-of-arms blazoned on its door. He looked again at the annoyed girl, then he threw back his head and emitted a guffaw. 'Well, I'll be damned!' he said. 'Come in, madam—I'm most extraordinarily honored.'

Miranda threw him a furious glance and swept past him. The cottage had but four small rooms besides the kitchen in back. The front room and surgery were full of men, a dozen at least, and one weeping woman who hastily wiped her eyes when she saw Miranda.

'Look what I found at my door!' cried Jeff, still chuckling. 'Miss Van Ryn, no less—' he made a sweeping bow to the bewildered Katrine, who put her finger in her mouth and clung to Miranda's skirts.

'—And—' continued Jeff with even greater impressiveness, 'the exquisite Miss Wells. She too is tinged with royalty, folks, for she is the patroon's cousin.'

A murmur ran round the room. A small, slight man with mouse-colored whiskers pulled at Jeff's arm and whispered something.

The woman stood up, her threadbare gray shawl falling off her thin shoulders. 'Aye,' she said bitterly. 'The Van Ryns can mince in silks and velvets while I and my children go hungry.' She sidled past Miranda, who stood her ground, her heart beating fast. The woman went out the front door.

'We'll meet later, men,' said Jeff. 'It's maybe wise to make new plans in view of this.' He motioned toward the Van Ryn carriage. There were exchanged looks of understanding. Several nodded. They filed silently from the room, leaving only the small slight man and Jeff.

Miranda found her tongue. 'That was a down-rent meeting!' she cried indignantly.

The two men looked at her accusing face and Jeff laughed. 'It was indeed, Princess. Allow me to introduce Doctor Smith Boughton.'

The small man bowed coldly.

Smith Boughton, she thought. Fenimore Cooper's words at the banquet came back to her. 'Tuppenny little doctor, skulks about preaching rebellion and defiance of the law.' This, then, must be the one who was organizing the farmers.

'I should think you'd be ashamed,' she said to him hotly, 'stirring up trouble, telling people to do wrong. They were happy enough on the manors until you came along.'

The two doctors exchanged glances. Though Boughton was the older they had both been medical students at Castleton, Vermont. Always they had been friends. Since Boughton, burning with fervor and the true crusader's spirit, had come to Columbia County, Jeff had done what he could to help the cause. But Jeff had balance and a sense of humor, which the other did not. Now the little doctor stepped up to Miranda, his eyes blazing. She saw that he was neither mousy nor meek.

'You parrot words you've heard,' he shouted at her. 'The farmers have never been happy on the manors. My own people were Rensselaer tenants and I know. You feather-brained girl, d'ye realize why your forefathers left the old country? It was to find freedom and be quit of tyranny. All the length and breadth of this great land white men are free, except here on these manors. I tell you 'tis a black and rotten spot here. A stinking survival from the past!' He clenched his fist and Miranda stepped back. Katrine, wide-eyed, peeked around the edge of her skirt.

'But it's the law!' said Miranda weakly. She felt force in the little man's oratory, but she was not in the least convinced.

'The law is wrong,' said Boughton more temperately. 'And it shall be changed.'

'Without violence,' put in Jeff on a warning note, adding directly to his friend, 'Our cause will suffer if there's violence.'

The other nodded and sighed. 'See you later,' he said to Jeff. He bowed curtly to Miranda and went out.

'Now, young lady,' said Jeff, smiling at Katrine, 'let's see the finger that brought you here at this interesting moment.' He took the child's hand and led her gently to the surgery. It was a small room with a red drugget carpet. Besides the scrubbed oak bench on which lay iron forceps and a couple of scalpels, there was only a cabinet filled with bottles and pill-boxes, a stone mortar and pestle, some medical books, a table and two chairs. A beam of sunlight fell through the single uncurtained window.

Miranda reluctantly admired the deftness with which Jeff's blunt fingers unwound the bandage, and the reassuring way he spoke to Katrine. But she found nothing else to admire. She loathed his thick-set, aggressively masculine body, his boorish manners—and above all his treacherous alliance with the down-renters. She chafed to be gone and tell Nicholas. She consulted the surgery clock. Already it was past one-thirty.

'There's nothing wrong with this finger,' said Jeff, raising his head after a careful examination.

'No,' she answered, 'I didn't think there was.'

Jeff straightened and folded his arms. 'I find that most interesting. Dare I hope, then, that I've aroused a secret passion in your maiden breast? Can it be that it was solely from the hope of seeing me again that you came today? This condescension overcomes—'

'Fiddlesticks!' Miranda burst out, and was immediately horrified. Well-brought-up young ladies did not shout 'fiddlesticks'; that was a deplorable lapse into her childhood. And now the insufferable man was laughing again.

She pulled up her yellow gloves and straightened her bonnet. 'We came today, Doctor Turner, because Nicholas—' she corrected herself instantly—'the patroon wished it. I now bid you good day.'

Her little slip and the tone of her voice as she had said 'Nicholas' sobered Jeff. He scrutinized her sharply. Her fragile gold-and-white beauty did not appeal to him. He preferred a buxom bosom and high spirits along the lines of Faith Folger, who flouted her Quaker background with rosy cheeks and hearty laughter, and a passion for wearing cherry-colored ribbons in her dark curls.

Miranda, with her little pretensions, had irritated him as much as he had her. Moreover, knowing her to be a farm girl of simple upbringing he thought her a traitor to her class. The girl's head had been turned by luxury. But, he now thought, perhaps it was deeper than that. It would be a pity if the little goose fancied herself in love with Van Ryn, who was undoubtedly a handsome and romantic-looking fellow. There would be no solution to that situation, except heartbreak for the girl. Worse yet, suppose Van Ryn seduced her. Even as the idea occurred to him he rejected it. Whatever the man's faults, a desire for shoddy intrigue was not one of them. Jeff was as sure of that as he was sure of his own name.

'Did Van Ryn come with you to Hudson today?' he asked abruptly.

'Yes,' said Miranda. '*Mr.* Van Ryn escorted us.' Her eyes flew to the clock with transparent longing. She moved definitely toward the door.

Jeff on impulse put his hand on her arm. 'Miss Wells,' he said earnestly, 'why do you stay at Dragonwyck? Don't you miss your home and your family?'

Miranda colored angrily. 'You're impertinent, sir!' she said, throwing off his hand; and sweeping up Katrine she made a grand exit.

Jeff, shrugging his broad shoulders, watched her glide into the waiting barouche. He stayed frowning at the window until a knock on his door aroused him. A frowzy old woman stumbled in.

'Oh, doctor,' she whined. 'My pains're back again. I need more of the medicine.'

'Come to the surgery, then, Mrs. Potts,' he said kindly. 'Maybe we can get to the root of the trouble this time.' And in examining the aching body and searching for illuminating symptoms, he forgot everything else, as he always did.

The newly rebuilt Hudson House on Warren Street provided the Van Ryn party with an excellent dinner. Their table was set in a corner of the white-pillared dining-room, and the watchful proprietor saw to it that no lesser mortals approached the patroon. Except, of course, three anxiously hovering waiters.

Miranda told Nicholas at once about the down-rent meeting and Smith Boughton, but he made light of it. 'It's nothing but childish hysteria. I'm surprised that so sensible a man as Turner should have part in it. But it'll soon stop. I've spoken to the sheriff.'

He was in no mood for unpleasant matters. He too was enjoying the day. He had bought Katrine a rag doll and a paint box. There was something for Miranda too. A gold-and-enamel vinaigrette for smelling salts. She and Katrine were both in an ecstasy of gratitude.

The afternoon passed too quickly. Miranda dreaded the hour of return and Nicholas made no move. They wandered to Parade Hill, the promenade terrace at the foot of Warren Street, and walked leisurely about admiring the view of the Hudson and two old schooners, whalers both, which lay beside the docks below. Soon there would be no more whalers, and in a few years trains would come snorting through the peaceful river bank and deluge the terrace with soot and sparks.

But today it was quiet. There were other promenaders—girls in Quaker bonnets and demure fichus, laughing children with hoops which rolled merrily round the central fountain, old gaffers stretching their legs in the crisp sunlight.

Miranda and Nicholas spoke little. A soft contentment held them both. Nicholas, who so often retired into a remote place where she could not follow, was that afternoon all hers, responsive to her interest in the lively waterfront scenes, smiling with her at the children's antics.

And then unpleasantness marred the golden afternoon. They walked past a secluded bench on which sat two old men with pipes and mufflers.

'Ain't that the Van Ryn?' crackled the high-pitched voice of the deaf. 'For sure that's not his lady with him?'

'Indeed 'tis not! His lady's monstrous fat and doesn't go abroad.' The other voice exploded into senile chuckles. 'By hokie-nettie! Perhaps it is his—' Sudden discretion obliterated the last word, but even to Miranda the meaning was clear. Sharp misery shattered her happiness. For hours she had managed to forget Johanna.

Nicholas gave no sign that he also had heard. The red sun dipped behind the Catskills and a chill breeze sprang at them from the river. It whipped the ready color into Miranda's cheeks, fluttered her curls and green bonnet ribbons. She shivered.

He looked down at her. 'We must go home now, Miranda.' He put the faintest emphasis on 'home' and she responded with a bitterness she could not control.

'Dragonwyck's not my home. I'm there only on sufferance, and because you—' she hesitated, 'because you have not yet sent me away. —Johanna doesn't like me,' she finished very low.

They were descending the steps to the street, and though he took her arm it was with so light a touch that she could scarcely feel it. And he was silent for so long that she was frightened. She shouldn't have said that. Perhaps he was annoyed that she had seemed to criticize his wife. Or perhaps he thought her ungrateful and pleading for more of his bounty. That would be dreadful.

He handed her into the waiting barouche, and still he did not speak. She settled miserably into her corner. Katrine yawned and stretched out on the seat opposite them, Cristabel, the new rag doll, and the paint box all hugged tight in her arms. Miranda covered the child with a carriage robe.

She stole a pleading look at Nicholas. In the shadows she could barely see his profile, the thin aquiline nose with flaring nostrils, the full, compressed lips, the planes of his jaw beneath the shadow of dark hair on his cheek. Despite his stillness there was intensity in his attitude, an effect of concealed violence which had no outer manifestation. The day's sympathetic companion had disappeared once more, and she was alone.

Before they again crossed the Stockport Creek it was black night outside. The horses slowed down to a walk. The oil carriage lamps threw a flickering and uncertain light on the fir trees which hemmed the road. They entered a thick wood with underbrush so close that it scratched against the sides of the carriage. Miranda could bear the silence no longer.

'Are you angry with me, Cousin Nicholas?' she asked faintly.

He turned his head, but before he could answer they were both jolted from their separate preoccupations. A weird clamor broke from the quiet forest, war whoops and the tooting of horns. Beneath these the steady beat of a fife and drum, and defiant voices singing to the tune of 'Old Dan Tucker.'

The barouche was surrounded with dozens of masked figures in lurid calico costumes shouting and gesticulating as they waved pitchforks and spears and clubs. The near horse shied violently, and the carriage stopped.

'Batter the coach in!' yelled one of the figures, and a heavy blow from a pitchfork rebounded from the carriage's sturdy roof.

'Stop that; that's not the way!' shouted another man in a blue sheepskin mask. 'Down with the rent, Van Ryn! Get out so we may talk to you.'

Nicholas was already out of the carriage. Though her heart was beating fast Miranda was not frightened. In spite of the weapons, there was more comedy than threat in this crazy collection of childish masks and calico nightgowns.

'It's all right, dear,' she said to Katrine, whom the racket had only half wakened. 'Go back to sleep.' The child subsided.

Miranda, moved by curiosity and a desire to be near Nicholas, also got out.

He walked up to the man in the blue sheepskin mask who seemed to be the leader. The others pressed close around them in a menacing circle.

'Well?' said Nicholas to the blue mask. 'Pray what is all this?' He spoke as casually as though this were a garden party on the Dragonwyck lawns, and before the leader could answer, a large figure in pink calico with a headdress of turkey feathers broke from the circle and brandishing a torch in Nicholas' face shouted: 'Ye know very well what we are. We're Indians! We've banded together on the warpath to right a grievous wrong!'

Nicholas' eyes traveled slowly from the speaker's muddy hobnailed boots beneath the home-dyed nightgown to the rawhide belt from which dangled a tin horn. Finally he raised his eyes to the clumsily painted mask.

Nicholas' lips curved. 'I've no objections to your playing at Indians, though it seems a childish amusement for grown men. But kindly play your games elsewhere; you're blocking the road.'

A threatening growl issued from a dozen throats. The group moved closer, but as well as the hatred which flowed from them toward the man in their midst, there was uncertainty. His attitude confounded them, for they saw that he was not bluffing, that their demonstration provoked in him no emotion but contempt and annoyance that his carriage should be delayed. And allegiance to the patroon was in their blood, violently as they resented the system.

The group wavered, several of the masks turned toward the one in blue sheepskin as though for guidance. 'You tell him, Blue Eagle,' muttered the man in turkey feathers.

The leader nodded and raised his hand toward Nicholas in a gesture of command. 'We're warning you, Van Ryn,' he said in a stern voice muffled by the mask. 'You won't collect the next rents. We Indians will see to that. Our chief Big Thunder has promised the farmers. You can send all the sheriffs and mealy-mouthed bailiffs you've a mind to but you'll not collect the rents.'

'Indeed?' said Nicholas. 'And now, having conveyed your message, I take it we may proceed.'

There was a silence. Even Miranda passionately admiring Nicholas felt the discouragement which emanated from the leader and gripped the others, and she amazed herself by feeling a twist of pity for them—the utter unreason of trying to assault the patroon's impregnability with puerile warnings and masquerade.

At last the blue mask dipped in assent. 'You may proceed.'

As Nicholas turned toward his carriage a few pitchforks were waved, and there were scattered tootings from the tin horns, but their defiance had flattened.

'Oh, you were so splendid!' cried Miranda as they once more seated themselves in the barouche. 'So—' Her voice broke into a frightened scream.

The glass windows in the doors on either side of them shattered simultaneously, and above the crash there was a report and the high whine of a bullet.

Without conscious thought she threw herself into Nicholas' arms. They tightened convulsively around her, holding her pressed against him. Her bonnet fell to the floor, and bending his head he touched her hair with his lips.

As soon as the coachman had managed to control the terrified horses the left-hand door was thrown open and Jeff Turner's anxious face peered in at them. 'You all right?' he cried. By the light of the torch he had seized as he ran to the carriage he saw Miranda's bright head against Van Ryn's breast, and even in his dismay he had a swift thought—Oh, Lord, so that's the way it is—before Nicholas put the girl gently from him.

'That bullet was a mistake, Van Ryn,' said Jeff. 'I'm mortal sorry. One of the men lost his head and we'll deal with him. We don't mean violence.' His quick eyes saw that no one had been hurt. Katrine, who was now wailing, had been protected from the falling glass by the carriage robe, and the bullet had passed harmlessly in and out the windows.

Still trembling, Miranda pulled the frightened child onto her lap, glared with the anger of ebbing terror at Jeff. So did Nicholas, who except for unusual pallor was composed again. They both saw the blue sheepskin mask which Jeff had hastily shoved down below his chin when he heard the shot.

'So Doctor Turner is Blue Eagle,' remarked Nicholas without particular emphasis. 'Don't you think you might keep your companions in better order?'

'Yes, of course,' answered Jeff impatiently. 'I told you I'm sorry, but there's no harm done, and it's no wonder one of us lost control. You're mighty provoking, Van Ryn, with your god-like airs and your stubborn refusal to see any viewpoint but your own. Don't you realize these men are desperate—you fool!'

Jeff snapped his mouth shut against his rising temper. Neither violence nor abuse was the way to right this injustice that was unfortunately backed by law. The two in the carriage infuriated him. But for Nicholas he felt an unwilling admiration. The man was cool and brave enough.

'It's you who are the fool, Doctor Turner,' said Nicholas indifferently.

Jeff turned and walked slowly back to the group of disgruntled maskers. Silently they all watched the carriage speed down the road and disappear between the pines. They had accomplished nothing, except to put themselves in the wrong and in danger of the law by that reckless pistol shot.

'Never mind, men,' said Jeff, tacitly admitting the affair's failure. 'Take heart, we'll win out yet. We'll show 'em we mean business over at Ancram next week!'

There were mutters of assent. They formed a straggling file, the fife and drums began again. A few voices took up the refrain:

'The moon was shining silver bright,
The sheriff came at dead of night.
High on a hill an Indian true,
And on his horn a blast he blew.
Get out of the way, Big Bill Snyder,
We'll tar your coat and feather your hide, sir.'

Singing doggedly, the calico Indians plodded down the cold, muddy roads to their various farms.

In the Van Ryn carriage Miranda was trying hard to control hysterical tears while she soothed the whimpering child on her knee. It was not only the fright and danger, nor shame at the way she had thrown herself into Nicholas' arms. It was the realization that he had pulled her violently against him and she had felt the hard pressure of his face on her hair. This time there could be no doubt of his response, and beneath the exultation of that knowledge she felt a corroding fear. She could not look at him: above Katrine's head she kept her face turned toward the blackness of the broken window through which an icy wind blew. Though her teeth were chattering she scarcely felt the cold.

I must go home, she thought wildly. I must get away. It's true I must go. Tomorrow I'll tell him. No, now—quickly, before I lose my courage.

'Cousin Nicholas,' she said, her voice high and strained, 'it'll soon be Christmas time. I should be home. My mother will need me. There's always so much to do. I think I should go at once. Tomorrow or the next day—perhaps—'

Nicholas reached out in the darkness and put his hand on her arm. At his touch she fell silent.

'Be patient, Miranda,' he said in a quiet tone of absolute command. 'You will go back to the farm in due time. In due time—' he repeated on a lower note. He took his hand from her arm.

What is there to be patient for? she thought with anguish. I can't go on like this. But she had not the strength to protest. Her head drooped against the cushions. Later, she thought, when I'm in my room alone and warm again, I'll be able to think clearly. I'll know what to do.

She shivered as they emerged from the forest and the wind from the river blew through the broken panes with redoubled force. Katrine was dozing again. Heavy as a stone against Miranda's breasts the child's round head rolled in rhythm with the motion of the carriage.

8

MIRANDA DID NOT GO HOME. SHE MENTIONED THE possibility in a letter to her mother, but Abigail, suppressing her longing for her favorite child, wrote back by the next post that Miranda must not think of returning if the Van Ryns were willing to keep her. 'I can see that you are learning many gentle ways and becoming quite the lady. Mind you take full advantage of this rare opportunity.'

So it seemed foolish to insist on going, particularly as Miranda found her sudden panic inexplicable when coolly examined in the morning light. There had, after all, been nothing shameful or astonishing about that moment in the carriage. What more natural than to turn for protection to one's escort, and Nicholas' behavior—that had been really nothing more than chivalry and the affectionate impulse of an older relative. Even Ma wouldn't think it queer if she knew, thought Miranda. But she had not mentioned that episode to her mother.

Life at the Manor House went on as though the day in Hudson had never been. Nicholas sent to New York and Boston for books. Boxes of them arrived on each boat and were carried from the dock straight up to the tower room, where he now spent most of his time. An Albany schooner homing from the Orient brought a fresh consignment of foreign plants, and to Miranda's regret all the exquisite Persian oleanders were removed from the conservatory to make room for palms, an aloe, and some bulbous Ceylonese ferns that she thought hideous. She had admired the oleanders' waxy rose blossoms and the vivid green of their lance-shaped leaves, and she missed the fragrance which had delicately penetrated to the dining-room. But Nicholas seemed to have lost interest in flowers.

By early December everyone had a more vital interest than the placing of shrubs. The anti-rent wars were gathering momentum.

December the sixth was Saint Nicholas' Day, and according to

Dutch custom the time for giving and receiving presents. Several of the neighboring children had been invited to celebrate with Katrine, and by three the guests had all arrived: Dominie Huysmann, the pastor, with his wife and three solemn children, the Verplancks from Kinderhook with their brood, two Van Rensselaer grandchildren, and the little Dejongs from Stuyvesant.

It was Nicholas himself who represented his name saint, not in the later convention of a jolly Santa Claus, but in the original conception of a fourth-century ecclesiastic. The blue satin robe stiff with embroidery, the gold miter and episcopal staff, had come from Holland, as had the traditional ceremony which Nicholas invested with an awe-inspiring solemnity. Though he produced no faggots for the punishment of naughty children, Katrine and the others sat terrified while he lectured them on their sins in the prescribed manner. Even when he raised the crook high over his head and slashed open the muslin bag which released a clattering rain of sugar plums onto the floor, the children waited until he vanished through a side door before precipitating themselves on the candies.

After they had sated themselves with the sugar plums, the double doors to the Italian drawing-room were thrown open to disclose a long table covered with damask upon which lay a row of wooden sabots gilded at the tips. These sabots also waited from year to year with the Saint's costume in an attic room. On each one had been pasted a child's name and they contained besides a wisp of hay—for Saint Nicholas' horse—a quantity of small trinkets and toys.

There were no gifts for adults, New Year's Day was the proper time for that; and while the children examined their presents the elders gathered in the Green Room for gossip and refreshment.

Miranda sat apart from the group in a chair designated by Johanna. The girl no longer resented these continual reminders of her inferior position, for since the day in Hudson she had felt a nervous desire to propitiate Johanna—an unreasonable desire, Miranda told herself, for had she not conclusively proved that there was no basis for guilt?—still she now made constant efforts to please the mistress of Dragonwyck and had even taken to confining her ringlets in a net.

The general conversation which flowed past her was dull enough talk of the river families until Nicholas, dressed in his own clothes, joined the group. At once Dominie Huysmann turned his lean, apprehensive face to the patroon.

'Oh, mynheer, that was shocking about the canopy,' he cried, his

Adam's apple working. 'I trust mynheer understands that I knew nothing about it. They're ruffians. I think they've gone mad!'

Miranda looked at Nicholas. What was all this about the canopy? She had no doubt that some new down-rent demonstration was referred to, and she soon heard the details.

While she had been busy helping to fill the sabots, Johanna, Katrine, and Nicholas had that morning driven to the village church for the saint-day services. They found that the carved oaken canopy which covered the Van Ryn pew had been chopped down in the night. Splintered wood and mangled carvings littered the aisles. There had been a sign tacked on the pew door: 'Canopies are for kings and we'll have no kings here.'

'It was dreadful,' put in Johanna to the sympathetic audience. 'I assure you there were splinters on all the cushions.'

The Dominie listened respectfully to his patroness's complaint, then turned back to Nicholas. 'But mynheer, the matter is getting desperate. What shall we do?'

'Do?' repeated Nicholas. His eyes rested on the pastor with detached amusement. 'Why, we'll build the canopy again tomorrow. I've already given orders. I think this time it'll be of black walnut, somewhat in the gothic manner but more delicate. And the Van Ryn arms shall be blazoned in sable and gules upon the front panel.'

Huysmann swallowed. 'It'll make the tenants very angry. They—they might harm you, or—' he squirmed, scarcely daring to link himself with the patroon but made bold by fear, 'or me and my family. They know I'm loyal to the manor.'

The ladies rustled and looked at each other anxiously. The Dominie's wife bit her pale lips and clasped her reticule to her skinny bosom as though it were one of her children. Nicholas frowned.

'There is nothing to fear from my tenants. Nothing. Do you think we can't guide and control them as we have done this two hundred years? This hysteria will pass as it has before.'

The Dominie, after a quick glance at his patron's face, bowed his head. 'Yes mynheer. Doubtless you are right.'

The ladies subsided. After all, this was men's business, and if the Lord of Dragonwyck believed the matter unimportant it must be so. None of them had had any first-hand contact with the down-renters. Only Miranda was not so sure. She had the memory of the sullen meeting in Jeff Turner's surgery, of the pitchfork rebounding from the carriage roof—and the pistol shot. Could Nicholas possibly be wrong?

Nicholas was not wrong in so far as the immediate outcome of the rebellion affected him personally. And no broader consideration interested him. That the events of the next few days—events in which he took no part and ignored until they were over—were eventually to mould his life he neither knew nor would have believed.

The unrest in Columbia County culminated outside of Dragonwyck Manor on Van Rensselaer lands. On December 12, in Copake, Sheriff Henry Miller and a deputy attempted to dispossess two farmers who were behind with the rent. They were met with violent opposition. The little doctor, Smith Boughton, disguised as Big Thunder, inflamed three hundred of his calico Indians with his oratory. They seized the sheriff and burned his legal papers in a tar barrel. After this they allowed the disconsolate officers to ride back to Hudson with jeers and the tooting of horns for accompaniment.

By December eighteenth matters had come to a head. Big Thunder called a mass meeting at Smoky Hollow near Claverack. Nearly a thousand Indians gathered on the square before the tavern, a whooping, yelling mob in masks and gowns. This time there were many guns and the tavern's cellar full of whiskey was raided. The combination produced tragedy.

While Doctor Boughton from the tavern balcony vainly tried to quiet his rioting Indians, a stray shot killed one of them—young Bill Rifenburg, a gentle boy from a near-by farm, the only son of a widowed mother.

The suddenly hushed crowd flocked around the still figure on the ground gaping at the spreading stain of red on the calico shirt. Someone snatched off the boy's fox-shaped mask. Jeff, not yet disguised, had been upstairs with Boughton. The two doctors exchanged a look of horror. 'That's done it!' cried Jeff. 'See if you can quiet 'em down, while I do what I can for that boy.'

Big Thunder leaned over the balcony railing; Jeff pelted down the stairs and knelt by the quiet body. There was nothing to be done. Jeff was still kneeling there wondering how to break the news to Mrs. Rifenburg, and bitterly regretting the tragedy and inevitable blow to their cause, when Sheriff Miller and five deputies galloped through the subdued crowd.

'So it's murder too, along with the other charges!' cried the sheriff, taking in the situation. Then seeing the figure up on the balcony he cried exultantly, 'Come, boys—we've got Big Thunder at last!'

With pistols cocked the officers rushed into the inn. They found Boughton flattened against the fireplace in the upper room, his mouth twisted with despair. For a few minutes he resisted arrest, exerting his slight strength and cursing. The six men hustled him downstairs and bundled him on a horse.

Jeff watched helplessly. He could do nothing for his friend then, and a further brush with the law would damage them irreparably. The sheriff paid no attention to him. He had no warrant for Doctor Turner, whom he knew and liked, and he was in a hurry to get away from the dazed, silent mob before they turned threatening. He slapped the rump of the horse on which Boughton was tied: he and his men mounted swiftly and herded their prize down the road to Hudson.

Jeff helped carry Bill Rifenburg to his mother's house and did what he could for the widow. Then, heartsick, he too returned to town.

Big Thunder was in jail, but the authorities were nervous. The tooting of horns continued all that night from the near-by hills. The down-renters sent threats. They would release their leader by force. They would burn the town down. The Hudson Light Guards mobilized, the Albany Burgesses came down river to help. Finally as the panic grew a message was sent to New York City, and Captain Krack's troop of German-American cavalry steamed up the Hudson on a chartered ship.

Jeff stood on the doorstep of his house and watched the dashing troop prance from the dock along Front Street toward Warren. They were preceded by a brass band whose martial din made eloquent accompaniment to the splendor of gold epaulettes and braid, metal helmets with white plumes and gilded eagles, dangling scabbards, and glossy patent-leather boots.

All this to subdue a handful of farmers in bedraggled shirts and one small imprisoned man. Jeff turned wearily and went back to his surgery. He sank into a chair and rested his head on his hands.

Rillah, the grizzled old colored woman who tended him, shuffled into the room and put a mug of mulled wine at his elbow. 'Drink dis here, massa,' she said. 'Den you won't be so down in de mouf.'

'What would I do without you, Rillah?' said Jeff.

'Sames you done befoh I come, but I ain' gwine let you try,' announced the old woman, wagging her turbaned head. She was an escaped slave from a Georgia plantation who had managed three years ago to reach this particular station on the underground railway to Canada before collapsing with exhaustion and pneumonia. Jeff had cured her and she had attached herself firmly to him ever since. 'Now you stop studying 'bout dem pore farmers,' she added, patting his shoulder. 'Dey time foh freedom comin' someday just like niggahs' time comin' someday. Never did see such a man foh frettin' ovah other people's troubles. Quit it now, dis minute.'

Jeff drained his mug and smiled absently. He was used to her affectionate scoldings. No, the time is not yet ripe, he thought. Someday the farmers will surely win, but it can't be done with rioting and violence. We're fighting for democracy and we must use the democratic system. Election's the only way. We'll put our own man in the Governor's chair, fair and square.

He sighed. That would take a lot of doing and in the meantime the Manor lords had won again. Boughton's trial was postponed until March and Jeff had no hope of the outcome. Against the little doctor and his farmers would be all the power of wealth, prestige, and established fact.

Jeff got up and putting on his hat and greatcoat walked out of the house toward the jail, where he intended to console his friend as best he could. As he forced his way through the crowded streets, jostling gaudy uniforms at every step, he thought of Nicholas Van Ryn. The man would be more arrogant than ever now. 'Damn him,' said Jeff under his breath. He had a second of impotent hatred.

The Livingstons and the Van Rensselaers had finally bestirred themselves in the anti-rent war; their complacency had been shaken, they had even been frightened. But not Nicholas, entrenched in superiority, so sure that nothing could change the world which he had inherited, or threaten his own supremacy.

I believe the man's really dangerous, thought Jeff. God help the person who thwarts him, if indeed anything can pierce his armor. And he thought of Miranda. Affected little ninny! Perversely clinging to that atmosphere of decadent luxury, pretending she was an aristocrat, openly worshiping the dark, unpredictable ruler of Dragonwyck. Her wings would be badly singed before she got home where she belonged. Honest work, she needed, with those smooth white hands she was so obviously vain of, honest work and a simple, honest man to knock the nonsense out of her and give her a houseful of babies.

She's healthy enough for all that she needs a bit more meat on her bones, thought Jeff irritably.

So preoccupied was he that after crossing First Street he bumped squarely into a soft body. There was an explosion of giggles and a pair of black eyes looked up into his. 'Mercy on us, Doctor Turner, thee needn't run a person down!'

It was Faith Folger, her seductive figure clothed in Quaker gray, no cherry-colored ribbons today in the dark curls beneath the demure bonnet, because her mother had caught her before she left the house and inflicted severe chastisement. But Faith needed no ribbons to catch and hold the male eye. Even now while Jeff laughingly apologized for his clumsiness, two of the cavalrymen had drawn their horses to the curb and were ogling her hopefully.

'And what are you doing, my girl, running about in this mob of bawdy soldiers?' asked Jeff with a teasing inflection.

Faith tossed her head, not neglecting a sidelong glance at the two cavalrymen. 'I'm but going on an errand to the pharmacist's for Ma,' she said demurely, pouting her lips and looking up at Jeff through her lashes.

Jeff glanced at the red mouth, as he was meant to. He had several times stolen kisses from it and enjoyed the process immensely. Now, suddenly, Faith did not tempt him as she usually did. She seemed a bit lush and full-blown.

'Well, mind you don't break any military hearts,' he said lightly, and raised his hat.

The girl was startled. 'Will thee not escort me, Jeff?' she asked. Always he had been eager for her company. And though nothing definite had been said as yet, she knew that her family approved and she herself was more than willing to settle down as Mrs. Turner.

'I'm mortal sorry that I can't now,' said Jeff, who could have perfectly well. 'I'm on my way to see poor Boughton.'

'Oh,' said the girl. She gave him a small, bewildered smile. For the remainder of her walk to the pharmacist's, she kept her eyes cast down as a Quaker maiden should and ignored the two cavalrymen, who walked their horses on the street beside her making to each other loud complimentary comments on her charms.

It had always been the Van Ryn custom to close Dragonwyck after New Year's and embark with servants for New York and the town mansion on Stuyvesant Street. This year Nicholas vetoed the plan.

'But why not?' asked Johanna pettishly. 'This place is dreary enough in winter, and I can't see reason for owning a town house if we don't use it. Besides, I'm quite longing for the theater.'

It was evening and they were sitting in the Red Room. Johanna, having decided to make good use of Miranda's proficiency with the needle, had loaded her with a great pile of new damask napkins to hem. The girl sat sewing in the far corner by the harpsichord in a small straight chair which had gradually, by an intangible ruling, become her only rightful place. Katrine was in bed. The evening differed from a dozen recent evenings in which Johanna yawned, read a word or two in a magazine, and yawned again while the gold-and-ormulu clock ticked off the minutes to bedtime, in that Nicholas was with them.

Usually now he left them the instant dinner was over, and they heard his steps ascending the winding staircase to the tower. Unless he went to the pianoforte in the music room and played to himself, sometimes softly, sometimes with torrential chords and dissonances. But tonight he sat in a chair opposite his wife.

'This winter I prefer to remain at Dragonwyck, my love,' he repeated. 'If you need new clothes you may send for a dressmaker to come here.'

Johanna's big face puckered, she moistened her lips. 'But why, Nicholas? I had made so many plans.'

He rose from his chair, walked around the center table, and smiling slightly stood looking down at his wife. Her red-slippered foot, which had been beating an irritable tattoo on the footstool, gradually ceased to move.

'It can't be because of the rebellion. You said yourself that was all over now Boughton is imprisoned,' she persisted, but her voice had grown fainter. 'And it's damp here in the winter, I shall get one of my heavy colds—'

Nicholas made a hardly perceptible motion with one hand. 'That would be most unfortunate, my dear. You must take every precaution. But we'll stay at Dragonwyck.'

Johanna shifted in her chair. Her eyes dropped under her husband's gaze. For a moment Miranda felt sorry for her, an emotion immediately eclipsed by relief. The move to the city would certainly have resulted in her being sent back to Greenwich. They would hardly have included Miranda in the New York household too.

Yet why don't I want to go home! she thought passionately. What is there that keeps me here? She lifted her head and looked at Nicholas. The soft candlelight cast his shadow against the red-papered walls. He dominated the room as he dominated the two women. As though he felt her gaze he turned his head and looked at Miranda.

Again the girl felt a little shock that in that dark face the eyes should be so light and vivid a blue. It was this anomaly that gave the curious effect of blankness, of shuttered windows which showed no sign of the life which moved inside. A chill passed over her, but with it a fascinated compulsion so strong that had he held out his arms to her she would have run to him, blindly forgetting Johanna and all decency.

Instead he bent over and picking up Johanna's handkerchief, which had fallen to the floor, restored it to her with a bow.

'Good night, ladies,' he said softly. 'May you rest well.' And he left them.

For the remaining half-hour until Tompkins came in with wine and cakes the mistress of Dragonwyck sat silent in her chair, her eyes fixed on the handkerchief which lay where Nicholas had placed it on her lap.

January and February passed swiftly for Miranda. The river was blocked with ice and the roads nearly impassable, so that there were no visitors. The days were outwardly monotonous, but she did not find them so. There was tension at Dragonwyck. A subtle sense of mounting expectancy which seemed to have no cause. Each morning she awoke to excitement which each quiet winter evening denied. There was no change, and yet the excitement recurred.

In the middle of March there was a blizzard, and Johanna kept to her bed nursing one of the heavy colds which she had feared. The sounds of coughing and violent nose-blowing penetrated even through the shut door of the great bedchamber. Miranda, passing the door on her way to the schoolroom, saw Magda run in with a basin of mustard and water and a pitcher of steaming negus; heard Johanna in a clogged voice demanding fretfully whether the buttered toast were not ready yet.

Even when she's sick she thinks of nothing but eating, thought Miranda contemptuously, and passed downstairs to call Katrine for her lessons.

The schoolroom was bright with a fire on the hearth; snow piled up softly against the windows, though the wind blew with diminishing force. The two blonde heads, flaxen and amber gold, were bent together over a scrawled slate when the door opened. Nicholas walked in and the child's round eyes repeated Miranda's astonishment.

'How nice to see you—Cousin Nicholas,' she stammered. 'We—I was just correcting Katrine's sums.' It was the first time he had ever entered the schoolroom. And her amazement was increased to see a trace of uncertainty in his manner. She felt that he had wanted to say something to her, but that now suddenly he had changed his mind.

He walked over to the window, stood a moment staring out toward the gray river which was nearly hidden by eddies of snow.

'Is the child doing well?' he asked without interest.

'Oh, yes. She's learning fast. She's good at figures. I think she's ready for a textbook on arithmetic. Perhaps we could send to the city—?'

Nicholas glanced at his daughter. Her cheeks were flushed, her fingers whitened with pressure as she nervously clutched her slate pencil. He gave a short laugh.

'Why bother with a textbook! A little addition and subtraction are enough for *a girl.*'

Still further bewildered by the bitterness in his tone, which seldom betrayed any emotion, Miranda said timidly, 'It—I suppose it must be disappointing that you have no son.'

A peculiar expression ran over Nicholas' face. 'I do not brook disappointments,' he said, and going to the fireplace held his hands out to the blaze.

She colored. It had been presumptuous to mention such matters to him. But did he mean that he would not allow himself to feel disappointment over the failure of an heir to carry on the unbroken Van Ryn line, or did he mean that he and Johanna yet might—?

The pain that shot through her at this unfinished thought rushed her into speech.

'I think it'll stop snowing soon; I mean there seems to be a lightening in the west.'

'I trust so,' said Nicholas. 'Or the doctor will be delayed.'

'Doctor?' she repeated blankly.

'Certainly,' he answered with increased coldness. 'Mrs. Van Ryn is ill, and I have naturally sent for a doctor to attend her.'

The girl was hurt by his tone as well as by his saying 'Mrs. Van Ryn.' It was as though he were deliberately putting her in her place.

'I didn't realize that Cousin—that Mrs. Van Ryn was that ill.'

Nicholas did not answer. He deserted the fire, walked with quick restless steps back to the window. He jerked together the heavy portières, turned back into the room, and said to Katrine: 'When you are through with your lessons go to your mother. You pay her little enough attention.'

'Yes, Papa,' said the child. She hesitated, then overcame her awe of her father and asked, 'Will Doctor Hamilton let me play with his chiming watch like he did last year when I had measles?'

Nicholas frowned. 'It won't be Hamilton who's coming. I've sent for Doctor Turner.'

Miranda raised her head quickly. Why? she thought. Why that Turner, who is a boor and a down-renter? There were other doctors available besides Hamilton.

Jeff, in Hudson, when he opened his door to a stable boy in the Van Ryn livery and received the summons to Dragonwyck, had wondered the same thing. He had made a rueful face at the snowdrifts and thought of refusing. But curiosity had won, curiosity and a feeling of gratification. If Nicholas had so much faith in him as a doctor as to overlook their clash, he might well be generous too.

Jeff saddled his horse, and lashing his carpetbag full of pills and instruments to the cantle, plodded away after his guide through the snow.

It was dusk by the time Jeff reached Dragonwyck village. Lights from scattered windows looked warm and comforting. The parsonage in particular gave an impression of cosiness. The Dominie, Mrs. Huysmann, and three of their children were gathered around the lamp on the center table, which was covered with a cheerful red cloth. As Jeff's tiring horse walked past the window he noticed many homely details, a moon clock on the mantel which chimed five times, an iron kettle steaming on the hob beside the fire. The pastor's pinched face looked relaxed. He peered benevolently over his spectacles at his wife, who was mending a small pair of breeches while a sleepy baby leaned against her knee.

It must be pleasant, thought Jeff, shivering in his greatcoat. A scene like this to come back to after long hours in the saddle. Instantly he pictured Faith in the place of Mrs. Huysmann; the babies that would be with them were nebulous, but there was nothing vague about his reconstruction of another scene. Faith and himself upstairs in a billowing feather bed shut in against the world. Here there would be warmth and vitality and comfort.

Tomorrow, he thought, I'll ask her.

The horse dragged himself up the last long slope and stumbling a little on his snow-packed shoes rounded the bend before Dragonwyck.

In the twilight the great pile of stone looked gigantic as its turrets and gables loomed against the dark sky. The portières had all been drawn and no light showed. Here there was neither warmth, vitality, nor comfort. It's evil and unhealthy, this place, thought Jeff. It belongs to a dying age.

Though he was the most practical of men, Jeff had an instinct of repulsion so strong that he very nearly turned his horse before they reached the porte-cochère. He could ask for shelter at the parsonage or at one of the farmhouses—and give what excuse for having covered all those miles to no purpose? thought Jeff, angry with himself. Ridiculous fancies, my lad.

Besides, there was a sick person inside who needed him, and this call Jeff would never deny.

He banged the silver door-knocker. At once the door was opened by Tompkins.

'Good evening sir. I fear you've had a nasty ride. They've been expecting you this two hours.'

Jeff blew on his fingers and advanced to the farther end of the long hall, where there was a fire. Firelight and candlelight did little to relieve the effect of luxurious gloom. Jeff pulled up his coat tails and tried to warm his chilled legs.

'I hope Mrs. Van Ryn's not very ill,' he said. 'How's she feeling now?'

'Better, I think, sir. But my lord has been anxious for you to come. He's always so solicitous for his lady's health.'

Is he indeed? thought Jeff. He couldn't picture Nicholas as a solicitous husband. But he might be wrong. With unusual humility Jeff admitted to himself that he didn't understand these people.

Tompkins ushered him upstairs and Magda received him at her mistress' room door. Johanna greeted him sulkily.

'I can't think why Mr. Van Ryn didn't call Doctor Hamilton as usual.' She held out a fat hand, which she withdrew at once, letting it fall to the bed as Jeff touched it.

'I'm sorry, ma'am,' he said with some embarrassment. 'But I'll do my best to cure you.' And he proceeded to make a thorough examination, undeterred by Johanna's grudging co-operation, or by Magda's disapproving eyes.

Except for the heavy cold there was nothing wrong with Johanna. Considering the vast bulk through which it was required to pump blood, even her heart was in good condition.

'Nothing to worry about, ma'am,' he told her cheerfully. 'Take these drops three times a day, and a bit of scraped onion in sugar for the cough. You'll soon feel right. One thing more, though—' said Jeff, seeing a sodden pile of nibbled sweetmeats on the bedside table. 'The diet should be light for a few days. Gruels and tea, a boiled egg or so. Nothing more.'

He was dumfounded at the anger which transformed her face.

'What nonsense!' she cried. 'Everyone knows one should stuff a cold. One must keep one's strength up!'

'Why ma'am,' said Jeff temperately, 'you won't lose strength in a day or two in bed, and it's wise to rest the digestion.' He felt inclined to laugh at the violence of her reaction to his simple directions.

Johanna's mouth set stubbornly. 'I shall eat as I please,' she said. 'Magda, be sure they are making that tipsy cake I ordered, I'm longing for it.' Her little eyes threw Jeff a look of defiance.

Jeff shrugged his shoulders. He had an inkling of the true state of affairs. Eating was to her the greatest sensual satisfaction. Baulked of other passions, she had gradually poured all her desires into one channel. It's a form of lust, he thought with pitying distaste, and in itself a disease.

'Your cold will mend faster without the tipsy cake,' he said. 'But it will mend anyway.' This was a fool's errand he had come on, and he wished very much that he were snug at home and within reach of really sick people who might need him. He cast around for some remark with which to close the fruitless interview. His eyes roamed over the frowsy room, lighting on the most attractive thing in it.

'What superb flowers!' he said pleasantly, pointing toward a low shrub which stood in a cloisonné pot upon the large table. The blossoms, which grew thick as red stars amongst the long green leaves, gave forth an agreeable fragrance. The anger faded from Johanna's eyes.

'It's one of Mr. Van Ryn's Persian oleanders,' she said slowly. 'He had it brought here today to brighten the sickroom. It is pretty, isn't it!'

She spoke in a curiously strained voice. Evidently the patroon did not often trouble himself to bring his wife flowers, thought Jeff, and in truth, were I married to this lump of suet, I wouldn't either.

He smiled vaguely, agreed that the shrub was pretty, and retired from the room.

On his way downstairs he passed Miranda, who was standing at her own door. The girl gave him a cold nod and a resentful glance from the corner of her long beautiful eyes. In the green dress trimmed with cream lace at the throat and with her lightly poised head and undulating walk she put him in mind of a valley lily. He returned the nod as coldly, annoyed by her continued hostility.

A hostility not shared by Nicholas, he discovered when his host came forward to greet him downstairs. The patroon was at his most charming. He listened attentively to Jeff's account of his wife's health, saying at the end: 'Yes, I'm sure you're right. The cold is already breaking up, but it's well to be sure that the lungs are not affected nor any sudden complication threatened. Don't you think so, sir?'

Jeff agreed and added brief mention of his efforts to reduce Mrs. Van Ryn's diet.

'Did she agree to that?' asked Nicholas.

'Indeed not,' laughed Jeff on a rueful tone. 'She ordered a tipsy cake instead.'

There was a short pause, then Nicholas said, 'Ah, yes, I fear my wife is very much given to the pleasures of the table,' and he smiled indulgently. The smile and the tone were just that—indulgent, the half-pitying, half-amused attitude one has toward a wayward child.

Natural enough, and yet deep in Jeff there was a little psychic tremor, a faint unease. He looked sharply at his host and the tremor disappeared. The smile on Nicholas' handsome face seemed genuine. His startling blue eyes expressed nothing but courteous interest in his guest.

Jeff enjoyed that evening. A guest room had been prepared for him and Nicholas overruled his objections to spending the night. It would have been folly to set off on the long ride back at that hour.

Miranda joined them at supper, and though at first the girl was very quiet and constrained she gradually responded to Nicholas' conversational brilliance as Jeff did.

It was a species of magic that their host made that night around the damask-covered table. He told them stories of his travels in Europe, using rich and vivid words so that they saw the castle on the Rhine where he had met the mad countess, or the dingy alleyway in Florence where his purse had been stolen. He spoke of events nearer home, the coming of the Croton water to New York two years ago, when the populace went mad over the fifty-foot fountains of free water which gushed from the new-laid pipes. Or he told them of the theater, the delirious night when the divine Fanny Elssler mislaid her ballet slippers and danced 'La Tarantule' in her stocking feet to the accompaniment of a pelting of roses and love notes from the ecstatic audience.

But Nicholas did more than simply dazzle those two who knew nothing of Europe or the theater. It was in no sense a monologue. Using that most subtle of all flatteries he constantly included them and their opinions.

He described the divine Fanny's costume and appearance. 'She wore white, you know, though many thought red or green would have better suited her brunette beauty. What do you think, Miranda?'

Or to Jeff when telling of strange customs or food he would ask, 'How does that seem to you from the medical side?' and in each case listened intently to the answer.

They were at once stimulated and relaxed. They were scarcely conscious of each other, both concentrated on their host.

It was nine o'clock when he rose from the table and Miranda, seeing that the evening was ending, gave a sigh of disappointment which Jeff inwardly echoed. Nicholas had made him feel important and brilliant, and Jeff was too human not to have enjoyed it.

'I'm going up now to see Mrs. Van Ryn,' said Nicholas.

Jeff uncrossed his legs. 'Shall I have another look at her?' he asked without much enthusiasm.

'No. I'll call you if I think there's a reason,' and Nicholas left the room. Miranda's eyes followed him.

'Yes,' said Jeff, noting her expression, and laughing. 'I must admit that he can be very charming.'

She blushed, bringing a bemused gaze to his face. 'You do see it now, don't you?' she said. 'How wonderful he is—and—'

'Never mind,' said Jeff crossly. Though he felt more admiration for Nicholas than he had ever expected to, he didn't relish that look in the girl's eyes.

'I can't think why you always treat me like a child!' she cried indignantly.

Jeff pushed his chair back. 'I'll spare you the obvious answer.' As she flounced from the room, he thought that it would be a great satisfaction to spank her. His palm tingled.

He went upstairs to his bedroom, took off his coat, and put on the dressing-gown which he found laid out for him. It was of yellow brocaded satin with velvet reveres. He fastened it gingerly and looking at himself in the great pier glass burst into laughter. His sandy head, heavy neck, and hairy chest looked ridiculous in that elegant garment. 'Fine feathers'll never make a fine bird out of you, my lad,' he said, and sat down by the fire to wait in case Nicholas summoned him. An hour passed and nothing happened, so he clambered into bed.

Miranda too had gone upstairs, her mind filled with irritation at Jeff. When she reached the landing she turned and went down the hall to Katrine's room meaning to say good night to the child, though nearly certain that she would be asleep. She opened the door and peered in. The night light burned by the bed and she was surprised to see Katrine sitting bolt upright, her eyes wide open.

'Why aren't you asleep, dear?' chided Miranda.

'I can't,' said the child. 'There's so much noise downstairs.'

'Noise?' Miranda smoothed the pillow and straightened the bedclothes. 'There isn't any noise, pet. You've been dreaming.'

The round eyes stared incredulously. 'Don't you hear it? The piano's going and going. And some lady keeps laughing, high and clear.'

Miranda listened a moment. There was no sound but the drip of melting snow from the eaves. She shook her head.

'Lie down, dear. You musn't make up stories.'

The child pushed her away. 'You're being mean, M'randa. I hear it just as plain. You listen in the hall.'

To humor her, Miranda opened the door. So far from being noisy the house seemed unusually quiet. There were no servants about; all the bedroom doors were tight shut. She wondered unhappily if Nicholas were still in there with Johanna behind the big door at the end. There was the faint guttering of a spent candle, but no other noise of any sort. The stillness was heavy, pressed down.

'Now you hear it, don't you?' cried the child. 'The laughing's so loud, except it doesn't sound like happy laughing. It sounds as if it came from the Red Room.'

And suddenly as though a hidden water gate had burst, fear drenched the child. 'It's Azilde,' she moaned. 'It's what Zélie said. The piano and the laughing. Make it stop—please, please make it stop.' Her eyes were black with terror.

Miranda seized the little shoulders and shook them. 'Listen, Katrine—' she cried, trying to penetrate through the panic. 'There isn't anything. I don't hear anything. Zélie's a stupid old woman and you mustn't believe her crazy stories.'

The child held her breath, listening. In spite of herself Miranda listened too while an icy prickle ran up into her scalp. There was still no sound of any kind. The child lay back with an exhausted sigh.

'It's stopped now,' she said.

'Nor ever started.' Miranda's voice was sharp, but Katrine did not listen. Her eyelids fell, her stormy breathing gradually lessened. In a few minutes she was asleep.

Miranda went back to her own room, annoyed with herself because of a desire to run through the hall and tug at her bell pull to summon anybody who would come and talk to her for a moment.

Utter nonsense, she told herself. I didn't hear anything, nobody else heard anything. It's only the fancy of an excited child.

After a while she became calmer, but not calm enough for sleep. She lay on top of the bed in her white dressing-gown and watched the dying fire. Repeatedly she pushed away the thought of that soulless laughter the child imagined she had heard, and replaced it with memories of Nicholas' fascinating talk. 'Lake Como,' she said the little name to herself lingeringly. He had described a marble palace amongst cypress trees, had made her feel that she was there with him listening to the lap of the water, the singing of a nightingale, the love serenade of a boatman on the lake. *'Piangi, piangi fanciulla,'* he had sung for them the first line. She hadn't known that he could sing.

She raised her arms above her head and stretched. She was at last becoming sleepy. She thrust her feet into the bedclothes, then drew them out again and sat up, wide awake. There was the stamp of running footsteps in the hall, a murmur of voices, then thunderous knocks on a distant door.

She put on her slippers and went out into the hall. Servants were distractedly running about with candles. Magda stood wringing her hands, her shrewish face gray. Under her directions a footman was banging on Jeff's door, who that moment appeared.

'What is it?' he asked, calmly alert, though his speech was thick with sleep.

'Mevrouw is taken bad!' cried Magda. 'Hurry, sir.'

Jeff picked up his bag, pulled the magnificent dressing-gown close around his nightshirt, and went to Johanna's room. Miranda followed.

There was a horrible noise in the room, the sound of retching, steady, almost rhythmic. On the bed, a shapeless figure threw itself backward and forward in a monotonous, mechanical way.

Jeff stood for a moment appalled, then he groped for the pulse, which was terrifyingly slow and irregular; the flesh beneath his fingers was clammy as an eel.

'What's happened?' he said sharply to Magda, who stood moaning beside the bed. The woman's fright had conquered her resentment of the new doctor.

'It began sudden, near an hour ago. Vomiting and purging. I thought it would pass.'

'Did she eat that?' asked Jeff. On the table by the bed were the remains of an enormous tipsy cake, its moist crumbling sweetness soaked in sherry and filled with preserved fruits. A silver nutmeg mill stood beside it. Johanna was fond of nutmeg.

The maid nodded. 'She ate a lot of it. Mr. Van Ryn asked her not to, but her heart was set on it.'

'Where is Mr. Van Ryn?' snapped Jeff. He was doing what he could for his patient, forcing down ammonia spirits to help the flagging heart, but she could not retain the draught. He put hot cloths on her head and distended abdomen, but she knocked them off.

'He's up in the tower; I sent for him.'

Acute indigestion? thought Jeff swiftly. Inflammation of the bowels? The cake would explain it, all that rich stuff taken into a depleted system. And yet he wasn't satisfied. Johanna's rolling pupils were distended so that her eyes appeared to be not blue but black. Some drugs do that, thought Jeff.

'Has she had any medicine of any kind?' he asked Magda.

The maid shook her head. 'Nothing, sir, except those drops you gave her.'

The drops were a harmless little carminative.

'What has she eaten since I saw her last? Think, be careful.'

'Nothing but the tipsy cake.'

Jeff went on working grimly, but while the retching grew less, the pulse also got slower and a bluish tinge was suffusing Johanna's face. He knew that Nicholas would be there any moment and that he must hurry with the question which he didn't want to ask and had not time to phrase properly.

'Did Mr. Van Ryn give her anything at all?'

The maid shook her head. 'I was in the room all the time putting things away. He handed her the cake when she asked for it, that's all.'

I'm a fool, thought Jeff, frantically chafing the fat, chilling arms. Nicholas strode in, pushing past Miranda, who stood paralyzed by the door.

He went up to his wife and she seemed to feel his presence. Her eyes focused painfully and her swollen lips moved. Her breathing became shallow and gasping.

'What is it?' cried Nicholas, turning a white face to Jeff, who made a hopeless gesture.

'Acute indigestion. I fear the heart is failing,' he whispered. He piled blankets on her, he had fresh warming pans brought. He held her up so that she could breathe. Nicholas stood as though dazed, motionless.

Twenty minutes later, Johanna ceased to breathe at all. Magda gave a scream and rushed sobbing from the room.

Jeff drew the sheet up over the staring eyes and sank into a chair profoundly shamed and miserable. He had been here all the time, somehow he should have been able to save her. Had he missed some symptom in his examination this afternoon? There might have been disease he had not discovered. And I was so cocksure, he thought bitterly.

Nicholas turned from the bed, moving as though awakened from sleep.

'Her foul gluttony has killed her,' he said. There was no emotion in his voice except a faint sadness. It was a statement of fact. Nor was it until the next day that it struck Jeff as a strangely unfeeling remark, for it was what he had been thinking himself.

Nicholas walked to the door and saw the frightened girl.

'Go to bed, Miranda,' he said. 'It's all over.'

She gave a smothered gasp. From the moment of approaching that room the events had had the unreality of nightmare. She was stupefied. She obeyed Nicholas and walked back to her room like a somnambulist.

The patroon, going out into the hall, called the awed servants together and gave instructions.

Jeff raising his head saw that he was alone in the room with the sheeted figure. Scarcely knowing why he did it, he broke off a piece of the tipsy cake and wrapping it in the napkin, stuffed it in his pocket. Then he picked up his bag and prepared to leave that dismal room. On his way he passed the little oleander bush. He remembered Johanna's apparent pride in it. Poor woman, he thought, there has been mighty little pity or tenderness about her passing.

Soon, as he left the manor behind him he heard, as did everyone else in Dragonwyck, the tolling of the village church bell. Dong, Dong, Dong, clanged the great iron clapper. Thirty-four times, one for each year of Johanna's completed life.

9

BY EVENING OF THE SECOND DAY AFTER JOHANNA'S death Dragonwyck teemed with strangers. Coach after coach, the curtains drawn down, rolled up to the black-wreathed door to discharge the Van Tappen relatives from Greenbush, from Albany and Watervliet. The halls and stairs resounded with the shuffling of countless feet as friends, tradesmen, tenants—anybody who felt the wish to do so—mounted to the bedroom and paid their last respects to the Lady of the Manor.

She lay there in state upon the ancestral bed between two burning tapers, a black velvet pall covering all but her face. There were flowers enough now in Johanna's room, masses of white tuberoses and lilies to replace the oleander.

Messengers from Hudson had brought bolts of black materials for which all the drapers had been ransacked. Magda and the maids sewed furiously.

By four o'clock Miranda had completed her own dress. The untrimmed black gave her a vivid distinction, but for once she had no interest in her appearance. She was numb with horror and unbelief. It can't be true, she repeated to herself. Death can't happen like that so quickly. She didn't seem very sick.

The girl had not left her room since Nicholas ordered her into it. Her food had been brought up to her on trays, and Magda, who had assumed control of the household since the patroon had locked himself into his room as a bereaved husband should, made it clear that Miranda would not be welcome downstairs amongst the Van Tappens. But the great bedroom at the end of the hall drew Miranda with a morbid fascination. At dusk she crept out and joined a group of strangers who were murmuring in shocked undertones before Johanna's door. She walked with them into the silent room and took her turn at filing past the bed.

That's not Johanna! she thought appalled. For on the still, waxen features there lay a quiet dignity that had never been there in life. The grossness had gone; it seemed in the soft light of the tapers that the actual flesh had been purified. And the bloodless lips were curved into a faint, subtle smile.

Miranda made an involuntary sound; heads turned and stared at her curiously. Controlling herself with effort she hurried back to her own room.

Where had it come from, that dignity, that look of power which transformed the face she had never thought showed anything but discontent and greed? Could it be that deep hidden in Johanna there had been qualities never realized, never guessed? And that smile—as though in death she had discovered a secret and triumphant illumination. Had Johanna really been like that—or was it only a trick of the great magician, an accidental part of the ultimate mystery?

I wish I hadn't hated her so, thought the girl; and suddenly tears ran down her face. For she hadn't known until that moment how much she had hated Johanna.

It was Magda who brought Miranda's supper tray and flung it on the table.

'You'll be leaving, of course, after the funeral,' said the woman rudely.

Miranda swallowed. 'I suppose so,' she said. Yes, of course she must go. She couldn't stay here alone with Nicholas. Nicholas! The girl clasped her hands tight and walked over to the window, hiding her face from the maid's spiteful glare. When the woman had gone, Miranda pushed the tray away untouched.

Nicholas was immeasurably farther away from her after this tragedy than he had ever been. For him, too, his wife in death must have assumed a strange new importance. How much sorrow and loss he felt, she wasn't sure. She had never been sure what Nicholas felt for Johanna. And yet she was his wife—the mother of his child—he must feel it terribly. And Miranda buried her face on her arms. After a while she undressed and went to bed, exhausted by the previous night's sleeplessness.

At midnight the house was quiet. No more footsteps shuffled down the hall. The Van Tappens had long since retired. Miranda slept heavily so that she did not waken when the door opened and shut again. But she heard her name, and opened dazed eyes to see Nicholas looking down at her. She lay mute, her beautiful eyes staring and still clouded with sleep.

He put his candle on the table, came back by the bed. She saw the black mourning band on his arm and could not look past it, nor raise her gaze to his face.

'Miranda!' he said. 'Look at me.'

Slowly she obeyed him, dragging her eyes upward from the black band. He drew a harsh breath. With one violent motion he jerked her up against him. He kissed her savagely, and against her shrinking breasts she felt the pounding of his heart.

'No, no—' she whispered, terrified, struggling to push him back.

He raised his head, withdrawing his arms so that she fell back against the pillows. He stood up, gave a short laugh. 'If I wished "Yes," do you think your silly "No, No" would stop me?'

'I—I don't know,' she whispered. His tigerish ferocity had frightened her, but now that he stood apart from her, again cool and controlled, her eyes filled and she looked at him with pleading.

'Get up and put on your dressing-gown,' he said. While she did so, he turned his back, went over to the fire and poked up its dying embers.

When she was ready she went to him, stood tall and slender in her white robe, her hair pushed childishly back behind her ears and cascading down about her shoulders.

He reached forward and took her left hand. She watched uncomprehending while he pushed a massive ring onto her third finger. She stared at the ring. It was of old gold made into the likeness of two tiny hands with diamond tips which clasped a dark red carbuncle roughly heart-shaped.

'It's the Van Ryn betrothal ring,' he said.

She lifted her bewildered gaze from the ring to his face. 'I—I don't understand.'

'Ah, yes you do, Miranda,' he said softly.

An incredulous joy leaped in her and died. She drew back. For not fifty feet away lay that still sheeted figure smiling the strange little smile. 'Johanna,' she whispered.

Nicholas' eyes hardened. In the moment of silence she heard the unhurried ticking of the clock on the mantel, a dog barked somewhere out by the stables.

'She never wore the ring,' he said. 'Her finger was too thick.'

Thank God, she thought in confusion, it must be all right, then. Of course it's all right if she never wore it.

'You will do exactly as I say,' said Nicholas.

The dark red stone on her finger glowed in the firelight, the tiny diamonds sparkled.

'Yes—oh yes,' she whispered. 'Always.'

'Hide the ring. Mention it to no one. Friday you will go home. In exactly twelve months I shall claim you.'

'Twelve months—' she repeated.

'Naturally, there will be a year of mourning.'

'But Nicholas,' she cried, clasping her hands and looking at him in despair, 'I can't believe—I never hoped or thought— Do you really love me—you haven't said so—'

Nicholas smiled. He put his hands on her shoulders. 'I've asked you to share my name. Tender speeches are for schoolboys. Live for the future, Miranda—as I shall.'

He bent and kissed her swiftly. Then he was gone, and the girl alone by the fire sat staring as though hypnotized at the betrothal ring.

At the same moment in Hudson, Jeff in his locked surgery, the curtains carefully drawn, finished the last of the experiments he had been making. He had no book on toxicology, but had found some pertinent data in one of his pharmacological textbooks.

On a plate before him lay a few crumbs, all that remained of the specimen of cake he had abstracted from Dragonwyck. The rest he had examined through his microscope, which was weak, but powerful enough to have shown up any tiny grains of white or gray powder. There were none. Following the directions in his book he had burned a portion of the cake in a retort, and on still another piece had poured certain chemicals. All the results were negative.

Now with a sudden revulsion of feeling he picked up the plate and shied it into his stone sink, where it smashed to splinters.

I ought to be ashamed of myself, he thought. My suspicions are nothing but childish pique that my medical knowledge was at fault and I lost a patient.

He shut the textbook and put it back on the shelf to accumulate dust. He tidied up the surgery and went to bed, resolving never to think of the matter again.

10

JOHANNA WAS BURIED WITH ALL THE POMP BEfitting her station. There were the twelve pallbearers—Livingstons, Van Rensselaers, Schuylers, and Van Tappens—to head the funeral procession. Each had a small white satin pillow to support his share of the coffin's weight. None of the coffin itself was visible, for it was covered with the traditional 'dood kleed' of black wool from which hung fifty silken tassels which swayed with the bearers' labored tread.

Behind the coffin walked Nicholas alone in his black silk suit, his face expressionless, his eyes on the ground.

Katrine followed with her mother's relatives. Miranda found herself relegated to a position barely ahead of the servants.

It took half an hour to cover the half-mile to the church, and by that time the pallbearers' faces were running with sweat.

Of the funeral service Miranda heard nothing, for as she seated herself in the corner of the back pew assigned to her she was aware that someone was staring at her. She turned and encountered Zélie's eyes. The old woman's fixed gaze was both knowing and malicious. She nodded her head once, and her shriveled mouth widened in a melancholy smile.

The girl's hand flew to her bodice and touched the outline of the hidden ring. And at once anger at her own folly jerked her around in the pew. As though Zélie could possibly know!

She did not turn again, but the service was over and Johanna's coffin carried to its final resting place in the churchyard before Miranda was sufficiently composed to pay attention.

The rest of the day passed in the traditional ceremonials.

The black-draped dining table was loaded with elaborate side dishes besides the baron of beef, the roast hindquarters of a lamb and a baked carp. To these the company did full though solemn justice, aided by copious draughts of wine and punch.

Nicholas presented to each of the pallbearers a 'monkey spoon,' a small trinket of carved silver with a tiny figure on the handle, supposed to represent one of the twelve Apostles. Nicholas gave each spoon with a courteous murmur of thanks, and everyone thought him the model of dignified sorrow.

'Poor, poor man,' murmured Mrs. Henry Van Rensselaer, resting her knife and fork and looking at him with sympathetic admiration. 'So young to be bereaved—and so handsome.' Her thoughts turned to her four unmarried girls. But it was too soon to think of things like that. She picked up her knife and fork again.

Miranda took no part in these proceedings. No one invited her to do so. She stayed alone in her room. And the next morning she started on her journey home.

The river being still closed to boats, Nicholas sent her in the light coach with Dick, the second coachman, to drive, and Greta, a middle-aged chambermaid, to chaperone her. They would have to spend two nights on the road, the first at the Beekman Arms in Rhinebeck, the second in Peekskill; and a young lady could not stay alone in an inn.

There was a dismal feeling of indifference, almost of disgrace, about Miranda's hurried departure at seven in the morning. She went to Katrine's room to say good-bye, but the child was sleepy and unresponsive; all her interest was centered on the projected visit to Aunt Van Tappen in Albany. Far worse than Katrine's indifference was Nicholas' absence. The girl had been sure that he would appear to wish her God-speed even if they had no chance for a private word. But he did not.

Greta, plump and stolid in black alpaca, already waited in the coach; Miranda's parcels and new trunk filled with the clothes she had acquired at Dragonwyck were neatly lashed on top. Dick's red face was impatient and the horses snorted and stamped, anxious to be off into the chilly spring morning.

There was nothing to do but get in. The heavy door slammed and the coachman cracked his whip. Miranda pressed her face to the window pane and looked her last at Dragonwyck. Its tower and gables shone bright as brass in the rays of the rising sun. Desolation seized her and the image of the great house dissolved in a mist of tears.

Her hand crept to the ring in an effort at reassurance which was becoming habitual, and she sank back on the seat trying to hide her face from Greta. The woman opened a string bag and drew out a letter, which she tendered Miranda.

'Here, miss,' she said. 'Mynheer said to give you after we leave.' Her stupid face showed no curiosity. She was a good, obedient servant, incapable of iniative or speculation. It was for this reason that Nicholas had picked her to accompany Miranda.

The girl's heart beat fast as she opened the letter. It said:

> I regret very much not bidding you farewell. It's better not, and there is that between us that needs no words to express. Already one day of the appointed time has passed, my dear one.—N.

Forgetting discretion, Miranda pressed the note to her lips, then looked nervously at the silent Greta wondering if she had been observed. But the woman had gone to sleep. Miranda tucked the letter in her bodice next the ring. Her desolation was forgotten. A year was not so very long to wait.

I'll be so good, she thought; I'll study and improve my mind so as to be worthy of him. Then there was much to be done, dozens of dainty underclothes to be made and linen to be monogrammed. She would not come to him empty-handed. She suppressed the disquieting thought that all this preparation would be hard in view of Nicholas' command to 'tell no one.' She would manage somehow.

With each mile that separated her from Dragonwyck the horror and gloom of the last few days dimmed. Her relationship to Nicholas changed and became as she wanted it to be. He loved her and she loved him and soon they would be married—the natural termination of any romance. She shut her memory against Johanna, as against Nicholas' black and inexplicable moods. One must never look back, she thought blithely, feeling mature and philosophical. It's only the future that matters. Just as Nicholas said.

The coach was passing through Hudson when she reached this conclusion and she thought briefly of Jeff Turner. Even the thought of him had the power to make her uncomfortable, and resentment rose in her.

But soon they left behind the town of brick houses and church spires. The horses trotted vigorously along the highroad to Poughkeepsie and Miranda noted with pleasure passing glances of admiration for her equipage—the smart liveried coachman on the box, the matched bays with their jingling silver harness, the impeccable maid beside her. Miranda held her chin high.

After noon on the third day they passed through Bedford Village and continued down the North Way. In a few more miles Miranda recognized landmarks near home. She welcomed these with eagerness and her long submerged yearning for her mother at last claimed her. When they reached Stanwich she leaned forward hanging out the window, excitedly directing the coachman and straining her eyes for the first glimpse of the farm.

Still when at last she saw the square white frame house beneath the elm trees, she was dismayed. It was so small, so insignificant.

And in the yard before the kitchen door stood the farm wagon steaming with a load of manure which Tom and her father were pitching from a pile by the stable. Both men looked up as they heard the carriage approach: she saw that they were unshaven, sweating, and dirty.

The coachman had nearly passed the farm road by before she found her voice. 'Turn here,' she called to the box in a small, defiant voice. 'This is where I live.'

She suffered under the man's stare of astonishment. He pulled up the horses and guided them through the narrow gate. Greta, stolid as ever, glanced at the farm with incurious eyes.

The coach stopped just short of the manure pile, and Dick, opening the door for Miranda, waited respectfully, hat in hand. Tom and Ephraim stood transfixed, then the boy's jaw dropped.

'Gosh almighty, Pa. It's Ranny!' he cried.

Ephraim recovered from his surprise and his bearded face set in disapproval. 'So I see.' He advanced to the girl, who stood nervously on the carriage step, unwilling to risk her delicate kid slippers in the barnyard muck.

'Well, miss,' said her father, 'did your fine folks get tired of you and pack you back again?'

'Oh, no, Pa—' she cried, flushing. Though she was not particularly glad to see her father she had expected a warmer welcome. 'Mrs. Van Ryn died last Monday, and of course I came home. There was no time to write.'

'Indeed,' said Ephraim, wiping his hands on a spotted red handkerchief. 'I'm sorry to hear of the poor lady's passing, but we're all mortal and the Lord strikes where He will. Home is the place for you and always has been. Stop swaying on that step like a chicken with the pip. You'll find your ma around to the back in the herb garden. She'll likely be glad to see you.'

Thus commanded, Miranda gathered up her silk skirts and descended gingerly.

Ephraim turned to his son. 'Tom, I reckon we can find room to stable these horses, but the coach'll have to stay outside. As for you,' he paused, having just discovered Greta inside, and clearly not knowing what to do with her and the coachman, 'Miranda'll cook you up some supper, we'll find you beds somewhere.'

'Oh, no, Pa!' Miranda cried again in embarrassment. She saw the twinkle in the coachman's eyes at the thought of her cooking him up some supper. She who at Dragonwyck had always been served by a dozen hands. 'Mr. Van Ryn has made arrangements for them to return at once. They'll spend tonight on the road. Good-bye,' she added quickly to the servants. 'Thank you very much. My brother'll help you get my trunk off.' And she fled around the corner of the house.

She saw a thin figure in an old gray sunbonnet stooping over the herb patch, and forgetting her shoes and skirts she flew with a cry of joy. 'Ma, dear! Oh, Ma, I'm so glad to see you!'

Abigail straightened and was startled out of her Yankee reserve by the sight of the slender fashionable figure. She opened her arms and caught her daughter to her breast.

There began for Miranda a period of difficult adjustment. Nearly a year had passed since she left them. Home had not changed, but she had—immeasurably; and except for Abigail, her family that first evening appeared to her as rather uncouth strangers. The baby did not know her, and screamed with terror at the scented and ringleted lady in rustling green silk.

All three of her brothers eyed her in wary embarrassment after a stiff greeting. Tabitha, flushed from tending the oven, her apron awry, cried, 'My land, Ranny! I'd never have known you,' and the sisters exchanged a brief kiss. But there was no warmth in Tibby's greeting, either. Her scrutiny of Miranda mingled envious resentment with disapproval. Silk dress, low-cut bosom, lace, kid slippers—and she's got *powder* on her face, thought Tabitha, horrified. She tightened her lips, and while they all sat down to supper around the kitchen table, she glanced at her father, sure that he was sharing her disapproval and would soon voice it.

Nor did Ephraim disappoint her. When he had finished grace, he rested his carving knife and fork on the home-cured ham hock before him, and surveyed Miranda. 'You aiming to do the dishes in that ridiculous rig?' he inquired.

Tabitha giggled, and the smaller boys nudged each other.

Before Miranda could answer, her mother leaned forward and said quickly: 'It's just for tonight, Ephraim. Ranny was tired from the traveling. She'll get into the hang of things tomorrow again.'

Ephraim grunted. 'She'd better. I'll have no idle, furbelowed, fiddle-dee-dee girls around here.' He picked up the carving knife, and said no more. The family, who were braced for a protracted lecture, settled in some surprise to their food.

Miranda's appearance discomfited her father. He could not help but see that the girl had grown extraordinarily pretty, and that in both her dress and her manner she now resembled the fine ladies he had seen at the Astor House. He was grudgingly impressed by her arrival this afternoon, the blazoned coach, the two servants, the sleek horses in their silver harness. Mr. Van Ryn must have thought a lot of the girl to provide her with such state. But now she was home again, any high-faluting nonsense she had learned must be knocked out of her. He helped himself to fried potatoes and shoved the dish toward Abigail.

Miranda toyed with her food. She was not hungry and the salty ham, greasy potatoes, and even Tabitha's fresh bread cut into thick slabs were unappetizing to a palate used to Dragonwyck's sophisticated cooking. She noticed things that had never bothered her before. Had the boys always gulped like that, and wiped their mouths on the back of their hands? And after Nicholas' chivalrous politeness, it was disconcerting to see that her mother and sister must wait for each dish until the hungry males had helped themselves.

Being at home again was like settling slowly down into the narrow end of a funnel. Everything oppressed her: the farm talk, the family prayers and Bible reading—in her absence Ephraim had finished the New Testament and was back into Deuteronomy—the eight o'clock bedtime, the sharing of her bed with Tabitha.

'It won't be for long,' snapped Tabitha, seeing the look of dismay which Miranda cast at the bed that seemed to her incredibly narrow. 'Soon you'll have it all to yourself.'

Miranda examined her sister's plump, triumphant face. 'Why—what do you mean, Tibby?'

'Ob and I are being married next month,' said the younger girl, thinking: and that's more than you'll be, for all your fancy clothes and that you're two years older.

Miranda sat down on the bed, remembering Obadiah's broad face, his little stutter, his thick hands. 'Are you in love with him, Tibby?' she asked gravely.

The other girl nodded, embarrassed. One didn't speak of love right out like that, but Ranny had always been queer.

'Then I hope you'll be very happy,' said Miranda, her voice not quite steady. Nicholas—she thought with a paroxysm of longing. The year now stretched forward an eon. Will it ever be 'next month' for me, too— She longed to tell Tabitha, just for the pleasure of speaking his name. But she knew that she must not. The ring was safely concealed beneath the high-necked nightgown.

'I have two silk dresses,' she went on quickly. 'Choose either one you want, Tibby, and I'll make it over to fit you.'

'Oh, Ranny, thank you!' cried her sister, overcome. 'That's real sweet of you. You always were much cleverer with the needle than me,' she added, determined to be generous too. She dropped most of her touchiness as she discovered that Miranda did not mean to patronize her. And that far from having to listen to long accounts of the glories and refinements of Dragonwyck, Miranda did not want to talk about her visit at all. Instead she listened patiently to Tibby's description of Ob's virtues, and the three-room cottage which was being built on a corner of the Brown farm for the young couple. 'Parlor, kitchen, and bedroom—*and* the parlor *papered,*' whispered Tabitha exultantly to the quiet figure beside her in bed. 'Of course later—the house won't be big enough,' she added, blushing into the dark. 'Ob said—said he hoped we'd have to add more space every year. Wasn't that awful of him!'

'Shocking,' agreed Miranda. She tried to picture Nicholas and herself in a three-room cottage. It was impossible. The image of Nicholas was inextricably mingled with magnificence, with brocades and gilt and invisible service, the somber and regal atmosphere of Dragonwyck.

She put her hand down the collar of her nightgown and felt for the ring. The heart-shaped carbuncle was warm from her body. She slipped her finger through the gold circle.

Long after Tabitha had gone to sleep she lay staring up at the low-raftered ceiling, making no sound, but slow tears trickled down her face onto the uncomfortable cornhusk mattress.

11

TABITHA WAS MARRIED ON SATURDAY THE THIRTY-first of May in the Second Congregational Meeting House on the hill. The church was crammed with representative Greenwich families—Meads, Reynoldses, Pecks, Closes, and Husteds.

Ephraim and Abigail in a front pew nodded decorously at these friends and neighbors who had all turned out to honor the young couple. Ephraim's satisfaction was increased by the absence of the Reverend Noah Coe, whose eight years of unpopular ministry had culminated last week in his stormy dismissal by the Society.

Well, Coe's gone at last and good riddance, thought Ephraim, eyeing the Reverend Clark, the young substitute pastor, who had been brought in temporarily until the Consociation should decide on a permanent incumbent. A sound minister and a fine new stone church, that's what we need. I daresay I can squeeze out a couple of hundred, Bob Mead and Eliphalet Peck'll do considerably better— He started as Abigail nudged him.

'Hurry, Ephraim; they're waiting,' she whispered. Recalled to his duty, he hastened down the aisle and took Tabitha on his arm as the congregation cleared their throats and struck up 'Rock of Ages.'

Tibby looks lovely, thought Miranda with pride as she followed her sister and father up the aisle. Tabitha wore Miranda's watered gray silk trimmed with ruching. The difference in their heights had made it possible to cut enough from the bottom to piece out the bodice and waist, which were much too small. Miranda had also donated tiny green ostrich feathers to trim the poke bonnet. A white wedding dress would have been unthinkable extravagance for a farmer's wife, and without Miranda's generosity Tabitha would have been married in a serviceable cashmere or alpaca.

Obadiah waited beside the pulpit for his bride, his broad face scrubbed and shining.

Ephraim handed over his younger daughter, and stepped aside with

Miranda. The Reverend Clark opened the Bible and raised his hands. The congregation bowed their heads—all but Abigail. She clenched her worn fingers on the front of the pew and gazed at the group beneath the pulpit. Obadiah's mother glanced sideways at the tense figure beside her and whispered sympathetically, 'It's hard to have them leave us, Abby, but Ob'll be a good son to you, and they're not going far.'

Abigail nodded. It was not at Tabitha that she had been looking but at Miranda. For she had surprised on the girl's downcast face an expression of suffering, and a pain so obvious that the mother's heart was shocked.

I knew it, thought Abigail, deeply troubled; something has happened to the girl that she's not told me. While searching for the cause of Miranda's unhappiness, an unhappiness which Abigail had felt and tried to deny to herself during this past month, the marriage service was finished, and she realized with compunction that during Tabitha's supreme moment she had had no thoughts for her younger daughter at all.

Some thirty guests drove down the turnpike to Stanwich Road and then to the Wells farm for the spread: apple, dried peach and rhubarb pies, ham, doughnuts, coffee and cider. Abigail and her daughters had been cooking for days.

Ephraim would serve no intoxicating liquor, but some of Ob's young friends had fortified themselves with a jug of Connecticut rum, and before the afternoon shadows cast by the wineglass elms had even touched the east wall of the farmhouse, the merriment had grown rough and rowdy.

The older people sat apart beneath the trees and watched the young ones play kissing games. Even Ephraim saw no harm in that at a wedding, nor did any of the other farmers, who might enforce their blue laws, but enjoyed a strenuous and unrefined frolic just the same.

Miranda longed to go off by herself to the quiet of the little attic room which she would no longer have to share, but she dared not, knowing that her absence would annoy her father. She tried to keep out of the way, busying herself with carrying pies and plates back and forth from the kitchen, and the young people let her be. Some of the men made sheep's eyes at her, but they were afraid of her. She was tall and lovely and remote in her green silk dress.

'Stuck up, she is,' whispered little Phoebe Mead to Deborah Wilson in the corner of the barn where they had both run for refuge from

Zach Wilson, who was 'it' at the moment and lurched blindfolded now this way, now that, trying to catch one of the girls in his outstretched arms.

Miranda shrank behind a tree as she saw her former admirer stumble in her direction, and would have escaped him except that Ob, her new brother-in-law, seized her around the waist and shoved her toward Zach's groping hands. Everyone stopped running to watch. There were titters. She stood stiff as a fencepole while the rough fingers pawed her dress, her hair.

' 'Tis Ranny!' shouted Zach, and tearing off the blindfold he gave her a wet smacking kiss on the mouth. Quick as thought she slapped him hard across his fat face, and he stumbled backward.

There was a shocked silence. A kiss was the usual forfeit for being caught. If one didn't like the kisser one might giggle and duck, but this blaze of disgust and anger on the white face—and the mark of her fingers standing out livid on Zach's cheek! He rubbed at it, bewildered. 'What in creation's the matter with her!' he muttered.

'Catch yourself an iceberg next time, Zach,' shouted a male voice. 'Leastways they don't slap.'

Miranda turned slowly. She saw Tabitha's indignant look. Ranny making a scene, spoiling everybody's fun, and at the wedding too.

Color rushed to Miranda's cheeks. 'I'm sorry, Tibby,' she whispered; then catching up her skirts she ran into the house.

Abigail had seen the whole incident, though Ephraim fortunately had not. 'I'll just go look at the oven; it cools down mighty quick,' she murmured, and followed her daughter. She found Miranda upstairs, face down across the bed, and crying so hard that she did not hear her mother's light footstep. But she felt the touch on her hair and jumped up.

'Ranny, lass,' said Abigail gently. 'Tell me what ails you, I can see—' She stopped, staring. Against Miranda's bodice there hung a carved gold ring with a heart-shaped red stone. The girl covered it quickly with her hand, but her mother shook her head and pulled the ring from under the clutching fingers. 'What is this, Miranda?' she said sternly. 'And why are you hiding it?'

Shouts and laughter from the renewed game of Blind Man's Buff carried through the open window into the hot room. A fly circled lazily, buzzing against the rafters.

'I'm waiting, dearie.' She put her arm around the girl's shoulders, and Miranda with a choked sound hid her face on her mother's thin chest.

'It's the Van Ryn betrothal ring,' she whispered.

Abigail, completely bewildered, felt sharp dismay. Could it be that Ranny had taken the ring in some clandestine way, and afraid to admit her fault, therefore hid it? It was obviously of great value. Her protecting arm fell away.

'How do you come by it?' she snapped.

Miranda lifted her head. Now that it had been forced on her, it could be no breach of faith to tell. 'He gave it to me,' she said proudly. 'Nicholas.'

For an instant her mother was conscious only of relief. It was not surprising that Mr. Van Ryn should have made the girl a present at parting, since he had been most generous throughout. Then her bewilderment returned.

'But why a betrothal ring? And why do you hide it? And—' she added with growing apprehension, 'You called him Nicholas; surely that's not respectful, Ranny.'

Miranda got up, she moved slowly from the bed to the little deal table on which she had arranged her toilet articles. The bottle of lustral water was misplaced; she shifted it, picked up her horn comb and laid it down again. 'I'm going to marry him, Ma,' she said.

'What!' cried Abigail. Miranda turned. Her chin was lifted a little, her long eyes were both frightened and defiant, but on her mouth there was a small smile. 'I am, Ma, next spring.'

'But Ranny, it's not possible! You must be mad, girl.' Abigail laced her hands, all her usual decisiveness dissolved in confusion. 'He's too old for you—' From the many crowding objections, this was the first that came to her. Her picture of Nicholas as a settled, middle-aged gentleman.

Miranda gave a soft little laugh, remembering that her mother must still think of Nicholas as they had imagined him last summer. 'Oh Ma, he's only thirty-two, and the handsomest man in the world. He looks like—like—' If only she had a picture of him, how often she had wished it. 'Wait a minute!' she cried, and falling to her knees opened her horsehair trunk. Pinned to the lid was an illustration which she had cut from a gift book, 'A Garland of Roses for 1844.' She thrust it at her mother. 'This is something like him, though Nicholas is far better-looking.'

Abigail frowned at the picture of a tall, dark young man, leaning negligently against a balustrade. It was titled 'Lord Allingham awaits his bride.' She placed the illustration on the bed.

'I see that he is not as I thought him, Miranda,' she said gravely. 'But it makes no difference. How can it be that his wife died on Monday, and you left on the Friday, and yet he gave you a betrothal ring?'

Her voice fell like a cold stone through the little room. The girl made an involuntary gesture of defense. The eager, happy light which had shone in her eyes as her mother examined the picture was snuffed out.

'Yes,' she said, groping for words, 'I know it seems—I know it's hard to understand, it wasn't exactly that way—' She swallowed. Suddenly she flung herself down beside her mother, clasping the spare knees and looking up at Abigail with a desperate pleading.

'I love him so, Ma. I loved him from the beginning, I think. Oh, won't you try to understand, please? And he—he never was happy with Johanna.'

Abigail slowly relaxed, allowing her love for this child to stifle the doubts which afflicted her. The ways of gentry are different, she thought, and who am I to judge them? She was silent, stroking the girl's hair, and there came to her gradually a half-guilty pride. It would be a very grand marriage.

'Your pa—' she began, still trying to adjust herself to the staggering idea.

'Pa mustn't know for a long time,' said Miranda quickly. 'No one must know. *He* said that—Nicholas.'

Frowning, Abigail turned from her daughter's appealing gaze. She saw the reason for secrecy: all of Greenwich would be scandalized if they knew Miranda's plans. And yet this hole-and-corner business—Something wrong about it, something snide, thought Abigail. But the lass loves him. She'll be a great lady. I'll not spoil her chances.

She rose briskly, smoothed down her poplin dress. 'Wash your face and see if the fresh pies are ready. I'll keep your secret, Ranny.'

Tabitha's wedding day ended in a boisterous skimelton party, a kind of local charivari. She drove beside her husband on the spring wagon to the new cottage on the adjoining farm, and no sooner had the young couple retired upstairs than the racket broke out. Twenty of Ob's friends serenaded them with catcalls and the banging of kettles. Two of the Mead boys fired muskets into the air at great peril to the yelling bystanders. Nat and Seth, proud to be included amongst the men, and swelling with additional importance because they were brothers to the bride, marched around and around the house with a fife and drum. The noise kept up until midnight and made sleep impossible for any of the near-by farmhouses.

'Tibby's got a rare send-off,' said Ephraim, kicking off his best shoes, and settling into his chair with a tired grunt. 'She and Ob are well liked, and no mistake.'

Abigail and Miranda were cleaning up the kitchen; neither answered Ephraim, who was relaxed and pleased with life. It had been a good wedding, tribute to his standing in the community.

A muffled boom rattled the window panes. It was followed by shouts and huzzahs.

'Consarned if they haven't brought the old cannon from Cos Cob,' said Ephraim, chuckling. 'Hasn't been such a skimelton in years.' He glanced at his older daughter, who with a checked apron tied over her dress was neatly washing dishes. 'Likely you'll soon be having one too, Ranny,' he said kindly.

Heaven forbid, she thought. Nicholas would be disgusted by this method of starting marriage. Would he perhaps be disgusted by her whole background, she thought, dropping the greasy dish rag in sudden panic. She looked at her father's stocking feet, which were propped comfortably on the table.

'But ye'll never get yourself a husband 'less you drop those high and mighty airs,' continued Ephraim, his good temper waning at her silence. 'Men don't like it. Ye'll be an old maid yet, if you don't mend your ways.'

'I hope not, Pa,' said Miranda. She took an empty pie tin from her mother, and the women's eyes met in a quick glance.

'You dry,' whispered Abigail, 'I'll finish the washing. You mustn't let your hands get rough.'

She gave her mother a look of fervent gratitude. There was comfort in having shared her secret. The sharing had made it real. For there were times when it seemed that she must have dreamed Dragonwyck and all that had happened to her there. Suppose Nicholas forgot her—suppose he hadn't really meant it—suppose he met someone else—

The summer days dragged by, and Miranda's fears grew. Abigail spared her many tasks, but the inexorable farm routine demanded every pair of hands, and now Tabitha was gone.

Baking, boiling, and washing, milking the cows, the care of Charity, who was a lively two-year-old, and into everything, through these chores, Miranda moved automatically, preoccupied and dully miserable. Nor was she efficient. She let the bread burn, or the fires go out. Once she scorched an entire kettle of the precious blackberries which Abigail was cooking into a winter's supply of jam.

'Land's sake, Ranny, you're no more use than Charity!' snapped her mother, exasperated, when she discovered this last tragedy.

The girl's eyes filled. 'I'm dreadful sorry, Ma. I'll pick you some more berries. I was stirring the kettle, and then somehow I got to thinking —and I forgot—'

'Take the baby for a walk, and keep out of the way, do—' Abigail took the blackened sticky kettle from her daughter. 'I'll clean it. Rather do it myself than watch you mooning and puttering. Go on out—scat!'

Miranda obediently took the baby's hand. Charity gave a crow of delight. 'Pick f'owers, Ranny!' she commanded, tugging at her sister. 'Make w'eath for baby.'

Abigail watched the two wander across the north pasture. The girl's heartsick, she thought. It's a wonder he wouldn't write to her. All these months, she's been pining.

She attacked the kettle vigorously, her lips compressed. Abigail too was beginning to have doubts.

By the end of September, Miranda could stand the silence no longer. She could not eat, she slept badly. Her talismans, the ring and the note from Nicholas which she had received on the morning of her departure from Dragonwyck, no longer served to reassure her. It was true that she had intuitively accepted the fact that he might not write her.

And she knew as surely that there had been a tacit interdiction against her writing to him. Yet why not? thought Miranda feverishly. What could be more natural—a few words thanking him for his kindness to her, asking about his health. A letter that anyone might read without suspicion.

One morning when the men were working in the fields, and Abigail had gone down the road to see Tabitha, Miranda stole into the front room and sat down at her father's cherry desk.

She made four drafts, and finally copied the last one onto a sheet of lined paper, from the back of Ephraim's ledger. There was no other paper.

Stanwich Road, Greenwich,
Sept. 25th, 1845.

Dear Cousin Nicholas:

It seems eternity [she scraped this out with a penknife and substituted 'a long time'] since I left Dragonwyck.

I trust that you are in good health, and Katrine as well. My thoughts ever turn to you—[she stopped, hastily added an *r*] your kindness and hospitality. Please [she erased that] I would esteem it a great favor to hear if you are quite well.

She laid the pen down and gazed with miserable eyes out of the window into the rustling elm leaves. How to sign it? Not 'sincerely,' not 'affectionately.' There was no word that she dared write.

She picked up the pen, and put down 'Miranda,' carefully embellished with the flourishes she had learned at the Academy.

She folded the sheet, sealed and addressed it. That afternoon, she walked three miles to the Horseneck Post Office, had the letter franked, and walked back again through fields of goldenrod and up the shady Stanwich Road, and her heart was lighter.

Surely he would understand, would read between the lines and send her a word of reassurance.

But weeks passed and there was no answer.

The girl's going into a decline, thought Abigail, watching her daughter anxiously. I wish she'd never gone to Dragonwyck, or heard of that Nicholas. She was always over-romantic, and to my everlasting shame I guess I encouraged her. 'Eat your vittles, Ranny,' she would urge with irritation born of worry. 'You look like a picked crow.'

'Aye,' agreed Ephraim on one occasion, wiping his mouth and examining his daughter. 'What ails you these days, child? You wear a face long enough to eat oats out of a churn.' He had been better pleased with her lately. She was quiet and biddable. It had occurred to him that she seemed a bit mopish, but girls were unstable, moody creatures, full of silly whims.

'Well,' he continued, with an idea of cheering her, 'next week's Harvest Festival in Peck's barn. I hear they've got a fiddler coming from Stamford. It'll liven you up. Likely catch yourself a beau.'

Miranda said nothing, sat as she so often did now, her lids dropped, staring vaguely at the table.

Her father frowned and opened his mouth to speak when Nat created a diversion. 'Looky—' he cried, peering through the kitchen window—'there's a stranger on a roan horse just turned through our gate!'

Miranda started. Against all reason, wild hope set her heart to pounding. She crowded with the others to the window. They all watched the approaching horseman: strangers were an event.

'It can't be a peddler,' said Nat. 'He has no pack.'

The roan horse walked slowly, its head drooping. The rider was concealed by his woolen cape and battered beaver hat.

'Someone who's lost his way,' suggested Abigail. A thought struck her, the same that had come to Miranda. She glanced at the girl, and saw from the hopeless disappointment in her face that at any rate this was not Nicholas.

'I'll see what he wants,' said Ephraim, going out the door. At that moment the stranger raised his head, and Miranda gave a cry of surprise.

'Why, it's Doctor Turner!' She stared at the powerful shoulders, the square, smiling face, hating him because he came from up-river, because he reminded her poignantly of Dragonwyck, and yet was not Nicholas. He might have news, though, she thought with rising excitement. Of course he would have news.

She ran down the steps as Jeff alighted.

For a moment he hardly recognized her. Her golden hair was braided and pinned tight around her head; she wore pink challis and an apron. She was too thin and pale, so that her long hazel eyes now looked enormous in her sharpened face. Her lips trembled as she smiled at him.

'Oh, Doctor Turner—' she cried impulsively—'have you—did you—?' She broke off, conscious that Ephraim was staring at her.

Jeff took her hand in his, hardly hearing what she said. He thought that eagerness, that glad crying of his name, were for him, that she was happy to see him. Warmth flowed over him. In her simple clothes, she seemed to him far more beautiful than she had in the fashionable silks and ringlets she had worn at Dragonwyck. He was touched by hollows in her cheeks, and the shadows beneath her lovely eyes.

'And who may this gentleman be, Ranny?' inquired Ephraim sternly.

Jeff dropped her hand and grinned in some confusion. 'I'm Jefferson Turner from Hudson, Mr. Wells. Perhaps Miranda has mentioned me.'

'She has not, sir,' said Ephraim. He too misinterpreted his daughter's behavior. This young man must be the reason for the girl's pinings and sighings. But though he liked Jeff on sight, as people usually did, he had no intention of unbending until he had been given a full explanation.

Jeff was soon established at the table, while Abigail plied him with roast pork and pie. Miranda saw that her own questions must wait until her father's had been satisfied, and she moved from the stove to the table and back to the stove again in a fever of impatience.

It seemed that Jeff had made a trip to New York. 'For there's a fine doctor there, Doctor John Francis. He has a new treatment for cholera. The old whaler "Nellie B"—put into Hudson in July and she brought us some cholera from India. We only had five cases, praise be, but I lost two of them.' He put down his knife, and his face sobered.

'I hope they were good Christians, and died in the faith of our Lord,' said Ephraim. Jeff nodded. 'Oh, their souls are safe enough; it's the welfare of their bodies that concerns me.'

'Young man—' said Ephraim, 'that remark smacks of levity. The body is but dust and ashes. Still—' he went on, because he was interested, and despite a possible laxity of principle, the young doctor seemed a fine, upstanding man, 'did you find a new medicine for the cholera in the city?'

' 'Tis nothing in the world but clay—' said Jeff ruefully. 'Chinese clay. Doctor Francis has tried it and it works well.'

'To eat, you mean?' put in Nat. All three boys were listening intently, delighted with this break in their lives. Only Miranda paid no attention. What did she care for cholera and its treatment when her whole being was centered on one subject? The meal seemed to her interminable. Even after everyone had finished eating, Ephraim ignored the lengthening shadows outside and sat on at table talking to the guest. And this in spite of the filled wagon in the yard and the team ready harnessed to drive a load of late potatoes to the dock.

Jeff explained the uses of clay in cholera, and he told them of his trip from Hudson. He had come by horseback because he wished to stop along the way in Poughkeepsie and Fishkill and White Plains to see friends and confer with other doctors.

'This morning I was in Rye,' he said, smiling, 'and finding myself so near Greenwich, I thought to come and see Miranda.' This was not entirely true. He had meant from the beginning to call on the Wellses. But he did not himself clearly understand why he had wanted to see her again, and the fact embarrassed him.

'I'm glad you came,' said Ephraim heartily. 'You'll stay with us to-night, of course. You can share Tom's bed.—Ranny,' he turned to the silent girl, 'you might walk about a bit with the doctor. Show him the orchard; I'm certain they don't grow apple trees like that where he comes from.' Ephraim had made up his mind. No doubt the young fellow had come a-courting. He would have preferred one of the neighbor boys, but Jeff had passed muster. I'll not be harsh with the girl, thought Ephraim; she might have done far worse.

So with her father's approval, and followed by a puzzled look from her mother, Miranda and Jeff went for a walk in the apple orchard.

'You're not looking very well, Miranda,' said Jeff gently. 'I think I must give you a tonic.'

She walked fast, anxious to get out of hearing of the house. She brushed his remark aside, and climbed swiftly over the stone fence. He followed, and when they stood on the bumpy ground amongst a few worm-eaten russets, she turned to him with urgency.

'Tell me, have you been to Dragonwyck? Have you seen Mr. Van Ryn?'

So, he thought, surprised to see how much he minded, that breathless eagerness of greeting was not for me at all. She is still obsessed with the lord of the manor.

'Dragonwyck's closed,' he said; 'has been since June. Mr. Van Ryn is traveling, down South somewhere. Didn't you know?'

She shook her head, trying to hide her face from him. But he had seen the tears start to her eyes.

'I did see him once in September, at poor Boughton's new trial,' he said unwillingly. He had not meant to tell her this, nor of the message Nicholas had given him for her, for he had persuaded himself that she would have forgotten Nicholas, now that she was back home. And he profoundly believed that it would be better for her if she had. But in the face of her anguish, he could not deny her.

'How was he?' she asked breathlessly. 'Oh, please, please tell me.'

'He seemed very well. I only saw him for a minute.'

He sighed, remembering the crowded little Hudson courtroom where Smith Boughton had stood his second trial for sedition against the Manor lords, the first one having ended in disagreement.

This time things had gone as badly as possible. The steely-eyed Circuit Judge John Edmonds had presided. Boughton's lawyer, Ambrose Jordan, had lost his temper, had actually provoked a fist fight with John Van Buren, who represented the manors. From the beginning, Jeff had had small hope of the outcome, but the verdict was even worse than he had feared. Smith Boughton had been sentenced to life in Clinton Prison.

They had been sorry after that, some of those who had persecuted the little doctor. There had been tears in the courtroom; Mrs. Van Rensselaer had fainted. Jeff had watched them all with hatred—the well-fed, smug lot of them ensconced in the white-paneled gallery, so avid for their dubious rights, so terrified of one small, white-faced man who had dared to threaten their wealth and power.

Nicholas had been amongst those in the gallery, conspicuous in his black suit. He had watched the proceedings impassively, his handsome head turned a little, his blue eyes showing little interest.

As soon as the verdict had been pronounced, he had risen and left the gallery. Jeff too had quitted the courtroom, moved by an impulsive and quite impossible wish to go to his friend. The guard soon disabused him, no one might now see the prisoner; and he had been walking sadly down the courthouse steps, when he felt a touch on his arm.

It was Nicholas, who said, 'Good day, Doctor Turner. This must be a bad time for you.'

'At any rate, it's a pleasant one for you,' said Jeff, starting to walk on.

'The verdict is just but harsh,' said Nicholas calmly. 'Were I he, I would kill myself. He'd be far better dead than in prison.'

I really believe he means that, Jeff had thought, and he had answered: 'I don't agree with you, Mr. Van Ryn. Life is precious, and what's more the sentence may be commuted some day. Now if you'll excuse me—I leave soon for a trip to New York and I've much to do.'

'Indeed?' asked Nicholas politely.

'When I'm thereabouts, I may call on Miss Wells,' added Jeff, more from curiosity as to what Nicholas would say than anything else.

He had said nothing for a moment and the peculiar shut expression had appeared in his eyes. 'If you do see her,' he said at last, 'you might tell her that I shall come down-river in April.'

'Certainly,' said Jeff, thinking it a very trivial message. He had continued to think so up to this moment, and now he wondered.

When he delivered the message to Miranda, he no longer wondered. She was transfigured by a blaze of joy.

'Did he say that?' she cried. 'Oh, thank you, thank you, Jeff.' She was unconscious of her use of his name, half-laughing and half-crying in her relief. It was all right then. Nicholas hadn't answered her letter because Dragonwyck was shut and he was traveling. But he would be with her in April as he had promised.

She no longer doubted or even wondered why he did not write her. He had his reasons, he was different anyway from all other men. He had given her his word, she had been shameful to need the confirmation. But oh, it was sweet to have it.

She smiled at Jeff, including him now in her joy.

'You're easily pleased,' said he crossly. It was plain enough now that she hoped to see Nicholas in April—six months off—and on this distant meeting she must be building a foolish romantic structure—the little goose. The real facts never occurred to him. He knew that Miranda had been but three days in that shrouded house of mourning, and he had heard how during that time the widower had shut himself into the tower study with his grief.

'Miranda,' he said on impulse, 'why do you make yourself unhappy, always hankering after things you haven't got? Can't you be content here at home? This farm is beautiful—'

'Beautiful!' she repeated in amazement, looking around her.

The orchard where they stood was on higher ground than the farmhouse, which nestled like a white dove beneath hemlocks and the tall protecting elms. The fields, checkered by stone walls, undulated gently toward the sapphire strip of the distant Sound. A late October haze, faintly lavender, filtered the clear air and intensified the perfume of burning leaves. Maples on the Cat Rock Hills blazed red and gold, colors repeated even more strongly by a riot of sumach and goldenrod against the gray wall of the little burying ground. In the adjoining pasture Buttercup's bell tinkled rhythmically, as Seth guided her toward the barn and the evening milking.

'I suppose the country's pretty enough,' said Miranda vaguely, 'but it has no refinement, no elegance; and as for the farm—it's nothing but work.' She looked down at her hands. Despite her care they had reddened a little; two of her almond-shaped fingernails were broken off short.

'Work's not such a bad thing,' answered Jeff. 'There's joy in getting things done, in being useful. It makes a pattern. Bread that is worked for is sweeter far—' He shut his mouth, seeing that her eyes held the look of passive endurance which descends on a congregation toward the end of a tedious sermon.

'D'you think for one minute—' he shouted, suddenly angry, 'that your precious Van Ryn with his estates and his carriages and his idleness is as happy a man as I am, or your own father?'

He was pleased to see that he had startled her, but otherwise he produced no effect. She gave him an indulgent smile, and said softly, as though she did not want to hurt his feelings, 'I should never think of comparing you or Pa to Mr. Van Ryn in any way.'

'Miranda, you're—' he began, and then he laughed. There was no reaching her. 'Come and show me the rest of the farm, I'm interested in it even if you're not.' And taking her arm he helped her back over the stone wall.

Jeff stayed several days at the Wells farm, because on the night of his arrival the baby developed a virulent sore throat. Some hours later, the dreaded white spots appeared and the terrified Abigail, who had lost one child from this cause, did not need Jeff to tell her that Charity had diphtheria.

She did not need Jeff for diagnosis, but she needed him badly when the suffocating membrane threatened to close the little throat, and only his promptness in making and inserting a hollow reed to the trachea saved the child. Jeff and Abigail worked together for three days and nights, sponging, poulticing, and making inhalations of turpentine.

Miranda, who had never had the disease, was banished from the sickroom, despite her protests.

When it was all over, and Charity with the elasticity of childhood had started on a quick recovery, the family embarrassed Jeff by its gratitude. 'I'll never forget what you've done—never,' sobbed Abigail, exhausted by strain and relief.

And that night at family worship, Ephraim abandoned the chapters which should have been read in favor of the Good Samaritan. In his prayer he thanked the Lord devoutly 'for that Thou hast sent us one to succor us in our hour of need.'

Ephraim accepted Jeff's refusal of any payment for his services, because of the conviction that the young doctor would soon be his son-in-law. He was therefore amazed when Jeff mounted his horse one morning, and after warm farewells to each one of them, departed for Hudson without having asked permission to woo Miranda.

'I can't make it out,' Ephraim told Abigail that night in the conjugal bed. 'I made sure he'd speak for the lass, and she brightened up like a spring morning directly he got here.'

His wife sighed, turning restlessly on her pillow. She knew, now, why Miranda had brightened and that it had nothing to do with Jeff. Would that it *were* Jeff the girl loved. She and Ephraim were of one mind in that. But Abigail was loyal to her daughter—and there was that betrothal ring—Ranny had given her word elsewhere even if she had not, as she so patently had, given her love as well.

'I can't understand the young people nowadays,' Ephraim growled. 'Flighty, don't know their own minds.' A new thought struck him. 'Very like Jeff's gone home to make arrangements there before he speaks. He'll be back again. That's what it is.'

'Perhaps,' said Abigail faintly. She knew better than to upset her husband before it was necessary.

12

NICHOLAS ARRIVED IN GREENWICH ON THE SECOND of April, exactly one year from the day on which he had last seen Miranda. He went to Weed's Tavern on Main Street, found the accommodation offered him cramped and noisy, for his rooms fronted on the Boston Post Road, where market wagons, carriages, and stages continually clattered by; so he had his coachman make inquiries, got back in the coach, and traveled through spring mud up the North Street to Stanwich, where he took over the second floor of a little inn.

As soon as he was settled, and the flustered innkeeper, who seldom had guests nowadays, had unpacked for him, Nicholas ordered a glass of Madeira. Then he opened his writing case and began a note.

An hour later a stable boy delivered this note at the Wells Farm. It was addressed to Ephraim, who was sluicing his head and face at the pump preparatory to eating supper. He stamped into the kitchen, where Miranda and Abigail were laying the table. He held the note out in his wet fingers. 'I'll be consarned if this don't beat all!' he cried. 'Your fine Cousin Nicholas is stopping in Stanwich, and he's coming to see me on a matter of the "greatest importance." '

Miranda took one look at the well-remembered handwriting. The kitchen stove, her mother and father, spun slowly around her. She clutched the edge of the table and shut her eyes. Then quite suddenly she was calm. The long uncertainty was over. There would be trouble now, Pa would be difficult; but she knew that Nicholas could handle him, could do anything in the world that he wished to.

'What in tunket could *he* want?' grumbled Ephraim, running a comb through his beard. 'Ranny—' he turned to his daughter, but Miranda had slipped upstairs. The green silk dress, long unworn, was ready. She took it from the lavender-scented bag where it had hung, waiting.

She parted her hair and brushed it around her finger into curls on either side her face and rolled the rest into a heavy coil on the nape of her neck. She touched the heliotrope Cologne to her wrists and forehead, and when she stood fully dressed, she untied the silk cord and, drawing the betrothal ring from its hiding place, she kissed it and put it on her finger.

There was the sound of carriage wheels outside when she got downstairs. As she entered the kitchen, they heard a knock on the front door, the one that was never used.

Ephraim went to open it and all the family crowded after him into the chilly front room. He unbolted the door and Nicholas walked in. He bowed to Ephraim, paused by the threshold, his head nearly touching the low ceiling, while he searched the other faces which he did not know. Then he saw Miranda, who had held back, her heart pounding, her hands shaking, now that the moment had actually arrived.

Nicholas' face lighted, his eyes burned into hers as though he asked her a question which needed no answer except the expression on her face. He moved swiftly across the room and before the gaping boys and thunderstruck Ephraim, took Miranda's hand and raised it to his lips.

'What's the meaning of this, sir!' shouted Ephraim.

Nicholas released the girl's hand and turned to confront the astonished father. 'May I speak to you alone, Mr. Wells?' His tone plainly indicated that he was in a hurry to have done with a boring task. He made a gesture of dismissal to the others and they obeyed it at once; not even Abigail thought to look at Ephraim to see whether he also wished them to go. The door of the front room shut behind them.

'Well—' whistled young Nat, sinking into a kitchen chair and staring at his sister. 'So that's your Mr. Van Ryn! You're a deep one, Ranny.'

She stood proudly amongst them, her head thrown back, a little smile on her lips. Her whole body seemed to glow and bloom.

The boys gazed at her as though they'd never seen her before. Her mother glanced at her and felt a sharp dismay. This Nicholas was all that Miranda had said and more. She had never seen a man so handsome, nor one who seemed more masterful. There had been tenderness and the proper homage in his greeting of Miranda. You couldn't ask more of a husband than that he should be masterful and tender, especially when wealth and position went with it.

What's the matter with me, then? thought Abigail. She opened the oven door and turned the loaves. Come what might, the baking had to be done. The bread was doing well. She shut the oven and seizing a knife began to pare apples with vicious jabs. After the second apple she laid the knife aside. Might as well face it. From the instant that he had walked through the door into their house, Abigail had felt a queer revulsion, not quite fear but akin to fear. No reason for it, she told herself—but the feeling of recoil and apprehension remained.

'Get to your chores, boys—' she addressed her sons briskly. 'This matter doesn't concern you.'

They rose, pausing as they heard their father's voice raised in angry protest, and the calm slow tones which answered. Reluctantly they filed out, Tom to the evening milking, Seth and Nat to the woodpile. On the way they covertly examined the shining carriage, the sleek, beautifully matched horses, and the coachman, who entirely ignored the boys.

In the kitchen the two women drew closer. Miranda took her mother's hand and held it tight; a shiver ran through the girl's body as the parlor door burst open and Ephraim shouted, 'Miranda, come here!'

Nicholas stood at the fireplace, he wore his usual air of detachment; but Ephraim sat in his armchair, his fingers beating a tattoo on the table, and Miranda saw that his empurpled face showed not only anger but perplexity.

'He says he wants to marry you,' said Ephraim to his daughter, in a tone of grim disbelief. He drew his bushy brows together. 'Says you know all about it.'

She hesitated a second, then she nodded. 'Yes, Pa. I'm going to marry Nicholas.' She walked to the fireplace and smiled timidly up at her lover. His eyes kept their expression of controlled annoyance, for he found this scene with Ephraim tedious and unnecessary; but he put his arm around the slender waist and drew the girl to him.

Ephraim stared at them both and suddenly his daughter became to him a stranger. He hunted for words with which to confute these two, to forbid the marriage, to order Van Ryn from the house. But he could not find the words. There *were* no valid objections, as Nicholas himself had contemptuously pointed out.

'What d'ye think about this strange business, Abby?' Ephraim turned to his wife, who had followed Miranda into the room.

She too looked at the couple by the fireplace. Already she's gone from us, Abigail thought with pain, for the girl's face reflected some of Nicholas' remoteness and condescension. It seemed to the mother as though a black chasm had opened across the oak planks in the flooring and the two of them stood alone upon the farther side. She put her hand on her husband's shoulder. 'I think it is to be, Ephraim. And we must make the best of it,' she said quietly.

Ephraim made a few more protests, but he was helpless against Nicholas' implacable purpose, and Miranda's feverish desire. He was outraged to discover that the marriage arrangements had already been made. Nicholas had called at the parsonage and engaged the Reverend Clark for three o'clock on the next day but one, engaged him to come to the Wells farm.

'It's indecent, it's too soon!' roared Ephraim. 'And my girl must be married in church like a good Christian. I'll have no hole-and-corner wedding here.'

'Our marriage shall not be solemnized before a lot of gaping strangers,' returned Nicholas. He considered that he had already made sufficient concession in securing the Wells' own pastor rather than importing a Dutch dominie who would have been more suitable to a Van Ryn wedding. 'As for the day—' he continued, 'I can see no reason whatever for waiting.'

'But she has nothing ready—' put in Abigail. 'No wedding gown.'

'She needs nothing. There's an entire wardrobe awaiting her at my house in New York.'

Abigail's mouth tightened; she looked at Miranda, wishing that the girl would stick up for her rights, would insist on every bride's prerogatives of naming time and place herself. But the hazel eyes fixed on Nicholas were blind to everyone else.

Miranda was therefore married at three o'clock on Sunday afternoon, April the fourth, in the farmhouse parlor, with no witnesses but her family and Obadiah. Tabitha and her young husband huddled together in a corner behind the cherry desk, both bewildered by this extraordinary turn of events. I don't envy her, thought Tabitha, she'll be a second wife, and he's so much older. But she looked from Nicholas to Ob's patient, ox-like face and sighed unconsciously.

Outside it was raining hard, not a spring shower but a steady downpour from which drops spattered against the window panes with tiny hissing sounds. Dankness seeped through the parlor and found its way to Abigail's heart. She closed her eyes to shut out the picture of the minister in his black robe, Nicholas' erect back in dark blue, and Miranda in the green silk dress, very pale, making her responses in a muted, trance-like voice.

Green is unlucky for brides, thought Abigail. Not only the green dress, but everything about this marriage was unlucky. She was sure of it, though how or why she knew so surely she could not have told.

Ranny child—don't! don't! she cried silently to the slender figure. You'll never know happiness, you'll tear your heart out against him—

But the golden head bowed for the final prayer. It was already too late.

'Come, perk up, Abby,' said Ephraim, joggling her arm. 'No use wearing a long face now. The girl's made her bed and must lie in it. No doubt she'll do well enough if she obeys Holy Writ, looks to the ways of her household, and eats not the bread of idleness.' Now that the thing was done, he saw no point in further protests and misgivings.

Abigail had prepared a wedding supper, but Nicholas would not stay for it. 'I wish to leave at once. I want you alone,' he said low to Miranda. These were the first words he spoke to her after the ceremony. Nor had he touched her. But all during the hurried farewells his eyes were on her.

She clung to Abigail when the moment came, but Nicholas allowed her no time to feel the full sorrow of the parting.

'Come, Miranda,' he said, and indicated the waiting carriage where beside the open door the coachman stood, his cockaded hat in his hand.

'It won't be for long! I'll see you often, often!' she cried to the silent family group on the steps. They were now inexpressibly dear, all of them, even Ephraim and Tibby. Oh, what have I done! Why am I leaving them like this? Oh, Ma—darling— She stretched her arms out to them, in an abandon of longing, but Nicholas lifted her into the carriage. He shut the door, beckoned to the coachman. The horses started forward.

She flung herself to the window. Through the gray drizzle she saw the boys wave half-heartedly, saw Abigail pick up the baby and lay her cheek against the soft curls as though for comfort. They all turned, and for a moment the kitchen door stood open, outlining a rectangle of glowing warmth and light in the gathering darkness. Then the light vanished and the farmhouse melted into the twilight.

A sensation of unreality seized her. She leaned against the blue velvet cushions and closed her eyes. This is not I, she thought, it can't be that I'm married. When I open my eyes I'll be back in the little attic bedroom. Ma is down there in the kitchen setting dough, the baby is crowing in her cradle waiting for me to pick her up. Pa and the boys are out in the fields.

She opened her eyes and saw Nicholas watching her. She raised her left hand, staring in unbelief at the heavy golden band on her finger.

'Yes,' said Nicholas. 'We're married, Miranda.' His words increased her panic.

But I don't know you, she thought. How can I be married to you when I don't know you? Again she stared at the wedding ring. She saw another hand, a fat one with a gold ring not unlike this on its puffy finger, saw it lying on the black coverlet, clear in the light of two tapers. She made a small sound and shrank to the farthest side of the seat.

Nicholas' eyes narrowed. He put his hand on her shoulder, his fingers closed so that her flesh beneath the green silk was bruised. He pulled her to him and kissed her once. His kiss effaced Johanna as it effaced the memory of Abigail's strained face. She tasted fear and beneath the fear a strange and shamed delight. He released her and laughed.

'We'll soon be home,' he said. 'This is no place for love-making.'

She was hurt by his laugh, it was as though he had triumphed over her and having seen her submission had lost interest.

The cream-colored horses trotted tirelessly. When they reached the Post Road and turned west toward New York, the rain stopped, and the surface of the road improved so that they no longer bumped through puddles and mudholes. From time to time a cluster of lights emerged from the darkness and they slowed a little for the main street of a town, Port Chester, Rye, Mamaroneck; but soon each one was left behind and the night closed around them again.

'How did this year of separation pass for you?' inquired Nicholas, breaking the silence, and she understood from his tone that he wished her answer to be as casual as his question. She had yet fully to comprehend that he welcomed emotion of any kind only when it initiated with him, and that it amused him to control his own emotions as a chess player controls his pieces; but she obeyed his tone, saying as lightly as possible:

'Why, it seemed very long. I tried to keep busy. You—you were traveling, weren't you?'

'Yes. I went through the Canal to Lake Erie and then down the Mississippi as far as Memphis. But I found nothing in the West to interest me. Everything is barbarous and uncouth. I spent the past winter visiting friends on a plantation near Savannah. This type of life I liked better. In the South they have both culture and beauty.'

'Oh,' she said. How many girls he must have met during this past year, wealthy and beautiful girls; even Miranda, ignorant as she was about the geography of her country, had heard of the languorous and tempting beauty of Southern women. Had he ever repented of his promise to claim her, had he ever made love to any of those others—that dazzling multitude which she wistfully pictured?

He did not enlighten her. He talked instead of the plantation system and slave labor, of which he heartily approved. 'It's deplorable that our short-sighted laws no longer permit it up North,' said Nicholas, 'though it's true our climate's against the blacks' working efficiently.'

He talked of the loveliness of Southern gardens, of the charm of old cities like Savannah and Charleston, and the coach rolled steadily onward.

At Pelham he turned to her, saying, 'There's a tavern here where we can get some wine and food if you want to, though everything's prepared for us in town.'

She was chilled and faint, but she saw that he did not want to stop. 'No,' she murmured, 'I'm all right. Let's go on if you want.'

'Good,' he said softly, in the darkness. 'We shall go on.'

Go on to what? she thought, and panic broke through.

Last night when she had gone to the little attic room Abigail had tried to talk to her. 'Ranny—I hardly know how to—how to prepare you—' Her mother had paused, slow color flushing her thin cheeks. She had turned from Miranda, fixing her unhappy eyes on the room's farthest corner. 'You must submit to your husband, even if it—no matter what—you must do as he wishes. You see—'

'Yes, Ma—I know,' Miranda had interrupted. She too was embarrassed, but stronger than that was the feeling of desecration. Even her mother might not touch on any aspect of the miracle that was occurring, the unbelievable joy of her union with Nicholas.

She had stopped Abigail from further speech by running to her trunk and making pretense of last-minute packing. She remembered now her mother's look of pity and the sudden mist in the sharp anxious eyes.

She had resented the pity, thinking how little her mother knew of love, and that whatever marriage proved to be—and she had lied to her mother, for she had only the haziest idea of its intimacies—how could she fear it with Nicholas? Their love would make everything simple and easy, she had thought, forgetting how often she had feared him in the past.

And now they were married, and the magic ceremony had not yet transformed them into two different human beings as she had expected. She knew him no better than she had before. But it will be all right, she told herself. I'm foolish to feel frightened. All brides feel this way. Even Tabitha did, I know she did.

She gave a choked sigh, and Nicholas looked at her.

'We're nearly home,' he said. 'See, these are the lights of Yorkville; only three more miles.'

'Is your house right in town?' she asked, now as anxious as he for the relief of impersonal talk.

'Yes, and at the rate the city is growing it will be downtown soon. The house is built on the site of one of the Van Ryn farms, next to old Petrus Stuyvesant's own bouerie.'

'Oh—' she said, 'and what is a bouerie?'

He explained briefly that it was Dutch for farm, and while the carriage continued down the Post Road, which was now called Third Avenue, he pointed out various landmarks—the Potter's Field at Fiftieth Street, the dim bulk of the Croton Reservoir at Forty-Second Street, Peter Cooper's residence on Twenty-Eighth.

On Tenth Street they turned east to Stuyvesant Street and the horses, knowing their nearness to the stable, broke into a canter. She saw a flash of open iron gates, the curve of a short drive, and the carriage stopped before a large, three-storied brick house with a graceful white portico.

Nicholas took her arm and ushered her through the front door into a paneled hall which seemed to her, tired as she was and giddy with excitement and weariness, to be filled by bobbing, white-capped heads.

'This is your mistress,' said Nicholas, thrusting her forward, and a confusion of voices chorused, 'Welcome, Mrs. Van Ryn.'

Startled, she stepped back and looked behind her. Nicholas scowled, his grip tightened on her arm.

'Your servants are greeting *you,*' he said.

She stiffened, holding her cloak tight around her, forcing to her lips a faint apologetic smile.

The aprons and caps, the maroon liveries filed out.

'They're all strangers—' she whispered, while underneath her brain repeated dully, Mrs. Van Ryn. I am Mrs. Van Ryn. Miranda Wells is Mrs. Van Ryn.

'Of course,' he answered, leading her into a small breakfast room where a table was spread by the fire. 'I dismissed all the Dragonwyck servants. Eat now, my dear—' he indicated the table. 'You must be famished.'

'All those servants are gone,' she repeated, wondering. Tompkins, Annetje, Magda, all part of the Van Ryn household for years. Thank God they were gone: they would never have accepted or obeyed her. Was that why Nicholas dismissed them? Had he seen how hard it would have been for her? She looked at him gratefully.

'And old Zélie?' she asked.

"Zélie is dead. When I dismissed the others she refused to leave. She stayed on alone. The bailiff wrote that she died in the winter.' He moved to her side with a quick motion. 'Darling, this is our wedding night. Now that we are at last home, shall we not forget everything but us? Here's a glass of wine for you. Drink it.'

The supper was exquisitely prepared. There was cold capon in jelly, an oyster-and-mushroom patty, an elaborate frosted wedding cake topped by a spun sugar wreath of orange blossoms. But though the wine refreshed her a little, Miranda found that she could eat nothing. Nor did Nicholas; and seeing that she had not touched her food, he rose.

'Come,' he said.

Color drained from her face and her throat grew dry as sand.

They mounted the stairs through the quiet house; he threw open a door on the landing and led her into the room he had prepared for her.

He had had it redecorated in the Empire style: the finest woods both gilded and inlaid, azure satin draperies embroidered in rose. She saw nothing of this. It was the perfume of a hundred flowers that assailed her at the threshold, white roses and lilies which stood in porcelain vases upon the tables and shone with luminous whiteness in the light of long wax tapers. Two of these tapers had been placed in golden candlesticks, one on either side the bed. Her eyes slowly focused on these, moved to the masses of bridal flowers.

'Nicholas—no,' she whispered, throwing out her hands with a convulsive and imploring gesture. 'Oh, don't you see—the flowers and those candles by the bed— Don't you remember—'

She gave a cry as he turned on her, his eyes blazing. She thought he was going to strike her and she recoiled against the wall.

He did not strike her. He walked to the two tapers and blew them out. Then he came back to her.

'No—' she cried. 'No, no, please—'

He picked her up and threw her across the darkened bed.

At five o'clock the bells of Saint Mark's, half a block away, rang the hour through a cold and misty dawn. A faint light stole between the blue draperies at the window. She had been waiting for this, her aching, tearless eyes fixed on the windows, as they had been for hours.

She moved her body cautiously an inch at a time away from that other who slept beside her. With infinite care she raised her head, straining through the gloom to discover the things which she must put on. If she could assemble them, there must be some place that she could dress, some way to slip out. Though she had no money, her desperation would persuade someone, a teamster, or peddler, to take her along the road.

The light strengthened and she moved again nearer the edge. She raised herself on one elbow, and on the white skin of her arms and breasts were livid marks. She moved her head farther, calculating how she might slide from the bed in one silent motion; but her long flowing hair impeded her. She reached in back of her head and tried to loosen her hair, but she could not. She heard the difference in the quality of the breathing behind her, and she held her own breath.

Saint Mark's bell clanged once for the half-hour, and a chorus of chitterings arose from starlings who nested in the pear tree outside the window. She heard a distant cry on the street in front of the house. 'Milk, ho! Come buy my nice fresh milk!' The town was awakening. She must hurry, hurry, hurry—

She dug her fingernails into her palms. Stealthily as if it moved without her knowledge, her head turned and she looked down at the figure beside her.

Her terror ebbed in diminishing waves, leaving amazement. This was not the same man who had inflicted on her the lurid-streaked blackness of those hours just past, who had violated without pity her soul as well as her body. This was not the aristocratic lord of Dragonwyck, nor even the charming and responsive companion she had known once or twice. This was the sleeping face of a young and defenseless man; almost a boy he looked with his black hair rumpled as she had never seen it and the cruel lines about his mouth smoothed away.

He sighed a little as she stared down at him, and moved his hand. She saw then that his cheek and his right hand lay on her hair, and her throat tightened, for his unconscious position and movement were unmistakable. It was as though he turned in appeal, blindly seeking comfort in the soft masses of gold that lay outspread on the pillow.

His eyes opened and he looked up at her. She braced herself for the change to the expression she knew so well, the cold intensity that held no kindness. But he gazed at her quietly seeing the sharp inrush of fear in her face.

'Miranda—' he whispered, with pleading.

Still she hesitated, her body curved and poised for flight.

His lips twisted into the shadow of a smile, a smile tinged with sadness. 'You can't leave me,' he said. 'Don't you know that? Nothing but death will ever separate us.'

'No,' she whispered. 'I don't know. I'm afraid.' Tears began to roll down her cheeks.

He raised his arms and pulled her gently down to him. Her taut body relaxed. This is the way he really is, she thought. I must never forget that no matter what he does or says, he's really good and he does love me. It was the beginning of a long and painfully maintained self-deception, for the precise type of goodness and love for which her heart yearned had not existed in Nicholas since he was twelve, and his mother died.

13

THE FIRST WEEKS OF MIRANDA'S MARRIAGE WERE happy. Nicholas, during that period, was usually the husband she had dreamed of—tender and indulgent. The horror of her wedding night faded, for Nicholas showed her no more violence. She forgot her fears, and began to bloom with a softer and maturer loveliness. Her arms, her bosom, and her throat filled out, all sharpness disappeared from her face. Her beauty, no longer ethereal, became seductive, and was enhanced by the magnificent wardrobe which Nicholas provided for her. Some of this wardrobe she found ready waiting in the closets of her dressing-room. It had been made by Madame Duclos from the old measurements. But Nicholas also furnished her with a list of other shops, mantua makers and milliners, directing her to buy whatever she liked. She spent many hours reveling in the fairy-tale unreality of ordering not one, but six leghorn or satin bonnets trimmed with *point d'esprit,* imported French flowers, or the finest ostrich plumes. In her excitement she bought far more than she could hope to wear, even if she changed her whole costume five times a day, and she made some mistakes. She wasn't able to resist a vermilion taffeta dress which darkened her hair and dulled her complexion. But on the whole her natural clothes sense guided her. Nicholas put no curb on her buying orgy, saying: 'I want you to be well dressed, Miranda, as befits your position as my wife. Soon we'll begin to entertain a little; you must learn to take your proper place in society.'

This prospect frightened her, for Nicholas expected a great deal. She must be beautiful, cultured, and witty and she must be a brilliant hostess, so that the Van Ryn reputation for discriminating hospitality might not only be maintained but acquire added luster.

During Johanna's lifetime this hospitality had been largely Nicholas' concern; the first Lady of the Manor had had no interest in anyone who did not belong to the river families, and to all other guests had shown a passive indifference.

But from Miranda he demanded active co-operation. She must understand current topics: the stormy Oregon question, the annexation of Texas as a slave state, the immediate probability, in view of President Polk's attitude, of a war with Mexico. She must be able to discuss Mr. and Mrs. Kean's Shakespearean productions, the singing of Madame Borghese at Castle Garden, or Donizetti's new music for Sir Walter Scott's 'The Bride of Lammermoor.' She must be able to express an opinion on the remarkable results of mesmerism.

She must above all take an intelligent interest in the new books which were appearing from England: Sir Edward Bulwer-Lytton's strange romance, 'Zanoni,' a Mr. Thackeray's 'Notes from Cornhill to Cairo,' Mr. Dickens' scandalous treatment of America in 'Martin Chuzzlewit.'

Miranda raced through these as Nicholas gave them to her, paying dutiful attention to the passages he marked, for each morning after breakfast they went to the little study off the drawing-room for an hour of concentrated instruction.

He was a good teacher, stern over any negligence in her study, but gifted with the ability to make a subject vivid. She slipped easily into the pupil-teacher relationship with him at these times, and was grateful as she began to appreciate the completeness of her former ignorance.

She had little intellectual curiosity and she accepted all Nicholas' pronouncements without question. He said that Walter Scott's historical romances were overrated, and that Dickens' novels were vulgar, so she must waste little time in reading them. He was enthusiastic about Emerson's Essays; their militant individualism agreed perfectly with Nicholas' own conviction. He required that she learn by heart certain passages from 'Self-Reliance.'

'Let us bow and apologize never more. A great man is coming to eat at my house. I do not wish to please him; I wish that he should wish to please me. . . . A true man belongs to no other time or place, but is the center of things. . . . Let a man then know his own worth and keep things under his feet.'

This she accepted without question as applying to Nicholas or perhaps any man; it never occurred to her to make application to herself. But there was one sentence from the same essay which shocked her. 'As men's prayers are a disease of the will, so are their creeds a disease of the intellect.'

'Oh, Nicholas—' she cried when she read this. 'What a dreadful thing to say! Doesn't the man believe in God?'

He looked up from the book and regarded her with tolerant amusement. 'My dear child, no intelligent person believes in God. Only the immature and ignorant need a prop from without; there is no god but one's self.'

'I don't believe it!' she cried indignantly. It was true that the family prayers and incessant Bible reading had sometimes bored her, and that in church her mind often wandered, but she had guiltily recognized these derelictions as faults in herself; they had nothing to do with the eternal verities, Heaven, salvation, and God. 'You can't really mean that,' she persisted, thoroughly aroused. 'It's wicked, Nicholas, and if you aren't a true believer why do you go to church?'

His amusement deepened. He had never before seen her spirited and indignant. It became her. Her long eyes flashed hazel fire, her pouting mouth was mutinous. He shut the book, leaned back and crossed his legs.

'I go to church at Dragonwyck simply as an example to my tenants. The lower classes need idolatry, it steadies them.'

For the first time she felt resentment at this calm superiority which she had always admired. 'And what about me?' she said hotly. 'I believe in religion, is that because I've come from the "lower classes"?'

He shrugged his shoulders and stood up. 'Very likely, my dear one. But you'll get over it. I'll see that you do.'

'No—' she cried, 'never!'

He stood quiet looking at her averted head. She felt the changing quality of the silence.

'Come here, Miranda—' he said softly.

I won't, she thought, I won't go to him or look at him. She felt the power of his will beating on her. Her head turned. Slowly she raised her eyelids.

He sketched a brief motion with his arms, and while her mind still resisted, her body obeyed him. He embraced her with a roughness he had not shown her since the first night. But now his violence gave her a dark pleasure. She clung to him, yielding. At once he released her, withdrawing his arms so abruptly that she lost her balance and swayed against the table. He gave a short laugh.

'Arrange your dress, my dear, the servants might come in.'

She flushed scarlet, pulling up the shoulder of her blue morning gown. Even her humiliation was overshadowed by a sense of being degraded, of having lost part of her integrity. She turned from him and went to the window, staring blindly at the passers-by on the sidewalk outside the gate.

He watched her bent head, the white neck with its tendrils of gold curls, and his gaze softened.

'This afternoon, we might visit the American Museum,' he said. 'It's a pity that the theater season is over.'

She pressed her cheek against the window pane, not moving. I'm not a child, she thought, to be shamed one minute, and offered a treat the next. But she knew that Nicholas was making an extraordinary concession. She had longed to see Mr. Barnum's collection of marvels, whose fame had long ago reached Greenwich, but Nicholas had refused to take her. Such exhibitions were cheap and fit only for yokels.

Except for her drives in the closed carriage to the dressmaker, she had seen nothing of New York. Society had left them to the conventional seclusion of the honeymoon period; no one would call on the bride until signaled to do so by receiving invitations to a party.

She turned at last from the window and Nicholas met her with one of his astonishing changes of mood.

'Shall we pass the remainder of the day exactly as you'd like to?' he asked, smiling. 'You shall see whatever sights you want, and I'll not object, I promise.'

I'll never understand him, never, she thought, staring at his smile, which was frank, open, and almost gay. Impossible to believe that an hour ago he had been the impersonal schoolmaster, or that half an hour ago he had treated her to a brutal passion followed by indifference.

'Come, my dear one,' he said. 'What shall it be? Barnum's freaks? The minstrel show? The pantomime at Niblo's Gardens? Or all of them?'

'Oh, Nicholas, could we?' she cried, dazzled out of her resentment by this catalogue of amusements which she had longed to see.

He jerked the bell-pull. 'I'll order the carriage. You change to a walking costume, not too elegant, for I don't want you to be conspicuous.'

She chose a simple sapphire-colored cashmere with a modified hoop, black gloves and shawl, and a black satin bonnet trimmed with sapphire ribbons. She found when she joined Nicholas on the stoop that he was also dressed in a subdued manner—slate-colored suit, plain white shirt, and buff cravat.

'You look most charming for our democratic expedition,' he greeted her. He was then still interested and eager to please her. He had even ordered the open victoria, to which he usually objected because he disliked curious stares.

The May day was warm and brilliant; along Lafayette Street the budding elms and maples were tipped with fresh tender green. Geraniums bloomed in window boxes and reflected rose on the faces of the passers-by, who walked alertly, buoyed by the electric sparkle of the New York air in spring.

Miranda, basking in the sunlight, excited by the people, the motion of the carriage, and anticipation, pressed her gloved hands tight together in the old childish gesture of delight. The day was perfect. If only Nicholas doesn't—if only he—she thought, unwilling to be more specific. It would be foolish to spoil this pleasure by dread of the moods which transformed him between one minute and the next.

When they reached Mott Street, he said: 'It's after two. Shall we dine before we go to the Museum, and what sort of an eating place would you like? The Astor House, perhaps, or Delmonico's?'

She considered a moment. 'I'd like something different, please. Lots of people laughing, and music, and do you suppose I could have fried clams and crullers?'

He laughed. 'Certainly you may.'

'But—' she added, 'could we go to the museum first—Oh, look!' she cried, interrupting herself and forgetting that it was rude to point. 'What a queer-looking man! Oh, what is he?'

Along the eastern sidewalk there shuffled a figure in black silk with a high-necked jacket. His face was yellow, his arms were folded in his loose sleeves, a small black cap surmounted a shaven head from which dangled a long tail of coarse hair.

'That's a Chinaman, my dear,' said Nicholas. 'There must be about a hundred Chinese living in that section. The first ones came some years ago, when a Chinese junk sailed home without them. Our country,' he added with a trace of annoyance, 'is being overrun with all types of foreigners. It'll be increasingly hard for the ruling class to govern them properly.'

'Maybe they'll all mix up together,' she said vaguely. She knew little of the torrent of Irish, Germans, and Scandinavians which poured into New York. Still less of the black stream which flowed steadily from the Congo to the Southern States.

'Oh, there's the museum!' she cried, happily gazing at the high white building on Park Row. It was decorated with American flags, and painted on its façade, one between each window, were the oval portraits of impossible animals tastefully picked out in crimson and gold.

Nicholas dismissed the coachman, paid twenty-five cents admission for each of them, and they joined the crowd of farmers, sailors, immigrants, and children who had come to be thrilled by Barnum's marvels.

Miranda rushed from exhibit to exhibit, tugging in her excitement at Nicholas' arm but grateful for his protection and the expert way in which he opened a passage for them through the jostling throng. She was charmed with the 'Educated Dogs' and the 'Industrious Fleas'; horrified by the Fat Boy, the Giants, the Albinos, and the thirty-foot boa constrictor which lay torpidly coiled around a large egg. This egg, said a sign over the cage, contained 'a fearsome juvenile sarpint,' which added to the horror.

She was impressed by the Moving Diorama of the Funeral of Napoleon Bonaparte, and the 'very particular identical' club which killed Captain Cook in the Fiji Islands. Still more awed by an old colored woman, who doddered and chattered to herself upon a high platform. 'Joyce Heth,' said the sign, 'is 161 years old. She was George Washington's nurse, and used to dandle him on her knee.'

'How wonderful!' breathed Miranda, staring with all her might at this remarkable being who had bridged the distance from the dim historical past of the country to now.

Nicholas forbore to tell her that this was the third Joyce Heth so exhibited, her two predecessors having inconsiderately died.

At last they came to the gem of the collection. At the far end of the hall separated by red velvet ropes from the lesser attractions, General Tom Thumb dressed in full military uniform lolled upon a miniature golden throne. He was no bigger than a six-months-old baby, and although he was actually a child, his tiny good-humored face was shrewd and knowing.

'Oh, isn't he sweet!' cried Miranda, adding her bit to the chorus of feminine admiration. A heavy man with a beard stood behind the tiny General's throne; he looked sharply at Miranda and then at Nicholas, bent down and whispered in the dwarf's ear.

The little creature jumped up and advancing to the edge of his platform held out his hand to Nicholas. 'Mr. Barnum is honored to see you in his museum, Mr. Van Ryn,' he piped. 'Shall I dance the Highland Fling for you?'

The crowd drew back murmuring and staring at the Van Ryns. Miranda flushed at their sudden prominence, and not knowing that the great showman made it his business to recognize anyone of the slightest importance, felt a glow of flattered vanity.

Nicholas, however, frowned; but he touched the infantile hand, answering that they would be gratified to see the Highland Fling.

When the dance was finished, Nicholas hurried Miranda away before Barnum could come around in front and accost them.

'Yes, I'm ready to go. It's been splendid, but just one more exhibit, please, Nicholas.' She pointed to a red-and-white sign which said 'To the Egress' and was further embellished by an arrow which indicated a mysterious passageway. 'Oh, do let's see the Egress!' she pleaded.

He looked down at her serious, expectant face. 'Certainly, my dear. It's of all things what I most want to see.'

Delighted with his enthusiasm, and still unsated, she pressed ahead eagerly as they entered the dark hall which presently turned into a flight of stairs that ended in a door. This door precipitated them onto Ann Street.

Blinking in the sunlight, she looked around her. 'Where's the egress?' she asked, puzzled.

He gave one of his rare laughs and indicated the door. 'You just passed through it. That's Barnum's way of getting rid of the stupid crowds.'

You might have told me, she thought. Might have prevented me from making a fool of myself too. The trivial incident hurt her. If one really loved a person, one protected them from humiliation, one did not laugh. But he does love me, she thought fiercely. He is doing all this today just to please me.

And, indeed, Nicholas lived up to his bargain as he would always fulfill any program upon which he himself had decided.

They walked to Franklin Street and dined at Contoit's 'New York Gardens' at a small wooden table under a chestnut tree. A German band provided the noise for which Miranda had longed; she had her fill of fried clams and crullers and her first taste of beer. This plebeian fluid made her feel both sleepy and contented. The sleepiness passed, but the contentment sharpened into bliss, for it seemed that they had barely begun their rounds of diversion.

They picked up the carriage and drove to Palmo's Opera House to see the black-faced minstrel show. With absorbed attention she followed the jokes which flew from the end men to 'Mr. Bones'; her small slippered foot tapped time to 'Doo-dah, Doodah. Gwine to run all night. Gwine to run all day.—Bet my money on de bobtail nag—Somebody bet on the bay.'

And after that there was still Niblo's. Here they had ices and wine, before strolling through a gallery of paintings, and attending the Ravels' marvelous pantomime of Hades, complete with devils, ghosts, and skeleton deaths. Besides the theater and the picture gallery, Niblo's amusement palace offered an exhibition of exotic and indigenous plants.

'Here's something you'll really enjoy, Nicholas!' cried Miranda as they passed the entrance of the Botanical Hall. 'Though I guess they haven't anything as fine as you grow in Dragonwyck greenhouses. Look, there are orchids and camellias and oleanders.'

He was silent so long that she thought he hadn't heard her. She looked up inquiringly and saw that he was staring not into the perfumed dampness of the hall but at her. The coldness that she dreaded had suddenly appeared in his eyes, but they held as well a faint ironic questioning.

'Don't you want to see the flowers?' she asked nervously.

'Not particularly,' he answered. He drew out his gold watch. 'We'll be late for the pantomime if we don't hurry.'

He doesn't want to be reminded of Dragonwyck yet, she thought. The memories are still too painful. A jealous misery stirred in her. Since the moment of their meeting at the Wells farm neither of them had ever mentioned Johanna's name. Can it be, she thought with sudden anguish, that he misses her? No, it isn't possible. It isn't.

Is it because I'm so young and so ignorant of men that I never know what he is really feeling? she wondered as they drove home up Broadway. It was late; moonlight silvered the brownstone houses and the Gothic splendor of the newly completed Grace Church. It eclipsed the disheartened flicker from the gas street lamps. Few sounds disturbed the quiet—an occasional snatch of song or laughter from the shuttered houses, the steady clop-clop of their horses' hoofs on the cobblestones.

'Have you enjoyed yourself, Miranda?' he asked as the carriage turned east on Eighth Street.

'Oh, yes—' she cried. 'It's been wonderful!' And moved by an impulse of loving gratitude, she slipped her hand into his. His fingers remained slack and unresponsive, her hand lay unwelcomed.

She withdrew her hand and averted her head. The passing gas lamps blurred and ran together. Why did he act that way? Why wouldn't he respond to her simple, natural gesture?

A flash of bitter insight answered her. Nicholas was neither simple nor natural; these qualities were as absent from his treatment of her as they were absent from his complex personality.

She had not, as yet, enough introspection to realize that part of his fascination for her had arisen from his unpredictability, and her conception of him as a mysterious being from a superior world who had miraculously condescended to desire her. Nor did she realize how tightly she was enmeshed by his physical attraction, a bondage woven not only from the magnetism of his body but from the very fear and pain he caused her.

'You're crying, Miranda?' he asked in a tone of amusement. 'Kindly spare the coachman your sorrows anyway. It's a singular way to end what you assure me has been a happy day.'

She pressed her handkerchief against her mouth, controlled the shaking of her shoulders.

The carriage drew up to their stoop; she stumbled out before it had fairly stopped, frantic to get away, to be alone, locked into a room—alone. Her foot missed the carriage step and she fell to the gravel on her right ankle. She gave a sharp cry and Nicholas was beside her on the instant. He picked her up in his arms, carried her into the house and upstairs.

The ankle was not badly wrenched, and as the pain abated she watched her husband with amazement. For it was Nicholas who bathed and bound it for her, touching the swollen foot as tenderly as would a woman. He refused to call the maid and himself undressed her. He ordered port wine and held the glass, watching her anxiously while she sipped it.

When he had made her comfortable in bed with her foot on a pillow, he lay down beside her and drew her head to his shoulder. He held her without passion, as though she were a child.

How can he be so cruel to me at times—and then like this? she thought. And again her awakening perceptions gave her the answer.

He would hurt her himself, take pleasure in doing so, but he would not allow her to be injured by anyone or anything else.

A week later a few select members of New York society received engraved cards bidding them to a soirée and supper at the Nicholas Van Ryns' on Thursday, May the twenty-eighth, at seven o'clock.

Miranda's début was not to be a large affair and Nicholas had hand-picked the list: Schermerhorns, Brevoorts, and the Hamilton Fishes to represent the 'Knickerbocker' aristocracy. Old Philip Hone and his wife, because Mr. Hone who had once been Mayor of New York, was amusing, and went everywhere. After some hesitation all the Astors had been invited: the senile John Jacob, the William B.'s and their son John Jacob, Junior, with his fiancée, Miss Gibbes. That the Astors were the richest family in the country influenced Nicholas not at all, and certainly did not outweigh their lowly German background. But he approved the fine new mansion on Lafayette Place and young John Jacob's cool gravity. Moreover, his fiancée, Charlotte Gibbes, came from an excellent Southern family.

Any other host of Nicholas' standing would have stopped there or rounded out the list with a few more of the élite, the Aspinwalls perhaps or the Verplancks, but he was indifferent to the high boundaries which separated the sections of New York society, knowing that any gathering was enlivened by a touch of the exotic; accordingly he asked Madame Teresa Albanese, who had been singing at Castle Garden, Mrs. Elizabeth Ellet, a sharp-tongued poetess from the Ladies' Literati Group, and Herman Melville, a young sailor who had just published a book called 'Typee' which was startling the reading world not only by the originality of its vivid prose but by its titivating descriptions of naked Polynesian maidens.

For days Miranda had been worrying about the party which was to present her publicly as Mrs. Nicholas Van Ryn. Her nervousness overshadowed President Polk's declaration of war against Mexico. After all, everyone had expected the war, and whatever was happening was so far away in places with outlandish names, Palo Alto and Resaca de la Palma. In this she reflected Nicholas' own lack of interest.

'I believe that we have no particular moral right to declare war,' he said, 'but I daresay we'll win and the country will be much enlarged. At any rate there'll be another slave state for the South.'

'Won't the North mind?' asked Miranda, remembering the Abolitionist torchlight parade that she had watched from her window.

'Very likely,' he answered, shrugging. 'I don't doubt that the North and South will be at each other's throats some day.'

'You mean they'll fight each other?' she asked, startled. 'Oh, but they couldn't, it's the same country. Why can't things go on as they are?'

'Because men are fools,' said Nicholas, and changed the subject. 'By the way, the little Count de Grenier is back in New York. He arrived on the Celtic yesterday and sent me a note. I've asked him to the soirée. His wife didn't come with him this time.'

'Oh?' she said, diverted, remembering the plump Frenchman and his gaiety and compliments at Dragonwyck. How long ago it seemed! The night of the Fourth-of-July Ball! The Coryantis Waltz with Nicholas. That was when I first knew that I loved him, she thought, and there was pain in the memory. She had been happy that night for a while, but there had been humiliation too—from the Van Rensselaer girls—from Johanna.

'Nicholas,' she said abruptly, 'when are we going to Dragonwyck?' Her heart beat fast as she waited for his answer. Yet why should she be frightened of so natural a question? The Manor House was his real home, as it was now hers.

'Why, it won't be ready until the end of June,' he said. 'The workmen are there now, painting and making certain changes. I think we'll leave here in a fortnight and go to the Mountain House at Catskill to escape the heat before we go to Dragonwyck.'

She gave a sigh of relief. How silly she'd been! Imagining that he avoided not only the mention of Dragonwyck's name but any thought of living there. She was completely wrong, as she so often seemed to be with Nicholas. It's like Ma used to say, she thought ruefully; I've a head stuffed full of silly fancies.

She went upstairs to her writing desk and wrote a long, rapturous letter to her mother, detailing her happiness and Nicholas' virtues as a husband.

When Abigail received this letter three days later and first read it, she was reassured. She passed it on to Ephraim.

'Seems contented as a pig in clover. I told you to stop fretting about her,' he commented, handing the letter back.

But Abigail, again running her eyes over the flowing script, frowned. 'I don't know, though; she says almost too much. Seems like she was trying to convince herself as well as me.'

'Land o' Goshen, Abby!' snapped Ephraim, stamping to the door.

'If the Good Lord handed you a golden crown you'd worry for fear maybe it was plated. Ranny's happy and she says so. What more d'ye want?'

'Nothing, I guess,' said Abigail, sighing. She plunged her fingers into the soft feathers of the goose she was plucking when Miranda's letter arrived.

On the afternoon of the party, Miranda lay in the darkened bedroom and tried to rest. The hairdresser had come and gone and she dared not move her head for fear of disturbing his handiwork. Everything was ready, thanks to Nicholas and the staff of experienced servants, who neither needed nor welcomed her timid suggestions. 'Don't fash yoursel', madam,' said Mrs. MacNab, the Scotch housekeeper, when Miranda asked if the ices had yet arrived from the caterers. 'The Maister's given strict orders, and Sandy and me'll tak' care of ever-r-a thing.'

They treated her like a charming but useless child, and Miranda overcame annoyance with the realization that she was in truth completely inexperienced.

It would be fun to meet people, she thought with rising excitement, shutting her eyes determinedly, though sleep was impossible. Except on the day of their expedition, and on occasions when she had gone to services at Saint Mark's Church around the corner, she had during these weeks seen no one but the servants—and of course, Nicholas.

Not that, she told herself hastily, she wanted anyone but Nicholas. It wasn't that she was lonely, but sometimes she longed for a friend. Another woman with whom she might discuss silly things like clothes or embroidery stitches. With another woman one could laugh and say the first words that popped into one's head. Instead of being on guard, and anxious.

There was a knock on her door and Mrs. MacNab came in holding a letter. 'Just came for you, madam.'

From Ma! thought Miranda eagerly. But it wasn't from Abigail. The handwriting was unfamiliar and the postmark was Hudson, New York.

She broke the seal and looked at the signature. 'Jefferson Turner.' How strange that he should write to her! She had seldom thought of him since the week that he had stayed on the farm, and so compelling had been her preoccupation with Nicholas at that time that aside from gratitude for his help in saving Charity he had made little impression on her except as an instrument for delivering Nicholas' message.

My dear Miranda [said the letter]:

I have recently heard of your marriage. I confess it was a great surprise. I hope you'll be very happy.

When you come up-river, I shall not be here to congratulate you because I've joined the army and leave at once for Mexico. I don't know what sort of a soldier I'll make but I guess they need doctors anyway.

Please remember me to your family when you write. I hope all will go well with you. God bless you.

It had taken Jeff a long time to write that letter. He never would have written it but for the war, and the consequent knowledge that he was very unlikely to return. If a Mexican bullet didn't do the job, yellow fever or dysentery almost certainly would.

He had understated the matter when he wrote that Miranda's marriage was a surprise. He had been thunderstruck, then this emotion had given way to blinding anger, a veritable fury at Nicholas. The fury had been enlightening, and when he calmed down he faced its origin squarely. Jealousy, and a feeling for Miranda which would not in the least tolerate the thought of her as another man's wife.

Ephraim had not been far wrong when he had told Abigail that Jeff would return to Greenwich, for that had been in his mind. All along, Jeff realized now, he had been marking time, waiting for Miranda to recover from her obsession. And yet this feeling had stolen upon him so gradually that he had been unaware of it.

'Why in the name of all that's foolish do I want that girl?' he asked himself derisively when the news of her marriage shocked him into the knowledge that he did want her—badly. But being Jeff he wasted no time in moping. He translated his feelings into action. He would have enlisted in any case, not being troubled by any hairsplittings as to President Polk's exact motives. The country was at war, and he was needed. That was enough for Jeff. But a decided unwillingness to see Miranda ensconced at Dragonwyck as Nicholas' wife speeded up his decision.

Then he wrote to her.

Miranda, knowing nothing of this, was puzzled and touched by his letter. There had been antagonism between them from the first.

Even during his stay at the farm she had thought that he disliked her. Now it seemed that he did not.

She was still staring at the sheet of paper when Nicholas opened her door and looked in. 'You're not resting?' he said disapprovingly. He walked over to the bed. 'What are you reading?'

'A letter from Doctor Turner,' she answered. There was a pause. Nicholas stretched out his hand. 'Let me see it.'

She gave it to him, a trifle surprised. He never showed any interest in her letters from home. She watched him while he read and was puzzled to see tenseness vanish from his face, and in his eyes a fleeting impression of—what?—satisfaction—relief—she couldn't be sure.

He handed back the letter. 'I find his tone rather familiar. Since when does he know you well enough to invoke the blessings of deity upon you?'

'He spent a week with us at the farm last fall, you know,' she answered nervously. Nicholas' question had held the frequent note of irony; she wasn't sure whether he was really displeased or not. And if he were displeased at her receiving a letter from another man, why had there been that undoubted flicker of relief?

'I didn't know he stayed a week,' said Nicholas without particular emphasis. 'But he's a pleasant young man and a patriotic one, I see. No doubt you enjoyed his company—?' There was no mistaking the sarcastic inflection this time.

She turned her head wearily, settling back on the pillow. 'No—' she said, 'I thought only of you.'

The little Count de Grenier arrived first at the soirée. He had grown stouter during the year he had been back at Lyons directing the silk business, of which certain matters of export had required this new trip to New York. His plum satin suit and embroidered vest fitted him like the casing on a sausage, but his black eyes were as lively and curious as ever, his waxed mustaches quivered with the same zest.

He had been very much interested by the change in the Van Ryn ménage, and was impatient to see Miranda in her new rôle. When she came, preceding Nicholas down the stairs, moving with her own peculiar grace and hesitating a minute on the threshold to master her nervousness, his Gallic heart was overcome.

'But she's veritably beautiful!' he thought, jumping up to kiss her hand. 'She's incredibly changed.'

He saw at once as no man but a Frenchman would have that part of the change came from outward adornment; the cleverly cut white satin gown with black Chantilly lace ruffles, the touch of coral salve on the lips, the increased blondness of her hair, which she owed to the hairdresser's camomile rinse. And then, of course, the Van Ryn diamonds sparkling on her bosom! It was the first time that she had worn any of the jewels which had been presented to her by Nicholas; she had done so tonight only because of his express command. Her resistance had died away when she saw how becoming were the newly cleaned and dazzling diamonds, but the great ruby pendant, the pendant Johanna had worn on the night of the ball, she felt that she could never touch. She had never even lifted it from the jewel case.

The change in Miranda was, however, by no means entirely due to clothes or jewels or grooming. The Count examined her admiringly. Her voice had grown richer and lost its provincial tone. She smiled and murmured with surprising poise, 'I'm so happy to see you, Count.' And her long eyes no longer met his with transparent innocence.

She was waking up, the little one, as well she might married to this handsome enigma. He reluctantly released Miranda's fingers and turned to greet Nicholas.

Ciel, what a couple! Standing side by side in the doorway they were like one of Winterhalter's smooth, impossibly perfect portraits. But it was a fairy tale come true, this marriage!—Cendrillon—he thought—the fat wife considerately dies, and the little country mouse captures her rich and handsome prince. Now they will live happy ever after. Where but in this amazing country could Fate be so kind?

The Count continued to enjoy himself. He delighted Mesdames Schermerhorn, Brevoort, and Fish by his gallantry and compliments. He knew this type in France—solid, well-born matrons who were grateful enough for masculine attention while their husbands drifted together by the fireplace and discussed the iniquities of the administration, the progress of the war, or, with increased tempo, the convenient manner in which ancestral farm lands on Manhattan turned themselves into valuable city real estate.

That was the basis of all their fortunes, thought the Count, catching a phrase here and there while he amused Mrs. Fish with chitchat of Louis-Philippe's court. The Van Ryns' too. He felt a prick of envy, knowing that Nicholas had never had to think of money. He had an honest agent, shrewd enough to sell the Van Ryn holdings to an advancing city at good profit. But it didn't take much shrewdness. *Ça marche tout seul,* the Count reflected gloomily, and making graceful obeisance to the three ladies he maneuvered over to another group in the adjoining parlor. Here he found the Astor family clustered around old John Jacob, who persisted in going out of an evening though he invariably fell into a restless doze, his shrunken chin sunk on his chest, so that he presented to the company only a bald scalp, mottled brown with age.

The Count had met the Astors before on his previous trip and had not found them stimulating. William and young John Jacob were both tight-lipped and dour men who took so long to answer a question that the Count's volatile mind had forgotten it before they began. He had derived some amusement at parties in Paris from mimicking this trait of the richest family in America, but that was *vieux jeu* now. He bestowed an appreciative and sympathetic glance on Miss Gibbes, who was about to join her future to that of the sour-faced John Jacob, but then his eyes wandered.

Over in the corner near the rosewood piano he saw Miranda talking to a big man with an astonishing golden beard which gave him a Jovian appearance and conflicted with the youthful awkwardness of his gestures. Beside them sat a sharp little woman like a squirrel, her bright, malicious gaze fixed flatteringly on the bearded man, who seemed embarrassed.

I must see what's going on there, the Count promised himself, and cast around for some way to extract himself from the Astors.

This way Nicholas provided, for he came up to them with the Philip Hones and the Count was released. He paused long enough before starting across the room to admire the effortless way in which Nicholas managed his guests. By a word, a smile, or a question he amalgamated the three groups—the men by the fireplace, the forsaken ladies by the window, and the Astor family. Soon he had them all talking and even old John Jacob woke up and contributed mumbling comment.

He is suave, that Nicholas, the Count thought. When he wishes to be charming, he is irresistible. But I doubt very much that he always wishes to be charming.

He approached Miranda and her two companions. She rose at once and said: 'Count, may I present you to Mrs. Ellet, she writes such delightful poems, and this gentleman is Mr. Herman Melville, who has just given us that fascinating book, "Typee."—The Count de Grenier,' she added to the others.

Bravo, ma chère! the Count applauded her inwardly. This graceful introduction worthy of a duchess, except that duchesses always had bad manners, showed the vast distance she had come from the tongue-tied, nervous girl he remembered.

'I have heard of your so exquisite poetry, madame,' he said quite untruthfully, bowing to Mrs. Ellet. 'And it is a great pleasure to meet two American authors. I have longed for the opportunity.'

He examined Melville curiously. He had not read 'Typee' but he had heard of it, chiefly that it was indelicate according to the Anglo-Saxon standards set by the young English queen, and that it was so well written that most of the literary critics doubted that it could really be the work of an uneducated sailor.

'You have had an interesting life, monsieur,' offered the Count, for the bearded young man seemed disinclined to say anything.

'Oh, yes, Count,' cried Mrs. Ellet, clasping her hands in pretty pleading. 'Mrs. Van Ryn and I are just dying to hear all about Mr. Melville's experiences in the Cannibal Islands—too, too dreadful.'

Melville turned his massive head and contemplated Mrs. Ellet with calm, sea-colored eyes. 'The Marquesans are not cannibals,' he said, 'but I wouldn't blame 'em if they ate up the missionaries.'

Mrs. Ellet gave a piercing scream of laughter. 'Oh, my, how very droll you are! Why, I give five dollars every Sunday to send to the missionaries who convert the poor, naked heathen.'

'Then you'd better save your money, ma'am; they're much better off as heathen.' He lowered his gaze to Mrs. Ellet's *décolleté,* which revealed a great deal of craggy bosom. 'And they're no more naked than you are,' he added with emphasis.

The lady flushed furiously. The Count quivered with repressed mirth. But Miranda, horrified by this contretemps, for surely an accomplished hostess would have prevented it, brought out the first thing she could think of. 'Mr. Melville comes from a Dutch family too, you know,' she said hastily, with a confused idea of mollifying Mrs. Ellet. 'His mother was a Gaansevoort.'

'Indeed,' said the insulted lady, dripping ice.

'Ah, look who is coming, here!' cried the Count, tactfully creating a diversion and recognizing a familiar European figure. 'It is La Albanese herself. Now we shall have a treat!'

They all turned to see Nicholas greeting a vision in orange satin and rhinestones. The Italian singer radiated good nature and peasant vitality from her oily black hair to the broad feet on which she wore dirty red slippers.

She pumped Nicholas' hand in a cordial grip, seized Miranda's, and pulling the girl toward her crying *'Ah, que bella! La bimba!'* implanted a garlic-laden kiss on Miranda's forehead. She waved to the Count, whom she had met in Paris. 'So 'appy to see everywan,' she boomed, describing a sweeping gesture. 'Now I seeng for you.'

She surged over to the piano, leaving a trail of musk through the rooms. 'Who will accompanee me?' she cried, drawing a sheaf of music from under her arm.

'I shall give myself that pleasure, signora,' said Nicholas, bowing and seating himself on the stool.

Mrs. Schermerhorn raised her lorgnette and peered doubtfully at La Albanese. An Italian opera singer in the drawing-room! Most startling! In any other house she would have been affronted. But Mr. Van Ryn's reputation for conservatism and *savoir-faire* was impregnable. And his blood was of the bluest.

Before the rich earthy voice had finished the 'Casta Diva' from 'Norma,' Mrs. Schermerhorn had relaxed and was wondering if it would be possible to persuade Madame Albanese to appear at a little soirée next week.

Gradually according to their separate natures they all succumbed to the spell. The singer had great artistry, her flexible voice fell pure and true on the exact middle of each note, but far more persuasive than that was the vitality that flowed from her, the unashamed and wooing passion.

She gave them 'Voi Che Sapete' from the 'Marriage of Figaro,' and the mad scene from the new 'Lucia.' And the applause was much louder than the decorous gloved spatter expected in a drawing-room.

La Albanese bowed, flashing a toothy, delighted smile. 'Never 'ave I seeng so good,' she announced, beaming. But she knew what none of the audience had enough musical knowledge to guess, and she swept 'round dramatically, extending her hands to Nicholas. 'But eet ees you who inspire me, signor. You play *con fuoco, con amore—maraviglioso!* Nevaire do I teenk to find soch playing een America.'

'You do me too much honor, madam,' murmured Nicholas, smiling.

Tiens, thought the Count, craning to see his host, who was hidden behind the music rack, that's true. Who would expect to find so much fire and brilliance in a man like that? The Count ran over to himself the many social gatherings he had attended in this country. At none had he ever seen a gentleman concern himself with music, beyond lending an embarrassed tenor to a duet with a young lady. Piano playing was entirely relegated to the fair sex. And yet no one could possibly think Nicholas effeminate.

He was unclassifiable, thought the Count crossly; like all his countrymen he liked analysis which resulted in things being neatly labeled and docketed.

'Now I geef you a song een Eenglish,' announced Madame Albanese proudly, and the Count moved his chair a trifle so that he might see Nicholas.

The diva sang Maritana's plaintive ballad, 'Scenes That Are Brightest,' contriving somehow to invest the trite words and simple melody with an indescribable pathos. The tragedy of vain hope, of unfulfilled love.

During the singing of this ballad, the Count saw Nicholas turn his head so that his intense blue gaze rested on Miranda's averted face. There was longing in that look, an appeal. But when the girl shifted her position, unconscious of his glance, his eyes fell quickly to the music.

So, after all, maybe there's something not right between those two, the Count reflected. Suddenly he was bored with his own speculations and delvings. *Zut alors,* he said to himself, stretching his plump legs, I make mysteries like an old woman. He wondered how long it would be until supper.

He had not long to wait. The recital finished with a gay Italian folk song; then amidst the chorus of appreciation, Madame Albanese bowing and smiling made her way to Miranda. 'I want the W.C.,' she announced with simple Latin realism. 'Weel you show me ze way?'

'Oh—oh yes,' stammered Miranda, blushing scarlet and hurrying the prima donna from the room.

More embarrassment awaited her upstairs, for her guest gave a cry of delight when she saw the bedroom. She admired the curtains, the rugs, the bed. 'Your 'usband mus' be verra fine lover,' said La Albanese enthusiastically, patting the bed. 'I can tell. You are lucky, *bambina,* and verra happy. No?'

For a moment Miranda was outraged, and then she responded to the genuine friendly interest in the shining black eyes.

'Of course,' she said, 'very happy.'

La Albanese frowned, unsatisfied. 'But you are too serious!' She put her large orange silk arm around Miranda, enveloping the girl in scent and garlic and good will. 'Look, *bimba*—In my country we have a—how you say?—a proverb. *Amare, cantare, mangiare.*—Loving, singing, eating—these are God's three gifts. You don' need more.'

Miranda smiled. How wonderful it would be if life were as easy as that! But why can't it be? she thought suddenly. And under the influence of that vibrant personality, she felt lighthearted and gay.

When they got downstairs the guests were starting toward the dining-room. Nicholas came over to her and whispered, 'Everyone is delighted with you. The party is going well,' so that her new mood was easy to maintain, and she found herself talking and laughing at the supper table, all nervousness forgotten.

Nicholas had placed Madame Albanese between the Count and Herman Melville, knowing that the other gentlemen might find her a bit overpowering. But Melville did not; he talked with animation and from time to time his laugh boomed out. Whereupon Mrs. Ellet glared at him across the table.

She was placated, however, when Nicholas asked her about Edgar Poe, in whom she had a proprietary interest. The lady bridled, shaking her sparse ringlets. 'Poor Mr. Poe. Such misfortunes—his little wife—dying, I fear—and they've moved miles out in the country to a positive hovel.'

She lowered her voice to a piercing whisper which immediately stopped all other conversation at the table. 'I feel so sorry for him —his terrible failing, you know—too dreadful; and then this scandal with Mrs.— Oh—' she cried with a little scream of confusion. 'Everyone is listening!'

Everyone was, but with a collective start they began politely to talk of other things. None of them except Nicholas had much interest in the poet's misfortunes; they had simply been hypnotized by Mrs. Ellet's whisper.

Nicholas, however, felt otherwise, and to Miranda's astonishment, for she thought Mrs. Ellet a vulgar and unpleasant woman, he engaged her to drive out to Fordham with them on Monday and introduce them to the Poe household.

'But why, Nicholas?' Miranda asked him later after the guests had gone. 'Why are we going to meet the Poes, and don't you think that so much of Mrs. Ellet's company will be tiresome?'

'I do,' he answered. 'But we can hardly appear there without someone to introduce us.'

'But why go at all?' she persisted. The expedition seemed to her highly unattractive, a hovel in the country, a drunken, and some said unbalanced, man with a wife who was dying of consumption.

Nicholas' mouth set. He disliked being questioned, nor was he accustomed to the slightest opposition to his arrangements. She sat before her dressing-table brushing her hair, which fell like a rich gleaming mantle nearly to the floor. In her cream lace négligée she looked very fresh and lovely, and she had behaved well tonight, had profited to perfection by his careful coaching. He suppressed the sarcastic and final reply which he had been going to give her. 'You wouldn't understand, my dear,' he said.

She put the brush down and turning on the satin seat looked up at him. 'Why wouldn't I?' she cried passionately. 'Why do you always shut me out? Tell me sometimes what you're thinking and feeling, before—' she stopped. She had nearly said 'before it's too late.' How had so much emotion been aroused in her by so little? No wonder he stared at her.

He was silent for a second, then he pulled his violet dressing-gown closer around him and sat down in a chair opposite her.

'My love,' he said, smiling, 'I had no idea that my motives in wishing to meet Poe were so important to you. I'll gladly explain them. I admire the man's genius, I sense in his writings a strong kinship with my own mind; they have a macabre quality, a voluptuous flavor of mystery and evil which attracts me strongly. And I am curious to see his present degradation. It interests me.'

His ironic voice ceased, and she made a hopeless little gesture, while tears came to her eyes. Her mind was closed to the meaning of his words, some of which she did not know—'macabre,' 'voluptuous.' She had thought for a moment that he was really going to confide in her, to answer her appeal with frankness at last. It never occurred to her that under the masking lightness of his tone he had told her the simple truth.

And he, seeing this, laughed. 'Come, my pretty one. It's very late. Go to bed and don't perplex yourself with matters you don't understand.'

14

ALTHOUGH MIRANDA DID NOT KNOW IT FOR THREE years, the visit to the strange and unhappy little household at Fordham had far-reaching effects on her life.

On Monday she and Nicholas dined very early at one, picked up Mrs. Ellet at the exclusive boarding-house where the lady resided when she visited the city, continued up Broadway, crossed the Harlem River, and arrived at last upon the Kingsbridge Road.

The day was exceedingly hot, typical of this summer of 1846, which was to be the hottest that New York remembered. Inside the closed brougham it was oppressive and made Miranda feel languid; she and Mrs. Ellet both used surreptitious handkerchiefs to remove tiny beads of perspiration from their upper lips. But Nicholas, who seemed impervious to temperature, was cool as usual while he questioned their guest on the various recent accomplishments of 'the starry sisterhood,' as the feminine literati, Mrs. Anna Cora Mowatt, Margaret Fuller, Mrs. Osgood, and Anna Lynch, had come to be known to the irreverent.

Eliza Ellet considered herself a whole blazing constellation amongst the starry sisterhood and was delighted to tell him of the salon's brilliance, even more delighted to recite little snatches of transcendental verse which she had herself indited 'in that hushed hour between midnight and dawn when Morpheus' sable hands touch the rosy finger tips of Aurora and even the fairies are slumbering on their flowery couches,' said Mrs. Ellet with a rapt look.

But she spoiled this pretty fantasy by an uncontrollable sniff, and sudden, glistening pallor. 'It's so warm, and there seems to be an odor of—' she paused, '—of boiled ham.'

'Oh, I'm so sorry, Mrs. Ellet,' said Miranda, rousing herself, for the transcendental snatches had not held her attention. 'It must be the hamper we're taking to the Poes. You know you said it was the custom to take them something.'

A large wicker basket crammed with provisions, a roast chicken, a game pie, calves'-foot jelly, and the offending ham had been placed under the seat. At the last moment Nicholas had added a bottle of port wine and a bottle of brandy. 'The port for the invalid, and the brandy for Poe,' he explained to Miranda.

'Oh, but Nicholas—should we take spirits to him—if he has that—that failing?' she had protested.

'I hear he's far more interesting when he's drunk, and I intend to find out,' said Nicholas.

She did not feel quite the shock that this speech would have given her two months ago; she was living in a new country where the moral precepts that had formed her conduct no longer prevailed.

Now, while with courteous apology that his guest should have been made uncomfortable, Nicholas spoke to the coachman and had the hamper moved outside to the box, Miranda rested her head against the cushions and thought: I suppose I'm too serious. Madame Albanese said so.

The Poe cottage was not a hovel, but a small workman's frame house with two doors and a porch wreathed in jasmine and honeysuckle. It stood on a slight rise of ground under a shading tulip tree, bees droned around the honeysuckle, and as the Van Ryn carriage approached, the monastery bells of the near-by College of Saint John clanged melodiously on the hot, still air. There was here a paradoxical effect of rustic peace.

Paradoxical, because there was no peace within the house where a dying girl and a half-crazed genius were ministered to by the harassed and kindly mother, Mrs. Clemm. She hurried out of the kitchen door to greet Mrs. Ellet, who introduced the Van Ryns.

'Happy to see you, I'm sure,' said Mrs. Clemm. 'Eddie likes company, and my poor Virginia does too, though this is one of her bad days—poor lamb. Doctor Francis is with her now.' She sighed, her plain middle-aged face puckered with anxiety. She was immaculate in her black dress and white cap with long lappets, but the dress was shiny and frayed, and Miranda noticed with pity that Mrs. Clemm's right shoe had split and been neatly mended with a piece of plaster painted black.

'If Mrs. Poe is ill—perhaps we shouldn't intrude?' said Nicholas, at the same time motioning to the coachman to bring the hamper.

'Oh, no, it'll do 'em good, poor children, to see you and dear Mrs. Ellet. Come on in, do.'

She accepted the hamper gratefully without false pride, just as she accepted the Van Ryns' visit. A good many people found their way out to Fordham—literary critics, editors, and feminine admirers—and it was on their occasional contributions of food and delicacies that the family largely subsisted. For poor Eddie never seemed to make any money, and somehow or other he always seemed to get at odds with the men who could help him.

Mrs. Clemm ushered the visitors through a tiny whitewashed passage onto which opened a cubbyhole of a bedroom. There were but two other downstairs rooms, the kitchen and the parlor, both meagerly furnished and small, but all was scrubbed and shining with cleanliness, the checked matting on the sitting-room floor, the whitewashed walls, even the low raftered ceiling.

Virginia lay on a makeshift sofa by the window; her little wasted body hardly raised the covering quilt. Her face, of an unearthly pearly white, was framed by black hair, glossy and neat from her mother's careful tending. Her eyes, brilliant with fever, were upturned to the elderly physician who sat beside her holding her wrist.

As Mrs. Clemm motioned the others into the room, Poe rose from the rickety writing table where he had been hunched in apathetic despair. How short he is! thought Miranda, surprised, for she and Mrs. Clemm both topped him by inches, and Nicholas' height completely dwarfed the poet.

She had come to judge all masculine appearance by the standard of Nicholas' classically etched features, and though many women had found Poe attractive, Miranda did not. His high forehead bulged beneath straggling dark locks and seemed to overwhelm his mouth and chin so that his sallow face was pear-shaped. His mustache was unkempt; ill-health and misery had lined his skin, which was slack beneath his eyes, gray eyes which could be magnetically piercing and alert, but were now dulled by a recent dose of laudanum. He looked much older than his thirty-seven years.

His greeting of Mrs. Ellet was unenthusiastic, for he knew her to be a malignant gossip whose tongue was largely responsible for the blackening of his platonic relationship with Mrs. Osgood. Miranda, seeing this coldness, wished more than ever that they had not intruded themselves on the distressed family, but Poe's dullness lightened and his tone warmed when he turned to the Van Ryns.

'It's good of you to make the long drive from the city,' he said, bowing to Miranda, and shaking Nicholas' hand. 'I'm sorry that we are at some disadvantage in welcoming you.' He indicated Virginia's couch.

'I admire your work immoderately, Mr. Poe,' answered Nicholas at his most charming, 'and I couldn't leave the city without giving myself the pleasure of meeting you and telling you so.'

Poe was at all times susceptible to flattery, and he brightened still further at the sincerity in Nicholas' voice.

'You've read some of my stuff?' he asked eagerly, adding with bitterness, '"The Raven," I suppose. Such fame as I have appears to rest entirely on the plumage of that gloomy bird.'

'I've read everything you've ever published,' replied Nicholas, obeying the other's motion to seat himself on one of the stiff-caned chairs, 'both fiction and poetry. I find your stories provocative and fascinating, although I confess that I prefer the verse. There it seems to me that your genius reaches its highest peak.'

Poe thought so too, and when he found that Nicholas actually knew most of his poems by heart and could quote even from the obscurer ones, those which the public had long since forgotten, 'Tamerlane' or 'The Sleeper,' the gratified poet pulled his chair over and conversed animatedly.

While the two men talked and Mrs. Ellet hovered beside them trying to interject literary appraisals and daintily turned appreciations of her own, Mrs. Clemm drew Miranda to the couch, where the doctor had finished his examination.

The sick girl looked up at Miranda. 'So nice of you to come and see Eddie—' she whispered. 'How pretty you are—' she added, with naïve sweetness.

Miranda smiled, and clasped the transparent little hand. She was touched by the patience and gentleness of the childish face. For though Virginia was actually older than Miranda, neither poverty nor illness had aged her: she was the same docile child who had married her cousin Eddie ten years ago.

'I'm sure you'll be better soon,' said Miranda, and knew immediately how hollow was that conventional phrase, for the red spots of the consumptive rushed to Virginia's pale cheeks, a paroxysm of coughing shook the small body, while the handkerchief she pressed to her mouth was flecked with scarlet.

'Come away, ma'am,' said the doctor brusquely to Miranda. 'She mustn't talk just now.' He took the girl's arm and propelled her toward the kitchen.

'No room to sit in here,' the doctor explained in answer to Miranda's look of surprise. 'Too many people already.'

It was true, the sitting-room's three chairs were occupied by Mrs. Ellet, Poe, and Nicholas, while on the far side Mrs. Clemm bent over her daughter, whose eyelids were drooping with exhaustion.

'Well, well—' said the old man as they entered the kitchen, and his eyes twinkled. 'That poor creature in there's right. You're a well-shaped piece of woman-flesh, m'dear. Glad to meet you. My name's Francis. John Wakefield Francis. Expect you've heard of me, hey?' And he chucked her under the chin.

Miranda drew herself up, but it was impossible to resent Doctor Francis. His bonhomie, his genial appreciation of pretty women, and his vigor were only equaled by his generosity. His professional skill and purse were always at the command of the needy.

'I don't think—' she began. 'I've been in New York such a short time—' And yet his name did have a reminiscent ring, though she was positive she hadn't heard it recently.

'Sad household here,' said the doctor, shaking his gray head. 'Sorry for all of 'em. Poor worms. Nothing but failure and trouble and sickness. Guess you don't know much about those things—hey?' He peered at her rose moiré dress, her lace-covered bonnet, the pearl earrings and brooch.

'No,' she answered with a little inward shudder. 'I guess I don't.'

'Never be worth a damn till you do meet trouble and lick it,' said the doctor, suddenly thumping the table with a stubby and not very clean hand. 'Can't live soft all the time or you turn to mush. You don't want to be mush, do you?'

'No,' she said, laughing. She saw that the doctor thought her to be a pampered society girl, and this delighted her.

She had then eliminated all taint of the potato farm, the drudgery of manual labor. And it was Nicholas who had translated her, she thought with gratitude.

'I'd sell my soul for a cup of tea,' muttered Doctor Francis, seizing a poker and rattling the stove's grate. 'Long drive back, lot of patients to see tonight. Don't suppose you know one end of a teakettle from the other?'

She hesitated. A girl brought up as he thought she had been would never have been able to handle that balky stove. It would be easy to say no, to settle back with her hands folded and wait for Mrs. Clemm to come to the kitchen after finishing with Virginia.

But the old man looked tired, and also he reminded her of someone; somewhere below the surface of her mind there was a quiver of recognition, though as yet it sent up no conscious certainty. But the quiver was pleasant.

'Give it me,' she said, and took the poker away from him. She tied a clean cloth around her waist to protect the swelling rose skirts from the stove. In a very short time the kettle was boiling.

'You're not so useless as you look, my beauty,' said the doctor. 'Here's the tea.' He pulled a packet from his sagging pocket. 'Wouldn't do to use any of their tea—doubt they have enough for themselves.'

At the precise moment in which she poured his tea for him, Miranda recovered the buried memory. Last fall in the farm kitchen at home, she had poured like this for Jeff on the night of his arrival when he had bored her with talk of cholera—and Doctor—surely it was Doctor Francis!

She sat down on the other chair, startled—not by the coincidence, nor by the fact that despite the difference in age there was some resemblance between the two physicians, but by her own emotion at thinking of Jeff.

'Do you know a Doctor Jefferson Turner of Hudson?' she asked eagerly.

'To be sure I do!' the old man answered. 'But how do you—aye, I forgot, you Van Ryns live up-river there. Jeff Turner came to see me last year. I dunno as I ever took to anyone right off as I did to him. He's a splendid boy and a damn good doctor. I offered to set him up in New York, like to've kept him near me, but he's got some bee in his bonnet about caring for the community where he grew up. And he don't give a hang for money.'

'No,' she agreed, half-impatiently. From the beginning, Jeff's frank contempt for the Dragonwyck luxury in which she had reveled had caused friction between them.

Doctor Francis pushed his cup back with sudden explosiveness. 'This plagued war! Don't suppose you know, Turner's gone down to Mexico. Don't blame him, 'd go myself if they'd have me. But it's foul waste to let a boy like that get killed.'

'Oh, I guess he won't get killed,' she said, smiling.

A gust of anger swept the old man. He glared at her. 'What do you know of war, ma'am? Come to that, what d'ye know of life? You and your kind 're wrapped a foot thick in cotton wool; because your own precious hides are safe, you think there's no such thing as danger, or blood and death.—Of course he can get killed, and likely will be because he's got guts. He'll not only be out on the battlefield tending to the wounded, but he won't rest until he gets a crack at the enemy himself.' He stopped and said in a quieter voice, 'What's Jeff Turner to you, ma'am, anyway?'

Miranda averted her eyes. She had been staring at the angry old man with startled dismay. I don't know, she thought, what Jeff is to me.

'A friend,' she answered, at last.

His image rose before her now, the sandy hair, the gray eyes which quickly kindled into humor, the powerful hands that could be so gentle in touching a sick child, and with this image the feeling of confidence and the unsentimental sympathy which were as much part of him as his body.

'Yes, a friend, I think,' she repeated slowly. 'He made a lot of trouble for my husband on the Manor, but he also saved the life of my baby sister.'

The old doctor snorted. 'Both just like him!—Well, ma'am, I must be going. Likely you're dying to join that metaphysical-poetical confab that's going on in there.' He pointed a stumpy thumb toward the sitting-room. 'Sorry I bellowed at you. Pretty young things like you aren't really required to face unpleasantness. Might spoil that Dresden-china complexion.' He pinched her cheek, picked up his pill bag, and went out the kitchen door.

Miranda got up and washed the teacup, put another stick of wood on the fire, and straightened the tidy kitchen. She was anything but anxious to join the 'confab' in the other room. The familiar tasks which she had despised, this homely little room, seemed to her a momentary resting place in which to gather strength before plunging again into the tempest of dark emotions which whirled her around Nicholas.

Knowing him, as she was beginning to know some aspects of his nature, it was amazing that he had permitted her to be out of his sight so long. It could only mean that his interview with Poe was proving exceptionally interesting.

When she finally opened the low door into the other room, she saw that this must be so. Nicholas motioned her with his eyes to sit down, but paid no further attention to her. The two men had moved their chairs around the table, and in the middle of it stood the brandy bottle, half-empty, and two glasses. Mrs. Clemm had taken Virginia to the bedroom and stayed there with her. Mrs. Ellet, ignored by the two men, had moved to the vacated couch, where she sat fanning herself with irritated little flaps. Her malicious gaze missed nothing of the scene at the table, and she was mentally arranging its recounting. 'Poe was positively intoxicated, my dear! You never saw anything more shocking. Even after the first glass. I could see that poor Mr. Van Ryn —a gentleman to his finger-tips of course—was as embarrassed as I.'

Miranda quietly sat down on the third chair. Little light came through the small windows now, for the sun had dipped below the hemlocks which bordered the Kingsbridge Road. Shadows had gathered thick in the corners of the room, but there was still light enough to see the deplorable change in Poe, the constant tremor of his sensitive hands, the twitch which pulled at his slack lips and the glitter of his staring eyes.

Miranda turned her head away in horrified pity. Inexperienced as she was, she knew that this was more than simple drunkenness. The very smallest amount of alcohol acted as a violent poison on the poet's precariously balanced system, disintegrating all control.

And Nicholas sat there at his ease, his arms folded, gazing at the spectacle before him with sardonic interest. He had himself taken but a quarter-glass of the brandy.

Poe raised the shaking glass to his mouth. 'Fame!' he cried thickly. 'I said I despised it. 'Twas a lie! I dote on it.' He lurched forward, the glass fell from his hand and shattered on the floor.

At the crash Mrs. Clemm hurried in, took in the situation at a glance. 'Oh, Eddie dear, how could you again, when you promised!' she cried, catching up the bottle. She gave the guests a look of mortified apology.

'Don't take it away, Muddie!' Poe clutched the substantial arm feverishly. 'It's anodyne—the liquid Nepenthe. Give it back. Fool woman—give it back. Don't you see that with that golden liquid I become a king—a god? It points me the path to the skies, to the Lethean peace of the skies!'

'Yes, Eddie dear,' said the old woman, stroking his forehead. 'That's from your new poem, isn't it. Why don't you read it to them?' She hid the bottle behind her, pulled out the table drawer and extracted a quantity of foolscap.

'Pray do, sir,' said Nicholas, crossing his legs. 'We should be greatly honored.'

The poet scowled, shaking his head from side to side, his hand still clawing at Mrs. Clemm's restraining arm. Then from the bedroom came the sound of Virginia's agonized coughing.

A spasm of terror passed over Poe's face. His head jerked and was still, but his wild, unfocused gaze gradually sobered.

'Read them the poem, Eddie,' repeated the motherly voice. Through long experience, Mrs. Clemm had discovered this recipe for bringing him to if he had not already entered that terrifying borderland where no human appeal would reach him for days. She vaguely understood that his unintelligible poems—for she never could make out what they were about—represented an outlet for the misery which tortured him, an outlet like the far more dangerous liquor.

She sighed with relief as the clutching hand fell from her arm to the sheets of foolscap on the table. He jerked them toward him.

'The skies they were ashen and sober;
The leaves they were crisped and sere . . .'

His voice at first harsh and incoherent slowly gained timbre. Soon each syllable was accentuated with delicacy, each word rounded to the fullest melody. From his actor parents he had inherited the talent of communicating emotion to an audience.

Mrs. Ellet ceased fanning and leaned forward. They were all hushed —even Nicholas—as the voice throbbed and deepened in the weird evocative cadences.

It was 'Ulalume' that he read to them. The elegy that foreshadowed Virginia's death and the recurring defeat of his own soul.

The first stanzas meant nothing to Miranda, except for their inescapable music.

'And now, as the night was senescent
And star-dials pointed to morn—
As the star-dials hinted of morn—
At the end of our path a liquescent
And nebulous luster was born . . .'

But it was in the next stanza that the meaning caught her. It was as though the voice with its interpretation swung wide the iron gate and precipitated her into the mists beyond—'the region of sighs.' Sadness engulfed her like a shroud, sadness and an eerie foreboding. For a few seconds she was held by fear like that she had felt in the Red Room, and each word seemed directed at her.

'But Psyche, uplifting her finger,
Said—"Sadly this star I mistrust—
Her pallor I strangely mistrust:—
Oh, hasten! Oh, let us not linger!

Oh, fly! let us fly!—for we must."
In terror she spoke, letting sink her
Wings till they trailed in the dust—
In agony sobbed, letting sink her
Plumes till they trailed in the dust—
Till they sorrowfully trailed in the dust.'

Miranda, without conscious will, turned her frightened eyes to her husband. For the space of a heart beat that phrase echoed in her own soul, 'Sadly this star I mistrust.'

She made a slight motion, and Nicholas, seeing it, smiled at her and shook his head in warning not to disturb the recitation. Reality came flooding back. She relaxed. Here was nothing but a small roomful of people and a drunken, though eloquent, poet.

In her reaction, she listened impatiently to the rest of the poem, thinking it unnecessarily gloomy. She had had enough of this morbid, poverty-tainted little cottage. She was sorry for them all, terribly sorry; but she longed for the spacious elegance of her bedroom. Her head had begun to ache and the heat grew steadily worse.

'Well I know, now, this dank tarn of Auber,
This ghoul-haunted woodland of Weir.'

The poem was finished.

'Magnificent!' said Nicholas heartily, and to Miranda's relief he stood up.

'Too utterly divine—' observed Mrs. Ellet, also rising. She touched Poe's hand gingerly with her fingertips, murmured that it had been a great pleasure, gave a loud disapproving sniff directed at the brandy fumes which permeated the room, and scurried out to say good-bye to Virginia.

'It's not right yet—there are many changes to make,' said Poe dully. All vitality had drained out of him, his speech was sluggish again. He made a couple of futile pencil marks on the manuscript, then his head sank forward onto his outstretched arms. His breathing grew stertorous.

'Poor Eddie,' said Mrs. Clemm. 'He'll sleep it off now. Tell me, sir.' She looked up at Nicholas pleadingly. 'Did you really like the poem?'

'I think it one of his very best.'

The anxious face brightened. 'Would you help a little to get it published? I know you don't have anything to do with such things, but if you could just say a word here or there? Mrs. Gove heard it and she said she'd try.'

'I shall be most happy to,' answered Nicholas, and they left Mrs. Clemm to the tending of her two sick children.

That evening when Miranda and Nicholas sat down to late supper in their cool dining-room, she summoned the courage to ask him the question which had been in the back of her mind on all the long drive home.

'Was the visit what you expected, Nicholas? Are you glad we went?'

He put down his coffee cup and frowned into space. 'The man is worthless,' he said contemptuously, 'but I envy him his dreams.'

'His dreams—' she repeated, not understanding.

Nicholas nodded, but he shut his mouth firmly and did not explain. The man Poe had disappointed him. Nicholas had hoped for a kindred spirit, one as unhampered by petty morality or the conventional attitude toward evil as Nicholas knew himself to be. Instead he had found despicable weakness, a sick man clutching at his mother and crying out for anodyne, a man terrified by the thought of death.

There had, however, been one rewarding moment during the conversation with Poe, who had unknowingly suggested an unusual avenue of escape into the mystical realms of power and increased consciousness. An avenue not to be compared with the muddy downhill path which liquor represented. Some day, thought Nicholas, perhaps I shall experiment.

'Could you send the poor things some money—? Anonymously, of course,' said Miranda, seeing that Nicholas was through with the subject.

He shrugged and picked up his coffee cup. 'The sooner the wife dies the better for everyone, I should think, but I'll have Bronck send them something if you wish.'

She was as anxious as he to forget the Poe household and she soon did forget it. But as it was with Nicholas, one legacy from the visit remained with her. Hers was the memory of the unexpected pleasure she had felt in that dismal little kitchen at talking about Jeff. And the doctor had disturbed her. Though she did not think of Jeff very often, she nevertheless took to reading the war news. And whenever the casualty lists were published she scanned them anxiously, reaching the bottom name with deep relief.

15

BY THE MIDDLE OF JUNE THE HEAT HAD SETTLED into a succession of broiling days and muggy nights. Even in the Stuyvesant Street garden there was no relief, for the city pressed around it too close. Street smells—manure, garbage, and dust—completely overpowered the garden's mignonette and roses. All noises were magnified, the harsh shouts of the street vendors, the rattle of wagons on the cobblestones. And through that stifling air the bellowing of doomed cattle penned in the great market at Forty-Second Street added to the sleep-shattering confusion.

Everyone who could left the city, and the Van Ryns with them. On a Thursday morning Nicholas and Miranda boarded the Reindeer and started up the Hudson. They were to disembark at Catskill Landing, and proceed twelve miles by stage to the Pine Orchard Mountain House.

Miranda had hoped that as long as Dragonwyck was not yet ready Nicholas might take her traveling. During the past fortnight they had gone to parties given by the Schermerhorns and the Astors where Miranda had met many people with more ambitious summer plans than theirs. Some were going to the ocean at Rockaway Beach, some to the White Mountains; two couples were even going as far afield as Niagara Falls and Lake Erie.

'How I should love to see the real ocean! I never have, you know—or Niagara Falls, Nicholas,' she had said wistfully, but he would not consider any change of plan. He had had his fill of traveling during the year of their separation, and besides, he wished to be in the vicinity of Dragonwyck so that he could be present on the July Rent Day and oversee the opening of the house.

'We might go up to Saratoga for a few days if we tire of the Mountain House,' he said, and that was the end of the matter.

I suppose I was greedy and ungrateful to want more, she thought, leaning against the Reindeer's mahogany rail and watching the Palisades slide by. How strangely different this was from her first trip up the river! The boat looked much the same as the one on which she had sailed then; but the Swallow, the graceful Swallow with its name bird so bravely painted in blue on the wheel box, was now nothing but a mass of rotting timber at the bottom of the Hudson. The Swallow had raced the Express once too often, and the year before had split herself in two on the rocks of a tiny island called Noah's Brig. A dozen people had been drowned.

I wonder, thought Miranda, if I had a premonition that day, when the racing frightened me so. By turning her head she could see a corner of the deck almost identical with the recess on the Swallow where Nicholas had placed her on that other June day two years ago—a shabby figure in brown merino, clutching the farm basket and wearing that hideous cheap bonnet. How dazzled she had been by the boat's carvings and archways, chandeliers, red plush carpets and statuary! The Reindeer was even more elaborate, but now Miranda was accustomed to magnificence.

She looked down at her blue moiré traveling suit, watching the bell-shaped hoop sway in the fresh breeze. This costume had cost a hundred dollars, and she had not even thought it expensive. That other girl who had sat in the corner there would have been horrified, despite her love of clothes, at the thought of paying such a sum. It was as much cash as the farm often brought in in a year.

How I've changed! she thought; but beneath the surface pride of that thought was disquiet. She had her heart's desires, everything that the Miranda of two years ago would have considered a paradise—wealth, position, and Nicholas. Why then should she suddenly remember a Spanish saying she had read long ago in 'The Gipsy's Revenge,' one of those idiotic books she used to borrow from Debby Wilson: 'May all your wishes come true, and may they all curse you!'

I don't know what's the matter with me, she thought impatiently, and turned from the rail as Nicholas approached. 'Come to dinner, my dear one,' he said gaily, drawing her arm through his. 'The captain is waiting for us in his cabin.' He was enjoying the trip. He had a deep feeling for the stately river which flowed by his manor, and though he shared little else with most of mankind, he shared that feeling of holiday freedom which a boat ride gives.

In the deserted passageway before the captain's cabin, he bent down and kissed her. It was the type of tender kiss that any newly wed husband might give his cherished bride. She entered the cabin, glowing and happy.

The happiness lasted through the bustle of landing and the tedious ride in the stage up the mountains to the hotel.

The Pine Orchard House on South Mountain was considered one of the noblest wonders in the East. All foreign visitors were taken to see it as a matter of course. Harriet Martineau had written of it that she would rather have missed the prairies, the Mississippi, or even Niagara than this. The Mountain House's fame rested not on its excellent cuisine, nor its elegant Greek-revival façade with the thirteen white Corinthian columns, nor yet on the Beach family's efficient management; it exalted the romantic nineteenth-century heart by its location on the edge of a twenty-five-hundred-foot precipice and in consequence its spectacular awe-inspiring view.

When Miranda walked through the hotel and stepped out on the piazza, she gasped, as everyone gasped. The Hudson Valley lay spread out beneath her, its fertile fields stained mauve in the sun's afterglow. Eight miles to the east the great river, diminished to a brooklet, curled like a silver shaving from Albany to Rhinebeck. Fifty miles away in Massachusetts the Berkshires thrust dark, irregular humps against the horizon. From time to time a trailing cloud mist floated by, obscuring the farms so far below, and accentuating the feeling of dizzy height.

'Flying must be like this—' sighed Miranda. Always intensely affected by her surroundings, it seemed to her that living in the presence of that view one could be eternally joyous, one would get nearer to God, who had lately receded to a nebulous vagueness where her hurried and self-conscious prayers did not reach. Nicholas' amused contempt for religion had had its effect. She no longer read her Bible at all, and she had skipped church on the last three Sundays. Not that Nicholas prevented her from going exactly, but there did seem to arise many difficulties; even though Saint Mark's was around the corner from the town house, he insisted that she be accompanied by one of the servants and take the carriage. Nor would he go with her himself. Moreover, she was gradually sleeping later and later in the mornings, for there were social events in the evenings, and even when there were not, Nicholas was seldom ready to retire before midnight.

Her lifetime training had not been disrupted without a feeling of guilt. But here in this heavenly place, she thought, buoyed by that youthful conviction that a change of location inevitably produced inward change as well, here all would be simple and easy.

For some days she rejoiced in everything—their three-room suite, the coolness of the mountain air, the well-dressed, pleasant-looking people whom she saw in the dining-room at meals, or in the ballroom during evening concerts, or on the piazza, rocking and enjoying that wonderful view. She longed to meet some of these people, the young couple from Charleston, the noisy Benton family—mama, papa, and four assorted children who had traveled here from Boston and never tired of amusing the dining-room with humorous accounts of that journey—or even the trio of placid old ladies who pre-empted one corner of the piazza in which to knit and rock and sip lemonade while they gossiped.

But Nicholas, it seemed, had no intention of fraternizing with anyone. He snubbed one or two tentative overtures, and after that they were left to themselves. This remoteness produced no hostility, everyone knew they were on their honeymoon, but it did increase the other guests' interest in the romantic couple.

When they entered the dining-room all conversation ceased until the head waiter had ushered them to their private table. Every feminine eye sharpened to see what toilette Mrs. Van Ryn would be wearing this time. The two of them were so conspicuously handsome, so much the embodiment of the aristocratic bridal couples one read about that even the men were interested and listened tolerantly to their womenfolks' admiration.

Two weeks passed quickly, for though there was no relaxation near Nicholas, neither could there be boredom. It was in fact for dullness that she unconsciously longed, a slackening of the tension. Nicholas' comparative indifference to the marriage relation, an indifference which had lasted for weeks and which she in her innocence assumed to be normal, gave place again to violent passion.

These opposing cycles were to continue throughout her marriage, and it was not surprising that she never learned to anticipate them, nor dared receive either mood with anything but submission. Marriage, she thought, must always be like this, and if it weren't, there was no way of finding out. One would die rather than speak to anyone about such subjects.

Often there was the dark shamed pleasure, but always there was pain, and she felt that her body was to him only an instrument without personal identity. But one must submit, out of fear—for the slightest resistance increased his brutality; out of duty—a wife should always obey her husband. Under these lay like a layer of granite beneath quicksand the fundamental reason—the willing enslavement of her senses and soul.

On the first of July Nicholas told her that he was going to leave her next morning for three days, and she felt a wave of quickly suppressed relief.

'I've given orders for you to have all your meals served in the sitting-room while I'm away,' said Nicholas. 'Naturally I don't want you to appear alone in the dining-room.'

She knew it was useless to protest, but she was disappointed. She had vaguely hoped to make friends with the Benton family or even one of the nice old ladies who sat on the piazza. If only I had someone to talk to, she thought, and then reproached herself. A bride did not yearn for outsiders.

They were in their sitting-room now, having breakfasted, and her eyes turned to the window. The morning sun gilded the valley beneath; so clear was it today that behind the Berkshires appeared the shadowy peaks of the White Mountains. The glory of that view had been a constant joy, but now for three days it would be her only companion as well. It was, she thought with a faint, dismal humor, a good deal to ask of scenery.

'Come, my dear,' said Nicholas, ringing for the hotel valet, 'let's get dressed for our walk.'

This was the usual morning procedure; they had explored all the mountain paths for miles around.

Nicholas had sent his servants to Dragonwyck to help in preparing the house, knowing that the excellent hotel service would be sufficient for their needs. Miranda indeed had little use for a personal maid; she enjoyed caring for her lovely clothes herself. Her skill with the needle always gave her pleasure and she consumed many happy moments in running fresh rose and blue ribbons through her ruffled undergarments, in pinning sachets of heliotrope or verbena in the bodices of her gowns before hanging them away in the capacious closets. But there was a great deal of laundry and pressing to be done as well, petticoats to be starched, body linen daily renewed, morning caps freshened with the pinking iron, and this she could not do herself. This work was attended to by one of the two chambermaids who were assigned to their suite; silent automatons in calico aprons and mob caps who had no individuality for her except that she had noted that one of them was very young and walked with a slight limp.

It was this maid who presented herself this morning in response to an angry ring. For Miranda, on examining the freshly laundered pile of linen from the night before, had discovered that a ruffle on her best India muslin négligée had been scorched to shreds, then clumsily sewn together in a transparent effort to hide the damage.

'Do you know how this happened?' asked Miranda sharply, pointing to the gown.

There was no answer. The maid twisted her hands in her apron.

'Well?' Miranda persisted more quietly. 'Did you do it?'

The girl was painfully thin and nondescript, the pink uniform hung slack on her undernourished body, the perky mob cap was askew on lusterless brown hair. The square face with its prominent Celtic cheekbones made a dim setting for the staring, frightened eyes.

Miranda waited and at last the girl moistened her lips.

'The iron was too hot, mum—please don't tell, mum. They'll turn me away without a character.' She swallowed, her jerking hands twisted the apron into a ball. 'Oh, lady dear,' she added in a choking voice, 'I'm terrible shamed to be a-spoiling of your pretty things, but I'd niver a flatiron in me hand till I come here.'

Miranda put the scorched gown on the bed. 'Should you be doing the pressing if you don't know how?'

'No, mum.' The girl hung her head, she looked up at Miranda through black lashes, a faint impression of the irrepressible Irish twinkle appeared. 'But they don't know that, mum. Sure and I had to be telling a bit of a fib to get this job, the blessed saints forgive me.'

To her own surprise, Miranda felt attracted by the girl; she was appealing and might be pretty if she didn't look so much like a starved kitten.

'Is the job so important to you, then—what is your name, by the way?' she asked.

'Peggy O'Malley, mum, and I'm fresh off the boat last month. Sure and I'm as green as the shamrocks that grow in the fields at home, but as to the job, mum—' she sobered again, the light went out of her eyes. 'It's all I have in the wor-rld, my job. And not so easy to get for me.'

Miranda suddenly remembered the limp. No, it wouldn't be easy for a raw Irish immigrant to find another situation, especially when there were such hordes of husky, able-bodied ones to choose from.

'I'll mend the ruffle, Peggy, and you'll be more careful, won't you?'

The girl seized Miranda's hand and kissed it. 'The saints bless your kind heart, mum. I'll try ivery iron on me own skin before I touch it to anything of yours.' She bobbed a curtsy and hurried away down the hall. Miranda watched the girl's pathetic effort to control the twist of the right leg and pity awoke a new train of thought.

When she and Nicholas had taken the path toward North Mountain and the Artists' Rock, she brought up the subject. 'What happens to all these Irish who keep coming into the country? I mean, is there anything for them to do but go into service?'

Nicholas was amused. 'Since when do you concern yourself with social problems, my love? Why, they can go to the manufactories, I suppose.'

'But the working conditions are awful there!' she cried, remembering a farm girl who had left Greenwich to go and work in a weaving mill near Hartford. The girl had come back six months later with consumption, and a horrifying account of working in darkness and filth, sixteen hours a day with no time for rest.

'No doubt,' said Nicholas.

She would have pursued the topic, for her imagination was caught by that girl, who even younger than herself struggled alone in a strange land to force a living from a country which would be hospitable only if she allowed herself to be exploited.

But shouts and screams of laughter assailed them from around a bend in the path. The irrepressible Benton family from Boston flocked into view. The children in pantalettes and round straw sailors swarmed over the rocks like monkeys, snatching at wild flowers and shrieking. The smallest, a five-year-old boy in a pinafore, shrieked as loud as the others, but his scramblings were impeded by a small Spaniel puppy which he hugged to his chest.

The parents, in stout boots and dust coats, followed more sedately, but they made nearly as much noise as their offspring. 'Willie!' screamed Mrs. Benton to her youngest, 'come away from that tree, there's poison ivy. Samantha—see the pretty butterfly! Girls, put your gloves on again at once, you'll get warts! Willie, put doggie down; you'll hurt him squeezing him like that.' As Willie reluctantly obeyed, Mrs. Benton discovered the Van Ryns. 'Oh,' she cried to her husband in the same piercing tone, 'here come the honeymooners. How romantic!'

Nicholas made an exclamation of annoyance. 'Let's turn back,' he said to Miranda, ignoring the fact that they were already surrounded by Bentons. The lady bore down on them beaming, determined not to miss this excellent opportunity for meeting the unapproachable couple. She had held out her hand and begun,

'Isn't this a superb day for a stroll—Mr. Van—' when everyone was electrified by a blood-curdling yell from Willie. Its anguish quieted the other children who ran up.

'Oh, what is it, dearie?' cried Mrs. Benton, frantically feeling her child for injuries.

'Doggie, gone—' sobbed the little boy, pointing at the cliff beside the path. Everyone peered over the brink. There was a sheer drop of twenty feet and then a ledge. On this ledge lay a small brownish blob, and a faint whimpering noise came from it.

All the children began to cry; Willie buried his face in his mother's bosom. The puppy's doom seemed certain.

Mr. Benton tugged at his side whiskers and blew his nose. 'Poor creature,' he said. 'Hush, children. We'll get another doggie.'

Willie raised his swollen face, his eyes dilated with horror. 'You got to get him, Papa, you can't just leave him there. He's *crying*. I hear him.'

'It's impossible, Willie,' answered the father, peering down the cliff, and made brusque by his own distress. 'No one can get him.'

'I'll get the dog,' said Nicholas.

All the children stopped crying, and stared with their mouths open.

'It's very good of you to offer, sir,' said Mr. Benton, 'but I couldn't let you risk your life for a puppy. Besides, it's quite impossible.'

Nicholas raised his eyebrows. 'I never undertake to do anything that I can't carry out.' He took off his coat. 'Kindly give me your two coats.'

Confused, the two Bentons silently took off their long dust coats. Nicholas knotted them together with his, fastened one end to the root of a sapling.

'Nicholas, don't—please don't,' whispered Miranda.

He paid not the slightest attention to her. His mouth was set, his black brows drawn together, but his eyes held a glint of excited exultation. She had seen that expression before—on her first trip up the Hudson when the boats had raced each other, and the night when he had confronted the anti-renters.

The combined coats reached far down the cliff, and as Nicholas started down them hand over hand, Mrs. Benton gave a shriek and shut her eyes. 'He'll be killed—'

Miranda's heart hammered against her ribs as she watched, but she had no real doubt that Nicholas could do it. She knew so intimately the reserves of power that dwelt in that taut body, his ability to control his muscles by the force of his will. She realized, as the terrified Bentons never could, that his apparently miraculous descent of that cliff-side was possible because he had no fear and, unhampered by that, his quick eye and quicker brain could discover and use foot- and hand-holds in the rock's irregular surface. In sixty seconds he had reached the ledge and tucked the puppy into the bosom of his frilled shirt.

In two more minutes he stood again beside them on the path, his breathing scarcely quickened.

'That was m-marvelous, sir,' stammered Mr. Benton. 'I don't know how to thank you.'

The children clustered around, gazing at Nicholas with awed hero-worshiping eyes. He put the puppy on the pine needles, where it gave a little whimper and feebly licked at his hand. 'I daresay it will live; the bush down there broke its fall.' He put on his coat.

While Willie cradled his puppy, crooning to it and kissing the furry ears, Mrs. Benton joined her husband's paean of gratitude and admiration, but Nicholas would not stop to listen. He smiled briefly, and taking Miranda's arm hurried her down the path to the hotel.

'I'm so proud of you,' she whispered, when they had rounded a corner and the Bentons were left behind. 'Oh, Nicholas darling—I didn't think you—' In the aftermath of the excitement she felt sobs rising in her throat. She would not have thought it in his nature to risk his life for a puppy and a small boy's misery. He was then not as indifferent to sentiment as he professed to be.

'Won't you stop hurrying and let me tell you how brave and wonderful you were,' she said coaxingly, for Nicholas had not turned his head and continued to stride down the path. He did pause now.

'Miranda, my dear one, I applaud your wifely flutterings, but let's not wallow in syrup.'

Her hand dropped from his arm. For a moment she knew doubt, but only for a moment, then her consuming desire to believe in his essential goodness reassured her. Men were always embarrassed by reference to their brave deeds; to minimize them even with anger was natural.

'All right,' she said, smiling up at him, 'I won't say another word. But just the same it was a grand thing to do.' Never had she loved him so much.

Her conviction that she had found a secret softness in his character sustained her through Nicholas' cold refusal to recognize the Bentons, who had naturally expected that the morning's episode would establish acquaintance with the Van Ryns. It sustained her too through his indifference to the recovery of the puppy he had saved.

On the following morning at seven, Nicholas left the hotel by stage for Catskill Landing and the boat to Dragonwyck. After he had gone she moved restlessly around their rooms, unable to settle down to the few activities which Nicholas had permitted her. She might go out for a walk at eleven, but otherwise he expected her to remain in their suite. Young Mrs. Van Ryn must not wander unescorted around the public rooms of a hotel.

Well, there were letters to write home, plenty of books to read, and a copy of *Godey's* in which to study the latest fashions. There was her embroidery tambour on which she was creating a masterpiece of garden flowers in colored silk. And there was the view to admire. Enough diversions surely for three days.

But as the morning passed, she found that none of them appealed to her. Gradually she realized that part of her restlessness came from physical discomfort. There were fleeting twinges of nausea, a heaviness in her stomach.

Could it be the fish last night? she wondered. She went to the marble-topped washbasin behind the screen in her room and searched amongst the bottles of lotion and toilet water. There were so many that she had forgotten what they all contained, but she had no real hope of finding any medicine. Both she and Nicholas enjoyed superb health.

I must send out for some of Hutching's Stomach Bitters, she thought, remembering Abigail's pet remedy for digestive disturbance. The effort of ringing and giving the order seemed, however, tremendous and she lay down instead.

After a two-hours sleep she awoke feeling much better and extremely hungry. She ordered for herself an immense dinner, roast beef, cold tongue, chicken in aspic, cream kisses, and syllabub. When this meal arrived and the waiter had set the round table in the parlor, she found that after a few mouthfuls all her appetite had vanished. The sight of the laden dishes and hot plates revolted her.

She pushed back her chair and rang for the waiter, who had gone elsewhere on business of his own thinking that he had a clear hour at least before Mrs. Van Ryn could possibly do justice to that meal. So it was Peggy that answered the bell.

'Yes, mum?' she said, curtsying. 'You'd be wanting something?'

Miranda nodded, gesturing feebly toward the food. 'Get rid of this stuff please—at once!' She leaned her swimming head against the antimacassar and shut her eyes.

Peggy gave her a puzzled look and obediently limped to the table.

She looked at the thick slices of rare beef in the congealing gravy, the mountain of fluffy mashed potatoes down which ran rivulets of butter, the half ox tongue, the jellied chicken garnished with truffles, and she made a queer little sound.

Miranda opened her eyes. 'Whatever is the matter, Peggy? You can't clear away all those dishes yourself. Get the waiter—'

'Yes, mum.' The voice was muffled, and surprise pierced through Miranda's concentration on her own discomfort. Tears were rolling down the little maid's cheeks.

'Peggy!' cried Miranda starting up. 'What *is* the matter!'

The other girl bit her lips, began piling the dishes under the Britannia metal covers. 'It's just my foolishness, mum. It came over me all at oncet how just one wee part of all this, would've—'

'Would have what?' persisted Miranda, putting her hand softly on the maid's shoulder.

Peggy raised her head. 'Mither and the baby died of starvation on Saint Patrick's Day,' she said dully. 'There's famine in Ireland, mum.'

Miranda stared at the girl appalled. There had been occasional newspaper mention of food shortage in Ireland, but it hadn't impressed Miranda, nor as yet the rest of America, which would not begin to ship cargoes of corn meal to the starving people for another year when the potato blight had reached devastating magnitude.

'But that's awful,' she stammered, feeling how inadequate were any words to express sympathy for a condition she could hardly imagine. An abundance of food was an automatic part of life, plain food at the farm, elaborate dishes with Nicholas, but always plenty.

She realized how cruel it seemed to Peggy—this lavish display of food which had been wantonly ordered to no purpose.

'You're not hungry now, are you?' she cried, looking at the thin arms and cheeks.

The other shook her head. 'The pigs feed better here, mum, than does the Earl of Kenmare at home. Only it's hard to eat when you've lost the knack and your heart lies heavy as a millstone.' She looked up at Miranda with her quick sideways glance and smiled sadly. 'For why must I be ever worriting you with me troubles, I wouldn't be knowing, mum; it's the kind, beautiful face that you have.'

'I wish I could help you,' said Miranda slowly. Money, she thought, a huge tip, but she had no money, no more than a dollar in her purse. Nicholas would fee the hotel servants in exact proportion to their efficiency, and he had already remarked that Peggy was careless, and not well trained.

Peggy smiled the warm smile that illumined her plain little face. 'I'm needin' no help, bless you. I've got me two hands and soon I'll have enough to pay back to Father Donovan the passage money he lent me,' she said sturdily. 'Sit you down, mum; you look a bit white. Here I'm blabbering instead of doing what you told me.' She whisked around the table, vanished for a moment and came back with a tray, uttered an exclamation of concern as she saw Miranda, who had suffered a violent attack of nausea and tottered to a chair where she slumped, panting.

The maid flung the tray down and rushed to help. Even through the spasms of retching and vomiting Miranda was conscious of the gentleness of the hands that held her head, and of the soothing little murmurs. 'Poor pretty darlin', you'll do fine now. Put your head on my shoulder; here's a wet rag for your poor face. Now to bed with you—quick.'

Miranda found herself on the bed, the comforter tucked tight around her exhausted body, and Peggy anxiously leaning over her and stroking her hair.

'Thank you,' whispered Miranda, trying to smile. 'I'm so sorry. I guess the fish last night was tainted.'

The little maid's eyes twinkled. 'I wouldn't be thinking it was the fish, mum.'

'It couldn't be the cholera starting—' cried Miranda, alarmed.

Peggy laughed outright. 'Nor the cholera neither, I'll be bound.' She leaned over and whispered a question.

'Why, yes—' answered Miranda, mentally counting days and still puzzled. 'But what would that—?' She checked herself in astonishment. She had no biological knowledge whatever except that derived from observation of the farm animals, but suddenly she had a dim memory of Abigail's sufferings in the months before Charity was born.

'Well, then, mum,' said Peggy, both amused and touched. The dear, pretty lady, as innocent as a lamb, she was, with her tainted fish and her cholera. Peggy, the eldest of seven children, had been raised without genteel reticences. She had been spared no grimmest detail of either birth or death, and an unquestioning acceptance of these was as much part of her as the Irish sympathy and humor which had made them endurable.

'I can't believe it,' murmured Miranda, half to herself. There was no gladness, no realization of the inevitable changes, no thought even of Nicholas, nothing but this blank unbelief.

'It's nature, mum,' said Peggy briskly. 'First the bed and then the cradle, as me poor mither used to say. I'll be leaving you to rest now.'

'No, don't go, please.' Miranda held out her hand. 'I don't want to be alone. I'll make it all right with the housekeeper if you're worrying about the work; only stay and talk to me awhile.'

The maid looked at the pale face on the pillow. The forlorn note in Miranda's voice sped to her heart. As far as Peggy could see the poor lady had naught in the world to trouble her beyond she was a bit queasy in the stomach. And yet she was troubled; a blindfolded bat could see that. And to be sure the rich weren't always happy, hard as it was to believe.

'What'll I talk to you of, mum?' she asked gently.

'Tell me about your home in Ireland—unless it hurts you to speak of it.' Miranda cared little what the other girl said; she wanted companionship while she tried to adjust herself to this startling possibility that she was not ready to face.

So Peggy talked, her brogue thickening as she forgot herself and the lady on the bed in memories of home. She came from one of the loveliest spots in Ireland, the banks of Lough Leane at Killarney. Beneath the thatched roof of the sod shanty there had always been poverty, but there had been merriment too. No matter how thin the milk in the wooden bowls, nor how few the potatoes, there would be a crackle of wit from the handsome red-headed mother to make them forget the emptiness of their bellies. And then the little Kerry cow died, and there was no milk at all. Soon there were no potatoes either. One day the red-headed mother quietly lay down on the straw pallet with her month-old baby in her arms. Nor did she get up again. They would all have starved—for the neighbors were in like case—without the help of the parish priest and the squire. These two men, distracted by the increasing misery in their town, did what they could. They sent Peggy's father to Belfast, where there was still work and food. They boarded the three surviving O'Malley children in the charity school, and they contrived to ship Peggy and other grown youngsters from their district to America, the land of plenty.

But it was not on the past dreadful spring that Peggy dwelt, nor on the twenty-one days she had spent jammed into a stinking hold with other immigrants. She told of the beauties of Killarney and its three lakes shimmering like magic jewels in the soft haze beneath the mountains. She told of the roses that grew of their own accord and scarcely needed tending in that warm, moist climate, and of the arbutus wood which she and her brothers had delighted to whittle into fragrant boxes.

Then crossing herself, and flattered by Miranda's continuing interest, she lowered her voice and spoke of the ruins of the tower and church at Aghadoe. 'No mortal man has lived there since the time of the Black O'Donohues hunnerds of years a gone, but they do say the little folk dance in the tower at the turn of the moon.'

'The little folk,' smiled Miranda. 'D'you mean the fairies?'

'Hush, mum!' cried Peggy, looking around nervously. 'Don't you be naming of them; that makes 'em come.' She paused, then her eyes danced and she giggled. 'But 'twould be a brash wee one, indeed, would cross that heaving ocean packed in tight like kippers in a basket, and he'd never survive the poking and peering of the im-i-gration men at journey's end. Sure and I don't think we need worry at all, at all.'

Miranda laughed. 'Peggy, you do me good.' She had ceased thinking of her as an ignorant and handicapped little chambermaid; somehow during the past hour she had come to think of her as a friend. The sympathy between them cut through the difference in their upbringing and their stations. And yet their stations were not originally so very far apart, thought Miranda, with a shock of surprise. She too had been reared on a potato farm.

'How much do you make a month here, Peggy?' she asked suddenly.

The girl looked anxious. Trouble often swooped down from unexpected quarters. And the job was so precious. 'Four dollars a month, mum—not counting me tips when I get 'em.'

Miranda sat up in bed. 'Will you leave here and come to me as my maid? I'll give you—' she hesitated, knowing well that there would be difficulty with Nicholas. She went on quickly, 'Twenty dollars a month. That'll help with the younger children and to pay back Father Donovan, won't it?'

Peggy drew away from the bed staring at the lady whose face between the long braids of wheat-colored hair was as pleading as though she begged a favor.

'Holy Mither of God, you'd not be making game of me, mum?'

'Of course not. I want you, Peggy.' And as she said these words they crystallized her desire. She wanted Peggy desperately, as an ally, someone that belonged to her in a world dominated by Nicholas. Particularly at Dragonwyck, nor until this second had Miranda realized how much she dreaded the return to Dragonwyck.

Peggy kneeled down beside the bed and put her rough hand timidly on Miranda's slim fingers. ''Twould be the grace of Heaven for me, lady dear, but have you not forgot—' she swallowed, 'me leg that was broke when I fell from the haymow ten years gone and grew back crooked—not but that I'm strong and well able to work despite it,' she finished fiercely to forestall the pity she dreaded.

'That doesn't matter in the least,' said Miranda. She squeezed the hand which lay on hers. 'Then it's all settled?'

The little maid's face broke into a dazzling smile, then darkened. 'What will he say, mum?' she asked soberly. Him, she thought, that's handsome and fearsome as the Black O'Donohues ever was.

Miranda had no need to ask who 'he' was. 'It'll be all right,' she smiled with a confidence she didn't feel. She must present the case very carefully, never for a moment letting him guess that her desire for Peggy ran deeper than just a need for a maid. For he wanted her to have no intimacies whatsoever. She had been drawn to Miss Gibbes, John Jacob Astor's betrothed, and had innocently made an engagement for them to drive out together one afternoon before they all left New York. But it turned out that the horses were unavailable, and that Nicholas wished her to walk up Broadway with him and call on old Mrs. Stuyvesant. In the same way, without ever saying so outright, he had discouraged her acceptance of any invitations from the young matrons she had met. At first she had been happy to be thus islanded with Nicholas, it proved his love for her that he wished to share her with no one, but she had been disheartened to find that she seemed to be permanently cut off from her mother as well. She had expected to have Abigail visit her after they were settled at Dragonwyck. She could send Ephraim money to get a hired girl for a while, for what was the use of being rich if one could not make presents to one's own family? She had worked out all the details before suggesting the plan to Nicholas.

His contemptuous incredulity that she should have had such an unsuitable idea still made her cheeks burn. He would, however, gladly send money to the Wellses if she thought they needed it; he had reached for his wallet. She had stopped him. Ephraim and Abigail would never accept a casual sum, nonchalantly thrown at them like alms.

Later, Miranda had told herself, after they were really settled, she would find the courage to broach the visit again, and she had let the subject drop.

But, she thought, tightening her lips, I won't give in to him about

Peggy. I won't. Determined that the change should be already made when he came back, she sent at once for Mr. Beach, the manager.

There was no difficulty there; Peggy could be replaced at once, and even if she could not have been, Mr. Beach would never have thwarted such an important client.

So, by the time Nicholas was expected on the evening stage two days later, Peggy was established as Miranda's personal maid. Miranda had amused herself by dressing the girl in a new uniform. She had cut down and shortened one of her own dimity morning dresses, had made a coquettish cap and apron and taught Peggy to pin her brown hair into two tidy coils over her ears. The transformation delighted both girls. Peggy now looked trim and smart, she held herself proudly. In return she nursed Miranda through two bouts of morning sickness and attacked the freshening of her mistress's wardrobe with an anxious eagerness that made up for her lack of skill. At first she hung the steel hoops inside out, laced the tiny whalebone corsets backward, sewed a gold bodice button onto a glove, and put the best white *peau de soie* bonnet into the bandbox meant for overshoes. But she learned fast, and her dismay at these mischances was leavened with so much humor that Miranda was amused and never irritated.

Miranda set the stage for Nicholas' return with a subtlety she hadn't known she possessed. She ordered a delicate supper of the things he liked best, hot liver pâté, a filet of bass in aspic, chilled sauterne. With Peggy's help she washed her hair and brushed it the requisite hundred strokes.

'He likes it flowing,' she said thoughtfully. 'I believe he likes my hair better than anything about me—'

'Small wonder, mum,' replied Peggy, looking at the golden mantle that rippled down to Miranda's slender hips. 'Can you not leave it loose, then?' Both of them had entered into a tacit conspiracy, both knew without ever having mentioned it that the continuance of this new relationship that meant so much to both lonely girls depended on propitiation, on the use of every possible weapon.

Miranda shook her head. 'It's not seemly.' She compromised by stuffing all the shining mass loosely into a pink chenille net. The net matched her foaming mousseline gown, also the color of a pink seashell. Like all fashionably dressed women with unlimited means, Miranda had a special gown for every imaginable function. A walking costume could hardly be worn for midday dinner, still less for tea. A morning négligée, no matter how elaborately beflounced and beribboned, might never appear after noon even in the privacy of the bedroom. This shell-pink gown had been contrived by the knowing modiste for one purpose only—the gratification of a husband's eye at just such an intimate supper party as Miranda was planning. Its graceful skirt belled but slightly over a petticoat stiffened with horsehair, the tight bodice was cut very low into a heart shape to show the swell of the white breasts. The only trimming were tiny rose velvet bows sewn at random with a careless gaiety, as though a swarm of rosy bees had settled on a pink cloud.

'And now your jools, mum! Slathers of 'em!' cried Peggy, clapping her hands and gazing at the vision before her.

Miranda smiled and shook her head. 'This gown looks better without jewelry, except perhaps a cameo brooch— Wait a minute, though.' She paused in the act of pinning on the cameo. There *was* a jewel which would set the dress off to perfection. She hesitated, frowning. But after all, why not?

She sent Peggy to the hotel safe for the huge leather case, unlocked it and lifted out two trays. On the bottom in a velvet box lay the ruby pendant. She lifted it out and cupping it in her palm stared at it with a fascinated repulsion. Against how many breasts—now stilled forever —had it already lain, this cold and indifferent jewel? It seemed to her that the ruby shimmered with a baleful mockery.

'Whatever's wrong, mum?' whispered Peggy.

I envied her this thing, thought Miranda, bitter envy. She opened her hand and the pendant fell with a little thud onto the bureau.

'The last woman to wear this jewel is dead,' she said, half aloud.

'The saints preserve us!' cried Peggy, crossing herself. 'Don't wear it, mum. Put it back!'

Miranda did not move, she continued to stare at the pendant; then her gaze traveled slowly to the open case. 'All these jewels belonged to the dead. That's how they came to me.'

The maid shivered. The dear lady was almost fearsome, eyeing those baubles as though they were alive and talking in that faraway voice. Not much sense she was making neither, come to think of it.

'Well, to be sure,' said Peggy reasonably. 'Most of the gentry's gear does pass on to others after death. 'Tis but your condition a-giving you dark fancies. Whisht, mum, you should be thinking of the new life that's in you, not worriting over what's past.'

The shadow gradually lifted from Miranda's face. 'Yes,' she said, 'I guess you're right.' She picked up the pendant, slipped the fine gold chain around her neck, and bent her head so that the maid could fasten the clasp.

''Tis fair as a queen you are, mum!' cried Peggy, admiring the result.

Miranda smiled faintly and looked at the china mantel clock. 'Go now, please; it's almost time.'

The maid nodded and hurried out to her cubicle in the attic. She reached under her straw pillow for the rosary, made of arbutus wood it was, Killarney arbutus. She kissed the little crucifix and began to pray for the outcome of the interview downstairs.

Miranda saw in one quick, thankful glance that Nicholas had returned in excellent humor. The rent-day had passed quietly with no unpleasantness. Each tenant had brought his proper tribute. The bailiff asserted that the manor was running well. The house too was ready.

As he greeted Miranda and complimented her on her gown, his eyes rested a moment on the pendant. She had the impression that he stiffened. She thought in that moment that he stared at the ruby that he was going to tell her to take it off. But she was wrong. He laughed instead. 'I see that the pendant has at last found a setting worthy of it.' And he bent his head and kissed her breast just above the jewel.

After the little supper—and he complimented her on that too—he drew her to the open window. It was a night of stars, and a frail new moon hung high amongst them over the dark valley. The twinkling darkness, so vast that it seemed she stood at the edge of space, reached down and enveloped Miranda, bringing peace. She leaned her head on her husband's shoulder, and a happy confidence came to her. She thought of a verse of poetry that she had read in *Graham's Magazine.*

And the night shall be filled with music,
And the cares that infest the day
Shall fold their tents like the Arabs,
And as silently steal away.

That was so beautiful, and true. Why had she worried about telling Nicholas of Peggy, why did she constantly raise up bogies when there were none? Under the influence of the sublime night all her problems dwindled to nothingness. Of course he'll be delighted, because I'm pleased, she told herself happily.

She was soon disillusioned.

At her first laughing words, 'Nicholas, I've something to confess.

You see, while you were gone—' his arm dropped from her waist. He shut the window and drew the curtains.

'Well, my pretty one, what is it?' he asked lightly enough, but his eyes had hardened to that agate-like blue.

The reassuring beauty of the night was shut out, and there was no support in the conventional hotel room or the flaring oil lamps. She forgot her carefully thought-out speech, stammered and floundered.

'You mean—' said Nicholas incredulously, 'that you engaged that untidy little cripple to be your personal maid!'

Miranda clenched her hands. 'She's not untidy any more, and she's not a cripple. She's had a miserable life, she's—'

'My dear girl, that's a singular recommendation. If you want to hire all the sluts who've led miserable lives, we'll have to build a city at Dragonwyck.' Nicholas sat down on the plush-covered sofa and crossed his legs.

'You twist everything—' she cried desperately. 'Please—please try to understand. I want Peggy, she's bright and willing. You said I could have my own maid—'

'I've already engaged one. A well-trained Frenchwoman. She will join you at Dragonwyck.'

'But I don't want her. I want Peggy . . .' The childish hopelessness of her wail echoed in her ears. Despair seized her. He loathed tears, they never moved him to anything but amusement. She controlled herself with agonizing effort.

'Please, Nicholas, if you love me. It's so little to ask.' She moved over to him, her hands outstretched, instinctively in her desperation trying to use woman's ultimate weapon, the frank lure of her body.

He laughed, though he continued to regard her with chill implacability.

'Oh, yes, you're quite lovely, my dear. But all the same you'll dismiss your new acquisition in the morning.'

She drew a harsh breath, looking at him with a helpless fury. There was one last resort. She had not meant to use it nor had she any hope that it would work.

She threw her head back and spoke with a roughness foreign to her nature. 'I've been sick these last days. Vomiting. I think I'm going to have a baby.'

The change in his face petrified her. He jumped up, grabbing her arms at the elbows, almost shaking her. 'Do you mean it, Miranda? Are you sure?'

She nodded. 'Are you glad?' she asked angrily. 'Does that at least please you?'

She saw the exultation in his eyes. She did not need his answer.

'Can I have Peggy, then?' she pursued inexorably.

He took her hand and raised it to his lips. 'You may have anything in heaven or hell, Miranda, if you'll give me a son!'

Many times during the next months Miranda was to ponder over the extravagance of that statement, the tone of his voice as he made it. At the time she had been too much exhausted by her struggle for Peggy, too much relieved by her unexpected victory to attach any great importance to it. She had always known that Nicholas, like most men, particularly those with large property to pass on, had wanted an heir. It was natural enough. But his attitude, now that there was prospect of one, was not.

From that night at the Mountain House, his manner toward her changed entirely. Without exception his every word and action were directed toward safeguarding her health and tranquillity. Whereas before he had taken pleasure in thwarting most of her wishes and bending her will to his, he now humored her in every way. He cherished her, as one cherishes perforce the instrument which will fulfill one's desire.

16

FOR THE NEXT WEEKS MIRANDA'S PHYSICAL SUFFERings were too insistent to allow room for any other emotion. She had dreaded the return to Dragonwyck, but when the river boat Express churned up to the landing and she saw the familiar towered silhouette against the eastern sky, the manor represented nothing but a place in which to lie down in a darkened room and fight off the ever-recurring nausea.

She dimly heard Peggy's whispered gasp: 'Faith and 'tis a castle! 'Tis grander than the Bishop's palace at home!' But Miranda felt no thrill of gratified pride. Her whole being was concentrated on the effort of getting off the boat and up the marble steps from the dock before the dryness of her mouth and the swimming in her head should lead again to the inevitable conclusion. She pressed a handkerchief against her lips, and with the help of Nicholas' support and murmured encouragement she managed to reach the porte-cochère, then she gave a moan and swayed against him.

Nicholas picked her up and carried her into Dragonwyck.

'No, please,' she cried faintly. 'I can walk. It's too humiliating.' For she saw rows of servants ranged on either side the Great Hall waiting to receive them.

'It's entirely proper for a husband to carry his bride into her new home,' said Nicholas lightly. 'Don't fret, my darling.'

He was always like that now, kind and gentle, ministering to her embarrassing seizures with a tactful patience that continually astonished her, for he despised illness.

He carried her upstairs and put her down on a bed. For some time she was too sick to notice her surroundings. Peggy, who had followed close behind them, knew what to do—cold cloths soaked in vinegar for the forehead, a warming pan for the chilled feet, a stick of peppermint to hold in the mouth.

The nausea ebbed. There would be a weak but blessed peace for a while. Miranda opened her eyes and gazed past Nicholas' solicitous face. She saw three great windows in front of her and two northern ones on her right.

This is Johanna's room, she thought, and a chill that was not physical crept through her. But I mustn't be foolish, she thought, and raising her head a little she forced herself to examine the room and saw with grateful relief that everything had been changed. Green satin replaced the red-plush curtains, a fawn-colored Aubusson covered the floor. Gone was the untidy clutter of furniture with which Johanna had surrounded herself; there were now but three fine mahogany pieces, and a couple of small chairs. The spacious room was revealed in its true proportions.

All was changed—with one exception. Her tired eyes roamed upward and she stiffened. She had not at first realized, because the old brocaded tester had been replaced with green satin to match the draperies. But there was no mistaking the coat-of-arms on the headboard or the four massive columns.

Long ago in another life she had entered this room for the first time and stood submissively beside this bed with resentment and envy in her heart. How this room would be changed if it were only mine! she had thought. How had she dared to think that? And with this memory there came another, sharp as the cut of a hidden knife. A wrinkled brown face from which peered black eyes filled with pitying contempt. *'Ah, p'tite,* you want a thing very much, you make it happen *sure.'*

Miranda turned her head violently and shut her eyes.

'Feeling badly again?' asked Nicholas.

'No. It's not that.—Nicholas, I don't want to sleep in this bed.'

He answered her with unexpected patience, even explaining his reasons.

This was the Van Ryn ancestral bed, for generations all those of his blood had been born and died on it. It was here that the Lord and Lady of the Manor always slept; it was here that his child would be born. Any other request he would be glad to grant, but on this point he was adamant.

Let it be, then, thought Miranda wearily. What does it matter after all?

Soon the great bed would become as familiar as it was undeniably comfortable. She would no longer see that gruesome night when the tapers had stood on either side and it had supported that motionless figure with the little subtle smile on its pale face. She must never look back again—never.

She was now the mistress of Dragonwyck and a Van Ryn. The past was gone; she must have no trailing tendrils of guilt, or fear or even of pity. She must cooperate with Nicholas in his tacit elimination of all that might remind them of that previous year she had spent at Dragonwyck.

All those servants were gone—and Zélie. Much new furniture had been bought, and the old rearranged. Throughout the house everything was freshly painted and plastered and papered. Even this bed, the one continuing association, was after all but a frame. Its mattress and springs were new.

There was, however, one legacy from the past which she could not conscientiously deny. There was Katrine. Surely it was time that the child came back to her father.

Two days later she broached this to Nicholas.

'If you would like Katrine here for a visit, I've no objection,' he said. 'But I see no reason for it. She's well cared for by her aunt, to whom I make a handsome allowance. She has besides many little cousins to play with, I believe.'

This was reasonable enough, but she felt beneath his temperate words his aversion to the idea and the indifference he had always shown to Katrine.

'She's your daughter, Nicholas. Don't you ever miss her or want to see her?' cried Miranda with sudden vehemence.

He was silent for several minutes.

'I doubt that she would want to come here, my dear. She has been under other influences.'

At first she did not understand him. 'You mean that Katrine wouldn't want to see me?'

He shrugged, thinking of the outraged letters he had received from Johanna's relatives after the news of his remarriage had reached Albany.

'I think the child may be prejudiced, and she does very well where she is. I shall run up to see her someday.'

Miranda was silenced. It had been stupid of her not to realize that Katrine would suffer at being brought back to this scene of her mother's death, or that she might have been taught to resent Miranda as the supplanter.

It was not only the Van Tappens who disapproved of Nicholas' marriage. All the up-river families were horrified. The topic enlivened many a tea-party in the drawing-rooms of Claverack, and Kinderhook and Greenbush. 'The scheming little upstart!' they said. 'No birth or breeding, nothing but youth and a pretty face; why must men be such fools!'

Some, like Mrs. Henry Van Rensselaer, balked of an alliance for one of her daughters, were more bitter. 'There was something going on between those two—even in poor Johanna's lifetime. I saw it with my own eyes,' they whispered. 'The whole matter is disgraceful, shocking. Nothing would induce me to call on them.' Nor did they call.

Nicholas was profoundly annoyed, but he hid it from Miranda, as he protected her from every unpleasantness, at this time. He surrounded her with an anxious solicitude, constantly ordering dishes which might tempt her precarious stomach, sending her to bed at nine, taking her for short walks or drives from which they always returned before there was a possibility of her tiring.

He exerted himself to divert her too. Caught in the lethargy of advancing pregnancy, her intelligence obscured by a constant malaise, Miranda found all mental effort impossible. Nicholas therefore concealed his own boredom and patiently read to her by the hour—from the trashy new novels 'The Orange Girl of Venice,' or 'Nellie the Ragpicker's Daughter.'

And in the evening he played for her—the simple and sentimental ballads that pleased her best. 'Ben Bolt,' 'The Old Oaken Bucket,' or 'Nellie Was a Lady.' And on Sundays they went to church together.

All this contented and reassured her. Except that their scale of living was more magnificent than that of most couples, the Van Ryns represented the epitome of the domestic felicity of the time. Life was suspended, hushed into a pleasing monotony. There were no violences, no clashes. The past and the future both melted into distance.

The outside world had become unreal. She knew vaguely that the progress of the war with Mexico was gratifying. In September there had been a victory at Monterrey, and she had wondered about Jeff. Still the thought of victory somehow seemed to include safety, and Jeff was as shadowy as everything else. Even her disappointment that her mother could not after all come to her soon vanished.

Nicholas had reversed his decision about Abigail. If Miranda wanted her mother, she might by all means invite her. The letter had been sent at once.

The carefully unalarming reply gave no hint of the misery that had gone into the writing of it.

For years Abigail had suffered from periodic attacks of rheumatism which she bore with a grim and silent endurance. This time the attack did not pass; it swelled her fingers, her knees, and in her right hip there was a constant grinding pain. She could barely creep around the house. She could not have endured the trip to Dragonwyck.

Her letter minimized the pain and indicated another reason. 'Tabitha's time is coming soon, and I must bide with her. She hasn't a houseful of servants to care for her like you,' wrote Abigail. 'Later, very likely I can come, take care of yourself my dear child, but don't coddle overmuch. Be thankful you have such a good husband.'

For Miranda's letters were full of Nicholas' care and tenderness.

In November, even Nicholas' desire to protect her from any emotion which might possibly interfere with his child's development was not proof against a shattering calamity.

When the news reached them they sat after supper in the Red Room. No malignant or superstitious influences about that room now; Miranda sometimes wondered how she had ever been silly enough to imagine that there were.

The little harpsichord stood in its accustomed corner. Sometimes Miranda played it, finding its unobtrusive tinkle better suited to the tunes she liked than the grandeur of the pianoforte in the music room.

She and Nicholas sat on either side the center table in the warm circle of lamplight. At her request he was reading to her. Miranda absently netted a purse, while she listened. The story filled her with a pleasant melancholy, and it delighted her that Nicholas should read so tolerantly this novel of religious faith and the love of Jesus. How he had changed! she thought, looking affectionately across the table at his dark head. It was exactly as it said in these books they read. Conversion followed upon the touch of baby fingers.

They both looked up at the sound of galloping hoofs on the drive. 'Now, what could that be?' wondered Miranda without much interest. She turned startled to look at her husband, who had uttered a sharp exclamation. He threw the book on the table and stood up.

The door burst open and Dirck Duyckman, Nicholas' bailiff, clattered in. His moon-face glistened, his disordered homespun suit was flecked with horse-sweat. 'It's bad, sir. Very bad,' he cried, trying to get his breath.

Miranda stared blankly from one to the other. She saw a quiver pass over Nicholas, then he lifted his head. 'Out with it; don't stand there blabbering!'

The bailiff passed a grimy handkerchief over his face. 'Young is in, sir. He's to pardon 'em all—the skunks! Even Boughton! The state constitution's to be changed. It's the end, sir. The end of the Manor.'

Miranda gasped, her frightened eyes flew to Nicholas, who stood as though carved from the granite on which Dragonwyck rested. Last week he had driven over to Hudson on election day to vote. But he had told her nothing of the election's importance to them. He had expressed no doubts that Governor Wright might fail of re-election or that John Young, passionate anti-renter, might sweep the state.

'What does it mean, Nicholas?' she whispered. 'I don't understand.' As he did not answer, but continued to stand rigid, his narrowed eyes looking through both of them without seeing them, she turned to the bailiff, who shuffled uneasily, casting a nervous glance at Nicholas whom he had always feared.

'It means, ma'am, that the Manor can't hold together no more. The farms must go to whoever wants to buy 'em. The down-renters have won at last.'

'Never,' said Nicholas quietly.

This calm assertion frightened the bailiff far more than if Mr. Van Ryn had shouted and cursed as any other man would. He moistened his lips. 'You can't help it, sir. 'Twill be law. The Van Rensselaers have given in already. They say as how the patroon even said it was a good thing.'

'Perhaps it is, then, Nicholas,' put in Miranda timidly, hoping to wipe from his face that frozen look. 'If you refuse to sell, won't it mean a great deal more trouble, and after all would it make so much difference? We'd still have all these acres around the house.'

He wheeled on her, glaring at her with fury.

'You little fool—d'ye think because a prating idiot in Albany says so that I'll give up—' His eyes fell to the white lace shawl which concealed the slight distortion of her figure. 'I beg your pardon, my dear,' he said in his normal voice. 'I'm being exceedingly thoughtless.—Dirck—' he turned to the goggling bailiff. 'You may go.'

The man went out muttering. If the patroon wanted to battle law and the entire country, that was his business. He was pig-headed enough to try. But I'll have no part of it, thought Dirck; I've got my bellyful of threats and bloodshed and shots in the dark. Out West I'll go. Be my own master for a change.

Miranda readily forgave Nicholas his anger. She knew that the manor system meant more to him than it did to the others, and that to him any curtailment of power was unthinkable—literally unthinkable, in that he would refuse to recognize the possibility. She partially understood that the manor was to him a symbol. It was his kingdom and his birthright. Had he been the King of Naples or Prussia his attitude would have been no different.

But this was not Europe, and America was not a kingdom but a republic. Willingly or not, they were subject to the laws of the democracy in which they lived. The manor was a hang-over from the past, not even the past of this country but an abortive offshoot from medieval Europe. The expanding republic had lopped it off like any other dead branch.

Miranda did not realize how much of her ready acceptance of the situation she owed to Jeff. When he had been at the farm he had sometimes talked of the evils of the manor system, and she had closed her mind in a stubborn resistance mixed with contempt. But she had heard, nonetheless.

After all, she thought with feminine practicality, the breaking up of the Manor would affect neither their wealth nor their home, and it would certainly turn a hostile tenantry into peaceful neighbors.

If only Nicholas would accept defeat for once. She looked at him wistfully and knew how futile this hope was. He would never accept a thwarting of his will in any matter, great or small. If he seemed to do so, it was only that a stronger and more hidden purpose might be served.

'I don't see what you can do, Nicholas,' she said quietly. 'If it's the law now that you must give up the farms.'

'I shall never give them up,' he returned with equal quiet. 'The Manor will go intact to my son.'

But it's impossible, she thought. Did he really think that he could fight against the whole country single-handed? Even Nicholas could not do that. And Dirck had said that the Van Rensselaers, who had far larger holdings, were already accepting the inevitable.

He walked over to her and resting his hand on her shoulder said: 'Miranda, can you doubt that I am always master of circumstance? Would you be here with me, bearing my child, if I were not?'

She looked up at him, startled. His words were true enough, and yet it seemed that his voice carried a dark and secret emphasis. It was as though she heard a warning bell from shoals muffled by fog, a faint and sinister tolling from far away.

Her eyes widened. 'Why do you look like that, Nicholas?' she whispered.

He took his hand from her shoulder and smiled quite naturally. 'You must worry about nothing, my love. Nothing. The Manor affairs are my concern. You needn't give them another thought. You must go to bed now; it's getting late.'

He bent and kissed her forehead.

She obeyed him silently, walked past him and up the great curving stairs.

In her room, Peggy awaited her as usual. The peaked little face had filled out in these months, had acquired a pixie-like prettiness. She was happy at Dragonwyck, happy in her service to the lady of the manor. The other servants liked Peggy, for her ready Irish tongue was quick but never wounding and her infirmity touched them. So they forgave her the little important airs that sprang from her position as the mistress's personal maid, and they forgave her her jealous refusal to let anyone but herself tend Miranda.

''Tis late ye are tonight, mum,' the maid said anxiously when she saw her mistress walk in, her blonde head drooping. 'Ye'll not be too tired?'

Miranda smiled vague greeting and did not answer. The misty fear which had seized her when Nicholas touched her shoulder had receded, but it had left a clinging wisp of disquiet behind.

She dropped wearily into one of the needlepoint chairs, closing her eyes while Peggy brushed the loosened hair in long, soothing strokes. After a while physical comforts brought direct physical peace. The cedar-wood fire crackled cheerily and gave out a faint fragrance. The room was in exquisite order as Peggy had been taught to keep it. The great bed's sheet had been turned down, and a hot brick wrapped in flannel subdued the iciness of its lavender-scented linen. Peggy had forgotten nothing, the hot milk which Miranda must drink, the exact placing of the pillows so that they might best support a body that had grown clumsy and hard to rest.

'Better now?' asked Peggy tenderly as she tucked in the blankets and arranged the coverlet.

Miranda started to nod, then gave an exclamation of surprise. Her hands flew to her abdomen. 'Peggy,' she cried, 'what was that?'

The little maid paled. 'It wasn't a pain?'

Miranda shook her head. 'No pain. A queer fluttering like a bird inside there.'

Peggy clasped her hands. 'Oh, the saints be thanked! I've been so worried, mum. 'Tis life you're feeling, lady dear. Your little baby moving within you.'

Miranda pushed down the covers and gazed at herself in amazement.

'It never seemed real before,' she said, half laughing, half bewildered. During all these months of illness and lethargy, the baby had been an intellectual concept, nothing more. Even the furnishing of what had used to be her own old room as a nursery had given her no realization of the baby as a new and separate entity.

A thrill of awed gladness came to her now, an anticipation so poignant that it erased the last traces of the uneasiness which Nicholas had caused her.

'Why did you say you'd been worried, Peggy?' she asked dreamily. 'This sensation is wonderful, nothing to worry about.'

The maid hesitated, but it could do no harm to tell now that everything must be fine. ' 'Tis late you are in feeling it, mum, with you going into your seventh month. I've been watching you and waiting these six weeks.' She did not add that she had fortified her own considerable knowledge of midwifery by anxious consultations with Mrs. MacNab, the housekeeper.

Miranda, protected both by ignorance and this new bliss, laughed placidly. 'Well, perhaps he's a very plump baby and was too lazy to move sooner.'

Peggy laughed too. But as she pulled the curtains and placed the screen before the dying fire, she thought, The Holy Blessed Mother grant that she's right, and that it isn't that the poor mite was too feeble to make himself known.

A stormy November full of sleet and hail became a cold snowy December. It was after all unnecessary for Nicholas to make overt resistance to change on his manor, for as yet the new laws had not been passed, nor the new Governor taken hold. It was in fact to be eight years before the last of the litigation and state suits against landlords for the trying of titles finally simmered into peace.

In the meantime the tenants, having won their point and certain of eventual victory, settled down again more equably than they had for years.

On December sixth, the Manor House was again thrown open for the Saint Nicholas Day feast to the children. This year none of the neighboring river families' children were invited. Nicholas had no intention of risking refusals. Had it not been for Miranda's condition, he would before this have concentrated his will on the subduing of these families who dared hold aloof. He would have invited important guests from New York, enlisted the aid of old Martin Van Buren, and given a ball of such dazzling brilliance that the countryside would have come out of curiosity if nothing else.

As it was this must wait until spring, when Miranda had recovered and there would be an heir to Dragonwyck.

The children of the tenantry, however, flocked to the party—nearly a hundred of them. Their parents were no more averse than the rest of the world to getting something for nothing, and many of them had sadly missed this festivity last year when the Manor had been shut. There was no denying the patroon did them well. Cunningly hidden in the gilded sabots there were gifts and candies for each child. There were showers of marzipan bon-bons in the muslin sheet suspended from the ceiling which Nicholas ripped open for them with the traditional crook. There were unlimited supplies of gingerbread and olykoeks fried to a succulent crispness, there were flagons of beer and rum punch.

After the ceremony, Nicholas moved amongst his people exerting his magnetism upon each one, flattering them with personal inquiries, expressing his pleasure at seeing them. By not the slightest word or gesture did he indicate knowledge that many of these had been his bitter enemies, and had spent the past two years in violent struggle to escape from his hold.

His attitude of benevolent interest was precisely as it had always been during the ten years of his patroonship, precisely that of his father and grandfathers back to the first patroon in 1640.

When the last crowded wagon left, its runners gliding swiftly through the new snow, Hans Gebhard's fat wife looked down at her three happy children. They snuggled in the straw like puppies, their hands clutching the fine gifts they had received—a doll, a singing top, even a pair of skates. On their tongues still lingered the reminiscent delights of cake and candy.

'The patroon's naught so bad, Hans,' said Mrs. Gebhard to her husband thoughtfully.

'Don't you dass to call him the patroon, now that we're quit of him!' Hans turned his sour face angrily on his wife. 'Have ye forgot Klaas, woman? Will a few sweets and baubees wipe Klaas from your noddle and how the Van Ryn used him?' He spat morosely in the snow.

Aye, thought Mrs. Gebhard, poor Klaas that had cut his wrists and died when the patroon turned him off the farm two years back on rent-day. Hans' own cousin Klaas had been, and the whole business mighty bad.

'Still and all 'tis done with now forever,' she said. The manor rum punch filled her stomach with a pleasing warmth. She was tired of ill-will and recrimination. There would be no more rent-days; come July they'd likely own their own farm at last. No more kermiss neither! The thought struck her like a blow. That had been something to look forward to all spring—the Fourth-of-July Kermiss; the games and the feasting, the rivers of cold, delicious beer.

She cast a nervous glance at Hans, afraid he might somehow guess her traitorous repining. Once having started she could not stop the disquieting thoughts. You couldn't but own the patroon had saved them a good bit of worry. There was the shipping of crops to New York. For that he'd made all arrangements, sending the stuff from the farms in one lot. They'd have to manage for themselves now, each farm as best it could.

Then there was the mill the patroon had built for them. It stood on a corner of the Manor House land. He'd never let them use that free now any more, nor spread their nets for shad on his section of the river.

Mrs. Gebhard sighed and her fat cheeks quivered. Never the sweet without the bitter. She must be more strong-minded like Hans. No price was too high to pay for freedom, for the right to own the bit of land where the Gebhards had borned and labored and died for two hundred years.

17

IT WAS ON THIS SAME SAINT NICHOLAS' DAY THAT A troopship from New Orleans docked in New York. It landed a hundred wounded men, and caskets containing those who could no longer feel their wounds.

Jeff Turner was amongst those in the first category and still too much shattered to be thankful that he was not in the second. A Mexican bullet had ripped upward through his left arm and collar bone, laid open his cheek, and plowed a groove through the side of his skull before it vanished into the bright tropical sky.

Though all the wounds had promptly begun to fester, Jeff's sturdy frame could have withstood that and the disablement of his arm and shoulder. He would have directed the cautery and splinting himself, and then have proceeded enthusiastically with his division under General Worth to Saltillo. But the head wound was another matter. He had been unconscious for days.

He had been dumped on a gun carriage in Monterrey and dragged back to General Taylor's base at Cerralvo. Here he had received hurried treatment in a hospital tent, and as he still declined either to regain consciousness or to die, he had been bundled into an empty supply wagon with a score of others and eventually reached the Texan coast, where a sloop conveyed them to New Orleans. The good Sisters at the Charité cared for him there while the skull fracture healed enough to permit him to travel home.

Jeff had intended going up-river to Hudson at once, but as he lurched off the gangplank onto the pier he knew that he must have rest first. It was still a struggle to stand for long. He was subject to sharp attacks of dizziness. There were crowds of anxious relatives on the dock but none for him. He grasped his dilapidated carpetbag with his good hand and strode through the press, praying that he might not keel over and make a scene. A few sympathetic glances were directed at the scar on his cheek and the dangling left coat sleeve. Though the arm had healed, the collar bone was slower and still needed the support of a sling.

One lady in bombazine, seeing the pallor of his face, the gauntness of his body in the ill-fitting blue uniform, cried, 'Oh, the poor young lieutenant!' But otherwise no one noticed him, for which he was grateful. He had the usual masculine horror of being conspicuous.

When he reached the sidewalk, the city noises banged on his sensitive nerves like thunder; houses, drays, and hurrying people merged crazily, swimming around him in slow spirals.

Damn, thought Jeff, gritting his teeth. He tumbled into a hack, muttered, 'Hotel—cheap one, anywhere,' and shut his eyes.

The driver took him at his word, trotted his horse two blocks along South Street, and decanted Jeff at Schmidt's Tavern, where he found himself established in a bare, dismal room priced at fifty cents a day. It was clean, however, and it had a bed upon which Jeff flung himself after getting rid of Mrs. Schmidt, the landlady, who showed a sentimental German disposition to cluck and yearn over him.

He lay for two hours in a semi-stupor, until the throbbing in his collar bone roused him. He sat up and ran his fingers impatiently over a lump on his shoulder. Another pocket of pus had formed on the surface of the partly healed wound. He scowled at it as he screwed his head around trying to see it. There was no mirror in the room. A quick cut of the scalpel it needed, and a wet dressing. His bag of instruments was left behind at Cerralvo amongst the cactus and yuccas.

He made a sudden resolution, scribbled a note, and shouting for the landlady told her to have it delivered. Then he tottered back to the bed.

It was dusk when he heard heavy footsteps ascending the stairs and a knock on his door. Doctor John Francis walked in.

'Well, so ye're back again, my fine young hero,' he said, chuckling, and extending his hand as casually as though they'd met yesterday. His wise eyes missed nothing of Jeff's condition, but he would no more have expressed his sympathy than Jeff would have welcomed it.

'Been makin' love to a cannon ball?' he inquired genially, plumping his black bag on the floor and sitting on the bed. 'Could you not find something warmer and softer to embrace down there?—No, don't sit up; do as I tell you, you young squirt. Lie still; you think you know it all, I'll be bound, but you're not as good a medico as I am yet. Yes, yes—I see it, d'ye take me for a mole?'

While he kept up an affectionate grumbling, his gnarled fingers were busy palpating the arm wound, the abscess on the collar bone, the healed scar on the cheek, the depression in the scalp.

'You've not much improved your beauty,' he observed with a twinkle, kicking his bag over to the bed and bending with a grunt to extract a scalpel. 'How'd it happen?'

'Just one bullet,' confessed Jeff ruefully. He indicated its upward path with a quick motion of his thumb.

'Was the greaser in a hole, then, or were you maybe skulking in a tree?' inquired the old doctor, and while he spoke he jabbed the scalpel deep.

'Ouch!' said Jeff. 'No, I wasn't in a tree, but I *was* on a roof.—What are you dousing on that compress, sir? I never saw stuff like that. Plain water'll do—or maybe you should cauterize again?'

'Deliver me—' retorted the old man with a terrible frown, 'from treating another doctor, especially a young know-it-all. Mind your business, my boy, and let me mind mine. You called me in, didn't you? You want this dod-gasted mess of a shoulder to heal, don't you?'

'Yes, sir,' said Jeff, smiling. 'But what's that brown stuff? It burns like a red-hot poker.'

'It's seaweed and alcohol made for me by an old Chinee on Pell Street. And I don't *know* why it ofttimes keeps a wound from festering, so don't ask me. The Chinamen know a lot about medicine and I'm not too proud to try their drugs. No more should you be.' He tied up the sling. 'You'll do now, my lad. Couple months from now you'll be good as new, barring that scar on your cheek, though doubtless the ladies'll consider it highly ro-man-tic. If you rest a lot and act like a sensible human being, the dizzy spells'll pass too.' He dumped his scalpel, bandages, and the brown bottle pell-mell into his bag, which he snapped shut. He lit himself a black and foul-smelling cigar, settled his massive body on the one rickety chair, and turned a look of anticipation on Jeff.

'Now, what in blazes were ye doing on a rooftop in Monterrey?'

At first Jeff searched for words, struggling against the universal reluctance to talk of battle to those who knew nothing of it. But gradually the old man's eager interest had its effect. Jeff forgot the four musty walls about him; they expanded into desert and dust, into brown adobe and the blinding gleam of white plaster under the Mexican sun.

Old Rough and Ready Taylor had made shrewd plans for the capture of Monterrey. He had sent General Worth with eighteen hundred men—of whom Jeff was one—on a circuitous route to the other side of the city, while Taylor created a diversion on the eastern side to cover their march. On September twentieth, Worth had arrived at his position and the city of Monterrey lay between the pincers which inexorably narrowed down on it. One after another the Mexican forts fell; Federacion, Independencia, and the Bishop's Palace on the west; Teneria and Libertad on the east.

On the morning of the twenty-third the Americans advanced into the bewildered city from both sides. But instead of risking life in the streets, which were raked by artillery fire and covered by snipers from shuttered windows, the American soldiers were ordered into the houses, where they tunneled their way through the interior walls, progressing through a cloud of plaster and falling rubble toward the grand plaza.

Jeff paused, remembering the excitement of that march through the homes. Like a lot of terriers after a rabbit they'd been. Burrowing, knocking down, jumping from rooftop to rooftop, rushing headlong through lovely flower-filled patios. They were all drunk with the ease of conquest, and the childish joy of destruction. He as drunk as any of them.

It was only now that he remembered the terrified faces of black-clad women, cowering in corners of their ravished homes watching the shouting, exultant soldiers break their furniture, shatter the statues of the saints, rip rugs and draperies to shreds.

By sunset both halves of the army had reached to within one block of the plaza. Here the Mexican troops were huddled awaiting orders from their leader, Ampudia, whose efficiency did not match his courage.

General Worth called for volunteers to plant a small mortar on an exposed rooftop which would command the square.

'And I suppose ye jumped up like a jack-in-the-box,' growled Doctor Francis, 'when ye should have been back at the base caring for the wounded.'

Jeff reddened, then laughed sheepishly. 'Well, we hauled up that mortar and stuck it where it did a lot of good. The hot shells'd mow down a dozen of them at a clip. But they didn't let us enjoy ourselves long.' Jeff paused again. 'It's curious,' he said thoughtfully, 'but I saw my bullet coming. He was a handsome Mexican, had a fine face. I saw him squinting up along the barrel of his gun, down there on the street. For a second we looked right at each other, and I had a crazy feeling of liking him. Then I ducked, but not fast enough.' He grinned. 'That's all I know first hand of our capture of Monterrey, for I didn't rightly come to from the blackness and the haze until they dumped me in the Charité in New Orleans.'

'I kind of like that greaser of yours too,' remarked Doctor Francis grimly. 'You needed a bullet to knock some sense into you. Now you're here, you'll stay this time, my lad. Move into my office tomorrow, start learning the ropes. I'll not work ye too hard till your brains've got unaddled.'

Jeff sent the old doctor a look of affection. He perfectly understood the little plan to give him rest at a salary. For a moment he was tempted. If he went in with Doctor Francis, it would mean a big society practice, the idea of which he loathed, but it would also mean money enough for research, and association with a man whom he deeply admired.

But that was just the trouble. Jeff's fiercely independent soul wouldn't stomach the thought of being beholden to anyone, or of slipping easily into a ready-made practice. Besides, he was needed at home. He had been startled and touched at the dismay of his patients when he had enlisted.

The old man read his face. 'Yes, there you go,' he grumbled. 'I see that mule look. Independent as a hog on ice. Go on back to your little jay town, kill yourself for a parcel of flea-bitten yokels.' He blew his nose stertorously. Jeff's second refusal was a grievous disappointment. Every man of achievement longs for a disciple, a younger edition of himself with whom to share the accumulated wisdom and experience of the past. That few men ever find this disciple, Doctor Francis well knew. And now having found him it was hard to be balked. Still he understood Jeff's reasons and honored him for them.

Both men were companionably silent for a while. The old doctor wreathed himself in clouds of tobacco smoke, and the young one gazed absently at the ceiling.

'Saw a friend of yours last summer, seemed mighty interested in you,' offered Francis suddenly.

Jeff turned and looked his question.

'Right pretty girl; married, though—so you needn't get all het up. Mrs. Nicholas Van Ryn, wife to that high mucky-muck what-you-may-call-him up on the Hudson.'

Jeff expelled his breath and sat up. 'Where'd you meet Miranda?' he said sharply.

The other raised his bushy eyebrows. 'So, it's Miranda, is it! I met her at the Poes' cottage and she made me a cup of tea with her own lily-white hands.'

'How was she looking?'

The old man snorted. 'Far as I remember she'd a pink satin dress and some darn fool feather in her bonnet; she'd a mighty trim ankle and a mighty trim waist—all right, all right,' he said in response to Jeff's ejaculation. 'She looked healthy enough, if that's what you want to know.'

The old man gave him a satiric look and grinned. 'Waist's not so trim now, I'll be bound; she must be two months from term.'

'What!' cried Jeff violently.

Doctor Francis chuckled at Jeff's air of stupefaction. 'Anybody ever tell you about the stork, Jeff? Bird that's likely to come moseying along when a young couple's married? Or when they're not, for that matter.'

Jeff made an impatient gesture. 'How do you know she's—she's pregnant?' He had managed to forget Miranda quite completely during his months in Mexico, had shut the memory of her away in an airtight compartment and thought that any sentimental yearnings he had had for her were done with. He was therefore annoyed to discover how much he disliked the thought of her bearing a child to Nicholas.

'I know,' answered Doctor Francis, 'because the great Mr. Van Ryn wrote me about it. He favored me with a request—more like a royal command at that—wanted me to move up to his manor and hang around for weeks until his lady takes a notion to produce this marvelous infant.'

'Are you going?' asked Jeff slowly.

'I am not! I told him most politely that I'd better use for my time than to fuss over one healthy girl, counting every pulse beat. He can find himself some other tame puppy. Plenty'd be glad enough to get the fee he offered. Come to think of it, you can do it yourself now; you'll be right handy.'

'No!' said Jeff explosively.

The old doctor leaned back and contemplated the young man. 'Little bit smitten with the lady's charms, aren't you?'

'It's not that. But—well, Van Ryn wouldn't want me. I attended the death of his first wife.'

Doctor Francis nodded. 'What'd she die of, anyway? Wasn't it kind of sudden?'

'Acute indigestion. Very sudden,' Jeff answered curtly. The memory of his suspicions of Nicholas now shamed him. They must have sprung from unrecognized jealousy. His face grew hot when he thought of those bungling little experiments he had made on the tipsy cake.

'Whyn't you get married, Jeff?' The old man put down his cigar and laid an affectionate hand on Jeff's good shoulder. 'Must be some tidy little woman around who pleases you. And if you're not so fond of her at first, you'll get to be once she's yours.' He chuckled. 'Lots of truth in what old Benjamin Franklin said, "All cats look gray at night."'

Jeff smiled and thought of Faith Folger. On the day he had sailed down-river to join the army she had stood at the Hudson dock beside her mother. The black eyes had been full of tears. 'I'll be waiting for thee, Jeff,' she had whispered, 'until thee comes back.'

He had kissed her quickly while her mother pretended not to see. The kiss had meant little to him, for his mind had been full of Miranda, and in any case he had not really expected to come back. But now the thought of Faith was comforting.

'I think I'll take your advice, sir,' he said to Doctor Francis, 'as soon as I have two whole arms and a steady head to offer a woman.'

Hudson welcomed Jeff home with wild enthusiasm. Had he permitted it they would have made a hero of him, but as he refused to be lionized they contented themselves with flocking to his little house on Front Street and bringing gifts; calves'-foot jelly, pound cake, ducks and chickens already roasted. The old black Rillah had nothing to do but fuss over Jeff and serve the dainties which were provided.

By New Year's Day, it seemed to Jeff that he had never been away at all. His left arm was stiff but had regained its usefulness, the spells of vertigo diminished in frequency, and he could ignore them enough to take on a restricted practice.

He had not yet proposed to Faith. He did send her a New Year's present. 'The Golden Chalice—or Mental Draughts from Many Fountains'—a popular gift book that year, prettily bound in red leather tooled with gilt. Faith was encouraged. 'The Casket of Love' or 'The Wedding Guest' would have been more significant, to be sure, but any gift book was indicative of serious intentions, and she made her plans for a June wedding. Now that he was home again, she must on no account allow their relationship to slip back into the old half-teasing, flirtatious state. She wanted Jeff, and had turned down three flattering proposals for his sake. It was high time that he speak the decisive words.

But January passed and Jeff remained unaccountably elusive. He refused invitations, pleading the need for rest. When Faith, growing desperate, invented a persistent headache and trudged through the snowy streets to consult him at his office, he received her warmly, even tenderly, but he didn't 'speak.' He told her to avoid fried foods for a while and take a dose of calomel, then sent her away again baffled but not quite disconsolate. For she knew men, and there *had* been a special note in his voice, an admission of intimacy in his manner, and besides she knew she had no rival. There was hardly a girl in Hudson who hadn't tried to interest Jeff, and he paid no attention to any of them.

In fact Jeff intended to propose eventually, but he had a male reluctance to being stampeded or to committing himself irretrievably.

He finally decided that on Saint Valentine's Day he would take the plunge. Send her one of those sugary, sentimental effusions which delight the girlish heart, follow it up by a formal call at her parents' house.

But when the fourteenth of February came, poor Faith received no Valentine from Jeff. He was at Dragonwyck.

During the first weeks after his return he had heard nothing of the Van Ryns. He had rejoiced to find that the manors were at last to be broken up and that his friend, little Boughton, was to be pardoned, but aside from this general news, the inhabitants of Dragonwyck might have been in Kamchatka for all one heard of them in Hudson. The shore road was blocked with snow as the river was blocked with ice.

Jeff had again made up his mind to forget Miranda and succeeded quite well. An epidemic of grippe inflicted itself on Hudson, and in consequence he was too busy and too tired to think at all.

Then he got a letter from Doctor Francis in New York. Following the usual greetings and inquiries it said:

> Don't be surprised if you're called to the Van Ryns' after all, for I've taken the liberty to write the Grand Seigneur heartily recommending your skill. He's got Brown there for his wife—

Doctor William Brown from Gramercy Park. I know the man and he is able enough, but the trouble seems to be Van Ryn has got him terrified. Brown is in a funk, thinks matters aren't progressing just right and doesn't dare tell Van Ryn. He sneaked a letter out to me begging for advice, but I cannot make head nor tail of it. Sounds like a normal pregnancy to me. I wrote back to the poor numskull—(my private opinion is that the size of his fee has addled his wits)—telling him not to worry, delivering babies is simple as rolling off a log. Dame Nature does it for you (though we can't let the laymen guess that), but I ended up by telling him to get in touch with you if he needs help. Then I got a letter from Van Ryn himself, complaining about Brown and begging me to go up there after all. So I handed you to *him* too. All this pother! The Grand Cham of Tartary would not make half the rumpus about an heir, I'll be bound.

Jeff threw the letter on his desk. Even if they did send for him, he wouldn't go. Nothing would induce him to involve himself again with Miranda or the dark intricacies of Dragonwyck. Doctor Francis was right and it was all a ridiculous pother. She had one qualified physician on hand to attend her, and there was doubtless nothing wrong with her anyway. She had always been a healthy farm girl, strong as a horse despite her air of fragility.

It's all nonsense, thought Jeff angrily, rolled up his sleeves and went into his surgery to open a boil on little Jimmy Coffin's neck.

Next morning at eight his bell pealed and he opened the door to see Nicholas muffled in a fur coat standing on his doorstep, and behind him a red sleigh and panting horse.

The two men looked at each other silently a moment, then Nicholas held out his hand. 'Will you come back with me, Turner?' he said almost humbly. 'We need you.'

Jeff frowned and receded from the door.

'You have a doctor up there; I could do nothing more than he will,' he answered coldly. 'Doctor Francis wrote me.'

Nicholas shook his head. 'Brown's a fool. I don't trust him. I beg of you to come—to hurry. There are certain symptoms; Brown says labor is starting.' He spoke in jerks. His face was haggard. His eyes, devoid now of all condescension or irony, were simply pleading.

Jeff had dealt with many an anxious father, but Nicholas' tension seemed excessive.

'What reason have you to think that Mrs. Van Ryn is in danger?' asked Jeff gravely.

Nicholas looked at him. 'Miranda?' he said doubtfully. 'I don't know that Miranda's in any danger. Do hurry, Turner—I beg of you.'

Jeff was startled. Was this frenzy of apprehension then only for the baby? Why did this man never seem to be motivated by a normal understandable emotion? He felt a sudden sharp pity for the girl immured there at Dragonwyck.

He sighed and reached for his greatcoat, cramming his stiff arm into the left sleeve with difficulty. 'I don't know what I can do, but I'll come with you.'

They were silent on the breakneck ride back to the Manor. Nicholas drove with headlong violence and he lashed the horse unmercifully. The runners made a hissing sound on the packed snow, the silver sleigh bells jingled with an effect of hysterical merriment which suited neither of their moods. The cold wind beat on their faces, now and again icicles fell from the overhanging trees, but Nicholas never slackened; his jaw was set, his narrowed eyes strained on the white road ahead.

Jeff sunk deeper in his greatcoat and was unpleasantly reminded of the last time on which he had hurried to Dragonwyck through the snow. My so-called skill was of no use then, he thought bitterly; it's a marvel Van Ryn still trusts to it.

As they whirled up under the porte-cochère and Nicholas yanked the trembling horse to a stop, the door flew open and Peggy stumbled out.

'Oh, Master,' she gulped, her mouth working, 'Missis is took bad and they won't let me near her. Please let me go to her.'

Nicholas pushed her roughly aside, not troubling to answer, and together the two men hurried up the stairs.

Two people hovered over the great bed on which Miranda lay moaning, Doctor Brown and the German wet nurse whom Nicholas had also imported from New York. The doctor was normally a dapper little man with an ingratiating bedside manner which had won him many influential patients. But now his pomaded locks were in disarray, his neat beard glistened with the sweat that had run down his face.

'What's the matter?' cried Nicholas, turning on him furiously.

The little doctor gave his patron a look of concealed terror. 'N-nothing wrong, Mr. Van Ryn,' he stammered. 'Labor has started but everything is quite all right, oh quite—quite.' His air of false brightness deceived no one, not even the wet nurse, who muttered, *'Ach himmel!'* under her breath and stared round-eyed at Nicholas.

'Mr. Van Ryn, would you and the nurse mind going out while I consult with Doctor Brown?' interposed Jeff with a calmness designed to quell this atmosphere of hysteria. 'I'm sure there's no need for alarm.'

As soon as the door closed, Doctor Brown mopped his face and heaved a sigh of relief. 'Thank God you're here, Turner. I can't take the responsibility alone.' He no longer cared that he might have to share his magnificent fee; he would gladly have foregone the whole fee if he could have been allowed to return with honor to his safe and placid Gramercy Square practice. 'The man's a maniac,' he added somberly. 'I think he'd kill me if anything went wrong.'

'Nonsense!' said Jeff, moving to the bed.

'My dear chap—you don't know,' whispered Doctor Brown, glancing nervously at the door where Nicholas had gone out. 'I tried to resign from the case and he locked me in my room. He watches me all the time, glaring with those icy blue eyes; sometimes I think he's mesmerizing me.'

'Rubbish,' said Jeff, concealing a smile. He held up his hand for silence because Miranda gave a long shuddering moan and opened her eyes.

Doctor Brown had been giving her laudanum; she had been wandering alone in a dark world of fantasy where from time to time the shadows gathered force and welded themselves into shafts of white-hot pain. Her pupils focused slowly on the face which bent near her.

'Jeff?' she whispered on a little questioning note like a surprised child. 'You're in Mexico, aren't you?'

'No,' he answered, smiling. He smoothed the matted waves of golden hair from her wet temples. 'I'm here with you.'

From miles and miles away the pain sent again its first tingle of warning; in that shadow world there was no room for anything but acceptance, and the pain. She groped blindly for Jeff's hand, deriving from its strong comforting grip the first reassurance she had had. The demon flung itself on her quivering body, wrestling, grinding, tossing, until, once more slaked, it threw her aside.

Doctor Brown said, astonished, 'I didn't know you knew Mrs. Van Ryn.'

'Yes,' answered Jeff briefly. He profited by the interval of peace to make a quick examination. Everything was entirely normal and going well. He saw no reason at all for concern and told his colleague so.

The little doctor brightened. 'Glad to hear you think so. Must be the atmosphere of this gloomy place gave me the jim-jams.—Don't know, though. I think there's been something queer about the foetal heart beat. Awfully hard to catch through the stethoscope.'

'It often is,' retorted Jeff. He now thoroughly agreed with Doctor Francis and Nicholas that the man was a fool, and that his nervousness had obscured his judgment.

At four o'clock of the following morning, Valentine's Day, Miranda was delivered of a son. The baby was well formed and handsome, as he could hardly help but be, having sprung from exceptionally good-looking parents. He had a good deal of dark hair and straight brows like his father, and at the corner of his mouth appeared a tiny mole like Miranda's. His arrival was greeted with wild rejoicing. The Dragonwyck church bells clanged welcome, as signal to the tenants that there would be rum punch and beer served all day from the kitchens. The servants poured themselves mug after mug, unchecked by any discipline.

Peggy crept away to her room to offer a prayer of thanksgiving to the Blessed Virgin. She had been reinstated in the sick-room for the last hours of labor as soon as Jeff had understood from Miranda that she wanted her little maid.

As for Nicholas, he refused to leave the cradle in the nursery where the baby lay nestled in silk and lace, but stood motionless gazing down at its little face.

It was Jeff who stayed with Miranda. She was floating in the drowsy peace that follows childbirth. In this state of confused joy no one seemed very real, but she was faintly conscious of hurt that Nicholas had not come to her after her ordeal; more sharply conscious of gratitude to Jeff. He had been the rock to which she clung through it all, his quiet, soothing voice the only comfort. To the passionate gratitude which most women feel toward the physicians who deliver them, Miranda added something more. Though she was not to suspect it for a long time, it was during those hours after her baby's birth that Miranda first felt love for Jeff. She knew now only that she was at peace and happy.

But for him there was neither happiness or peace. He had known from that moment in which she blindly reached for his hand that there would never again be question of marrying Faith or anyone else

This disquieting revelation he pushed aside to be dealt with later. There was a more important fact to be faced right now, and he sat rigid by Miranda's bed trying to determine what to do.

Doctor Brown's nervous forebodings had after all had a basis, though the man was too stupid to realize it, and was getting pleasurably drunk in his room on Nicholas' best brandy.

Jeff had instantly noted the bluish tinge in the baby's skin, the clubbing of the tips of the tiny fingers. As soon as he had dared leave Miranda he had placed the wooden tube of his stethoscope on the little chest and found his worst fears confirmed. The heart beat was spasmodic and so feeble that it seemed each sighing breath the infant drew must be its last.

I may be wrong, thought Jeff grimly, I've been wrong before. But he knew he was not. The baby's heart was defective; it might live an hour, it might live a month, but longer than that was an impossibility.

Miranda shouldn't know until she's rested, but I've got to tell Van Ryn, he thought, and I'd rather be hung, drawn, and quartered.

He walked down the hall to the nursery and found Nicholas still standing beside the cradle, while the wet nurse sat and rocked in the corner of the room and suckled her own baby.

Jeff took a deep breath. 'Mr. Van Ryn—' he said gently, 'I've got to tell you. The baby's not well. He has a bad heart condition.'

He waited, but by not so much as the quiver of a muscle did Nicholas indicate that he had heard. What's the matter with the man? thought Jeff, angry because this strained immobility made him nervous in spite of himself. He had a quick presentiment and peered into the cradle, but the baby still breathed.

So Jeff tried again. 'It sometimes happens like this. I can't tell you how sorry I am. At least your wife has come through beautifully and—' he paused, went on with stony disregard of his own revulsion. 'Someday there can be other babies.'

Nicholas raised his head in a quick darting motion and the young doctor instinctively stepped back. There was menace in that poised body, and Jeff felt a sharp, atavistic fear.

'My son is entirely well,' said Nicholas softly. 'I appreciate your services and they shall be suitably recompensed. You may go now.'

A hot anger rose in Jeff, the site of his head wound began to throb. 'You won't believe me, will you!' he cried roughly. 'You never believe anything you don't want to believe, do you!' He clamped his mouth shut, struggling for control. The baby gave a weak, gasping cry, pitifully unlike the usual cry of the newborn. Jeff bent quickly over the cradle, sensing as he did so the defensive gesture from the other man as though Nicholas would ward him off.

'Listen, Van Ryn,' said Jeff, all anger gone, for suddenly he saw pathos in this stubborn guardianship of a hopeless cause, 'you've got to face it. This baby won't live. It's a miracle he wasn't stillborn.' And far better if he had been, he added mentally. 'The heart is malformed, probably a constricted aorta. No amount of care or nursing will help. It's nobody's fault, nothing could have prevented it. It's just a tragic accident.' He had chosen his words carefully, striving to break through that impenetrable wall which was reared against him. He saw with despair that he had made not the slightest impression.

'You have great confidence in your opinion, Doctor Turner,' said Nicholas politely enough, 'but in this case I have none.' He left the cradle and walked to the window. 'The sleigh is waiting below to take you back.'

Silence fell on the room, broken only by the lusty gurgles of the other healthy baby at the wet nurse's breast, and the creak of her rocking chair.

'At least,' Jeff cried, 'let me prepare Miranda. Whatever you may wish to believe, it's damnable cruelty not to warn her.'

Nicholas turned from the window. 'There's no reason whatever for you to see Mrs. Van Ryn again. Good day, sir.' He ushered Jeff to the head of the stairs and stood there, so that there was no possibility of communicating either with Miranda or Doctor Brown. Propelled by the force of Nicholas' will, Jeff descended the stairs. After all, a physician thus summarily dismissed can neither plead nor argue. Had it not been for Miranda he would have angrily washed his hands of the whole matter. Brown would doubtless accommodate Nicholas with the desired opinion on the baby's condition before he too was sent away. And then Miranda would be alone.

I can't leave her like this, he thought, alone to face tragedy, alone with that madman. Even as he thought 'madman' his scientific training rejected the term as inaccurate. Nicholas was not conventionally insane. He was in fuller control of his faculties than most men ever could hope to be. Not mad but something far more dangerous, a powerful soul obeying nothing but its own desires and moving in a realm outside the normal. But this was no time for analysis; Jeff could do nothing about Nicholas. He stood irresolutely in the lower hall, until the sight of a servant scuttling past gave him an idea.

'Will you send Peggy to me at once!' said Jeff in a low voice. 'Mrs. Van Ryn's maid.'

While he waited he glanced uneasily at the stairs, afraid that Nicholas might descend to see why the sleigh had not yet gone. None of the morning sunlight penetrated into this huge hall; here it was always gloom. It seemed to him that the fading nymphs and satyrs on the wallpaper leered at him through the shadows and that the carved black chairs were pointing at him hostilely. Don't wonder this place gave Brown the 'jim-jams,' he thought; it's about as cosy as a mausoleum.

He heard the door to the servants' wing open and a light shuffling step. Peggy limped quickly up to him. 'Yes, sir. Did you be wanting of me?'

Jeff nodded gravely. 'Yes. There's no one but you can help.'

He told her, and the brown eyes filled with tears. 'Ah, the poor sweet mistress—'tis cruel hard. I was thinking the wee one didn't be acting right from the start.'

'You'll take care of her, Peggy, and help her to bear it.'

The girl swallowed. 'I love her,' she said simply, and seeing Jeff's change of expression, the corners of her mouth lifted. 'And I'm thinking you do too, Doctor dear,' she added softly. 'Now don't be furrowing your brow at me. I couldn't help but be using my eyes in those grim hours of the past night—and 'tis little enough of love there is in this strange great house.'

Yes, thought Jeff, chilled, that's true, perhaps. But Miranda had chosen this strange great house, had fervently desired the man who owned it. So far as Jeff knew she had never regretted her choice. Nicholas was of the type to fascinate a woman; they were ever attracted by ruthlessness and power, particularly when these were invested in a handsome physical covering. Motivated by his sense of justice and loathing of his own jealousy, Jeff leaned backward to believe that Miranda was happy, would be happy once the baby's tragedy was out of the way and Nicholas had accepted the inevitable. Even Nicholas could not deny death.

He picked up his bag and smiled at Peggy. 'I'm glad she has you anyway. If you're ever in Hudson, come and let me have a look at that leg; there might possibly be something to be done.'

'Tis kind he is, kind and good, thought Peggy passionately as she hurried through the baize door before anyone spied her in the front hall, not like him upstairs, with his eyes as cold as the winter sky.

There was no need for Peggy to prepare Miranda. She knew from the first instant that she held her baby in her arms. She had slept in exhaustion for twelve hours, and then the wet nurse came in to her bearing a tiny bundle.

'I nicht can make him to suck, *gnädige frau,*' the woman said sadly and laid the bundle beside Miranda, who raised herself on her elbow and parted the blankets. She gazed down for a long time, then her head dropped back on the pillow. She shut her eyes. 'Go away, please,' she said to the nurse.

When Peggy stole in later, she found them like that. Miranda with her eyes closed and slow tears sliding down into the baby's fuzzy hair where his head nestled against his mother's cheek.

'Och, darlint, don't—' cried Peggy, and knelt beside the bed. 'Sure and he'll be happier in heaven, the precious lambkin. 'Tis the Blessed Mother herself will keep him safe for you till you come.'

Miranda stirred and opened her eyes. 'He must be baptized at once. Get Dominie Huysmann,' she said faintly.

It was over this matter of the hurried christening that Miranda first discovered Nicholas' refusal to admit that anything was wrong with his son.

It was only after she shattered herself with anguished tears that he consented to let the Dominie go through the form as a foolish concession. Later in a month or two it would be done properly in church with the traditional ceremony and all the countryside as witnesses, Nicholas stated, and Miranda said nothing. Her heavy heart was lightened a little when the baby had been duly named 'Adriaen Pieter Van Ryn' and the horrified pastor had scurried back to his wife, who soon spread the sad news far and wide along the river.

The baby lived for six days, and during that time and despite Nicholas' angry protests, Miranda kept her son with her, allowing no one else to touch him but Peggy. She refused to admit the wet nurse, and it was from her own breasts that he drew a tiny amount of nourishment. But he had not the strength to suckle properly, and on a stormy Friday night he gave a little cry and ceased finding the strength to breathe.

While those six sad and dragging days passed, Miranda had thought much of God. She sent Peggy to fetch the Bible her father had given her. It had lain for months in the bottom of a drawer, but now she placed it beneath her pillow and read constantly. What had for years been jumbles of meaningless words resolved themselves now, in the light of her sorrow, into comfort and strength.

She held the baby close to her and whispered the Sixty-First Psalm for herself and him. 'Hear my cry, O God; attend unto my prayer. From the end of the earth will I cry unto thee, when my heart is overwhelmed: lead me to the rock that is higher than I.' And gradually some measure of resignation came to her.

For Nicholas there was none. When he walked into the room on that Friday night and saw Miranda's face, he gave a violent exclamation.

She shook her head, looking at him sorrowfully. 'Hush,' she whispered. 'God has taken him, Nicholas dear.'

He flung back the coverlet, staring at the small, still figure. His face was convulsed; he wheeled on Peggy, who crouched by the bedpost weeping quietly. 'It's you who've done this, you loathsome cripple!' he shouted, advancing on her. 'You've handled him roughly, you've let him fall—'

'Mother of God—' Peggy whispered, shrinking. Her hands flew to her throat, she backed inch by inch from that blazing murderous face.

'Nicholas!' Miranda screamed, trying to rise from the bed.

For a moment he hesitated, and Peggy drew a rasping, terrified breath. Then the fury drained from his face, leaving it gray, and he strode out of the room.

For three days he did not reappear; he locked himself in the tower room, which had been long unused. Frantic at her helplessness, for she was still too weak to get up, Miranda sent repeated messages and pleas by the butler and Mrs. MacNab. She didn't dare send Peggy. To these messages he answered through the locked door that she might make whatever arrangements she liked, nor would he say more.

The tiny white coffin traveled to the churchyard accompanied only by the wailing servants and Peggy, who had forcibly prevented her mistress from going.

On the morning after the funeral Nicholas came downstairs. He entered Miranda's room and greeted her with a brief kiss. 'Good morning, my love. You look very well. White always suits you.'

She stared up at him, stupefied. Her eyes turned blankly to her white bed jacket, then back to his face. It was thin and drawn and had a sallow tinge which it had never had before. His suit was rumpled, as was his cravat, and about him there was a very faint sweetish odor.

'Nicholas,' she cried, 'I've been so terribly worried about you.'

'That was foolish,' he answered, and he smiled. Behind the smile there was a warning. He walked to the window and parted the curtains.

'The ice must be three feet deep in the west channel, and deep enough by our pier. We must give a skating party. I'll make out a list at once.'

'Party—' she repeated—'Oh, I don't understand you—' She turned her face from him. She had been sure that when the first violence of his grief had passed then they would comfort each other, be drawn together closer than they had ever been by their mutual sorrow.

And now as Nicholas continued to talk lightly of invitations, of the state of the roads and the possibility of more snow, she saw with anguish how it was to be.

During the remainder of their life together he never referred to the baby, nor seemed to hear on the few occasions when anyone else did. It was as though it had never been.

18

THE RIVER FAMILIES WERE MOLLIFIED BY THE VAN Ryns' tragedy. One brisk March day the Widow Mary Livingston arrayed herself in the most imposing of her fluted white caps, and having passed the night visiting a friend in Valatie, she drove over to Dragonwyck.

After that visit she told everyone that Mrs. Van Ryn was a sweet little thing and had grown most ladylike.

'I don't blame Nicholas in the least for marrying her,' the Widow told Mrs. Robert Livingston of Linlithgow, who had come to 'The Hill' for tea. 'And for my part I think he's lucky. From a child he's always been difficult, you know. I remember how his poor mother—Katrina Brinckerhoff she was, from Rhinebeck—used to worry about him. He'd have gloomy fits, wouldn't speak to anyone, and pig-headed! She was the only one could manage him. He'd never listen to his father.' She paused to replenish her visitor's cup, and added reflectively: 'She was a pretty creature, Katrina was. Don't know as I ever saw such masses of lovely golden hair on anyone. Come to think of it, this new wife of Nicholas' is something the same type.'

'Is she?' said the other lady politely, helping herself to a seed cake.

'I wonder,' said the Widow Mary, pursuing her own line of thought, 'if Johanna was ever really happy with Nicholas.'

'Oh, but surely!' cried Mrs. Robert. 'She was mad about him, and he was always so devoted.'

The Widow inclined her stately head. 'I know, but Johanna told me once long ago before she got so—so corpulent and—' mindful that she was speaking of the dead, she suppressed 'stupid' and substituted 'slow,' 'she told me that he'd never forgive her for not bearing him a son. Those were her very words, "He'll never forgive me." Of course she couldn't have another try at it, you know—' The Widow leaned forward and whispered. The old lady had flourished in a franker age and was sometimes indelicately outspoken. Mrs. Robert Livingston blushed.

'Oh, well,' she said hastily, 'a disappointment, of course, but it happens to many.'

'That's what I told Johanna, but she just sat and stared at me with those pale round eyes of hers. "You don't know Nicholas," she said. The way she said it gave me quite a turn.'

'Indeed?' said Mrs. Robert, growing bored, for she had never known the Van Ryns very well. 'No doubt he'll have a healthy son yet. And if you think the new wife is acceptable, I too will call when I'm in the neighborhood.'

She did call, and the rest of the local gentry followed suit.

The young Van Ryns entertained constantly that year. Nicholas seemed possessed of feverish energy. Gone were the quiet domestic days they had enjoyed before the baby came. He invited people for weeks at a time, all kinds of people—New York or Albany aristocracy, English noblemen—there was always in New York at that period a ·tray foreigner or two with a portfolio of notes entitled 'My Observations of American Life.' He invited soldiers too, though no one below the rank of captain. In September Mexico surrendered and the Eastern States were crammed with returning victorious heroes.

Dragonwyck hummed with voices from the time that guests straggled down to the huge buffet breakfasts until after midnight, when they straggled up again, exhausted with festivities.

Most of them were dazzled by the constant entertainment provided for them—the boating parties, the rose fêtes in the gardens, the musicals and charades, the dances and elegant picnics on horseback accompanied by a cart and four servants to dispense hampers of capon or boned shad. Only a few of the more sensitive ones grew weary of constant regimentation, or sensed despotism in their host's arrangements.

One of the critical ones was Lady Hermione Basset, daughter to an obscure English earl. She was a middle-aged virgin and she was, of course, keeping a journal of her travels. It was called 'Little Gleanings from Across the Great Atlantic,' and it was written with an eye to publication once she should have finished gleaning and returned to London.

On the twentieth of September, 1847, Lady Hermione having arrived two days before and having since then danced, boated, inspected the greenhouses, ridden cross country, and taken part in archery contests, excused herself firmly, retired to her room, and vouchsafed to life at Dragonwyck some of her most penetrating observations.

'Situated upon one of the most picturesque of American estuaries,' began Lady Hermione cautiously, 'there rears itself a noble pile, a veritable castle, not inferior in magnitude or embellishment to some of the smaller seats of the aristocracy in England. The edifice is composed of gray stone upon which a creeping vine whose exact botanical nature I have not yet determined—(memo, must ask)—tenderly nestles, and this taken with carved gables and a commanding turret lend an air of antiquity. Imagine my astonishment to learn that the building was so constructed not ten years ago!

'In truth there is much to astonish the visitor in this estate. An esthetic taste and unlimited purse have combined with wild primeval nature to produce an effect of luxurious exoticism. How charming these bosky dells beneath the hemlocks! How moving to the responsive heart these marble gazebos by rippling silver streams, these velvety emerald lawns, this exquisite profusion of multi-colored blossoms!

'Within the hall too, all is of a Gothic and tasteful magnificence. And here the feast of reason and the flow of soul mingle around the groaning board with delicately seasoned viands, and the most impeccable of wines!'

Lady Hermione nibbled the tip of her pen and frowned. Was 'impeccable' precisely the word? Well, no matter, she could fix it later. She hastened on to the really interesting subject.

'You will be wondering, dear reader, what type of denizens inhabit this delightful abode, and I shall hasten to apprise you. Mr. X—, my host, is a gentleman of singular personal beauty. In stature he is tall and somewhat slender, luxuriant raven locks bestrew his lofty brow; his flashing eyes stir and startle the beholder, for they are of the most fiery and cerulean blue. Imagine if you will the prepossessing appearance of Lord Byron allied to the suavity of a Chesterfield and thus gain a partial impression of this gentleman, but only partial, for in my host I fear there is lacking the innate repose, the contemplative serenity which are the hall marks of true gentility.

'Alas, it is a flaw which I have frequently observed in this country! This restlessness of spirit, this headlong pursuit of one activity after another! Mr. X— excels in physical exercise, he rides like a centaur but at a pace which suggests that the Furies are pursuing him; he swims like Leander, surpasses all other contestants at archery or bowls, but—'

Lady Hermione laid down her pen. The point she intended to make was rather subtle, and was it after all particularly pertinent to philosophical comments on the United States? She was astute enough to realize that neither Dragonwyck nor Mr. Van Ryn were in the least typical, and perhaps it was not in the best of taste to criticize a hospitality because she found it demanding and excessive; because she had the uncomfortable feeling that the guests were by Nicholas shuffled and moved like pawns and had for him despite his surface courtesy no personal interest whatever.

There was pique in Lady Hermione's reaction. She had been very much smitten with Nicholas. It had seemed on her first evening at Dragonwyck that she and her host were entering upon a flirtation —oh, quite proper, of course, but exhilarating. He had given her a cluster of artemisia and made allusion to the flower's name and her own resemblance to the chaste and lovely moon goddess. She had felt feminine and seductive. But it hadn't lasted. His interest had disappeared just as suddenly as it started. She had watched with jealous eyes while he transferred all this flattering intensity to a Mrs. Gates—a little nonentity from New Jersey.

In Miranda, Lady Hermione was not interested. She saw simply a pretty young wife, exquisitely dressed but rather quiet, who expressed no opinions and did as her husband wished. No wonder she seemed tired, thought Lady Hermione, rubbing her wrist, which had been twisted in the last archery contest. This hectic atmosphere would tire anyone. She would leave in the morning, she thought while she shut and carefully locked her journal. She would go to Boston. There she had been told that she would find earnest thinking. It would be rather amusing to direct one's trenchant pen to the dissection of cultural pretensions. It would at any rate be restful.

Lady Hermione could leave, but Miranda could not. Life for her at this time resolved itself into a skimming along on the surface obedient to Nicholas' will. She was neither happy nor unhappy; it was as though she had started with him upon a frenzied race toward an unspecified goal. There was neither direction nor purpose, but the ceaseless activities, the pressure of people, and Nicholas' dominance gave her no time to realize it. It was only in dreams that she sometimes knew a bitter sadness and sense of catastrophic loss. From these she would awaken to find herself crying.

She had no time to consult her soul, and no privacy. Outside of her room there were people, and within it there was always Nicholas.

She had no friends. Several times one amongst the hordes of guests had attracted her; she had thought that here at last was someone who saw her as an individuality apart from Nicholas. But the situation never ripened. Without ever seeming to do so, Nicholas intervened, and soon the guest would depart again, having seen in Miranda just what Lady Hermione had—only a pretty young wife who adored her husband and had nothing much to say for herself.

In the same way the visit from Miranda's mother was repeatedly postponed. Abigail could have come now at any time; her rheumatism had improved, Tabitha's baby was doing well. When Abigail had received the letter telling of the death of Miranda's own baby, she had expected to leave for Dragonwyck at once. But the months went by and there was no more talk of her coming. Miranda's letters became very infrequent and brief. They read like society bulletins. 'Yesterday we entertained ex-President Van Buren and a host of others who have interest in the election,' or, 'Tomorrow we go to a ball at the Astors. I believe it is to be a brilliant affair.' Nothing personal in them.

Abigail hid her hurt under brusqueness of manner. Ephraim, the boys, and even little Charity suffered under the increased sharpness of her tongue.

And as for Jeff, until the fall of 1849 Miranda did not see him at all. She had thought for a while after the baby's death that she would see him often, that Nicholas—who must like the young doctor, for had he not twice called him in a crisis?—would invite Jeff to Dragonwyck.

Nicholas not only would not invite Jeff, but he forbade Miranda to see him for any reason. She might not take Peggy to have the leg looked at. She was to have nothing more to do with Doctor Turner.

Miranda had long since ceased trying to find reasons for all her husband's behavior, but she understood that he wished to see nothing and no one who reminded him of the baby's death. And she submitted in this too, all the more readily because she had a feeling of guilt about Jeff. Her interest in him, and her tenderness and gratitude, were not entirely fitting to a wife. So she did as Nicholas wished.

It was Peggy who suffered during this time. She tended her mistress faithfully, and Miranda was always kind, but the old close relationship was obscured. The missis was always in a hurry, morning, noon, and night. She seemed to think of nothing but her lovely clothes and the occasions for exhibiting them. There were no more little confidences and no more chance for them, because master was always in the way. And Peggy was afraid of Nicholas. He ignored her; when she was assisting Miranda with some detail of the toilet, he looked through Peggy, and almost never addressed her. She knew that he allowed her to remain because she had become very useful to Miranda—she had learned to sew and to press, she kept every detail of the elaborate wardrobe in exquisite order—but she never forgot the look in his eyes on the night the baby died. She understood that that outburst had been a reaction of blind rage at Fate, for which she had been the temporary and unwitting scapegoat; she understood even that as much as it was in his nature to regret anything, he probably regretted that loss of control. Nevertheless, she was constantly uneasy in his presence.

Besides the master, there was another cause for uneasiness at Dragonwyck. There had been a queer feeling about the house during the few days of the poor wee one's life. Not just sadness, but a nasty creepiness that gave you shivers up and down the backbone. This feeling was worst in the little Red Room, though the other servants didn't feel anything out of the way when they went in to clean. But Peggy did. One evening while the master was shut up in his tower, and the mistress was in bed with her sick little baby, Peggy had gone into the Red Room to hunt for a lace handkerchief that was missing. She hadn't stayed to search for it, because there had been someone else in that room. Someone you couldn't see or hear, but it was there. As real and as awful as the Black O'Donohue who galloped round Lough Leane on All Souls' Eve, real as the little folk who danced in the ruins of Aghadoe.

Peggy had run wildly from that room and locked herself into her own bedroom in the attic. Her hands had been soaking wet while she told her beads on the arbutus rosary.

Weeks later she had mentioned something of this to her mistress, but the poor sweet lady hadn't wanted to listen. She'd spoken quite sharply, while her eyes had held a bit of a strained, frightened look. So Peggy had said no more, and anyway the creepy feeling seemed to be gone.

Sometimes Peggy whispered to herself an old Gaelic charm. The red-headed mother had taught it to her long ago in the sod cottage near Killarney.

'Three things are of the Evil One—

An evil eye;
An evil tongue;
An evil mind.

'Three things are of God, and these three are what Mary told to her Son, for she heard them in heaven—

The merciful word,
The singing word,
And the good word.

May the power of these three holy things be on all the men and women of Erin for evermore.'

This was the sense of the charm, but Peggy said it in the ancient language as her mother had taught her. There was more magic in it that way. There was need for magic—good magic and prayers in that house—for never a bit of comfort did the poor mistress seem to get out of her own creed, after the baby died. The master laughed at her when she read in the Bible, and once he asked her what good all her superstitions and 'caterwauling to an imaginary image' had done her or anyone. Had they ever prevented sorrow or disappointment, he asked her in that quiet, sneering way of his.

And the Bible had pretty soon gone back to the bottom drawer. Small harm in that, maybe, thought Peggy, who knew little of the Bible and in any case could not read; but surely to goodness every soul, high or low, needed faith. She lit many a candle to the Blessed Mother and asked Her about it.

In New York this was easier, for there was a new church not far from Stuyvesant Street and she could slip out to early Mass. The mistress seldom rang for her any more until nearly noon.

It was in New York on May tenth of 1849 that this phase of Miranda's life came to an abrupt close, and the Astor Place Massacre was the cause of it.

The Van Ryns were bidden by the Clement Vandergraves to dine at four and go on afterward to the Astor Place Opera House, where they would witness William Charles Macready's interpretation of 'Macbeth.' All of fashionable New York was going, not only because performances at the Opera House were extremely elegant—it had been built in 1847 by a hundred and fifty gentlemen of wealth and social prominence—but because Macready's appearance tonight promised to be interesting. Three days ago on May seventh the ridiculous feud between the English Macready and the American Edwin Forrest had reached a minor climax when both actors presented themselves in 'Macbeth' on the same evening—Macready at the Astor and Forrest at the Broadway. There had been disturbance at both performances; each audience was composed of friends who cheered, and enemies who groaned and cat-called. Society on the whole was amused; everyone knew and discussed the rivals' relative rights to be incensed with each other.

Aside from the loss of dignity and lack of ordinary courtesy displayed by two talented actors, this spectacle would have affected nobody except that it got out of bounds and was seized upon by the malcontents in the city. The quarrel became a symbol of class war.

Macready was an Englishman and the favorite of New York society. Forrest was favored by the populace not only because he was an American but because he was most persuasive in such rôles as Jack Cade and Spartacus which personified the struggle of the underdog against entrenched privilege.

All over Europe at that time there were riots and insurrections born of class hatred. The same unrest trickled to America, where to be sure there was a democracy, but was it really working, that democracy? That was the ever-recurring doubt of the people. From this fear sprang many manifestations of revolt—large and far-reaching ones like the Abolitionist movement; smaller and less important ones like the anti-rent wars on the manors, and the Astor Place riot.

Nicholas and Miranda—in the barouche—set out from Stuyvesant Street at four o'clock on their way to the Vandergraves' in Gramercy Square. Miranda was happy. The May afternoon was fresh and fragrant. Nicholas was in a good humor, and there was the prospect of the theater with congenial companions. Miranda liked the Vandergraves and she adored the theater second only to opera, which had been for her an enchanted discovery. She thought with amusement and a trace of pity of the naïve girl who had been so excited over Barnum's shoddy freaks three years ago—and how beautiful she had thought that lurid pantomime at Niblo's!

Now she was accustomed to the best, could appraise the singing of Truffi in 'Ernani,' or the lovely Biscaccianti's phrasing in 'La Sonnambula.' She had long since passed her initial embarrassing confusion between Richelieu and Richard the III; she knew which speeches to appreciate, and when to applaud. She had not attained the blasé attitude affected by the society ladies. Her interest in the world of make-believe on the stage was too eager for that, but she had attained knowledge and poise.

She was conscious of looking her best tonight. Both she and Nicholas were in the ultra-formal attire which was expected not only from subscribers to the boxes, but from each member of the Astor Place Opera House audience. It was this emphasis upon full dress which particularly infuriated those of the populace who dared aspire to seeing the best opera or drama in the city. Without a black frock coat, white vest, and white kid gloves no gentleman would be admitted. To brighten the severity of his garb, Nicholas wore a very small carnation in his buttonhole and a set of sapphire studs.

Miranda looked at him admiringly. Whatever the inner disquiet in their relationship, or perhaps because of that disquiet, she had never come to take her husband for granted. She still saw him consciously, not with the blank eye of habit, but alertly. The firm chiseling of his dark profile above the frilled white stock, the blackness of his hair, and the always startling blueness of his eyes beneath their heavy brows—these things still had power to make her heart beat faster.

'Do you like my new dress, Nicholas?' she asked, hungry for the appreciation which he often withheld. But today he was generous. He turned and surveyed her, smiling. Her dress was of midnight blue—that color of all others most flattering to blondes, and the low heart-shaped bodice was cut as a basque. Of this Miranda was proud; it was a new fashion direct from Paris, and would not be adopted in New York for another year. She had daringly avoided all the frills and flounces which were considered essential, and used for ornament only a diamond bow-knot at her breast and a diamond arrow and tiny blue feather in her high-puffed hair.

Nicholas raised her white-gloved hand to his lips. 'You're beautiful, my love, you have excellent taste in dress. It's always pleased me.'

'Do I please you in all ways, Nicholas?' she asked wistfully. It was so seldom that he praised her, so seldom that he was approachable like this.

He was silent a minute and she thought instantly: What a fool I was to ask that! Neither of them had ever mentioned it, but she knew what he was thinking. She had not yet given him another son. She had gone secretly to consult Doctor Francis on this delicate point, and been reassured. There was nothing wrong whatsoever. It was just a matter of time. Nature was unpredictable.

'You wouldn't be sitting here with me in my carriage if you didn't,' said Nicholas, and he laughed.

Decidedly he was in a very good mood tonight.

They drove up Third Avenue so that they might see the famous Stuyvesant pear tree on the corner of Thirteenth Street. Again for the two hundredth time its ancient boughs were loaded with blossoms. How strange it was that it could go on renewing itself in exquisite youth, when the hands that had planted it had so long ago fallen to dust!

Nicholas got out of the carriage and plucked her a small flower. As she accepted it smiling, she thought that embodied in that little presentation of the pear blossom were the only three virtues which in Nicholas were invariable: his veneration for the Dutch tradition, his love of beauty, and his gallantry. On these three qualities alone could she always count—but it was enough, she told herself hastily, determined not to dim the gala evening.

The carriage stopped on the west side of Gramercy Park before a flight of steps which led to a white-trimmed doorway bright with gleaming brass. The Vandergraves were as trim and shining as their house, and as solid. They were both round and rosy and kind. As do many happily married couples, they had grown to look alike, and Rebecca's smiling face between two glossy wings of neat brown hair resembled her husband's smiling face between equally neat and glossy side whiskers. Upstairs in the attic nurseries, there romped eight little Vandergraves, all topped with neat brown hair and all as round and rosy as their parents.

It was a comfortable house, welcoming and cheerful. Miranda never entered it without a touch of envy, which Nicholas did not share. The Vandergraves bored him, but he suffered their acquaintance because their ancestors on both sides had landed on Manhattan Island with Cornelius Van Ryn, and they now belonged to that most conservative backbone of New York society, those of whom outsiders never heard. No function of theirs would ever be described in the newspapers; they would be buried and their daughters would marry in the same inner circle without causing the slightest ripple amongst the populace, who had already begun following every mention of Goelets, Lorillards, or Astors with greedy interest.

At half-past six when it was time to leave for the Opera House, whose performances began at seven sharp, Miranda was sorry to go. Neither the lengthy meal nor the conversation had been brilliant, but she had enjoyed herself. Rebecca's good-humored chatter, her assumption that everyone was as good and happy as she was, created an atmosphere of ease.

Miranda felt that Rebecca did not think her overshadowed by Nicholas as so many people did and that here at least she shone as a distinct personality. Intimate friendship was impossible, even had Nicholas allowed it, for to Miranda's twenty-four years, Rebecca's forty-two made an impassable gulf. And then there were all the children. No childless woman could share many interests with the mother of eight. Still, the visit had provided relief from the tension under which Miranda unconsciously lived, unconscious because she had grown so used to it that it had become her normal mental climate. When Rebecca said, 'Ranny, my love, I've rung for our wraps, I fear we may be late,' Miranda smiled and rustled reluctantly to her feet. Rebecca was the only person who ever gave Miranda her childish nickname, and she did it in serene oblivion of Nicholas' annoyance.

They all went together in the Vandergrave carriage, and when they reached Fourteenth Street, Rebecca, who had been speaking with tolerant amusement of 'Commodore' Vanderbilt's efforts to bludgeon his way into social acceptance, suddenly checked herself and cast an uneasy look at the street. 'Oh, dear,' she said; 'there seem to be a great many rough-looking men about, and they give us such horrid stares. You don't think there will be any trouble tonight, do you, Mr. Vandergrave?'

Her husband patted her hand. 'Of course not, my pet.'

At that moment the carriage paused to make way for the cross-town stage and a large poster intruded itself on the startled gaze of the carriage's four occupants.

In fiery red letters the poster exhorted:

AMERICANS! AROUSE!

THE GREAT CRISIS HAS COME!

Decide now whether English ARISTOCRATS ! ! !

shall triumph in this AMERICA's metropolis.

WORKING MEN! FREEMEN! Come out!

Dare to own yourselves sons of the iron hearts of '76!

'Oh, dear!' cried Rebecca again with increased alarm. 'What are they planning? Don't you think we should turn back?'

'Why, no, madam,' said Nicholas in genuine amusement. 'You surely would not let a few hysterical rowdies spoil your evening's pleasure. This silly actors' quarrel has nothing to do with us.'

The ladies looked relieved. Clement Vandergrave cleared his throat and swallowed the order he had been about to give the coachman.

But a sullen mob filled Astor Place. While carriage after carriage rolled through to discharge its occupants on the red carpet that stretched up the granite steps to the palisaded portico, this mob gave way just enough for the vehicles to pass, but a low growl like distant thunder hovered in the still twilight air.

As the Vandergrave party entered the theater, a man in a brown suit pushed past them and brandished his arms at the queue which had formed before the ticket office. 'You can't get in there, you poor fools!' he yelled, waving a bit of pasteboard. 'I paid for this ticket and they wouldn't let me in because I hadn't kid gloves and a white vest on! They shut the door in my face—damn the stinking nabobs—!'

The thundering growl outside rose higher in pitch, muffled but distinct through the Opera House walls.

Miranda looked up at Nicholas. 'It does seem more than just an actors' quarrel, doesn't it?' she asked hestitantly. 'I mean it seems to be directed against—people like us.'

'I daresay,' answered Nicholas, ushering her into their box and settling himself on one of the red-velvet seats. 'The lower classes are always jealous and trying to ape their betters.'

There was a distant crash and the diminishing tinkle of glass. A murmur of consternation ran over the audience. All eyes turned for reassurance to the group of frock-coated policemen who stood together in a far corner under the balcony. Their chief, Mr. Matsell, chewed on his fingernails and looked unconcerned. The audience settled back again and consulted their programs.

The curtain rose on time and the three weird sisters played to a quiet, waiting house. When Macready, tastefully arrayed in chain mail, strode on in the third scene and announced to Banquo:

'So foul and fair a day I have not seen,'

he was greeted with an ovation marred by a few hisses which the police suppressed, and supporters rushed a placard to the side of the proscenium which stated that 'The Friends of Order will remain quiet.'

The Friends of Order did remain quiet, but the mob outside did not. It worked itself into a fury. In the seventh scene just as Macready, beating his breast and flashing his eyes, began,

> 'I have no spur
> To prick the sides of my intent, but only
> Vaulting ambition—'

a handful of stones crashed through the upper windows and bounced harmlessly along the gallery; then clearly through those broken windows the frightened audience heard a shout. 'Tear it down! Burn the damned den of the aristocracy!'

Macready paused only a second and then went on at breakneck speed to Miss Pope, who made a valiant if pale and trembling Lady Macbeth.

Another clatter of stones fell into the theater; one of them hit the gorgeous chandelier, which shivered and tinkled threateningly. The parquet audience rushed back under the galleries. The play went on through the uproar, though the actors became inaudible and were reduced to the status of wildly gesticulating puppets.

Mr. Vandergrave rose. 'I'm going to take my wife home,' he said to Nicholas in a low voice, 'and I presume you will do the same. This is outrageous.'

'Why, no,' answered Nicholas, smiling and rising to help Rebecca with her shawl. 'I believe we'll stay. I'm fond of "Macbeth," and find this particular interpretation remarkably interesting.' He indicated the stage, where the third act was in resolute progress, though the actors had to skip over a stream of water which gushed from pipes which had been broken in Mr. Macready's dressing-room.

Vandergrave shook his head and presented his arm to his wife. They quitted the box and hurried with other prudent ones toward the Eighth Street exit, where a squad of policemen escorted them outside.

'Don't you think we should go too?' asked Miranda nervously. There was a constant banging of bricks, paving stones, and pebbles against the façade of the building; the balconies shouted and stamped to the accompaniment of the pandemonium outside on Astor Place.

'Are you afraid?' asked Nicholas, laughing.

She saw that he was exhilarated. He, who was so seldom amused by anything, derived from the hostility which surrounded them, from the mouthing, frightened players, the shrieking audience, a sardonic delight.

She twisted her gloved fingers together and tried to reason awav her panic. They were safe enough in the covered box, but what would happen later? Suppose the rioters succeeded in firing the opera house, or in breaking in? And even if none of this happened, when this nightmare performance was finally ended, what would Nicholas do? Danger was to him a joy and a challenge.

A sharp apprehension seized her, fear that was separate from the contagion of panic around her.

Though Macready's company begged for the descent of the curtain, implored him at least to make stringent cuts, he refused. The audience had paid for a full performance and that they would get, if they dared stay for it. No despicable Yankee mob doubtless incited by the even more despicable Forrest should feaze a British gentleman.

Toward the close of the last act there was a lull outside, occasioned, though no one in the theater knew it, by the arrival of the militia in Astor Place—sixty cavalry and three hundred infantry.

The last scenes became audible. The final curtain came down and Macready appeared bowing and was received with cheers.

The manager made a hurried announcement thanking those who had stayed and asking the audience to leave through the back door, where the constabulary would insure their safety.

Everyone obediently surged toward the indicated exit. Everyone but Nicholas. He adjusted Miranda's satin pelisse for her, put on his black cape, and blew some specks of dust from his gloves. Then he placed his tall hat under his arm.

'Where are we going?' cried Miranda as he ushered her from the box and turned down the deserted corridor to the right.

'Out the front entrance, as we came in, of course.'

She drew back, hanging on his arm. 'But that's where the—the disturbance is—oh, please, please, Nicholas, go with the others—I implore you—'

'The disturbance seems to have died down,' he said with the faintest tinge of regret. 'But in any case would you really contemplate our scuttling through the back door like mice?'

Yes, she thought passionately. I want to get home. I want to be safe. But she was silenced by her habit of obedience and the instinctive admiration for physical courage. The great front doors were barricaded from the inside. Nicholas removed the planks and held one of the doors for her to pass through.

At once they saw the reason for the silence. The troops were ranged along the base of the steps confronting the mob. Both factions were uncertain, eyeing each other warily. Now and again one of the rioters shied an isolated stick, stone, or rotten apple at the soldiers, who dodged as best they could and endured stoically. They had no orders to fire.

The flickering light of torches and such of the street lamps as had not been broken illumined the square. On the Bowery corner a fountain of water from a smashed hydrant gushed high in the air.

In the darkness of the colonnade around the theater no one had noticed Miranda and Nicholas. They might still have slipped down behind the troops and, mingling with the Lafayette Street crowd, who were mostly onlookers and curiosity-seekers, have walked the two blocks home.

The mob had exhausted its venom, and nearly exhausted its missiles too. It was nearing midnight, and in the absence of any victims and confronted by the impassive militia, most of the rioters began to think of drifting away. They had made their demonstration against 'foreign rule and the aristocracy,' they had inflicted a certain amount of damage on the hated Opera House. Perhaps that was enough. The frenzy for destruction ebbed with every passing moment; a good many of the older men were beginning to tell themselves it was a good thing there'd been no blood shed.

Then Nicholas walked down the steps and pushing through the astonished soldiers appeared in the front rank and gazed at the mob.

For a dumfounded instant they were hushed and then a hundred cries rose. 'Bloody bastard snob!' 'Spoil his pretty clothes for him.' 'Give it to him!' But still there was no concerted action. They seethed back and forth, fists were brandished, a few futile pebbles thrown, when suddenly a boy darted up carrying a bucket.

He had filled it at the hydrant, and laughing in an excited voice, 'This'll spoil his fancy duds!' he flung the water full over Nicholas. There were cheers and approving roars.

The crowd was willing now to be satisfied with horseplay rather than violence; the spectacle of a dripping aristocrat delighted them.

Nicholas' arm shot out in one quick, smooth motion. He seized the rifle of the soldier beside him, aimed carefully, and fired.

The boy dropped the bucket, the taunting laugh on his face crumpled into a look of foolish amazement. From the hole in his throat spurted a jet of blood, black as ink in the dim light. Before he fell to the cobblestones, fifty shots spattered across the square. The militia had started firing.

The mob, frantic now with terror, sent one last volley of paving stones before they fled. One of these stones hit Nicholas on the chest. He fell to the sidewalk not ten feet from the dying boy.

Two of the soldiers carried Nicholas back to the colonnade and laid him on the top step. Miranda knelt beside him, chafing his hands, easing his head on her wadded-up pelisse. The horror of the last few minutes receded. She no longer heard the screams and shots from the square. Her brain worked clearly. She knew exactly what to do. She saw that Nicholas, though unconscious, did not seem seriously injured, but he must be taken home at once.

'Go to the Van Ryn house on Stuyvesant Street,' she ordered one of the soldiers. 'Tell whoever opens the door that I want the carriage to hurry to the Eighth Street entrance of the Opera House. There must be three of our men, blankets and brandy. Then you will wait and show them where we are.'

The man went off without a word. She did not realize that that was the first command she had ever given in her married life, but she was aware of astonishment. Nicholas was, after all, not invulnerable! Mixed with this astonishment was a sick revulsion. She was too much confused and shocked to understand exactly what had happened—was still happening—in the square. She could only wait beside Nicholas and try to erase from her memory the black, spurting hole and contorted boyish face.—That face had reminded her of Nat at home.

Before the soldier came back to them accompanied by MacNab, a footman, and the coachman, the riot in Astor Place had ended. Amongst fifty who were wounded there were twenty corpses on the cobblestones. These included two bystanders, a little girl who had stolen from her house in Lafayette Street to see why the soldiers were shooting, and an old man who was on his way home to Jones Street after visiting his daughter uptown.

The troops marched back to their barracks.

To the north, Grace Church's new marble spire shone like an inverted icicle against the midnight sky.

19

A MONTH LATER WHEN THE VAN RYNS MOVED UP TO Dragonwyck, Nicholas had entirely recovered from the effects of the blow from the paving stone, which had cracked two ribs but done no other physical damage. His body had recovered, but his personality had changed. He wished to see no one. As abruptly as the phase of activity and continual hospitality had started, it now stopped.

During his convalescence in New York he lay day after day moody and silent, accepting Miranda's or Mrs. MacNab's nursing without comment.

Nobody knew of his part in the Astor Place Massacre. If any of his friends had heard the story, most of them would have considered that his action had been justified. They would have applauded his courage. What was the life of one vicious hoodlum amongst so many dead and wounded? And after all, the militia had fired at the same time.

It was Miranda alone who struggled through horror and doubt. She tormented herself with a hundred bitter questions. If Nicholas had not insisted on leaving by the front entrance to the theater, if he had not pushed down where everyone could see him, if instead of shooting he had knocked the boy down with his fist, would then the massacre have been avoided? Or would the soldiers eventually have fired anyway?

The conviction grew upon her that Nicholas too was suffering and that he felt remorse. This enabled her to bear his gloomy moroseness. In nightmares she repeatedly saw the blood spurting from the jagged hole in a thin boyish throat, and she thought that Nicholas saw it too.

That was not what Nicholas saw. He saw a man whose invincibility had been scathed by a chance blow, a man who had been unconscious and impotent for the first time in his life, a man who had to depend on strangers for safety—strangers and Miranda.

They returned to Dragonwyck and his moroseness and his silence continued. One day he mounted the tower stairs and locked himself into the room at the summit. He did not reappear for three days, and Miranda, remembering how it had been after the baby's death, left him alone.

When he came back to her he seemed more normal than he had since his injury, but upon his first greeting her she noticed the same faint sweet odor about his clothes, and his speech was slow, the words almost imperceptibly slurred.

Peggy noticed this too. Were it anyone else but the master, she thought, I'd say he'd been on a tout up there a-skulking by himself for three livelong days. But he's not got the smell of liquor about him, and he's not the kind of a man for a free and honest swig, not that one, he isn't.

A month later it happened again.

Miranda wandered about the house, which now that it was no longer filled with guests, had for her regained all its oppressive atmosphere. She avoided the servants' eyes, and pretended even to Peggy that Nicholas' conduct was in no way peculiar.

Toward twilight of the second day she made up her mind. She mounted the tower stairs, fifty feet of slow spiralings. The door at the summit was a six-inch slab of paneled oak. There was no answer to her first knock. She retreated a step and gazed at that dark, implacable door. A year—even a month ago, she would have accepted this silent symbol of Nicholas' orders, would have obeyed him as always.

Now she did not. She clenched her fists and pounded on the door until a muffled voice cried angrily, 'Who's there?'

'It's Miranda!' she called back resolutely. 'I demand that you let me in.'

There was silence, then the key turned in the massive lock and the door swung open. Nicholas, in a brocaded dressing-gown, stood and looked at her sardonically. 'Come in, sweetheart, by all means, since you demand it.' He closed and locked the door behind her, putting the key in his pocket.

She stared blankly at him and at the circular room. What had she expected? A bluebeard's chamber, a sable-hung and gloomy magnificence, exaggeration of the apartments downstairs?

On the contrary, the room was austere and nearly bare, furnished only with a plain table, chair, and couch. On the table were a row of shabby books and an unlit candle, on the floor a straw matting. Even though the sun had set across the river behind the Catskills, the four windows, each facing toward a different compass point, still caught ample light.

It was only after a moment that she noticed in the room a bluish haze and a pungent odor.

'You smoke here?' she asked vaguely, conscious of a baffled disappointment. She had for so long romanticized this locked room, had been so sure that once she penetrated its secret, she would at the same time penetrate the wall that guarded her husband's soul.

He stared at her steadily, so that she turned and answered his gaze, noting with surprise that in his eyes the pupils had shrunk to pinpoints. The irises appeared to be a solid blue.

'I smoke here.' He repeated her puzzled question with a sarcastic inflection. He reached out and seized her right wrist. His fingers closed around it in a brutal grip. He pulled her over to the couch, and she saw then that on its far side, hitherto hidden, there stood a small charcoal brazier and a tabouret on which lay a carved silver box, some fine wires, and three strangely shaped pipes.

'Behold the diamond gateway to all beauty and all power!' he said in that curiously slow voice.

She stared at the little pipes and the glowing charcoal. "What is it, Nicholas?'

He released her wrist and opening the silver box brought out a sticky black ball which he cupped in his hand. 'Opium, my love. The glorious fruit of the poppy!'

She looked from the sticky ball in his hand to his face.

'But that's a drug, isn't it?' she said uncertainly. She had never heard the word except once two years ago when she had skimmed through a newspaper editorial on the evils of the Chinese opium traffic.

Nicholas inserted one of the wires into the ball and twisting off a tiny bead began to toast it over the brazier. 'No drug for me—' he said, and his voice sank to a whisper. 'No drug, but a javelin to pierce the mist which separates us from reality. It is my servant. All things are my servants. For I am master of life and death. Don't you know that yet, Miranda?'

He turned his head and smiled through half-closed lids. Her heart began a slow pounding, but she managed to speak with calm.

'You're not well, Nicholas. I know that whatever this stuff is, it's bad for you. Come downstairs with me now—please.'

He laughed lazily and, placing the cooked pellet in the bowl of one of the pipes, he inhaled deeply, at the same time stretching himself upon the couch.

She began to edge cautiously away and his hand shot out fastening itself again on her wrist.

'Nicholas—' she said, looking down at him, 'I don't understand. What makes you do this?'

He did not answer her. He considered her question with an inward silent pleasure, viewing her and himself as through a translucent crystal. How delicious it was, this expanding of the faculties. His mind functioned by itself. It had withdrawn into cold star-spangled space, and out here in the vast infinity it gathered power until it became a flaming ball burning with an exquisite brilliance.

It had been on the visit to Poe's cottage that it had first occurred to him to try this instrument of power. Sometime after that he had gone down to a shuttered house on Mott Street. That experience had been distasteful, the poppy had not yet yielded to his mastery. He had not sought her again for a long time. There had been a reluctance. How shameful it now seemed!

He lay and contemplated that reluctance until it took form and he saw it as a small, creeping animal which must be crushed. Everything must be crushed which might obscure the flaming brilliance. He turned his head and looked up at Miranda. She too had taken on a luminous, fluid quality. In the dimming room her golden head was the only bright spot. His fingers tightened on her wrist until he could feel the small sinews move.

'Let me go,' she whispered. 'You hurt me.'

He saw that she trembled and that her long, beautiful lids were lowered to hide the fear behind them.

'Let me go—' she cried more loudly.

'Ah, but you don't want to go, my darling. Your soul and body are only a reflection of my will.' And he twisted her arm until she was forced down beside him on the couch. Her cries were stifled beneath his mouth. She shrank to a frozen stillness. The smell of the opium nauseated her.

At last his grip slackened. He pushed her from the couch, and reached for the silver box. 'Leave me alone,' he said dully. 'You weary me.'

He drew the key from his pocket and tossed it on the floor.

She bent to pick it up and gave an involuntary moan as pain shot through her swollen wrist.

Nicholas lay without moving, his eyes shut.

She unlocked the door and shutting it behind her walked slowly down the stairs to her bedroom.

Peggy, at her eternal task of putting away freshly laundered lingerie, uttered a sharp cry when she saw her mistress.

'Whatever is it, mum!' She gazed horrified. The missis' hair was falling down her shoulders and all tangled, her pretty rose bodice was torn, worse than that were the great staring eyes of her and the trembling of her pretty mouth. 'Och, and ye've hurt yourself, poor darlin'—' cried Peggy, touching the discolored wrist. 'Did *he* do that—the varmint?' she cried in sudden enlightenment. ' 'Tis the drink after all then he's a-closeting himself with up there!'

Miranda shook her head. 'It's not drink.' She moved restlessly to the dressing-table, picked up her brush, put it down again. 'Peggy, I want to see Doctor Turner. Heaven grant that he's still in Hudson.'

'He is that, mum. 'Twas only yisterday they was a-talking in the kitchen about him and the fine cures he does. 'Twould be for your wrist you were thinking of him?'

Miranda looked at her arm. 'Yes, yes, of course. It should be bound. I don't dare go to Hudson. I must get a message to him somehow—I don't know . . .'

'Leave it all to me, mum,' said Peggy with instant comprehension and sympathy. 'Write a bit of a note to send to him. I'll see that he gets it by midnight for sure.'

'But how can you—?' whispered Miranda, looking up doubtfully. 'How can you without danger of—?' In this house nothing escaped Nicholas, no orders were given without his approval, not the most trivial episode took place without his knowledge.

Peggy smiled demurely. 'There's a lad in the village, mum, Hans Klopberg the smith's 'prentice, wouldn't boggle at doing me a bit of a favor. He's trusty enough, for all he's a great hulking Dutchy.'

'Peggy dear—you're not—in love!' cried Miranda, momentarily shaken out of her own distress by the little maid's expression. She had come to take this fidelity and affection for granted. It had never occurred to her that Peggy might have a life of her own, might—and this thought filled her with desolation—want to leave and get married.

Peggy read her mistress's face, and her own sobered. 'I'll never be leaving you whilst you want me, missis dear,' she said earnestly. 'Never.'

But I can't keep her if she has a chance for happiness, thought

Miranda passionately, a chance to get away from this. And I don't know how I'll live without her. She felt that she hated this Hans Klopberg, whoever he was, and at the same time she despised her selfishness. Yet there were only two people in the world of whose love she was certain—Peggy and Abigail.

And neither of them had she repaid in kind, for always between herself and them there had stood the shadow of Nicholas.

'Come, mum, write the note,' said Peggy with brisk tenderness. 'I'm thinking we dare not have the young doctor to the house, for there's no telling when *he'll* be abroad again, nor yet what he can see from his turret and all. You must meet the doctor outside.' She thought swiftly, seeing that the poor dear lady was too deep in misery to plan. 'By the old mill on the creek, mum, as soon as it's light. Ye can slip out. Tell him that in the writing.' And Holy Mother of God keep that one from coming downstairs beforehand, she added to herself.

Her prayers were answered. All night long there was no sound from the tower room. Miranda lay alone and sleepless in the great Van Ryn bed. Her sprained wrist throbbed incessantly. At five she rose and dressed with Peggy's help. The November morning was chilly; both women's fingers grew numb and fumbling as they buttoned Miranda into a high-necked blue merino, topped by a hooded gray traveling cape.

Everything was arranged, Peggy whispered. Hans had ridden his father's plow horse to Hudson, giving as excuse a sudden pain in the foot which needed doctoring. 'Though,' said Peggy irrepressibly, 'divil a pain or an ache he's had in his life, that one, may the blessed saints forgive him for his untruthfulness.—'Twas artful of him, however, taking it all in all.'

Miranda smiled sadly at the girl's obvious pride.

'Yes, very artful, and then what—?' she urged.

Jeff had been awakened and read the note. 'He looked for a moment as dumfounded as a hen what's hatched a clutch of ducks,' said Peggy, quoting her admirer. 'Then he gives a bit of a start and a shake, and says he'll be there.'

Miranda leaned down and kissed Peggy. 'Thank you,' she whispered.

They stole together through the silent house, and on those thick rugs and carpets even the shuffle of Peggy's dragging foot was inaudible.

They had decided to use the little side door in the music room, which was at the farthest point of the house from the tower. The door was behind the grand piano, and Miranda, seeing the gilded instrument, was suddenly reminded of how long it had been since Nicholas had played on it. The keyboard was locked, and upon the painted garlands which decorated the lid there had gathered a thin powdering of dust. She saw him suddenly as he had been on her first night at Dragonwyck.

Just here he had sat and played to her 'I Dreamt That I Dwelt in Marble Halls,' and at her hesitant singing, he had smiled. A smile full of tenderness and indulgence. And back there in the Red Room, Johanna had been sitting alone, with her clumsy botched monograms. What had she been thinking of alone in there, while Miranda and Nicholas sang and played together 'I Dreamt That I Dwelt in Marble Halls'?

'Hurry, mum,' whispered Peggy, and Miranda started. She had forgotten the miserable present, forgotten even Jeff in the reconstruction of that scene of five years ago.

As Peggy stationed herself to wait by the door, Miranda slipped out. She kept close to the protection of the house, then ran ten yards across the lawn to the nearest hemlocks. From there she hurried shivering through the woods toward the mill creek. Her kid boots made little crunching sounds on the frozen ground. Ahead of her through the distant oaks and chestnuts a lurid red sun slid above the horizon.

Jeff arrived at the mill first. He tethered his horse and entered the deserted stone building. It stood on the edge of the Van Ryn estate proper, and Mrs. Farmer Gebhard's rueful prophecy had been correct. As soon as the tenants had started the long-drawn-out proceedings against Nicholas for their rights to the lands, they had been deprived of the mill, and the shad runs, and the threshing barns, and the market boat—all the perquisites that they had formerly enjoyed. Nicholas would not negotiate, he ignored their proposals to rent these conveniences—to share produce. In fact during the last year he had come to ignore his tenants. If he saw them in church or in the village, he looked the other way.

The bailiff had after all decided to remain, and it was he who collected the rents from those whose titles were not yet cleared; these rents he now forwarded direct to the Van Ryn agent in New York. The situation was pleasing, for since the patroon no longer bothered to check or supervise there were many agreeable opportunities for Duyckman to feather his own nest.

Jeff, knowing these things, looked at the mossy millstones, the machinery already corroded with rust, and sighed. The tenants had won but a Pyrrhic and inconclusive victory after all. They were ground, as the grains of wheat used to be ground between these millstones, by the ponderous slowness of the new laws, and by Nicholas' refusal to co-operate.

Jeff blew on his fingers and stamped his feet to warm them. The cold made his old shoulder wound ache, though that and the thin line of scar on his cheek were the only mementoes still left him of the Mexican campaign.

His life had been full and interesting of late. He had been tremendously excited by the new use of ether as an anesthetic. The famous operation at the Massachusetts General which publicly introduced it had taken place while Jeff was still in Mexico, and it was not until the following year that he journeyed to Boston to learn the technique of administering this miracle-worker. Since then he had used it enthusiastically, and discovered complete joy in surgery now that one no longer had to inflict agony on the patient.

Yes, the past two years had been pleasant enough. He had refused either to mourn or pine for Miranda, and by all accounts she had been involved with her husband in a giddy social whirl, so he had put her out of his mind.

He had, however, not married Faith, and that young lady, finally vanquished, settled down with a solid young lawyer who seemed to satisfy her very well. Jeff resigned himself to bachelorhood, though resignation was too strong a word for a circumstance to which he seldom gave a thought. And his was no monkish life. On his occasional holidays he could relax as well as the next man, could hugely enjoy a pint of good Barbados rum, and there had been a lusty adventure or two in Boston and New York.

When, last night, the brawny young blacksmith had delivered Miranda's note, Jeff had first read it with no reaction but astonished dismay. This summons to a secret rendezvous seemed to him melodramatic and ridiculous. When he re-read the note, he saw in the jerky writing and incoherent sentences signs of mental strain bordering on hysteria. He who never refused anyone who needed him could hardly deny Miranda, but he did feel a strong reluctance to subjecting himself again to the upsetting emotions which she invoked.

Still, here he was, cold, hungry for his breakfast, and certainly in no romantic mood.

He saw her slender gray figure come toward him through the bare tree-trunks. Despite her hurry and the tingling of her chilled feet, she moved with her own particular grace. He went to meet her, and she stretched out her left hand to him in a gesture half greeting, half supplication. 'Jeff—thank you for coming. I had to see you—talk to someone—it's about Nicholas.'

It would be, he thought grimly. But he smiled at her and drew her out of the wind into the shelter of the mill. He had forgotten how lovely she was. The last time he had seen her she had been ravaged by childbirth, but now under the ruffled gray hood her face was smooth and girlish, the skin as fine as porcelain. It was only her eyes that had aged; their hazel depths now showed disillusionment and anxiety.

'What is it, Miranda? Tell me,' he said quietly, seeing that now that she was here she scarcely knew what to say. She cast involuntary frightened glances in the direction of the Manor House, and the hand which clutched the cape tight around her chest, trembled.

She moistened her lips. 'I don't know why I came,' she said distractedly. 'There really isn't much to tell. It seems different now.'

He gave her a keen look. She obviously needed rest and a sedative. As both were impossible, he substituted the only remedy at hand. He unrolled his saddle blanket and spread it over one of the wheat bins. On the stone pavement near her, he hurriedly built a small fire. When the aromatic smoke began to curl toward the rafters, he sat down on the bin beside her.

'It feels good,' she said gratefully. She spread her hands out to the blaze.

'Hello,' said Jeff, 'what's happened to that wrist?' He noted her quick flush and motion of concealment while he examined the mottled swelling, which now extended from forearm to knuckles. 'I doubt that there's anything broken, but it's a nasty wrench. Cold cloths, arnica, and rest it needs when you get back.' He pulled a large cotton handkerchief from his pocket and fashioned it deftly into a sling. 'How did it happen, Miranda?'

She turned away from him. Here in this quiet old mill beside the fire, that scene in the tower became unreal, and the shock which had driven her to summon Jeff merged into an aching weariness. His presence brought her comfort and security at the same time that it seemed to banish her last weeks with Nicholas into the world of distorted fancy. She longed to lean her head against that powerful shoulder in the worn greatcoat, to shut her eyes and rest.

But Jeff persisted. He knew very well that it was not for the treatment of her wrist that she had summoned him by means of that frantic little note. He saw that both her nervous condition and her loyalty to Nicholas were now inhibiting her, and her manner convinced him that her injury had been caused by Nicholas.

'You've had a disagreement with your husband?' he asked gently. 'Tell me, my dear. You asked for my help, and now you must trust me. Think of me as a physician only, and one used to hearing all sorts of strange things.'

She nodded slowly. 'I know.' She bent forward gazing into the fire. 'He's been different lately. I guess he's always been, but—ever since the theater riot in May. I don't suppose you heard—he was hurt. But it isn't that—'

'My dear girl,' said Jeff patiently, smiling a little. 'You must begin at the beginning. Is your husband sick? Is it perhaps that he's taken to drinking too much?'

'No,' she said with sudden quiet. 'He smokes opium.'

'Smokes opium!' Jeff repeated, so much startled that for a second he wanted to laugh. He might have known that Nicholas' temperament would demand nothing as usual as liquor.

'It's not serious, then?' she asked, watching his face anxiously.

He sobered at once. 'I don't know much about opium, Miranda. A country doctor has no experience of such drugs, nor many city ones either, I guess. But tell me everything and I hope I can help you.'

She began haltingly, hunting for words. She briefly described the shooting at Astor Place and Nicholas' constant gloom and sulkiness afterward. She attributed this gloom to remorse. She told of his sequestrations in the tower room, and of her own discovery yesterday. But of the hour which she had spent locked in with Nicholas she gave no details. It was only from the expression of her lowered eyes that Jeff drew an inkling of what had passed.

He rose and busied himself in building up the fire, determined not to let his personal emotions intrude. He had offered his help to her as a physician, and this objective advice she should get. He walked to the glassless window and staring down at the mill stream, which purled and rollicked beneath a coating of ice, he shut out all thought of Miranda and tried to consider Nicholas dispassionately.

Had Jeff been born a hundred years later, he would have used to himself the cant phraseology of an, as yet, unrecognized science. But he needed no props beyond his own analytical perception and knowledge of human character to understand that the taking of opium represented to Nicholas—whatever he might choose to call it—escape from intolerable circumstances. And that in different degree his cycles of furious activity and his cycles of withdrawal from life represented the same desire for escape.

But what he's trying so hard to get away from, I don't know, thought Jeff, except that whenever his all-conquering ego butts up against something unpleasant he can't change, like the baby's death and the rent laws, he pretends they haven't happened.

He turned suddenly and looked at Miranda. 'Why don't you leave Dragonwyck for a while? Go home and visit?' he said brusquely.

She raised her head and looked at him with a sad little smile. 'That's what you always used to say to me, that first year here, remember? Go home. Go home. I couldn't then, and—' she paused. Her hood had fallen back and the firelight flickered over her bright hair. '—and I can't now,' she finished very low.

'Why not?' he asked angrily. 'Won't he let you?'

'No, he wouldn't let me. But I don't want to. I couldn't leave him. He—he needs me.'

'Rot!' snapped Jeff. 'I know enough to know that you can't do anything with a drug addict unless he wants to be cured. You can take away his opium, but he'll get more. He'll degrade you too. Do you want another wrist like that one—or worse?'

She slid off the wheat bin and stood up, looking at him coldly. 'You've always misjudged him,' she said. 'It's because he feels remorse for shooting that boy that he's this way now. I couldn't desert him, he needs help. Underneath he's really fine and good.'

Does she really believe that? thought Jeff, stupefied. 'You didn't feel that way when you wrote me that note—when you came here this morning!' he cried in exasperation. He wanted to shake her, he wanted to kiss her pathetic swollen arm.

'Yes, I did,' she said, lifting her chin stubbornly.

To his own dismay he suddenly leaned over and kissed her hard on the lips.

There was a silence. She put her hand to her mouth with a startled gesture. 'Jeff—' she whispered, staring at him.

'Sorry,' he said. 'But you needn't look quite so flabbergasted. Female intuition can't amount to much if you hadn't some idea of the way I feel about you.'

She shook her head slowly. 'No, I don't think I did.' Her first astonishment gave place to a more poignant emotion. She thought of the baby's birth and the strength she had drawn from Jeff. She thought of her talk with Doctor Francis in Poe's kitchen and the unexpected pleasure that had come to her at the mention of Jeff's name.

Seeing her troubled frown, he grinned with the humor that never deserted him for long. 'Don't let it worry you. I'm not a lovesick young calf nor am I going to force on you any indecent proposals. I don't as a matter of fact know just why my affections should have so inconveniently centered themselves on you.' He stopped, considering whether that were true. Part of her attraction for him was physical, of course; the slender body with its lovely grace of movement, the bright hair, the provocative set of her hazel eyes beneath straight brown brows—but other women had had for him as strong a physical appeal. It was her essential innocence and helplessness that had drawn him, that and paradoxically enough her blind concentration on Nicholas. In the beginning perhaps this had given her the glamour of the unattainable, constituted an unconscious challenge. But now it was more than that. The sweetness of her lips beneath his kiss had focused his love once and for all. And even while he spoke to her half-teasingly, he felt a heavy weight of longing and sadness.

'I must go, Jeff,' she said quietly, and she gave him an uncertain little smile, at the same time casting a frightened look in the direction of the manor.

'And I haven't helped you after all.' He frowned, kicking at the fire to dissipate the still glowing embers. 'I'll find out all I can about opium. I'll write you.'

'Oh, no, please. He'd see the letter. It doesn't matter. I'll manage. Probably it won't happen again.'

Probably it will, thought Jeff. But he could do nothing. He thought that she regretted having summoned him. He had failed her, not only in practical advice, but in that kiss which had changed their relationship. By his impulsive action he had thrown her back on herself again.

'Good-bye,' she whispered, not looking at him. And she was gone, running through the trees. It never occurred to him that she had longed to throw herself into his arms. And that the frantic pace at which she ran back toward the house, slipping on the thawing ground, was not caused by eagerness to return to her husband, nor yet fear of discovery. It was from Jeff that she ran, and the yearning which he had aroused in her. Upon her mouth she felt Jeff's kiss as though it were a red stain, and this moved her by revulsion to a guilty loyalty to Nicholas.

She had need of this loyalty when he came downstairs that afternoon. He walked into her room without knocking, stood looking down at her silently, his eyes narrowed. She sat by the window idly turning the pages of *Godey's,* since the injured right hand prevented her usual embroidery. She had hidden the sling under a lace shawl.

'You look unusually well, my dear. Your cheeks are quite rosy. Is it rouge, perhaps? Or might it be that you've been for a walk in the crisp November air?'

She shrank to wariness. Could he possibly have seen her as she crossed the lawn on her way back to the house?

'Why, yes,' she answered steadily. 'I did go for a walk early this morning. I didn't sleep very well. I thought the air would do me good.'

'That was sensible,' he said, and she saw that the subject of her walk had been a chance shot. He had some other purpose in mind.

'Just how *is* your health these days, my love?' He leaned forward, smiling with the exaggerated courtesy that always meant trouble. 'It interests me.'

Hot color spread over her face. His meaning was unmistakable, but she chose to ignore it, seeking refuge in a casual answer. 'It's good of you to be concerned, Nicholas, but I believe I'm very well.' She rose quickly. 'Will you come and have some food now? I'm sure you must need it.' His dark skin was tinged with yellow, his face was drawn and haggard. A muscle twitched beneath his eye.

He did not move. 'It would be a pity if you were barren, wouldn't it?' he said.

It's the opium, the drug, she thought. He's not well. It's nearly three days since he's eaten, and I can see that he's suffering.

She pulled herself together and tried to smile, saying as lightly as she could: 'That's a matter of the Lord's will, dear. And after all, we have each other. Surely you didn't marry me just for that.'

In the silence that followed, her last nervous sentence seemed to her to fall into space from whence it sped back into her consciousness like a gunshot.

'You didn't, did you, Nicholas?' she whispered. 'You loved me, me for myself. I know you did, you do. Underneath.—Don't look at me like that,' she added violently.

His unwavering gaze did not alter. 'Like what, my love?' he asked softly.

'The way you used to look at—' She bit her lips. 'Come downstairs, Nicholas. You must eat something.' She slipped her left hand through his arm, and the lace shawl fell to the floor, disclosing the sling.

He picked up the shawl, placing it carefully around her shoulders again. She saw his eyes flicker as they rested a moment on her wrist. He said nothing, but across his face there passed a fleeting uncertainty. He followed her to the dining-room, and bore with her efforts to make him eat and drink, concealing from her and denying to himself the revulsion of his outraged body.

They stayed at Dragonwyck that winter. It was Nicholas' wish, but Miranda was quite willing. She had no desire to be reminded of the Astor Place riot. The theaters and gaieties which had once seemed so attractive no longer appealed to her, and the whole of New York was for her overshadowed by the horror of their last weeks there.

She assumed that it was for this reason that Nicholas also preferred the calm of the Manor House. During those winter months their lives once more approximated the usual routine of country gentry. Nicholas did not go again to the tower room. He busied himself about the estate, planning a new road, reinforcing the dock, building a new barn for the prize-winning Jerseys he had recently bought. He resumed his long-lapsed interest in the greenhouses and harassed the gardeners, who had grown slack and perfunctory.

Before Christmas the MacNabs left, having saved enough money to buy themselves a farm in Michigan where their Scotch relatives awaited them, and Miranda, freed from their long dominance, gladly took over the household reins herself. She was no longer an ignorant girl, and the butler and housekeeper who replaced the MacNabs obeyed her orders as a matter of course. She was therefore busy from morning until night with domestic tasks which befitted the Lady of the Manor.

Nicholas displayed none of his temperamental peculiarities; he was courteous as always and showed to Miranda a rather remote consideration. He subjected her neither to the cold indifference nor the fierce lusts which she had suffered in the past.

And Miranda, profoundly grateful for this, lived determinedly on the surface, convincing herself that now at last they were settling into a normal, placid married life.

20

IT WAS ON FRIDAY THE TWENTY-FOURTH OF MAY that Miranda made her discovery.

She awakened that morning to an unusual sense of joy and freedom which she attributed to the lovely spring weather, unwilling to admit that Nicholas' absence from Dragonwyck might be the true cause.

During the last week the dark, restless mood had come back on him again, and two days ago he had suddenly announced that he was going to make a short business trip to New York. He had not invited her to go with him. She had grown so used to his constant company that for the first hours of his absence she felt blank and at a loss. But this sensation soon gave way to delicious ease and a holiday spirit. It was delightful to occupy the big bed alone, to eat when one wanted to, to walk or read or shut oneself into the bathroom and soak for hours in the great silver tub.

On this morning of the twenty-fourth, she awoke filled with energy and a desire to do something amusing. When Peggy came in with the morning tea, she found her mistress sitting up in bed looking very young and gay.

'Good morning, Peggy!' she called blithely. 'Isn't it a glorious day! I can smell it—buds and nice fresh sunshine.'

'It is that, mum, and you do be looking like a May morning yourself.'

The little maid helped Miranda into a rose mousseline bed jacket, thinking, Glory be that things had been better of late. The Master'd had none of his real wicked fits, had mostly been acting as pleasant and proper as ever did Squire O'Brien at home. And now with him away 'twas better yet.

'And how's your Hans, Peggy?' asked Miranda, smiling mischievously and wishing well to all the world. 'Would you like the evening off to see him?'

Peggy giggled and tossed her head. 'I see enough of him as it is. The great lout forever under me feet in the kitchen and the servants' hall. Him and his sheep's eyes. 'Tis hoping to be footman here, he is.'

'Is he?' asked Miranda, surprised. 'But I thought he was a blacksmith.'

'And a good one, mum.' Peggy hesitated. 'It's because of me he wants to come into service here. He knows I'll never leave you, so he's been thinking—maybe—'

'Of course,' said Miranda, putting down her teacup. 'I've been very stupid and selfish. Do you really love him, Peggy? Do you think he'll make you happy?'

The girl nodded. Her bright Irish eyes softened. 'He's willing to turn Catholic for me, mum. And he's so good. He doesn't—he's never said a word about—about my leg.' She turned and shook out Miranda's ruffled morning gown.

'You shall have a wedding in June, dear,' said Miranda quickly. 'A beautiful one. We'll get a priest from Hudson, or New York if necessary. And your wedding dress—white, of course. White India muslin. I've a length put away in the attic somewhere.'

'Oh, missis dear!' cried Peggy, laughing. 'White's only for gentry; 'twouldn't be proper for the likes of me.'

'Of course it would! It's the happiest color for brides.' She paused, remembering a girl in green silk, the sound of rain beating on the windows. Four years ago. Four centuries.

She jumped from the bed, thrusting her slender feet into the swansdown slippers which Peggy held for her. 'I'll hurry and dress. We'll go up and find the muslin. I know just how it should be made. Bodice tight, skirt very full but no hoop. Lace at the neck. I've a point de Venise collar in the lace box.'

Peggy twinkled affectionately. You couldn't make a white peacock out of a little mud hen with a twisted leg, she thought, but she held her peace. It was good to see the missis all bright and lively, that worried look gone from her.

After breakfast they went up to the attic together. This top floor covered the entire house, and the south wing was as familiar to Peggy as the back of her hand, for it housed the servants and one of the tiny rooms was Peggy's.

But they went through a green baize door into the seldom entered storage section, which contained a maze of unfinished cubicles and a raftered loft.

They found the lace box without difficulty, but not the length of

India muslin. Miranda had bought it during that first fall of her marriage, intending to make it up later for the baby. It must have been stored with other pathetic remnants of that brief and tragic period. Mrs. MacNab had attended to all that and Miranda had never had the courage to investigate.

She now found that there was amongst all the boxes and chests and trunks no trace of the tiny being upon whose coming had been lavished so much hope. Not even the cradle could they find anywhere.

It must have been Nicholas' orders, thought Miranda with certainty. His hurt had been so deep that he had banished from his house every reminder of the baby as he had banished them from his consciousness.

Her eyes filled with tears. Oh, why do I ever doubt him, she thought, just because he is a man and hides his tenderness? Swept by a sudden warmth of pity for her husband, she sank down on a broken chair in a corner of the loft.

When he came back she would redouble her devotion. So often in the past she had been wanting in understanding, had distorted incidents. The shooting at Astor Place—what could have been more natural to any proud and brave man? He had simply avenged an insult and at the same time he had been protecting her. And the opium—how grossly she had exaggerated that danger! Many a man took liquor in excess occasionally and wives thought little of it. Why, then, had she been so terrified by those small silver pipes? And after all, it had not happened again.

So thought Miranda, freed from the pressure of the disturbing presence and finding it therefore easy to believe what her heart told her that she must believe.

It was then that she saw the mattress. Peggy was busy in one of the small storage rooms, repacking a trunk which they had ransacked, and Miranda sat alone amongst a welter of discarded furniture.

A sunbeam struck through cobwebs in the eastern dormer and shed its dusty light directly on an enormous rolled mattress which stood upended against a painted Kas. There was something familiar about the Kas, she had seen those pealing roses and garlands before. She leaned forward idly and realized with a shock of distaste that it was the cupboard which used to stand in Johanna's room. All the furniture in this corner she saw had been Johanna's. There was the chipped table with something sticky still adhering to its veneered surface. And this mattress had come from the Van Ryn bed.

She rose abruptly and turned to go when a peculiarity about the mattress stopped her. Years of mice and damp had mouldered the ticking, which had split in a dozen places. From one of these a dark object protruded. She touched it gingerly and drawing it out found that it was a leather-bound book. She opened it and saw some pages of writing with the ink faded to brown. Puzzled she riffled the pages, and on the last one which contained writing a sentence leaped at her.

'And why does he bring me flowers, who never does—the pink oleander? I'm in mortal fear, but why should I be? Must be I'm feverish with my cold. Ever since that girl came—

'He's called a doctor for me, yet I'm not really ill. Not our own doctor, the new one—'

There was a space, and farther down the last entry:

'I've been so foolish. Nicholas was here and kind. He cut the tipsy cake and sprinkled nutmeg on it for me, the way he used to do when we were first married. He tells me the girl is going in a few days. I'm so glad. It will be all right now—'

There were more pages, but they were blank.

The diary slipped from Miranda's fingers and fell to the floor. She stood motionless staring down at it. After a moment she picked it up and put it in the pocket of the dimity apron with which she had protected her dress from the dust. She turned and walked out of the loft, unheeding Peggy's astonished call.

She walked down the two flights of stairs and out of the house. She cut across the gardens, through the formal beds of peonies and white iris, the banked lilies-of-the-valley which clustered about a miniature waterfall. She made for the south bluff beside the river where a grove of hemlocks had been untouched by Nicholas' improvements and she flung herself full length upon the needles. A gentle wind soughed through the thick-set branches above her head, and from far below came the murmurous lapping of the water.

She drew the diary from her pocket and opening it read the last page again, quickly. See—she told herself, there's nothing here. It means nothing. It's just that Johanna too sometimes found him hard to understand. Then he was kind to her. She says so.

Again she dragged her eyes from that sentence. 'He says the girl is going in a few days.' How had Nicholas known that she would be leaving Dragonwyck? There had been no such plan. It was because of Johanna's death—

'No,' she said out loud. 'I must be calm. I must think clearly.' Not half an hour ago in the attic she had resolved to avoid distortion and exaggeration.

It was for some other reason of his own, of course, that Nicholas had decided she must leave Dragonwyck, perhaps simply to please Johanna. And this thought, which would have been unbearable then, now seemed to her inexpressibly comforting.

She opened the book again and read the early passages. They were few and incoherent, but written in a neat, pretty writing that was so incongruous as having belonged to Johanna. As she read, Miranda's throat grew dry, for here was the evidence of a dumb and despairing misery.

'I think he hates me since that girl came. I know he never loved me as I did him, but we used to be happy. If I could only have a son—God help me, why does it have to be like this—'

And another entry.

'I finished the monograms on two of his handkerchiefs today and gave them to him. He said I'd better let Miranda finish the rest. The minx preened herself and smiled. Would to God she'd never come. She's always between us.'

Miranda raised her head. She remembered that speech of Nicholas', she remembered her own delight in it; and had she indeed preened herself, glorying in the petty triumph? She had been so contemptuous of those botched monograms, so pleased with the exquisite ones she herself had embroidered to finish the set. How pitilessly she had thrust home every small advantage in the secret struggle which the two women had had!

Once more she turned to the last page. 'Why does he bring me flowers, who never does?' There was nothing in these words, nothing on the page, and yet this time as she read them it was as though cold black waters were seeping upward toward her heart.

There was only one person who could reassure her, could help her get a true perspective. Only one who knew the circumstances.

She was seized suddenly with a feverish desire for action. She ran to the stables and told the astonished coachman that he must drive her to Hudson at once. She sent a groom flying to the house for a cape and harried the stable boys until a horse was harnessed to the open landaulet.

They made the trip to town in less than two hours, and all the way Miranda sat staring down the road ahead, the diary clasped tight in her hand beneath the cape.

Doctor Turner was in, but he was eating dinner, said old Rillah repressively, eyeing Miranda's informal attire with disfavor. They was mighty queer white trash often came to Doctor's office, but this one was as wild-eyed and fly-away-looking as any of 'em.

'Call him, please,' said Miranda. 'I must see him at once. Tell him it's Mrs. Van Ryn.'

That was different. Rillah grinned apologetically and bobbed her grizzled head, indicating a chair.

Jeff came out of his little dining-room, still chewing, the napkin in his hand. 'My dear girl. I'm delighted to see you, but I hope there's nothing seriously wrong.'

'I don't know. I've got to see you alone.'

He nodded, and ushered her into the surgery, closing the door behind them.

She dropped her cloak on a chair, opened the diary at the last page and held it out to him.

'Nicholas is in New York. I found this today in the attic. It was hidden in a slit in the mattress, the old one that Johanna had. It's her diary. I want to know what you think of it.'

Jeff looked at her set face and down at the book in her hand. A chill went over him, and a premonition.

He read the diary's last page and sank slowly down in the chair behind the desk. 'My God,' he said at last, very low. 'The oleander!' He read the entry again.

'What do you mean?' said Miranda sharply.

Jeff got up and went to his new bookcase. In it were over a hundred books he had not owned five years ago. He opened to the herbal section in Lunt's 'Toxicology.'

He turned his back on Miranda, carried the book to the window. '*Nerium Oleander. Family Apocynaceae.* A glucoside somewhat similar in its action to digitalis, but possessed of greater toxicity. The ingestion of three or four leaves has been known to kill cattle. Blossoms and bark equally poisonous.'

And at the bottom of the paragraph was the irrefutable list of symptoms. Sweat broke out on his forehead as he saw flung up at him in the small clear type the exact clinical picture of Johanna's illness.

'Vomiting and colic. Giddiness. Slow and irregular heart action.

Marked mydriasis of the pupils. Bloody flux. Respiratory paralysis. Death. Urine usually normal in color and appearance. May be difficult to diagnose, easily confused with any other acute gastritis.'

He shut the 'Toxicology' and put it back in the bookcase.

'What is it, Jeff?' whispered Miranda. 'What were you reading?' She had not moved since she had handed him the diary.

He sat down again behind the desk, instinctively trying for calm in this familiar position where he had solved so many problems. But there was no precedent for this.

She leaned forward, pressing her hands on the desk; her eyes, grown dark as the onyx brooch on her breast, regarded him steadily.

'Tell me what you're thinking, Jeff.'

He had not been going to tell her; his first instinct had been to reassure her quickly and send her away, until he could find his own bearings and decide what to do. He changed his mind as he lifted his head and met her eyes.

'I think,' he spoke slowly, careful to exclude from his voice the slightest trace of emotion, 'that in some way, by means of the oleander which he brought to her room, Nicholas murdered Johanna.'

She made a muffled sound. He ran to her side. She shook her head, pushing away his supporting arm. She walked from him and sat down on the small Windsor chair reserved for patients.

He took a bottle of ammonia spirits from his cabinet, poured a stiff dose into a glass of water.

'Drink this,' he commanded. 'I had to tell you, Miranda. If it were possible for me to spare you this—this horrible thing—I would. I've no proof. But I'm sure. And for your own safety, you must believe me.'

He began to pace the strip of drugget beside the desk.

For her own safety—that was the core of fear which he had discovered simultaneously with his acceptance of the fact of murder. If Nicholas had once scaled the barrier which separated normal humanity from the outlaws, there was nothing to prevent his doing it again.

Jeff turned and knelt down beside her, taking her limp hand in his. 'Miranda, you must never go back to Nicholas. I know this is a terrible shock and to you must seem unbelievable. I wouldn't believe it either except that I had a suspicion long ago at the time of—of the death. I was a fool, a criminal fool, not to have investigated more than I did. But I had nothing but a hunch to go on, and I couldn't find any trace of the common poisons, and I didn't know half as much as I thought I did.'

He spoke so as to give her time to recover and to collect himself. Both his nature and his training moved him to face reality squarely, no matter how intolerable that reality might be. She too must face it. She must emerge from this numb white silence and be convinced. Only too well he knew that he must battle her insensate loyalty for the man she had worshiped.

He began to speak quietly in a casual voice, trying to reconstruct objectively. 'He must have planned it ahead for a long time. I believe he waited until Johanna developed some trivial illness so that a doctor might be on hand. It was very clever.' Jeff paused to master a wave of bitter humiliation. Nicholas had very neatly used him as a cat's-paw. How shrewd to have chosen a young, inexperienced doctor, one too who was known to be a political enemy so that there was even less chance of suspicion in the countryside!

'It was,' he went on evenly, 'very like him to use flowers as an instrument of death. It would appeal to his fastidiousness. It happened, of course, when he was alone with her that night. And the tipsy cake, as I did suspect, must have been the agent. But how?' He thought a minute. 'The silver nutmeg mill, of course. He ground the leaves.'

He thought of Nicholas' peculiar remark: 'Her foul gluttony has killed her.' It had doubtless accorded with the man's sense of irony that Johanna's unhealthy passion for the cake had accomplished her death.

All too vividly Jeff now remembered the small green particles which had clung to the sticky slice he had examined. He had thought that they were angelica or citron. The rum with which the cake was saturated would have disguised any flavor.

'She was befuddled with her cold,' he said aloud. 'She wouldn't have noticed what he was doing with the mill.'

And at last Miranda stirred. 'What difference does it make how it was done?' she said in a dull, flat voice.

'It's only that you must believe the truth—to know,' he answered gently.

She raised her head and her lips parted in a blind and terrifying little smile. 'I think I've always known,' she said.

Jeff made an involuntary sound. She shook her head.

'No, not in the way you mean, not consciously. But in the dark, secret part of my soul where I never dared look.'

'Rubbish!' cried Jeff, made violent by relief. 'This is morbid, Miranda. Let's try to be sensible and face together what must be done. We must keep our heads and use them.'

She was not listening. She lowered her eyes and stared at the gold band on her left hand. 'I've been married four years to a murderer,' she said in the dull, thin voice. 'Enjoying the results of that murder.'

'You couldn't help it. You didn't know,' he said sharply.

'If it hadn't been for me, it wouldn't have happened,' she went on without listening to him. 'It was the weakness in me touched off the evil in him. Like flint and steel. Zélie knew, but I wouldn't listen.'

'Zélie?' repeated Jeff, bewildered. 'You mean that old half-breed servant of the Van Ryns'? But she was senile, her wits were gone, and whatever she knew or didn't know has nothing to do with you.'

He put his hands on her shoulders. 'Listen, my dearest girl. You must be brave and strong. You had nothing to do with Johanna's death. At worst you may have been the innocent cause, but you *were* innocent, and you must rid yourself of these morbid feelings of guilt. We can't change the past, but the future is clear. The murder must be exposed.'

She moistened her lips. 'You can't, Jeff. You said yourself there was no proof. No one would believe you.'

He frowned, releasing her shoulders. For a moment he quailed before the prospect of trying to indict Nicholas. Who, indeed, would take the word of a country doctor against that of the powerful patroon? Jeff would have to make a hash of his own reputation, admit to having been a dupe. There would first be the struggle to get an order for exhuming the body, and even then, he simply did not know whether analyzable traces of this particular poison would remain for so long in the viscera. This, of course, he could find out. And he thought with relief of Doctor Francis. The old man would help him. But suppose there were no traces. Then there was no proof at all. Nothing but a few ambiguous entries in a diary, and Jeff knew enough of the law to realize what Nicholas' counsel would make of those. There was, however—Magda. He suddenly remembered Johanna's embittered housekeeper. As he looked back on it now, he felt certain that the woman had had suspicions too. She had seen Nicholas give his wife the tipsy cake. Perhaps she could be found and brought to testify.

Doubtless she was with Katrine in Albany.

Jeff winced at the thought of what the exposure would do to Katrine, and Miranda too. He hadn't viewed it from this angle. With a sinking feeling he thought how hard it would be to prevent Miranda's dangerous involvement. She would naturally be considered an accessory, if not an accomplice.

Miranda had been watching him quietly. She saw the dismay in his face, though she only partially understood its reason. 'Yes,' she said. 'No one could touch Nicholas. He's stronger than anyone.'

'He's human like the rest of us, I suppose!' cried Jeff in sudden fury. 'And I shall see to it that he doesn't continue to go scot-free from punishment for a cowardly and loathsome murder. I hesitated only because of you. Miranda, you must not go back to Nicholas.'

'I deserve to suffer too,' she said. 'I married him.'

'And do you consider that you also deserve to be murdered?' cried Jeff, beside himself. He saw the startled flicker in her eyes, heard her indrawn breath. 'You little fool,' he went on bitterly. 'In your blind passion for this man, don't you realize that you yourself are in danger? You too can become an unwanted wife; you won't always be young and beautiful. You, no more than Johanna, have gratified his mad obsession for a son. Suppose he finds some other woman, as he found you; or without another woman, suppose you happen in some way to thwart his insane ego, his lust for power.—Do you think, Miranda, that you would be safe?'

She turned her head and a long shudder ran through her body. For suddenly she knew that he spoke the truth. A hundred unconsidered signposts came back to her. 'But what can I do?' she whispered.

He saw that she was near to breaking and that he must think for her.

'When does Nicholas return?' he asked.

'Tomorrow evening on the up-boat.' Her lips barely moved.

That's God's own mercy, thought Jeff; then, speaking very slowly and clearly, he said: 'You must be gone before he gets there. Tell one of the servants to flag the morning boat. Pack a trunk tonight. Take Peggy with you. When you reach New York, go directly to Doctor Francis.' He went to his desk and scribbled a note, pressing it into her hand. She nodded and slipped it in the bosom of her dress.

'Francis will hide you and take care of you for a few days until I get there. I dare not let you go home to Greenwich. That's the first place Van Ryn would look for you.'

'Yes,' she said faintly. 'I understand. But what will you—what can you do, Jeff?'

'Once you're safe, I'll go to Dragonwyck and confront Nicholas with our discovery.'

'Aren't you afraid?' she whispered.

As a matter of fact, I am, thought Jeff wryly. Not so much of what the man would try to do—Jeff had no doubt that Nicholas' first action would be an effort to get rid of the inconvenient young doctor—and then where would Miranda be! She could never fight Nicholas alone. But it was not fear for his own skin that concerned Jeff. It was the seemingly insuperable difficulties involved in accusing Nicholas, and the impossibility of guessing what he would do. I should have advice, thought Jeff, as to the best way to go about it. And a sudden inspiration provided him with the answer.

'I'll go directly to the Governor,' he said. 'Tomorrow. Lay the whole case before him.'

She got up, holding on to the chair back as she rose. Jeff put his arm around her and for a second she leaned against him.

'Be brave, darling,' he said softly.

She straightened, and fastened her cloak around her neck. She walked a little way to the door, then turning with her hand on the knob she gave a choked, mirthless laugh.

'Be brave—yes,' she said. 'Brave enough to understand that my love —that all my dreams, were evil.'

21

NICHOLAS DID NOT RETURN TO DRAGONWYCK ON the following day as he had expected to do. He arrived home at five o'clock in the afternoon at the exact moment that Miranda walked out of Jeff's house in Hudson and re-entered her carriage for the drive back.

The business matter which had taken Nicholas to New York had been quickly disposed of. It consisted in signing his name to the lease of three acres near Odellville at East Forty-Ninth Street, where an optimistic Irishman wished to open a country tavern in emulation of Mr. Odell, for whom the district was named.

Nicholas' presence had not really been necessary. Solomon Bronck had negotiated far larger and more complicated real-estate transactions with no help from his employer but an indifferent letter of acquiescence. The agent was therefore astonished to see Nicholas stride into the little office on Broad Street and demand to read the lease.

'Certainly, mynheer,' said the conscientious Dutchman, ringing his handbell for the clerk. 'I trust you're not dissatisfied in any way with my accountings.' He said this a trifle resentfully, for it was galling to make money for a man who neither took an interest nor made the slightest effort. It was Bronck, alone, who had continued the remunerative policy started by Nicholas' father—selling one of the original Van Ryn holdings for a good sum, buying cheap on the edge of town, and then, as the town advanced with incredible rapidity, repeating the process.

'I'm entirely satisfied with you, Bronck,' said Nicholas with a vague smile. When the clerk brought the lease he barely looked at it, and rapidly affixed his signature.

That isn't what he came to town for, then, thought the agent, puzzled. He noted his employer's air of abstraction, the jerky motions he made as he glanced through the papers which Bronck put before him.

'Yes. Yes,' said Nicholas, pushing them aside. 'All seems in order.'

'You've a deal of money not invested,' Bronck pointed out patiently. 'I thought maybe we'd buy a lot on the corner of Fifty-Seventh Street way up Fifth Avenue. Nothing there now but a shanty and a couple of goats, but you never can tell. Might be somebody'd want it some day and you can afford a long shot.'

'As you like,' said Nicholas. 'Send me the deed later.'

'Or—' went on the agent, determined to do his duty and trying to ignore Nicholas' obvious boredom—though if he was so uninterested why didn't the man go? Indecision was the last trait one expected to see in the patroon. 'Or—' said Bronck, 'would you fancy buying a share in the new river boat the Mary Clinton? The owner wants to sell. She leaves Friday on her maiden trip to Albany. And they say she'll be far and away the fastest thing on the river.'

Nicholas looked up. 'Fast enough to beat the Reindeer, or the Utica?'

Bronck frowned. 'I don't know, mynheer. I hope she doesn't try to race. The racing's a wicked thing, mighty dangerous for the passengers; look at all those that were lost on the Swallow. It's immoral, that's what it is.'

'Indeed,' said Nicholas. 'I find it most exhilarating.'

Bronck flushed, for Nicholas expertly conveyed by his expression that he thought the agent a milksop. If it's excitement the man wants, thought Bronck angrily, why can he not find it in some way that won't be dangerous to others?

'I'll go look at the boat,' said Nicholas, rising, 'and if she looks right, we'll close the deal tomorrow. I appreciate your suggestion, O most worthy Bronck. I can't think why it hasn't occurred to me before.'

The agent, left alone, fell into gloomy apprehension. I wish I'd never mentioned the damned boat, he thought, biting the end off a cigar. The patroon had changed, and yet for the life of him Bronck couldn't put his finger on the change. He had always known his employer to be a haughty and moody man, given usually to indifference, yet capable of rare but almost fanatical enthusiasms. Today had been no exception, yet for a moment the man had had a look—not normal. From this line of thought the agent shied away; he mopped his forehead with a red silk handkerchief. He called the clerk and issued orders for getting in touch with the Mary Clinton's owner, knowing that Nicholas would stand for no delay once he had made up his mind.

Bronck dared take no chances. There were five little Broncks in a cottage in Chelsea, and another on the way.

Nicholas bought a half-share in the Mary Clinton after he had examined her from stem to stern as she lay at dock in the North River.

She was a beautiful boat, built at the best yards in Hoboken—240 feet of clean, symmetrical lines. Her boilers and her engines were of the latest model and as new as the white-painted oaken decks and the giant paddle wheels. Nicholas could find no fault with her, and he changed his plans for return home so as to accompany her on her maiden trip Friday.

At first he was inclined to disapprove of the captain, John Hall of Jersey City, who seemed over-young and inexperienced to handle the new boat. But after talking with him Nicholas discovered that the young man knew every current and eddy in the river, and that he more than shared Nicholas' desire for speed. So Nicholas left the dock satisfied. He left the dock and dismissed the hackney cab in which he had driven to the river. He walked down Desbrosses Street until he came to Canal. At the junction of Canal Street and Broadway he hesitated. His natural route lay south down Broadway to the Astor House, where he was staying during his short sojourn, his town house being shut.

He hesitated so long that passers-by stared at him curiously, seeing in this tall, elegantly dressed man an abnormal immobility.

Two full-bosomed young women in false curls and frowsy lace shawls minced up Broadway, and on seeing Nicholas paused behind him and began to giggle. 'My, ain't he handsome; quite a swell too!' said one voice purposely raised. 'Like an image he stands, don't he! What's he looking at so hard?'

'Admiring of his self in the gutter I should think. Happen he'd look round he might see something else to admire too.' And both girls bridled, tossing their curls, from which floated a strong odor of patchouli.

Nicholas continued to frown at the pavement.

'Maybe he's afraid of girls!' cried the first one archly, still trying.

Of this whole conversation only one word in the last sentence did Nicholas hear. He swung around on them. 'I'm afraid of nothing in this world or out of it!' he shouted, and the girls shrank, stepping hastily backward.

'Lor', mister,' they babbled, 'we didn't mean anything—'

He did not wait to hear their frightened apologies; he walked with headlong, violent steps, jostling those that got in his way, until he reached a shuttered door in an alley off Mott Street. In here he stayed for several hours, and when he passed out again through that door there lay in his waistcoat pocket a small, sticky black ball wrapped in rice paper.

At no time to himself did Nicholas admit the true reason for his hurried trip to New York.

The Mary Clinton's first run was a success in that the boat made excellent time, easily outdistancing the Rochester, its only rival that day. So much so that there was no competition. Nicholas was profoundly disappointed. Jeff had been shrewd in his guess that to Nicholas danger was as voluptuous a stimulant as drugs. Had there been a frantic, pounding race, and had the Mary Clinton won—as of course she would have—then in the pleasure of victorious mastery there would have been less need for the release provided by the black substance in his pocket.

As it was he stepped off the boat onto the Dragonwyck landing, his mood flat and sullen, his frayed nerves crying for more of the opium that had been so long denied them.

Then he discovered that Miranda was not at home.

He mounted the turret stairs, placed the ball of opium in the silver box, but he did not linger in the tower room. He came down and sent for Peggy.

The little maid maintained a terrified but stubborn silence. She had no idea where the missis had gone—to call on one of the neighbors, mayhap. No, she didn't rightly know which one. No, missis hadn't been out at all before this, very likely she had tired with sitting in the house all the time. 'No, master. I don't know where she is.' And that's the Gospel truth, thought Peggy. I don't know where she is or what caused her to rush off like one demented, but I could be making a guess did I want to. She's in trouble and she's fled to the young doctor, but the saints forbid *he* should ever be guessing it, for he's come home in a fine filthy mood for sure.

She limped rapidly out of Nicholas' sight and stationed herself at an upstairs window with a confused hope of warning Miranda as soon as the carriage appeared at the bend of the drive.

But when Miranda arrived at seven, she did not see Peggy's anxious face or futile gestures; she saw Nicholas standing bareheaded by the front door waiting. And at the sight of him whom she had thought never to see again, she had a second of agonizing fear, and then she became calm. She felt now the detachment that Jeff had hoped for, and she strengthened herself slowly, deliberately, muscle by muscle and nerve by nerve, for the conflict that was coming.

'You have had a pleasant drive, my love?' said Nicholas, offering his arm as the coachman opened the carriage door.

'No,' she said. She ignored his arm and walked past him into the house. She turned toward the staircase, but Nicholas with a quick, gliding motion stood in front of her barring the way.

'Strange greeting to a husband you've not seen in three days,' he said softly. A softness which belied the cruel, eager light in his eyes. They missed nothing of her dishevelment. Her hands were still dusty from the attic, as was the little apron she had forgotten to remove in her headlong flight to Jeff. The evening wind and her hastily donned hood had both loosened her hair. The smooth waves were tumbled and one of the coiled braids had slipped to her shoulder.

'Yes,' she said. 'I am in disorder. Kindly let me go to my room, Nicholas.'

'Gladly, sweetheart. And I'll come with you. You interest me very much tonight, and you surprise me. I hadn't realized that you could surprise me.' He stepped aside and she mounted the stairs without answer.

How well she knew this snake-and-bird game in which he delighted! Let her dare to escape ever so little from his power and the situation slipped into its appointed groove. He would use sarcasm, his cold, soft anger, and ever mounting within these would be passion, the knowing subjugation of her body which translated itself into the subjugation of the soul, because she loved him.

Love, she thought, with a violent repulsion. Was it ever love? Can love be cemented in fear?

Together they entered the dark bedroom. Nicholas thrust a taper into the small fire which Peggy had started on the hearth. He lit the candles. He sat down in a chair by the fire and watched her while she poured water into the basin, washed her face and hands. She quickly recoiled her hair, smoothed out her dress. She removed the onyx-and-pearl pin, fastened the neck of her dress with the old hair brooch.

'Aren't you going to change?' said Nicholas. 'I want to see you in something light-colored and gay. Why do you put on that hideous pin? Wear some of your other jewels.'

'No,' she said, rising from the dressing-table and walking to the fire. 'I have a right to no other jewels but this.'

He regarded her with astonishment. She stood a few feet from him in her dark morning dress, extending her numb hands to the blaze.

'Where were you this afternoon, Miranda? The coachman will tell me if you don't.'

'I have no intention of lying. I went to see Doctor Turner in Hudson.'

She heard him make a sharp motion, and turning her head saw in his face an incredulous hope.

'No, Nicholas,' she said with bitterness. 'It's not that. I shall never bear you another child now. Any more than Johanna did.'

At that name the room seemed to spring to a listening stillness. There was no sound but the faint hiss of the fire.

'Why do you say that?' He sprang to his feet and stood beside her.

She reached blindly for the support of the mantel. Don't, said the agonized inner voice. Don't tell him. Maybe you're wrong. Maybe Jeff is wrong. You can't be sure. This is your husband, for better for worse—

'I'm very tired,' she whispered, 'and nervous. I scarcely know what I'm saying.'

The tenseness of his body relaxed. He gave a short laugh. He put his arms around her and pulled her toward him. His lips that had always had power to evoke an answer touched her mouth. She turned her head away, not violently but with a cold finality.

'No,' she said. 'It's finished, Nicholas.' For at his touch the weakness had passed from her. 'I loathe you now, you and myself. And I'm in mortal fear of you—as Johanna was—with reason.'

His arms fell away from her. For a moment his face blurred as though a giant hand had erased his sharp-etched features, dissolving them to blankness. At once they hardened again to watchful wariness. But Miranda had seen in his eyes the unmistakable leap of panic.

'Yes, Nicholas,' she said quietly. 'You're not as strong as you thought you were, are you! Even you can't break the laws of mankind and God without suffering. Not even you.'

They stood like that on either side the fireplace while a minute dragged by. Then Nicholas moved. 'I don't know what you're talking about, my love.' He turned and walked out of the room.

Miranda waited, her eyes fixed on the door. His footsteps died away. A burnt log fell to pieces on the hearth behind her and she started violently. The sudden noise released a rush of fear. She ran to the bell-pull, tugging at it so that the gold tassel came off in her hand. Again she waited. There was no sound but the ticking of the ormolu clock on the mantel. Ten minutes, fifteen. She opened the door, flinching from the still darkness in the hall, straining for Peggy's step. There was no sound. She yanked again and again at the bell-pull.

The clock gave a tiny gay chime.

She uttered a cry and her hands flew to her breast as she heard a noise from the north window—a succession of light taps. She backed slowly toward the other end of the room, when she heard a faint voice calling. And again a volley of taps on the pane. She slipped through the heavy curtains into the embrasure of the window. Twenty feet below on the ground she saw a white upturned face. Miranda unfastened the catch and leaned out.

'I can't get to you, mum,' whispered Peggy hoarsely. 'I've been throwing pebbles at your window. All the doors between the servants' quarters and your part are locked. And the outside doors too.'

Peggy's face blurred and wavered in the twilight. Miranda clutched the window sill. 'Where is he now?' she whispered, and saw the maid shake her head. The sound of Miranda's voice did not carry downward.

Miranda thrust back the curtain and stared into the room behind her. It was as quiet and deserted as before. She leaned out the window and spoke louder.

'He's in the tower room, I think,' answered Peggy. 'Leastways there's a light. Oh, mum, what's happened?'

'I've got to get out. Tell one of the servants to bring a ladder quickly.'

'They won't budge, mum,' came back Peggy's frightened wail. 'They're all scared of him. They won't let me in again. Shall I try and get Hans? I'll run to the village.'

'Yes. Hurry—hurry.'

As Peggy vanished amongst the trees, Miranda turned back into the room. She walked to the smouldering fire and put on a log—and another.

A long time passed.

I must get warm, she thought. Somehow I must get warm. I've got to think clearly, but I can't when I'm so cold.

In the dining-room there was a decanter of brandy. Brandy warmed you. She picked up a candle and opened the door into the hall again. Except for the pounding in her ears, there was no sound. She glanced quickly at the little door at the far end of the hall, the door to the tower stairs. It was shut.

Holding her candle high she ran to the dining-room. She found the decanter and raised it to her mouth, and her teeth against the crystal rim made little clicking noises. After a moment a fiery warmth filtered through her veins. She put down the candle and leaned against the buffet. Her mind cleared. The downstairs windows, of course.

They were locked at night, and shuttered and barred. It took a strong footman to attend to this, but nevertheless she could manage somehow. Or there was that little outside door in the music room; perhaps he had forgotten to lock that.

She picked up the cut-glass stopper, reached out her hand to put it back in the decanter when she heard a sound upon the stairs. The stopper slipped from her fingers and fell to the parquet. Her impulse to blow out the candle and run wildly was checked by a surer instinct. She stood and waited by the buffet.

Nicholas walked in and stopped just beside the doorway, staring at her with bewilderment. 'You are making merry, Miranda?' he said incredulously. 'I heard you laughing and playing the piano.'

She saw the abnormal brightness of his eyes and the quivering of the muscle in his cheek. Slowly courage seeped back into her. She lifted her head.

'Do you imagine that I would laugh or play tonight! You've been drugging yourself, Nicholas.'

His gaze slid from hers and there came over him an uncertainty. He stood with his head thrown back as if he listened for something.

'Why did you lock the doors?' she said.

He dragged his eyes back to her face, but he did not see her.

'I heard you laughing down here, Miranda. I heard the piano. It was very clear.'

And suddenly she understood. There was a current of fear in the shadowed dining-room, fear and hatred. But the current no longer touched her. It flowed past her to the dark, motionless figure which stood by the doorway.

'I believe it was Azilde that you heard, Nicholas,' she said quietly. 'As your child heard her on the night that Johanna died. She's laughing because there's disaster coming again to this house that she hated.'

'You're lying,' he said. 'It was you I heard.'

'No,' she said.

At her denial he took a quick step toward her. She saw his right hand go to his pocket—and a gleam of silver metal. She did not move.

'Yes, I'm quite helpless,' she said. 'You can do me any injury you like. But you won't get away with it this time, Nicholas. Too many people know. Peggy knows that you've locked me in. And Jeff Turner knows about Johanna. He's going to the Governor to tell him.'

His hands slowly fell limp at his sides. She saw the effort he made for control, saw his face compose itself into a semblance of the old assurance. 'My dear, you're full of sinister allusions and melodrama tonight. I can only assume that you're having an attack of female vapors.—And now when you add ghosts—'

He broke off so abruptly that it was as though a knife had cut his voice. He turned his head slowly in the direction of the Red Room.

The candle on the buffet dimmed and flickered.

He's hearing her now, thought Miranda, watching his appalled face. She stood frozen by the buffet, watching. She could hear nothing but the harsh noise of his breathing.

He put out his hand, groping for support on the top of the high walnut chair at the head of the table. His own chair. 'You hear it?' he whispered. 'You hear it too?'

She shook her head.

He made a quick gesture as though to close his ears to the sound of that high, mindless laughter. In that moment she felt pity at the expression of his eyes.

She clasped her hands and her lips moved soundlessly. 'Under His wings shalt thou trust: His truth shall be thy shield and buckler. Thou shalt not be afraid for the terror by night . . .'

She felt the subtle change in the atmosphere of the room, heard him give a long sigh. 'It's stopped,' he said.

His hand dropped from the chair. He straightened his shoulders and force came back to him. He laughed briefly. 'It was an hallucination. The opium, I'm afraid. I don't know how I could have been so credulous.'

He walked to the buffet and poured himself a glass of brandy.

'Will you join me, my love?' he asked in a perfect imitation of his usual courtesy.

She stared at him. Was it possible that he intended to act as though nothing had happened!

'Nicholas,' she said, 'I'm leaving Dragonwyck. You must know that. Wasn't that why you locked the doors?'

'I locked them,' he said quickly, 'simply on impulse because you were in a foolish, hysterical state. You're not leaving Dragonwyck, Miranda, nor will you ever leave me. Don't you remember I told you once that only death would part us?'

He leaned toward her smiling a little.

Yes, she thought, he told me that on our wedding night—'only death will part us'—Death—it was death that brought us together. Her hands crept to her chest in an effort to hide from him the agonized pounding of her heart. He stood, lithely poised between her and the doorway, behind her no refuge but the conservatory, from which there was no other exit. And even had there been, all the doors were still locked and the servants neither able nor willing to hear her call. I must be brave, she thought desperately, as I was a few minutes ago. She moistened her lips.

'Nicholas—' she whispered, but the last syllable ended in a cry, for a thunderous knocking shattered the heavy silence of the house.

Peggy, she thought in a great surge of relief, and knew at once that was impossible. She would never have heralded her approach like that.

The banging on the front door continued.

'We have an insistent caller, it would seem, my love,' said Nicholas softly, watching her through narrowed eyes. 'Would it interest you to find out who it is?'

He put his arm around her waist, pulling her with him into the hallway while from his left-hand pocket he took a key and unlocked the door. 'Ah, it's indeed Doctor Turner,' said Nicholas. 'I hoped it might be.'

His arm tightened painfully around Miranda's waist so that she swayed perforce against him and they stood like that in the rush of night air—a charming picture of devotion—the handsome master and mistress of Dragonwyck welcoming a guest.

For a second Jeff was fooled and dumfounded; then he saw Miranda's eyes.

'I was afraid of this!' he cried, advancing to her quickly, ignoring Nicholas. 'That's why I came. Are you all right?'

Her lips moved wordlessly, while Nicholas, releasing her, with one swift motion locked the door again behind Jeff. 'It was good of you to come, Turner,' he said pleasantly. 'As a matter of fact I sent a messenger for you a little while ago; perhaps you passed him on the road?'

'I doubt that I would have come again at *your* summons,' said Jeff, also quite pleasantly. He knew that he must play for time. He had no means as yet of knowing the exact situation, or how much Nicholas knew, but Miranda's eyes held terrified warning.

'I didn't think you would,' answered Nicholas, moving slightly. 'The message you would have received had you waited for it, my impetuous young doctor, would have been from Miranda, of course.'

Jeff looked at the girl, who shook her head in almost imperceptible denial. Her lips were drained white and her eyes as black as the shadows in the hall behind them.

This is going to be bad, said Jeff to himself, and there's no use hoping it isn't. For he had seen and recognized Nicholas' negligent unfinished gesture toward his right-hand pocket, and the faint silvery gleam there. Jeff had seen just such gleams in many holsters in Mexico.

'Let us,' said Nicholas, picking up the candle, 'go into the Red Room where we can sit comfortably and chat. We've always considered this room the coziest and most homelike in the house, haven't we, my love?' He smiled at Miranda, who caught her breath and stumbled in the direction he pointed.

They sat down, Miranda—and Jeff after a moment—on the two small horsehair chairs. Nicholas placed the candlestick on the center table where it flickered over the red rep cloth and piled books. He seated himself on the sofa and folding his arms surveyed them both with sardonic amusement.

Miranda sat as though hypnotized, her staring eyes on her husband's face, but Jeff forced himself to lean back negligently and cross his legs. He received Nicholas' gaze with a bland smile while his eyes watched the right-hand pocket, and his brain darted over the situation. Fool I was not to have brought a gun, he thought grimly. But his old army pistol had disappeared long ago, and in hurrying to Dragonwyck he had acted on impulse, never previsioning any such situation as this; he hadn't in fact believed in his hunch that Nicholas might return, he had simply been worried about Miranda.

'Miranda tells me that you think you've made an interesting discovery,' said Nicholas in a light and social tone.

'I don't think it, I know it,' answered Jeff. 'Though you were exceedingly clever.' So we're going to talk, he thought, fence for a while. Perhaps he won't shoot until he's enjoyed himself prolonging this, and before that happens I've got to act first. He measured the distance between them; a sudden rush might do it, but there was the certain danger that in that case the reflex shot would hit Miranda.

The candle flared suddenly and Jeff saw more clearly those blue masked eyes. He's had opium, thought Jeff; not much, but it may slow him up.

'You're a remarkable man, Van Ryn,' said Jeff. 'A genius, I believe. You could have been the most powerful man in the country—had you directed your talents more wisely.'

'Your kind opinion enchants me,' said Nicholas. 'Can it be, my love—' he turned to Miranda, 'that the good doctor thinks me susceptible to flattery?'

There was a silence. They sat there, the three of them, as though molded in lead. Against the rose-papered wall, Nicholas' shadow seemed to expand and darken.

Then Miranda made a small rasping noise, but she did not move.

Nicholas leaned forward. 'You're very quiet, my dear.' The slight smile was gone from his mouth. 'Aren't you interested in what the doctor thinks?—Oh, but I believe you are—' With a panther-like movement, Nicholas was on his feet. In the same instant so was Jeff. But Nicholas wheeled, and now the whole of the silver pistol was visible. With a violent motion of his other hand, Nicholas tore the net from Miranda's hair, roughly shook the gleaming golden mass until it fell loose over the chair back nearly to the floor.

'Look!' he cried, turning on Jeff. 'It's pretty, isn't it! Have you ever seen anything more seductive? But perhaps my wife—like this—isn't a new sight to you. I'm wondering if she hasn't permitted you to glory in it, already!'

He raised the pistol, forgetful of the girl beside him, secure in her long pattern of loyal worship, but Miranda's paralysis shattered. With her clenched fist she struck out from behind Nicholas and knocked the pistol from his hand. As the wild shot exploded through the room, Jeff leaped forward.

The girl shrank, panting, against the wall. In the dim light as now one struggling figure now the other was uppermost she could not tell which was Jeff. As she watched them, she prayed.

Jeff had great strength, but he was handicapped by the old wound in his arm, and Nicholas' strength, as always in moments of danger, was nearly superhuman.

The moment came when Jeff, partly wedged beneath the sofa, felt the long powerful fingers at his throat, and as the sweat poured from his face and there came a rushing and roaring in his head, he thought, This is it, my lad. God bless Miranda, somehow.

At first he couldn't believe it as he felt the murderous grip on his throat slacken. Blood coursed back to his brain in great surges.

He opened his eyes, focusing them painfully on the dark face above his. On that face he saw an incredible emotion—a dazed fear.

Nicholas sank back, completely off guard, his eyes dilated and staring—as though he listened.

Jeff jumped to his feet. 'Bring me that bell rope!' he shouted. Nicholas recovered himself then, but the violent strength had gone out of him, and Jeff pinioned the thrashing arms until the girl had yanked the long embroidered bell-pull from the cornice and run with it to Jeff.

He bound Nicholas securely, his nimble surgeon's fingers manipulating the heavy material as though it were twine. The body on the floor ceased to struggle. The head turned away from them.

'Hurry, Miranda!' cried Jeff. 'Get your cloak!' He pulled the key from the pocket of that motionless figure, and when Miranda came running to him, they passed through the great front door of Dragonwyck Manor—for the last time.

Jeff's horse, patiently cropping the sweet May grass, stood tethered to the hitching-post outside. 'Get on behind me!' cried Jeff, lifting the girl. The sturdy horse with its double burden trotted briskly up the river road to the north. Already it was light; a mauve and pink glow effaced the stars in the eastern sky.

'What are we going to do—Jeff?' she asked faintly.

He frowned, considering. After a few minutes he said: 'I'm going to put you on the morning boat at Schodack Landing; we'll just about make it. Then you'll go on to New York as we planned, and straight to Francis. I'll hurry on to Albany and the Governor. When he hears all the evidence and the story of this night, I'm sure we'll get action by tomorrow evening or the day after at the latest.'

'Nicholas may escape,' she said faintly.

'I know. But he won't get loose from those bonds until someone helps him. And with all the servants terrified and locked out, that shouldn't be for a long time. Anyway, I'm going to send a smart lad I know in Schodack down to watch the Manor House; if Nicholas does leave, the boy can follow him. He won't get far. But I've a feeling Nicholas won't leave Dragonwyck. It'd be more like him to shut himself up in his manor house and defy everyone. He's so cocksure of his own power.'

'I don't think so,' she said. 'Not any more.'

'Well, he's powerful, all right. He all but did for me,' said Jeff, grimly feeling his throat. 'I don't know what Heaven-sent thing threw him off guard a second. The opium, I suppose.'

'No,' she said. 'It wasn't that. It was Azilde. He heard her laughing again. I don't know if he really heard it or just in some dark part of his mind. But he's afraid of it. He fears as he never feared anything that symbol of his family's defeat and doom. Oh Jeff—' Her voice broke into a sob. From her seat behind him on the horse, she tightened her arms about him and laid her cheek against his shoulder. 'It *was* Heaven-sent, for it saved you.'

He turned in the saddle and kissed her gently. She had managed to braid her hair and bundle it somehow into a coil at the nape of her neck. Her little face was pale and shadowed under the gray hood.

'Try not to worry, darling,' he said with some confidence. The horse jogged steadily on. A rooster crowed from a near-by barnyard, and a cow lowed plaintively for her early milking. The morning sunlight flooded the pretty village of Schodack, and for Jeff life resumed again its normal values. Nicholas, the atmosphere of Dragonwyck, even the struggle in the little Red Room, seemed fantastic and unreal.

When they reached the landing and stood amongst several other passengers to watch the first morning boat steam up to them, he was detached enough to notice that it was a fine new boat in gala trim, all her multicolored pennants flying, the gilded eagle which perched on her foremast twinkling bright. And her name was the Mary Clinton.

As she set foot on the gangplank, Miranda clutched at him suddenly. 'Jeff, let me come to Albany with you. I'm frightened.' Her hazel eyes looked at him piteously.

He shook his head. 'We can't risk what people would think or say if you went with me. There's nothing to be frightened of now. Look at all the people on the boat, laughing and enjoying themselves. Sit amongst them in the air and sunlight. Try to get some rest.' He smiled at her and squeezed her hand under cover of her cloak. 'I'll be with you in a few days.'

She nodded like an obedient child and walked slowly up the gangplank to the crowded deck. At once the boat cast off and they hastened down-river.

She did as Jeff had suggested, sat down in a corner of the deck. When we pass Dragonwyck, I shall not look, she thought. But as the boat's whistle blew and the Mary Clinton threaded her way down the far channel past Houghtaling's Island, Miranda found that she could not help herself. She moved to the rail and stood there while the silhouette of the Manor glided slowly toward them. Then under her feet she felt a sharp slackening of speed, and the boat swerved to port. She lowered her gaze from the summit of the high tower and stared at the dock. For the red flag which signaled the boats to stop was fluttering in the wind, and beside it stood a tall figure.

The boat paused at the pier with an effect of quivering impatience, and Miranda looked down into her husband's eyes.

Of what use was it to run and hide amongst the other passengers, to barricade herself into a stateroom, to appeal wildly for help? A sensation of destiny and irrevocable fate settled over her, bringing calm. The wheel of fate had not yet turned full circle, the tie which bound them had not yet been loosed. There was more to come. This she knew with inner certainty, and from the mounting crescendo she could not escape.

She stood perfectly quiet while Nicholas set foot on deck and walked to Miranda.

Young Captain Hall dashed up to them.

'We'll have a rare race for you today, sir!' he cried. 'The Utica's close behind. Her runners have been up since dawn crying throughout Albany that she's the faster boat. But we got off ahead and we'll beat her into New York!'

As he spoke the Utica's slim gray hull rounded the island and she gave them a derisive hoot. Hall shook his fist at the rival. 'We must make up the time lost in stopping for you, sir. Had you not been owner I'd never've done it.' The young man hurried back to the bridge, never noticing, in his anxiety to have his new boat prove herself the fastest—and therefore the most desirable—on the river, that Mr. Van Ryn, who yesterday had been all enthusiasm, had not even answered him.

Nicholas stood beside Miranda on the deck. His dark blue suit, the same he had worn the night before, was wrinkled and one sleeve was torn. Across his hands were deep red gouges from the bonds tied by Jeff. The sun shone full on him and for the first time she saw gray in the blackness of the hair at his temples; his eyes were sunken and his mouth slack. Why, he's old, she thought with amazement.

'Miranda—' he said dully, without surprise, for he had withdrawn into a place which did not admit surprise. '—I had to—to get away—away from Dragonwyck.' His voice was slurred and uneven, not from the effects of opium, but from a far more deadly cause—the final realization of defeat. The hours he had spent helplessly bound, vanquished in his own house—by a man he hated, a man who was on his way now to the Governor bearing with him exposure and unbelievable humiliation—this had completed Azilde's work. It was only because a gardener working outside on the lawn had finally heard his master's despairing shouts that Nicholas had been released.

'Have you your gun with you?' said Miranda. 'Are you going to shoot me now?' she added with icy scorn.

He turned his head slowly from her. His eyes fixed themselves on the deck. 'I wouldn't have shot *you*—'

She pulled her cloak tight around her, and moved away.

'You're still my wife, Miranda,' he said in that strangely muffled voice. 'When we get to New York, we can take a boat, go to Europe, together we can find—'

'Nicholas,' she said in cold, slow tones, 'I'm not afraid of you any more, and after we get to New York I shall never see you again. And what I feel for you now is loathing and—pity. Yes, pity,' she repeated inexorably.

His hand went out in a quickly checked motion, as of appeal. He turned violently and stared out across the water toward Dragonwyck, whose faint outline was still visible against the blue sky to the north.

Miranda looked, not at Dragonwyck, but at Nicholas' slumped silhouette against the mahogany rail. This was the man I loved, whose child I bore, she thought, and then a compelling exhaustion deadened all emotion.

Numbness overpowered her. Her limbs seemed boneless. She sank to a deck chair and shut her eyes.

After a while, Nicholas sat down near her. She felt his presence and drew away, moving her chair a little so that her back was toward him.

Around them on the boat excitement grew. People ran to and fro along the decks, shouting and waving at the other ship—the Utica, which was now but an eighth of a mile behind. From time to time a passenger stared curiously at those who sat isolated in silence amongst the clamor.

Everyone by now knew who they were, and for a while they proved as interesting as the race. The ladies were disappointed in Miranda's clothes, which were remarkably plain and dull, and everyone agreed that they were not nearly as handsome a couple as report would have them; moreover, their lack of friendliness, their indifference to their fellow travelers, were condemned generally as evidences of a revolting snobbishness.

But as the Mary Clinton turned toward the Hudson landing, the Van Ryns were forgotten, for the Utica, instead of waiting for the pier, perpetrated a despicable trick. She skipped her scheduled stop entirely and glided triumphantly past in the far western channel.

The indignation of the Utica ticket-holders on the pier was as nothing to Captain Hall's fury. Even before the gangplank was raised, he gave orders to cast off and his boat leaped back into the river behind the Utica.

'May I fry in hell if I don't pay 'em back for that—' he muttered, and the consciousness of Nicholas' presence on board increased his anger. In deliberately cancelling her Hudson landing, the Utica had used the foulest of subterfuges, one never before attempted in these races.

And now the contest between the two boats passed the bounds of sport. Young Captain Hall hung over the wheel, his eyes never leaving the Utica's speeding stern except when he bent his head to shout through the speaking tube to the engine room.

Behind the pilot house the walking beam dipped madly like a frenzied seesaw. Green water roared through the paddle wheels. Downstream the Utica's gray stern grew more distinct.

'She's getting hot, man!' cried the pilot. 'I can smell it. You can't keep this up.'

'Won't have to for long,' retorted Hall. 'The Mary'll catch up all right. I know a trick or two.'

He hesitated; then his jaw set. He reached for the speaking tube.

Down in the stokehole the engineer received his orders. 'Skipper's in a lather, boys,' he said grimly to the sweating firemen. 'We've got to get more steam.' He shrugged his shoulders. 'Throw on the tar!'

The boiler room filled with a pungent smell. The engineer himself executed the other command and clamped down the safety valve.

Gradually the Mary Clinton responded and the excitement of racing seized many of the passengers who crowded the bow and cheered. But some of the ladies and the more level-headed gentlemen became alarmed. The decks vibrated so that the settees and stools set up a violent jiggling, and the whole ship pounded with a rhythmic banging.

A Mrs. Edwards from Vermont, who with her three-year-old Tommy was making a first trip to New York, grew increasingly upset. 'Oh, *why* are they trying to race that other boat!' she cried hysterically, clutching little Tommy tight. 'It's wicked—wicked!'

There were murmurs of assent around her, and a man named Davis went off rather sheepishly. He came back to report that he had talked to the clerk, who laughed and assured him that there was absolutely no danger. The other passengers accepted this and soothed Mrs. Edwards. She surged to the rail with the others as Captain Hall's revenge became clear, for the Mary Clinton caught up with her rival and then inched painfully past until the white bow extended some feet beyond the gray.

High on the bridge the Captain looked down at the startled faces which lined the decks on both boats. His clenched hands gripped the wheel with all his strength. The Mary Clinton swerved to starboard and plunged across the other's bow, stoving in a portion of the Utica's woodwork.

The impact of the collision threw Miranda from her chair. Nicholas was beside her on the instant helping her up. She shrank away from his touch. 'I'm all right,' she said coldly, 'but I don't understand what happened.'

'We've bested the Utica!' cried Nicholas, and she saw with astonishment that the apathy had left him. 'We'll shove her aground,' he added exultantly, 'unless she stops her engines and blows off steam.'

This conclusion had already been reached by the Utica. Captain Hall's triumph was complete. He grinned down at his crippled antagonist and snapped out new orders. His passengers were herded to the port side, the locked bows were thus freed, and with a hooting blast the victorious boat headed back into the center of the river.

Nicholas walked to the stern rail and gazed back at the Utica which was cumbersomely maneuvering into midstream.

Miranda seated herself again. Will this horrible trip never be over, she thought dully, shutting her eyes.

Captain Hall spoke once more to the engine room. With a relieved sigh, the engineer released the safety valve, but there were no orders to reduce steam. Not only did Hall mean to beat the Utica in, but he meant to beat her by hours if he could. So the quivering and pounding continued, and the smell of leaking steam grew stronger. On the hurricane deck cinders and sparks fell thick as tiny hailstones, and suffocating heat made the saloons nearly unbearable.

At one o'clock a delegation of five men approached Nicholas. Mr. Davis was again the spokesman. 'Mr. Van Ryn, we've just learned you're part owner of this boat, and we request you to tell the Captain to head off. He won't listen to reason.'

'If you're afraid, gentlemen,' answered Nicholas, smiling, 'you are at liberty to leave the boat at Poughkeepsie.' He made them a courteous bow of dismissal.

The gentlemen retreated, discomfited. Nicholas' manner had made them feel ridiculous.

A few passengers did disembark at the next stop, but Mrs. Edwards remained on board, and it was the sight of Miranda sitting so calmly in her chair on the after deck which had temporarily quieted her fears.

As they were passing Pollopel's Island in the lee of the Storm King, the Utica suddenly reappeared far upstream. Nicholas made a low exclamation and gripped the taffrail. From the bridge Captain Hall also saw the faint outline of the pursuing vessel. The Mary Clinton pounded and shook in yet faster tempo. The boat flung herself into the Tappan Zee.

Mrs. Edwards, leaning over to button her little boy's shoe, found the vibration so intense that she could not hold his foot still, and when her hand touched the deck, heat seared her fingers. She got up, dragging Tommy who began to whimper and ran to Miranda's secluded corner.

'Oh, ma'am—' she cried, 'are you sure there's no danger? They do say your husband laughed at the idea there might be, so I stayed on the boat. But I'm mighty nervous. It's so hot everywhere.'

Miranda raised her head. She looked at the woman's frightened face and then at the little boy. He had close dark curls and a sturdy body.

Mine would have been like that now, she thought.

'Answer me, ma'am!' cried Mrs. Edwards, her terror mounting at the dazed expression on Miranda's face. 'Is there danger?' She tugged at Miranda's cloak and the child imitating his mother put out his hand.

Miranda stared down at the little hand on her knee. 'I don't know,' she said.

'Look!' screamed Mrs. Edwards, pointing. A dense coil of smoke writhed through the door to the companionway, and a bright red glow flared suddenly from a near-by grating.

On the bridge Captain Hall stood petrified, looking down through the window at a scarlet tongue which licked up from the forward hatch.

'My God! She's on fire, you fool!' shouted the pilot, and he grabbed the wheel from Hall's flaccid fingers. The Mary Clinton veered sluggishly to port, then dashed full speed ahead for the Riverdale bank. The brisk south wind caught her amidships and the whole center section of the boat burst into flames.

The passengers were quiet during those moments when the blazing holocaust hurtled toward the shore. Then the crash came with a violence that flung over the smokestack. Some fortunate ones on the bow managed to pick themselves up after a stupefied instant and struggle to land. But the majority were aft as were Miranda and Nicholas. The stern lay over deep water. Between them and safety rose the advancing wall of fire.

Nicholas in those minutes on the burning boat was the only person untouched by panic. His calm voice rose above the screams. 'Throw the chairs and stools into the water!'

The men followed his example, hurling overboard everything movable which was not yet on fire. They hunted wildly for life preservers or small lifeboats. There were none.

'You must jump and take your chances!' shouted Nicholas. They all looked to him instinctively, and they obeyed his orders. As the last of the terrified passengers dropped to the water, he turned to Miranda, who stood numb with horror.

'Come, my love!' he cried, and his voice held the note of exultation, almost of gaiety.

'I can't,' she whispered.

Against the background of fire and smoke she saw only the violent blue of his eyes.

He tore off her cloak, which fell to the smouldering deck, and he picked her up in his arms running with her to the rail. In that second he spoke to her again, but it was to be many days before his words came back into her consciousness.

The cold green waters of the river closed over her.

Jeff learned of the steamboat disaster the following morning in Albany. He had spent the night in a waterfront hotel, and was dressing for his visit to Governor Fish, when he heard the excited cries of newsboys on the street outside. He paid no attention until he heard the words 'Mary Clinton' and 'Utica,' when he flung on his coat and joined one of the murmuring white-faced groups around a newsboy.

He bought a paper, and from the garbled scareheads which the new electric telegraph had so quickly sent a hundred and forty miles from the scene of the tragedy, the name Van Ryn leaped up at him.

'Hope wanes for noble hero,' said a column heading. Jeff clenched the paper with whitening fingers. His uncomprehending eyes raced down the paragraphs of hysterical conjecture and panegyric. He began again.

'Few details of this stupendous tragedy are yet known, but amongst many deeds of heroism, one name in particular must stand out with glorious luster. We refer to Mr. Nicholas Van Ryn, who—'

'My God!' said Jeff under his breath. He pushed open the door at his elbow. It led to the hotel's taproom, which at this hour of the morning was deserted and quiet. He sat down at a table and spread the paper out before him.

He forced himself to read carefully and slowly, seeking for truth beneath the mass of verbiage under which the journalist had buried the few available facts. There were so far at least forty known dead, including Captain Hall and the pilot. Nicholas Van Ryn had rescued his wife and subsequently a Mrs. Edwards and her child, after which he had been seen entering the water for the third time, obviously with the intention of helping those who were still floundering there. He had not been seen since.

A train had conveyed the rescued and the bodies of such victims as had been identified to New York. That was all.

Jeff wiped the sweat from his face. He went to his room, picked up his bag and hat. The New York boats had already left. He crossed the river by ferry and by hiring a horse and riding furiously he caught the train at Castleton on the recently completed shore road.

At eight in the evening his train passed the scene of the disaster. Not a hundred feet from the tracks the Mary Clinton's bow—all that was left of her—still smouldered on the bank. The peace of the river was repeatedly shattered by the booming of cannon fired to bring up the corpses of the drowned. The stench of charred wood and flesh hung like a miasma in the sweet May air.

Jeff's train stopped to pick up three more stiff, blanket-swathed bundles, and he took the opportunity to question the grim workers on the bank. They referred him to a pallid little man who stood gloomily by the smoking bow. It was Nicholas' agent, Bronck, who had remained on the scene of the wreck since the night before, after the first ghastly trainload had reached New York.

He raised a haggard face in answer to Jeff's question. 'No,' Bronck said, 'Mr. Van Ryn's body's not been found yet. I've checked every one of them. There's a dozen others not brought out yet, either. Impossible to tell just how many've been lost, as there wasn't any passenger list.'

'But what of Miranda—of Mrs. Van Ryn?' cut in Jeff. 'Where is she?'

'They took her to the Stuyvesant Street house. I guess she's all right,' answered the agent dully. A tremor passed over his face and he added with vehemence, 'God blast the day I ever mentioned the Mary Clinton to him. It was that wicked racing, I told him, I begged him—' The little man's voice broke. 'But he tried to repair the wrong, he died a hero's death, like a true aristocrat.'

The conductor shouted 'All aboard,' and Jeff hurried back to his train. Two hours later they jerked and rattled down Park Avenue to the wooden shack in the fields at Forty-Second Street.

Jeff boarded a horsecar and hastened down Third Avenue to Miranda.

22

MIRANDA'S RECOVERY FROM EXHAUSTION, SHOCK, AND exposure was complicated by pneumonia and consequent high temperature and delirium. For many days she recognized no one. She lay on the gilt bed, her marriage bed, in the Stuyvesant Street house, entirely unaware of her surroundings or the loving hands which nursed her. Jeff had immediately summoned Abigail when he arrived that evening after the disaster to find Miranda moaning and unconscious, tended only by the caretaker's frightened wife.

And two days later, Peggy had arrived from up-river. She and Abigail had exchanged one shrewd, appraising glance, then, mutually satisfied, had turned without more ado to the difficult nursing of their patient.

Jeff never left the house during the nine days before the crisis, but he dared not rely on his own skill where Miranda was concerned, and Doctor Francis was also in constant attendance.

On the tenth morning, Miranda opened her eyes and stared around the rose-and-gold bedroom. She gave a weak cry and at once felt the comforting support of arms around her.

'Oh, Ma,' whispered Miranda, still confused and knowing only the reassurance of that presence, 'I dreamed you were with me.'

Praise be, thought Abigail, she's come around at last. 'I've been with you right along, dearie. You've been pretty sick. Don't try to talk.' And the Lord help us when she begins to ask questions, added Abigail to herself.

Miranda's eyelids drooped, she turned her head against her mother's breast, sank back into drowsiness.

Abigail sat quiet in her cramped position on the edge of the bed. Her eyes smarted with painful tears. She looked down at this oldest and dearest daughter, who now looked helpless and young—as young as Charity. For the beautiful golden hair had been cropped short to lessen the fever's heat, and it now lay on the small round skull like a curly cap.

How were they to tell her that her husband was dead? There was much that Abigail did not understand. During her hours of delirium, Miranda had muttered many incomprehensible words. There had been gibberish about a tower room, and an attic and flowers—oleanders. All this the mother put down to light-headedness. But there was a dreadful ring of reality to the anguished desire for escape which accompanied all the other nonsense. Over and over the high strained voice repeated the same sentence: 'I've got to get away. Get away. But God won't let me. My fault too. I sinned.' And at no time did she mention Nicholas' name.

Neither Peggy, who understood the reason behind some of this, nor Jeff, who understood it all, enlightened Abigail.

On the afternoon of the day which marked Miranda's turn toward recovery, Doctor Francis and Jeff came downstairs after examining their patient, and at the latter's request they went into the morning room.

'I've got to talk to you, sir,' said Jeff. 'Got to.'

The old doctor was amused at Jeff's distraught air. 'The girl's all right. She'll do now. Healthy young wench. Nothing to worry about. She's had good doctors—and mighty good nursing, which is far more important than doctors in a lung congestion.'

'Yes, I know. It's not Miranda's health I'm worried about now, except that—' Jeff paused, biting his lips.

'You mean how's she going to take the news that she's widowed? Oh, she'll rally soon. She's very young. Besides, she can deify his memory, hero's death, saved her life—all very comforting to the bereaved.'

Francis spoke with deliberate flippancy. He thought that Jeff's trouble came from his obvious attachment to the sick girl upstairs.

'It's about Van Ryn I want to talk to you, sir. I've muddled and stewed over the thing until I can't think. I've got to get it off my chest.'

'Fire away, my boy,' said Doctor Francis, and eased himself into a chair. 'Now, what about Van Ryn?'

Jeff gave a harsh laugh. '"Nothing in his life became him like the leaving it,"' he quoted bitterly. 'You asked me once what the first Mrs. Van Ryn died of. And now I'm going to tell you.'

But before he could begin there was a tap on the door and Peggy appeared. 'The missis wants you, Doctor,' she said to Jeff. 'She wants to see you alone. No,' added the little maid in answer to Jeff's anxious frown, 'she's not feeling bad. 'Tis something else.'

Miranda was propped up on three pillows, and above the blue counterpane her face looked wan and pinched. But her eyes, huge now between the shadowed lids, held steadily to Jeff's.

'You look fine,' he said, smiling. 'Rather like a charming boy with that cropped head. Wasn't it the fashion in France at the turn of the century? You might set another fashion here, though of course it'll soon grow again.'

She paid no attention to his attempted lightness.

'Jeff,' she said quietly, 'Nicholas is dead, isn't he.' But it was not a question.

There was only one answer and Jeff nodded.

'Tell me what happened, Jeff.'

'He rescued you and a Mrs. Edwards and her little boy. He went back into the water again to help others. He overestimated his strength, I suppose, for he was never seen again.'

'No,' she said. 'He didn't overestimate his strength. He didn't mean to come back. He said to me—that last second on the burning boat—'

She paused, then repeated in a toneless voice, '"You shall see that I can save life as well as destroy it!"'

So he died as he lived, proving to himself and others that he was master after all, thought Jeff wearily. The ship's disaster had provided the ultimate opportunity for self-glorification.

'Yes,' said Miranda, as though he had spoken. 'You see we were all wrong about Nicholas, as wrong as he was himself. He wasn't strong. He was weak. The weakest thing in the world. A man who lives only for himself.'

He stared at her in amazement. For he saw that in that tired little voice she had pronounced a profound truth and the key to Nicholas' baffling character. Not strength but weakness or a fear of weakness had driven him to crime and the ruthless exploitation of others. Egomania, thought Jeff, that term he had read in the translation of a new book from Germany. And what incalculable harm to many innocent people could be done by one supreme egotist.

'Jeff,' she whispered, 'how soon will I be able to leave here? I want to go home to the farm.'

'Not for some time, dear. You must get well first.'

She lifted her hand from the counterpane. The gold ring on her finger shone dully as she gazed at it. She thrust the hand from sight beneath the sheet. 'I can't stay here,' she said. 'Surely you see that, Jeff.'

'This house is yours now,' he answered gently. 'All the Van Ryn possessions are yours.' He didn't know how much to say at present. Some days ago, after it had become certain that Nicholas' body would never be found, Bronck had come to Stuyvesant Street and had had a talk with the young doctor. The agent knew the provisions of Nicholas' will, for he had helped draw them, moreover, they were extremely simple.

Nicholas had never changed the will drawn in the summer of 1846 before the coming of the baby. In it he left everything of which he was possessed to his male issue, Katrine having been previously provided for by the settlement of a large sum. Bronck had tried to persuade him that this was inadequate and risky. But Nicholas would not listen to the agent's timid suggestion that there might after all be no male issue.

And now, in the absence of other heirs, all the property went to Miranda. She would be a very rich woman.

Jeff explained this to her, trying to conquer his own sadness at the thought of the wealth which seemed to separate them nearly as effectually as had Nicholas.

'Do you imagine that I would take it?' she cried with anger. '*All* the Van Ryn property belongs to Johanna's child, Katrine. I'll deed it over to her—except for one thing. Dragonwyck. And that shall be razed to the ground stone by stone until there is nothing left to show where stood that place of evil and misery.'

'And the land?' asked Jeff after a startled moment.

'The land shall go to the farmers, the workers. It's only the workers who have a right to things.'

'My dear girl!' protested Jeff, smiling. He did not believe that she meant it. He thought her to be suffering a natural reaction to the horror. It seemed impossible to him that she might see Nicholas' spiritual isolation, his total lack of kinship with his fellows, as responsible for the tragedy. The man and his way of living had been a deviation from the main line of growth. The growth of humanity and of the nation. Thank God he's dead, thought Jeff.

'I mean it,' she said gravely. 'I was afraid of work. I wanted things easy and soft. The evil in me brought out and abetted the evil in Nicholas.' She turned her head on the pillow.

He saw slow tears slip down her thin cheeks.

'Miranda, don't!' he cried. 'Don't blame and torture yourself.'

She didn't answer him, and after a minute he left her quiet, and went down to Doctor Francis, who still sat in the morning room. The old man was sipping a glass of sherry. He looked up as Jeff entered and waved the glass.

'Excellent stuff,' he said. 'Van Ryn cellars are famous. All Miranda's now,' he added, struck. 'She'll be a mighty rich young woman.'

'I don't think so,' answered Jeff slowly. 'She doesn't want it.'

'Want what?'

'The money, or anything that belonged to Van Ryn.'

'Fiddlesticks!' snorted Doctor Francis. 'Childish nonsense. She's the widow and has a right to the property. Or have you been filling her up with your own transcendental ideas?' he added suspiciously. 'Brook Farm communal-living trash?'

'No,' said Jeff with a faint smile. 'There's a real reason. Listen, sir, and I'll tell you what I started to before.'

Jeff talked for an hour, and after the first sentences the old man's expression of indulgence changed to startled intensity. He put down the sherry glass, leaned forward in his chair and listened. Nor did he utter a sound until Jeff had finished. Then he said, 'Suffering cats!' fished out his red pocket handkerchief and mopped his face. 'Were it not you, Jeff, I'd not believe a word of it.'

'I know.'

'It's a good thing you never reached the Governor in Albany that day. He'd have thought you mad, especially now that Van Ryn's a hero.'

'Yes,' said Jeff. 'He actually saved three lives in place of the two he deliberately murdered, Johanna and that boy in Astor Place. And whether it was a grim attempt at restitution or not I don't know. But come to that, the whole steamboat disaster was indirectly his doing, Bronck seems to think.'

The old man nodded. 'I guess every disaster, every tragedy in the world, my lad, is caused by someone's selfishness and refusal to recognize the rights of others. But thank God, there aren't many like Van Ryn.'

Both men were silent. Then Doctor Francis looked up and asked quietly, 'D'you still want the girl, Jeff?'

'More than anything else in the world, if she'll have me.'

'She'll have you, all right; just give her time,' said the old doctor.

In December his prophecy became a fact.

Jeff and Miranda were married two days before Christmas—married before the holly-wreathed pulpit in the Second Congregational Church by the new but already beloved pastor, Doctor Joel Linsley.

How different, praise God, is this marriage from t'other one, thought Abigail, as she stood beside Ephraim in the front pew. She put her hand on his arm and he grunted affectionately. He knew nothing except the bare outline of his daughter's marriage to Van Ryn. He had jibed a bit when he found that she had renounced all her property, for his Yankee practicality was upset. But he soon accepted Abigail's explanation that Miranda's life with Nicholas had been unhappy. There was little more than this that the mother herself knew or wanted to know.

When Ephraim was told that Miranda and Jeff wished to be married, he was pleased. 'Pity she didn't do it in the first place, but the girl was always flighty,' was his only comment.

Miranda was no longer flighty; even her father admitted that. She had developed a quiet strength and a seriousness of purpose in everything she did. She had dropped back into farm life without a murmur, relieving her mother of the most distasteful tasks. And look, thought Ephraim, turning his eyes on Peggy, who stood behind her mistress weeping into a pocket handkerchief—look what she did for that girl!

In July, Jeff had operated on Peggy's leg in the kitchen of the farmhouse on Stanwich Road. And it had been Miranda—white as the sheet which covered the little body on the scrubbed table—who had held the ether cone, steadily pouring the merciful drops in obedience to Jeff's terse orders. The operation had been a brilliant success. The dragging limp was gone, and now, on Miranda's wedding day, Peggy had followed her mistress proudly down the aisle with only the slightest hesitation in her gait to show where the trouble had been.

It was during the weeks after the operation, when Jeff and Miranda had fought the infection and fever which were considered the inevitable result, that they had discovered what their future life was to be. And it was she who broached it.

They had wandered out into a lovely summer afternoon, leaving Abigail in charge of the sick-room. They walked, as they often did, through the meadow to the apple orchard, and sat down on the stone wall by the little burying-ground. They sat in peaceful silence, soothed by the soft breeze, which smelled of apples and hay. Then Miranda spoke.

'Could you leave Hudson, Jeff? For good, I mean.'

He turned to look at her, wondering what she meant by the question. She seemed to him more beautiful than she had ever been, though she was thin, and her hair, grown out to shoulder length and confined in a net, was no longer brightly blond, but a warm chestnut. There was now about her an integrity and a sweetness, the unmistakable stamp of one who has suffered and emerged at last to complete awareness of the soul.

'I can go anywhere, if you'll go with me,' he said. 'I want nothing but you.'

'And your work?'

'Yes. And my work.'

She smiled at him. 'I've been thinking, Jeff, I could help you. In California they need doctors. Need them desperately. I—' she hesitated, went on in that mature, controlled voice which still surprised him, 'I never want to go up-river again. I couldn't bear it. Though that's perhaps foolish.'

'No, my darling. It's not foolish.' He thought of the site of Dragonwyck as he had seen it a week ago. Her orders had been carried out, quixotic as they seemed to the surrounding countryside. All the furnishings had been sold at auction, everything, including Miranda's own wardrobe. The proceeds had gone in an anonymous gift to the city hospitals, and a large sum to an astounded little parish priest in Killarney with directions to send Peggy's family at once to the States. 'And use the rest in any way you see fit.'

Peggy was to marry her Hans Klopberg in the spring, and Miranda had already arranged the wedding present, though the little maid did not know it. The fertile acres where Nicholas had grown his exotic trees and where the greenhouses were situated, these would belong to Peggy and her descendants forever. But the manor house at Dragonwyck had been demolished. Its site was now nothing but a filled-in patch of raw earth on which the wild grasses were already beginning to grow.

'No,' said Jeff. 'You must never go back. And you must never look back, Miranda. If you want to go West, we'll go.'

He put his arm around her drawing her gently against him, but he felt her body stiffen and saw with dismay that she turned her head from him.

'Never look back.' Words whose measured tolling mingled with the small wind that sighed through the elms above the burying-ground. She looked down at the quiet row of headstones. So peaceful they rested under the September sun—so safe . . . While *he* in the cold darkness . . . lying forever fathoms below the warmth and green of recurring summer, lying alone, as he had always been.

She made a choked sound, and Jeff felt a corroding jealousy as he saw the scalding tears gather in her eyes.

Will there always be this between us? Jeff thought.—Is she not yet free from him?

But then she turned suddenly and read his face and his heart.

'No, Jeff—' she said. 'It's not that. It's just that he was—so—so terribly alone.'

They were both silent, gazing out together across the fields toward the setting sun. Understanding came to him. She's right, he thought; all cruelty and passion must burn away at last to leave behind them only pity.

She slipped her hand into his, secure in the welcoming strong response. She shut her eyes and rested her head against his shoulder.

THE END